NEW YORK REVIEW BOOKS
CLASSICS

YOU'LL ENJOY IT WHEN YOU GET THERE

ELIZABETH TAYLOR (1912–1975) was born into a middle-class family in Berkshire, England. She held a variety of positions, including librarian and governess, before marrying a businessman in 1936. Nine years later, her first novel, *At Mrs. Lippincote's*, appeared. She would go on to publish eleven more novels, including *Angel* and *A Game of Hide and Seek* (both available as NYRB Classics), four collections of short stories (many of which originally appeared in *The New Yorker*, *Harper's*, and other magazines), and a children's book, *Mossy Trotter*, while living with her husband and two children in Buckinghamshire. Long championed by Ivy Compton-Burnett, Barbara Pym, Robert Liddell, Kingsley Amis, and Elizabeth Jane Howard, Taylor's novels and stories have been the basis for a number of films, including *Mrs. Palfrey at the Claremont* (2005), starring Joan Plowright, and François Ozon's *Angel* (2007).

MARGARET DRABBLE is the author of eighteen novels, including *The Needle's Eye*, *The Peppered Moth*, *The Seven Sisters, The Sea Lady*, and most recently, *The Pure Gold Baby*. Among her works of nonfiction are biographies of Arnold Bennett and Angus Wilson. She has edited the fifth and sixth editions of the *Oxford Companion to World Literature* and was made a Dame of the British Empire in 2008.

YOU'LL ENJOY IT WHEN YOU GET THERE

The Stories of Elizabeth Taylor

Selected and with an introduction by

MARGARET DRABBLE

NEW YORK REVIEW BOOKS

New York

THIS IS A NEW YORK REVIEW BOOK
PUBLISHED BY THE NEW YORK REVIEW OF BOOKS
435 Hudson Street, New York, NY 10014
www.nyrb.com

Published by arrangement with Virago Press, an imprint of Little, Brown
Group, London.

Library of Congress Cataloging-in-Publication Data
Taylor, Elizabeth, 1912–1975.
[Short stories. Selections]
 You'll enjoy it when you get there : the stories of Elizabeth Taylor / by Elizabeth
Taylor ; selected by Margaret Drabble.
    pages ; cm. — (New York Review Books Classics)
ISBN 978-1-59017-727-3 (alk. paper)
I. Drabble, Margaret, 1939– II. Title.
PR6039.A928A6 2014
823'.914—dc23

                   2014002275

ISBN 978-1-59017-727-3
Available as an electronic book; ISBN 978-1-59017-743-3

Printed in the United States of America on acid-free paper.
10 9 8 7 6 5 4 3 2 1

CONTENTS

INTRODUCTION

ELIZABETH Taylor is a shocking and disturbing writer. The lady-like middle-class image of herself that she projected during her lifetime was profoundly misleading, and encouraged her readers and some critics to regard her fiction as safe and domestic. We were all reading her too easily. Her work is full of treachery and passion, of horror and regret and foreboding, not all of it suppressed. W. H. Auden's famous lines of the 1940s, "And the crack in the teacup opens / A lane to the land of the dead" are apposite here, and a recurring and memorable motif in Taylor's stories is that of a carefully repaired and riveted porcelain cup, of a broken Dresden ornament. We live near the edge of disaster and are very fragile.

The stories move from the era of war damage and postwar austerity through rebuilding and reconstruction to an age of growing affluence, of coffee bars, transistor radios, motorways, and the package holiday in the sun. Taylor's sharp eye for the telling detail seems at times to be looking at objects in a museum, as though she was aware even at the time of the symbolic value and shortening tenure of now archaic female impedimenta such as corsets, dress preservers, hairpins, bath salts, skin food, and talcum powder. Talcum powder appears almost as frequently as riveted china. Even when writing within the period, she gives a sense not of timelessness but of immanent transience. In "The Rose, the Mauve, the White," one of her painful tales of adolescent anxiety, she describes three girls preparing for a dance (at which one of them rightly fears she will be a wall-flower) and shaking their Christmas talcum powder over one another's backs and armpits: "'What a lovely smell. It's so much nicer than mine,' said Frances, dredging Katie as thoroughly as if she were a fillet of fish being prepared for the frying-pan."

The ominous culinary image evokes with startling clarity one of those scenes which recur in Taylor's novels: the husband, returning from work, to a meal dutifully and unquestioningly prepared, sometimes at lunchtime by home help, or by a housebound wife in the evening. So many meals, so much repetition, so many hours of boredom, so many fillets of fish. So many wives, for whom the more or less superfluous home help was the only confidante.

Loneliness and boredom feature prominently in Taylor's work. "Tall Boy" is a heartrending story of a young West Indian in his London bedsit, but more often she describes female loneliness, endured by the many aging single or widowed women who people her world, the casualties of demography and war. Boredom is also predominantly female, as suffered by underemployed middle-class married women whose social status prevents them from finding satisfying work. She might herself have been one of the bored and lonely, had she not with great determination created for herself a successful career as a writer, drawing much inspiration from these frustrated lives and giving a voice to her neighbors—a voice they might not always have wished to recognize.

Elizabeth Taylor (a name which caused her some difficulties) was born Betty Coles in 1912 in Reading, Berkshire, some forty miles west of London along the Thames valley, and spent most of her life within the same area, in the neighboring county of Buckinghamshire, in what is now known as the commuter belt. This became her fictional territory, and the River Thames itself features, often lyrically, sometimes oppressively, in much of her work. She initially escaped from the discouraging lower-middle-class Coles family background by working as a tutor and librarian in more intellectual and bohemian circles, and in 1936 married John Taylor, whom she had met through an amateur dramatic society. He was (significantly: see the "civic function" title story of this volume, "You'll Enjoy It When You Get There") the son of a prominent local citizen, who was the owner of a successful confectionary business and at one period the mayor of High Wycombe. John followed in his father's footsteps, and Elizabeth officially became a well-dressed businessman's wife, mother, party giver, dinner party guest, and, less conventionally, though by no means secretly, a respected novelist. She also had a not-quite-secret lover, with whom she maintained a long, complex, and intimate relationship.

The material suggested by this brief outline supplied the plots, landscapes, and characters of most of her fiction, but there were surprising paradoxes in her life, some of them reflected directly, others obliquely, in her eleven novels and in her stories. The most improbable of these was her membership in the Communist Party of High Wycombe, a phrase which might seem to those who know conservative High Wycombe to be an oxymoron. She joined shortly before her marriage and was an active member, selling copies of the *Daily Worker* in the High Street on market days. Her political sympathies, unlike those of most of her neighbors and many of her literary friends, were well to the left, although left-wing activists often seem to be treated satirically in her work. Two stories in particular embody her social and humanitarian concerns: "Plenty Good Fiesta" describes the visit to a middle-class English couple of a spirited little nine-year-old Basque refugee from the Spanish Civil War, and "The Devastating Boys," the title story of her penultimate collection, records the summer holiday that two six-year-old "coloured" boys from London spend with a similar couple in the country, having been selected and sent by a charitable organization. Both stories are based on real incidents, and the latter is a subtle and risk-taking evocation of a complex relationship forged across the barriers of class and race, and of the hidden constraints within a long-lasting conventional marriage. One would not guess the biographical origin of either story, so carefully distanced is the tone, yet both betray a controlled depth of feeling.

Difficult marriages feature frequently, and one of her most remarkable and austere portraits of marital disharmony appears in "*Gravement Endommagé*," a powerfully atmospheric description of a couple on holiday in northern France, shortly after the end of

World War II. The blighted landscape reflects the desolation of their relationship, the wife, Louise, resolutely hostile and withdrawn, the husband somewhat hopelessly committed to reparation and reconstruction and another glass of Pernod. Like much of Taylor's work, it was first published in *The New Yorker*, appearing in October 1950 after having been submitted to the editorial scrutiny of her admirer William Maxwell. He urged her to cut references to the French setting and to a Japanese concentration camp in which, in the first draft, Louise had been interned. Taylor acceded to the second prompt but not the first, which is just as well, as the landscape with its poplars and plane trees and flaking houses and drab cafés is superbly drawn. She was always good on a sense of place. In the U.K., the story appeared in 1951 in *Woman and Beauty*, a not uncommon publishing pattern for her work: a highbrow and sophisticated outlet in the U.S., a middle-range women's market in the U.K.

The Englishness of the stories appealed to Maxwell and to her American publishers at Knopf, but it also at times irritated them. Her novels were difficult to sell in the States, despite her frequent and highly paid appearances in *The New Yorker*. The social nuances, the distinctions of class as opposed to wealth, the very decor were alien. What to make of the Kensington hotels for aging gentlefolk, the roadhouses for the brash new motoring classes, the ivy-clad preparatory schools clinging to the rituals of the past, the luxurious Thameside villas, the picturesque but poky cottages in pretty villages, the gossipy tearooms, the dirty shops, the deeply and depressingly English public houses? They were quaint and authentic, yet at the same time worrying. There was something unsettling about Taylor's England. Maxwell recoiled from and declined to publish her most sinister story, "The Fly-paper," suggested by the horrific Moors Murders of 1965, although it must be said that the low-key domestic tone of this tale of fatal entrapment seems also, initially, to have baffled her English publishers. Taylor's manner could be intentionally misleading.

Another of the paradoxical aspects of Taylor's life and work lies in her attitude to alcohol, to social and antisocial and solitary drinking. She clearly was well acquainted with hard drinkers, as we see in the characterization of the bored housewife Ida's gentleman-friend George Eliot in "Shadows of the World." (George's embarrassment about his name surely echoes Taylor's own—"His name was something he had to carry off.") George makes himself all too familiar with "what she called the cocktail cabinet," as they both wait for the return of Ida's husband, Leonard, who may or may not come home for dinner. "Just one of those village things," remarks George, urbanely, as Ida's suspicions and jealousy intensify. (Meanwhile, in astonishing counterpoint, a cat upstairs is giving birth to kittens.) In the wickedly cruel "Perhaps a Family Failing," drawn at the other end of the social spectrum, it is the public bar of the Seaferry Arms that ruins a honeymoon and probably a marriage. In the opening paragraph of "Flesh," a tragic-comic celebration of elderly lust, we enter the bar of a holiday hotel abroad, where Phyl is enjoying "what she called her *aperitif,* and which, in reality, amounted to two hours' steady drinking." Here is a writer who appreciates the importance of the role of alcohol in fiction, and the subtle gradations of indulgence and addiction.

One would have thought that Taylor, respectable wife of a prominent businessman, would have been more at home with the cocktail cabinet than the public bar, but there was something about the anonymity and the possibilities of the pub that appealed to her strongly, and she relished the conversations she overheard there. Her induction into communism had released her from the social timidity and fear of the working classes that plagued most women in her position, and her vocation as a writer gave her a license to explore the louche underworld so well evoked in one of her last stories, "Violet Hour at the Fleece." (She would have disliked that word, "vocation," just as she recoiled from praise of her "prose": she deplored pretension and self-importance.) There are hints that her lonely independence and her habit of drinking unaccompanied caused her husband some unease, but he seems to have been complaisant in this matter, as in others.

Her solitary wanderings revealed to her neighborhoods with

which housewives of her status would not in the normal course of life have been familiar: Her stories consciously document the changing face of postwar Britain. In an interview for *The Sunday Times* (by Geoffrey Nicholson, 1968, quoted by Nicola Beauman in her biography *The Other Elizabeth Taylor*, 2009) she said, "I am a great walker about strange streets and love to be alone in a town I have never visited before." Her detachment and her curiosity combine to sharpen her perceptions of landscape, architecture, town planning, domestic interiors, parks, and public places. Her topographical range may have been comparatively restricted, but within that range her observations are extraordinarily fresh and telling.

Yet she is not wholly and solely an objective observer. As a woman and as a writer, she inhabited two worlds and two ideologies, never quite reconcilable with each other. It is from this ambivalence and unease that some of her finest work springs. She cannot be labeled as a satirist, though she is often satirical. She is sharp, sometimes very funny, and can create monstrous characters and situations: Witness the tragically bored, frustrated, dangerous, and manipulative schoolmaster's wife, Muriel, in her novella "Hester Lilly," or Angel, the eponymous egotistical novelist protagonist of her 1957 novel. But sympathies can operate on a deeper level, and sometimes the reader may have cause to revise a first reading.

"Sisters" appears on the surface to be a short and simple narrative, inviting us to view with a sense of superiority the smug complacency of Mrs. Mason, a seemingly caricatured bridge-playing blue-rinsed small-town dentist's widow who has her own little set of friends and her own regular routine of coffee mornings and historical romances from the lending library. Her safe and cozy world is invaded by a literary detective, "a hideously glinty young man," seeking biographical information about her late sister, Marion, a celebrated writer who had lived a scandalously bohemian life in Paris in the thirties. Mrs. Mason insists that Marion's fictional version of their childhood had been full of lies and exaggerations. She tries to be discreet, but lets out, under pressure, and to her own dismay, the dangerous line "I think she killed my father."

This portrait of sibling rivalry can be read in many ways, and on closer examination it is not at all clear that Taylor condones the risk-taking famous writer and deplores the conventional home-loving dentist's widow. It is the nature of their interaction that she questions. Writers do betray, and maybe Marion had indeed driven Mrs. Mason into her padded retreat and into a life of denial by her literary intrusions and appropriations and by her mysterious but notorious death. There is a violence in the physical description of Mrs. Mason—whose husband, at the time of Marion's death, had been mayor—which exceeds satire. Something very powerful is at work in these few pages, and there are hints that Elizabeth Taylor herself, businessman's wife and mayor's daughter-in-law, is writing about something much bigger than a silly, frightened, and defensive old woman. She is writing about the need for responsibility and the impossibility of telling or knowing the truth. She is writing about the many ways in which we, sometimes unwittingly, hurt one another.

—MARGARET DRABBLE

YOU'LL ENJOY IT
WHEN YOU GET THERE

HESTER LILLY

MURIEL'S first sensation was one of derisive relief. The name—Hester Lilly—had suggested to her a goitrous, pre-Raphaelite frailty. That, allied with youth, can in its touchingness mean danger to any wife, demanding protectiveness and chivalry, those least combatable adversaries, against which admiration simply is nothing. "For if she is to fling herself on his compassion," she had thought, "at that age, and orphaned, then any remonstrance from me will seem doubly callous."

As soon as she saw the girl an injudicious confidence stilled her doubts. Her husband's letters from and to this young cousin seemed now fairly guiltless and untormenting; avuncular, but not in a threatening way.

Hester, in clothes which astonished by their improvisation—the wedding of out-grown school uniform with the adult, gloomy wardrobe of her dead mother—looked jaunty, defiant and absurd. Every garment was grown out of or not grown into.

I will take her under my wing, Muriel promised herself. The idea of an unformed personality to be moulded and high-lighted invigorated her, and the desire to tamper with—as in those fashion magazines in which ugly duckling is so disastrously changed to swan before our wistful eyes—made her impulsive and welcoming. She came quickly across the hall and laid her cheek against the girl's, murmuring affectionately. Deception enveloped them.

Robert was not deceived. He understood his wife's relief, and, understanding that, could realise the wary distress she must for some time have suffered. Now she was in command again and her misgivings were gone. He also sensed that if, at this point, she was ceasing to suspect him, perhaps his own guilt was only just beginning. He hated the transparency of Muriel's sudden relaxation and forbearance. Until now she had contested his decision to bring Hester into their home, incredulous that she could not have her own way. She had laid about him with every weapon she could find—cool scorn, sweet reasonableness, little girl tears.

"You are making a bugbear of her," he had said.

"*You* have made *her* that, to *me*. For months, all these letters going to and fro, sometimes three a week from her. And I always excluded."

She had tried not to watch him reading them, had poured out more coffee, re-examined her own letters. He opened Hester's last of all and as if he would rather have read them privately. Then he would fold them and slip them back inside the envelope, to protect them from her eyes. All round his plate, on the floor, were other screwed up envelopes which had contained his less secret letters. Once—to break a silence—he had lied, said, "Hester sends love to you." In fact, Hester had never written or spoken Muriel's name. They had not been family letters, to be passed from one to the other, not cousinly letters, with banal enquiries and remembrances. The envelopes had been stuffed with adolescent despair, cries of true loneliness, the letters were repellent with egotism and affected bitterness, appealing with naivety. Hester had been making, in this year since her father's death, a great hollow nest in preparation for love, and Robert had watched her going round and round it, brooding over it, covering it. Now it was ready and was empty.

Unknowingly, but with so many phrases in her letters, she had acquainted him with this preparation, which must be hidden from her mother and from Muriel. She had not imagined the letters being read by anyone but Robert, and he would not betray her.

"You are old enough to be her father," Muriel had once said; but those scornful, recriminating, wife's words never sear and wither as they are meant to. They presented him instead with his first surprised elation. After that he looked forward to the letters and was disappointed on mornings when there was none.

If there were any guilty love, he was the only guilty one. Hester proceeded in innocence; wrote the letters blindly as if to herself or as in a diary and loved only men in books, or older women. She felt melancholy yearnings in cinemas and, at the time of leaving home, had become obsessed by a young pianist who played tea-time music in a café.

Now, at last, at the end of her journey, she felt terror, and as the first ingratiating smile faded from her face she looked sulky and wary. Following Muriel upstairs and followed by Robert carrying some of her luggage, she was overcome by the reality of the house, which she had imagined wrong. It was her first visit, and she had from Robert's letters constructed a completely different setting. Stairs led up from the side of the hall instead of from the end facing the door. "I must finish this letter and go up to bed," Robert had sometimes written. So he had gone up *these* stairs, she thought in bewilderment as she climbed them now.

The building might not have been a school. The mullioned windows had views of shaved lawns—deserted—and cedar trees.

"I thought there would be goal-posts everywhere," she said, stopping at a landing window.

"In summer-time?" Muriel asked in a voice of sweet amusement.

They turned into a corridor and Robert showed Hester from another window the scene she had imagined. Below a terrace, a cinder-track encircled a cricket field where boys were playing. A white-painted pavilion and sight-screens completed the setting. The drowsy afternoon quiet was broken abruptly by a bell ringing, and at once voices were raised all over the building and doors were slammed.

When Muriel had left her—with many kind reminders and assurances—Hester was glad to be still for a moment and let the school sounds become familiar. She was pleased to hear them; for it was because of the school that she had come. She was not to share Muriel's life, whatever that may be, but Robert's. The social-family existence the three of them must lead would have appalled her, if she had not known that after most meal-times, however tricky, she and Robert would leave Muriel. They would go to his study, where she would prove—*must* prove—her efficiency, had indeed knelt down for nights to pray that her shorthand would keep up with his dictation.

From the secretarial school where, aged eighteen, she had vaguely gone, she had often played truant. She had sat in the public gardens, rather than face those fifteen-year-olds with their sharp ways, their suspicion of her, that she might, from reasons of age or education, think herself their superior. Her aloofness had been humble and painful, which they were not to know.

When Robert's offer had arrived, she had regretted her time wasted. At her mother's death she was seen clearly to be the kind of girl whom relatives must help, take under their roof as governess or companion, or to do, as in Hester's case, some kind of secretarial work.

In spite of resentment, Muriel had given her a pleasant room—nicely anonymous, ready to receive the imprint of a long stay—no books, one picture and a goblet of moss-roses.

Outside, a gardener was mowing the lawn. There, at the back of the house, the lawns sloped up to the foot of a tree-covered hillside, scarred by ravines. Foliage was dense and lush, banking up so that no sky was seen. Leaves were large enough to seem sinister, and all of this landscape with its tortured-looking ash trees, its too-prolific vegetation, had a brooding, an evil aspect; might have been a Victorian engraving—the end-piece to an idyllic chapter, hitting inadvertently, because of medium, quite the wrong note.

At the foot of the hillside, with lawns up to its porch, was a little church, which Hester knew from Robert's letters to be Saxon. Since the eighteenth century it had been used as a private chapel by the successive owners of the house—the last of these now impoverished and departed. The family graves lay under the wall. Once, Robert had written that he had discovered an adder's nest there. His letters often—too often for Hester—consisted of nature notes, meticulously detailed.

Hester found this view from her window much more pre-envisaged than the rest. It had a strength and interest which her cousin's letters had managed to impart.

From the church—now used as school chapel—a wheezy, elephantine voluntary began and a procession of choir-boys, their royal-blue skirts trailing the grass or hitched up unevenly above their boots, came out of the house and paced, with a pace so slow they rocked and swayed, towards the church door. The chaplain followed, head bent, sleeves flung back on his folded arms. He was, as Hester already knew, a thorn in Robert's flesh.

In the drawing-room, Muriel was pouring out tea. Robert always stood up to drink his. It was a woman's hour, he felt, and his dropping in on it was fleeting and accidental. Hugh Baseden stood up as well—though wondering why—until Muriel said: "Won't you sit down, Mr. Baseden?"

At once, he searched for reproof in her tone, and thought that perhaps he had been imitating a piece of headmasterliness—not for him. Holding his cup unsteadily in one hand, he jerked up the knees of his trousers with the other and lowered himself on to the too-deep sofa, perched there on the edge staring at the tea in his saucer.

Muriel had little patience with gaucherie, though inspiring it. She pushed aside Hester's clean cup and clasped her hands in her lap.

"What can she be doing?" she asked.

"Perhaps afraid to come down," Robert said.

Hugh looked with embarrassment at the half-open door where Hester hesitated, peering in, clearly wondering if this were the right room and the right people in it. To give warning to the others, he stood up quickly and slopped some more tea into his saucer. Robert and Muriel turned their heads.

"We were thinking you must be lost," Muriel said, unsure of how much Hester might have heard.

Robert went forward and led her into the room. "This is Hugh Baseden. My cousin, Hester Lilly, Hugh. You are newcomers together, Hester, for this is Hugh's first term with us."

Hester sank down on the sofa, her knees an inelegant angle. When asked if she would have sugar she said "yes" in error, and knew at once that however long her stay might be she was condemned to sweet tea throughout it, for she would never find the courage to explain.

"Mr. Baseden is one of those ghoulish schoolmasters who cuts up dead frogs and puts pieces of bad meat under glass to watch what happens," Muriel said. "I am sure it teaches the boys something enormously important, although it sounds so unenticing."

"Do girls not learn biology then?" Hugh asked, looking from one to the other.

Muriel said "no" and Hester said "yes": and they spoke together.

"Then that is how much it has all changed," Muriel added lightly. "That marks the great difference in our ages"—she smiled at Hester—"as so much else does, alas! But I am glad I was spared the experience. The smell!" She put her hand delicately to her face and closed her eyes. Hester felt that the lessons she had learnt had made her repulsive herself. "Oh, do you remember, Robert," Muriel went on, "last Parents' Day? The rabbit? I walked into the Science Room with Mrs. Carmichael and there it was, opened out, pinned to a board and all its inside labelled. How we scurried off. All the mammas looking at their sons with awe and anxiety and fanning themselves with their handkerchiefs, wondering if their darlings would not pick up some plague. We must not have that this year, Mr. Baseden. You must promise me not. A thundery day...oh, by four o'clock! Could we have things in jars instead, sealed up? Or skeletons? I like it best when the little ones just collect fossils or flint arrow-heads."

"Flint arrow-heads are not in Hugh's department," Robert said, although Muriel knew that as well as he, was merely going through her scatter-brain performance—the all-feminine, inaccurate, negligent act by which she dissociated herself from the school.

"They are out of chapel," Hugh said. The noise outside was his signal to go. "No rabbits, then," he promised Muriel and turning to Hester, said: "Don't be too bewildered. I haven't had much start on you, but I begin to feel at home." Then, sensing some rudeness to Muriel in what he had said, he added: "So many boys must be a great strain to you at first. You will get used to them in time."

"I never have," Muriel murmured, when he had gone. "Such dull young men we get here always. I am sorry, Hester, there is no brighter company for you. Of course, there is Rex Wigmore, ex-RAF, with moustache, slang, silk mufflers, undimmed gaiety; but I should be wary of him, if I were you. You think I am being indiscreet, Robert; but I am sure Hester will know without being told how important it is in a school for us to be able to speak frankly—even scandalously—when we are *en famille*. It would be impossible to laugh if, outside, our lips were not sealed tight..."

"If everything is to be said for me," Hester thought, "and understood for me, how am I ever to take part in a conversation again?"

From that time, Muriel spoke on her behalf, interpreted for her, as if she were a savage or a mute, until the moment not many days later, when she said in an amused, but matter-of-fact voice: "Of course, you are in love with Robert."

Muriel saved Hester the pains of groping towards this fact. She presented it promptly, fresh, illicit and out-of-the-question; faced and decided once for all. The girl's heart swerved in horrified recognition. From her sensations of love for and dependence upon this older man, her cousin, she had separated the trembling ardour of her youth and unconsciously had directed it towards the less forbidden—the pianist in the café for instance. Now, she saw that her feelings about that young man were just the measure of her guilt about Robert.

Muriel insinuated the idea into the girl's head, thinking that such an idea would come sooner or later and came better from her, inseparable from the very beginning with shame and confusion. She struck, with that stunning remark, at the right time. For the first week or so Hester was tense with desire to please, anxiety that she might not earn her keep. Robert would often find her bowed in misery over indecipherable shorthand, or would hear her rip pages out of the typewriter and begin again. The waste-paper basket was usually crammed full of spoilt stationery. Once, he discovered her in tears and, half-way across the room to comfort her, wariness overtook him. He walked instead to the window and spoke with his back to her, which seemed to him the only alternative to embracing her.

Twice before he had taken her in his arms, on two of the three times they had been together. He had met her when she came home from Singapore where her father had died, and she had begun to cry in the station refreshment-room while they were having a cup of tea. His earlier meeting was at her christening when he had dutifully, as godfather, nursed her for a moment. The third encounter she had inveigled him into. He had met her in London secretly to discuss an important matter. They had had luncheon at his Club and the important matter turned out to be the story of her misery at living with her mother—the moods, scenes, words, tears. He could see that she found telling him more difficult than she had planned, found it in fact almost impossible. Rehearsing her speeches alone, she had reckoned without his presence, his looks of embarrassment, the sound of her own voice complaining, her fear of his impatience. She had spoken in a high, affected, hurried voice, smiling too much and at the wrong moments, with a mixture of defiance and ingratiation he found irritating, but pathetic. He had had so little solace to offer, except that he was sure the trouble would pass, that perhaps her mother suffered, too, at the crisis of middle-age. At that, Hester had been overcome by a great, glowering blush, as if he had said something unforgivable. He did not know if it were some adolescent prudery in her, or the outrage of having excuses made for her enemy-mother. (For whom excuses might have been made, for she died not long after, of cancer.)

Now, as he stood at the window listening to her tears, he knew that she was collapsed, abandoned, in readiness for his embrace of consolation, and he would not turn round, although his instinct was to go to her.

He said, absurdly: "I hope you are happy here," and received of course only tears in answer.

Without physical contact he could not see how to bring the scene to an end. Bored, he surveyed the garden and thought that the box-hedge needed trimming. Beyond this hedge, hanging from the branches of fruit trees were old potatoes stuck with goose-feathers. He watched them twirling gaily above the currant bushes, not frightening the birds, but exciting or bemusing them.

She realised that he would not come to her, and her weeping sank into muffled apologies, over which Robert could feel more authoritative, with something reassuring to say in return and something to do. (He fetched a decanter of sherry.) His reassurances were grave, not brusque. He put the reasons for her distress sensibly back upon legitimate causes, where perhaps they belonged—the death of her mother, shock, strain, fatigue.

He sat by his desk and put on his half-moon reading-glasses, peered over them, swung about in his swivel-chair, protecting himself by his best old-fogey act.

"Muriel and I only want to make you happy."

Hester flinched.

"You must never let this work worry you, you know." He almost offered to get someone else to do it for her, his sense of pity was so great.

His reading-glasses were wasted on her. She would not look at him with her swollen eyes, but pointed her hands together over her forehead, making an eave to hide her face.

"But does Muriel *want* me here?" she cried at last.

"Could you be here, if she did not?"

"But do you?"

In her desperation, she felt that she could ask any questions. The only advice he ever wanted to give young people was not to press desperation too far, uncreative as it is; *not* to admit recklessness. Muriel had once made similar mistakes. It seemed to him a great fault in women.

"I shall only mind having you here if you cry any more. Or grow any thinner."

He glanced down at his feet. She was not really any thinner, but Muriel had begun her work on her clothes, which now fitted her and showed her small waist and long narrow back.

"You are bound to feel awkward at first with one another," Robert said. "It is a strange situation for you both, and Muriel is rather shy."

Hester thought that she was uncouth and sarcastic; but not shy, not for one moment shy.

"I think she is trying so hard to be kind and sympathetic," he continued, "but she must make her own place in your life. She would not be so impertinent as to try to be a mother to you, as many less sensitive women might. There is no precedent to help her—having no children herself, being much older. She has her own friends, her own life, and she would like to make a place for you, too. I think she would have loved to have had a daughter... I can imagine that from the interest she takes in your clothes, for instance." This was true, had puzzled Hester and now was made to shame her.

Muriel opened the door suddenly upon this scene of tears and sherry. Hester, to hide her face, turned aside and put up her hand to smooth her hair.

"Miss Graveney's address," Muriel said. She stood stiffly in front of Robert's desk while he searched through a file. She did not glance at Hester and held her hand out to take the address from Robert before he could bring it from the drawer.

"Thank you, dear!" She spoke in her delicately amused voice, nodded slightly and left the room.

Outside, she began to tremble violently. Misery split her in two—one Muriel going upstairs in fear and anger, and another Muriel going beside her, whispering: "Quiet! Be calm. Think later."

Hester, with her new trimness, was less touching. She lost part of the appeal of youth—the advantage Muriel could not challenge—and won instead an uncertain sophistication—an unstable elegance, which only underlined how much cleverer Muriel was at the same game.

Muriel's cleverness, however, could not overcome the pain she felt. She held the reins, but could barely keep her hands from trembling. Her patience was formidable. Robert had always remarked upon it since the day he had watched her at work upon her own wedding cake. There were many things in her life which no one could do as well as she, and her wedding cake was one of them. She had spent hours at the icing—at hair-fine lattice-work, at roses and rosettes, swags and garlands, conch-shells and cornucopias. She had made of it a great work of art, and with a similar industry, which Robert only half-discerned and Hester did not discern at all, she now worked at what seemed to her the battle for her marriage.

Conceived at the moment of meeting Hester, the strategy was based on implanting in the girl her own—Muriel's—standards, so that every success that Hester had would seem one in the image of the older woman, and every action bring Muriel herself to mind. Patience, tolerance, coolness, amusement were parts of the plan, and when she had suddenly said: "Of course you are in love with Robert," she had waited to say it for days. It was no abrupt cry of exasperation, but a piece of the design she had worked out.

Before Hester could reply, Muriel stressed the triviality of such a love by going on at once to other things. "If I were a young girl again I should have a dark dress made, like a Bluecoat Boy's—a high neck and buttoned front, leather belt, huge, boyish pockets hidden somewhere in the skirt. How nice if one could wear yellow stockings too!"

She rested her hand on her tapestry-frame and forced herself to meet Hester's eyes, her own eyes veiled and narrowed, as if she were considering how the girl would look in such a dress.

Hester's glance, as so often in the innocent party, wavered first. She had no occupation to help her and stared down at her clasped hands.

Muriel began once more to pass the needle through the canvas. Diligently, week by week, the tapestry roses blossomed in grey and white and blood-colour.

"Don't you think?" she asked.

She swung the frame round and examined the back of the canvas. It was perfectly neat. She sat sideways in her chair, with the frame-stand drawn up at one angle. Her full skirt touched the carpet—pink on crimson.

"Why do you say that?" Hester asked. "What makes you say it?" She sounded as if she might faint.

"Say what?"

"About Robert." Her lips moved clumsily over the name as if they were stung by it, and swollen.

"Robert? Oh, yes! Don't fuss, dear girl. At your age one has to be in love with someone, and Robert does very well for the time being. Perhaps at *every* age one has to be in love with someone, but when one is young it is difficult to decide whom. Later one becomes more stable. I fell in love with all sorts of unsuitable people—very worrying for one's mother. But by the time I met Robert I was old enough to be sure that *that* would last. As it has," she added quietly; and she chose a strand of white silk and began to work on the high-lights of a rose petal.

"I once fell in love with a young man who drank like a fish," she continued, for Hester seemed stunned into silence. "He was really an evil influence. Very flashy. You remember how I warned you about Rex Wigmore your first day here?" She began to shake with mirth. "Trying to be my own anxious mamma all over again. And all the time it was Robert! How lucky! For Robert is so gentle, so kind. He would never harm you. Nothing but good could come of a girl loving *him*. Yes, I can see Robert doing very well indeed, until the real one comes along. How furious he would be to hear us discussing him like this—men take themselves so seriously."

"I am not discussing him," Hester said, an ugly stubbornness in her manner. She snatched a handkerchief from her pocket and began to fidget with it, crushing it and smoothing it and staring at it in a bewildered defiance.

Muriel's white hand smoothed a woollen rose. "I always leave the background till last." She sighed. "So dull, going on and on with the same colour."

"It isn't true. He's my cousin, much older...your husband...I... does he know?"

"Well, I haven't asked him. Men are too vain. I dare say he knows all right, though. It's very good for them, at his age ... makes them feel young."

So Hester saw herself thrust into the service of nature, a coarse instrument, as good as anonymous. Muriel, spared such humiliation, could well smile, and congratulate herself. "Don't fuss," she said again in her most laughing voice. "If I had known you *would*, I wouldn't have said it."

"I wish I could go away." Hester wrung her hands and looked towards the windows as if she might escape through them. "You hate me being here. And now..."

"Now?"

"Now you believe this about me, how can you bear me to be here? No wife could."

At this, a stern, fastidious look came upon Muriel's face. She was silent for a moment, then said in a quiet and serious voice: "I ... as a wife; Robert ... as a husband; our private life together I must leave out of this. It is between us only, and I never discuss my marriage."

"There is no need to be rude to me," Hester shouted, so great her frustration, so helplessly she felt herself up against Muriel's smooth contempt. She was forced into childishness.

At her outburst—for all of today was working for Muriel, she thought—the door opened.

"But surely there is nothing sinister in that?" Beatrice Carpenter asked. She was Muriel's closest friend and they were walking in the park before dinner. "Young girls often cry. You rather surprise me, Muriel. You sound hysterical yourself."

"It was the atmosphere of the room. It trembled with apprehension, and when I opened the door Robert looked at me with a dumbfounded expression, his eyes opened wide over those awful half-moon glasses he *will* wear, they—his eyes—looked so *blue*—a little boy's look, little boy in mischief. 'Don't spank me, Nanny.' I hated him for a moment. Oh, I felt murderous. No, but I truly itched to hurt him physically, by some violent and abusive act, to hit him across the mouth, to..." She broke off in astonishment and looked about her, as if fearful of being overheard.

"You *are* in a bad way," Beatrice said. "The girl will have to go."

"I know. But how? I have to be clever, not insistent. I can't be put into the position of getting my own way, for it would never be forgotten. It would last all our lives, such a capitulation, you know."

Other married women *always* know; so Beatrice only murmured cosily.

Muriel said: "The self-consciousness is so deadly. When I go back, he will look at me to see how I am likely to behave. Every time I go into a room, he glances at my face, so that I can no longer meet his eyes."

"I never think embarrassment is a trivial emotion," Beatrice said.

"It has altered everything, having her here; for we were just at an age of being able, perhaps, to relax, to take one another for granted, to let ourselves slip a little. It is a compensation for growing old, and one must find a compensation for that, if one can."

"I cannot," Beatrice said.

"For a day or two I tried to compete, but I will not be forced into the sort of competition I am bound to lose." Muriel frowned and with a weary gesture unclipped her gold ear-rings as if she suddenly found their weight intolerable. She walked on with them clutched, warm and heavy, in her hand. Beatrice could not bear the sight of her fiery ear-lobes. She was upset, as when people who always wear glasses take them off for polishing and expose their wounded-looking and naked eyes. Muriel was never without ear-rings and might have caused only slightly less concern by suddenly unpinning her hair.

Beatrice said: "An experienced woman is always held to be a match for a young girl, but I shouldn't like to have to try it. Not that I *am* very experienced."

They sat down on a seat under a rhododendron bush, for now they were in the avenue leading to the house and their conversation had not neared its end, as their walk had.

By "experience" both meant love affairs. Beatrice thought of the engagement she had broken in girlhood, and Muriel thought of Hugh Baseden's predecessor and his admiration for her, which she had rather too easily kept within bounds. It was, as Beatrice had said, very little experience and had served no useful purpose and taught them nothing.

"And then," Muriel said, "there is the question of the marriage-bed." She was dropping the ear-rings from one hand to the other in her agitation. Far from never discussing her marriage, as she had assured Hester, she was not averse to going over it in every detail, and Beatrice was already initiated into its secrets to an extent which would have dismayed Robert had he known. "There were always so many wonderful excuses, or if none came to mind one could fall inextricably into a deep sleep. He has really been fairly mild and undemanding."

"Unlike Bertie," Beatrice said, and her sigh was genuinely regretful.

"Now I am afraid to make excuses or fall asleep. I scent danger, and give in. That may seem obvious, too. It is very humiliating. And certainly a bore."

"I sometimes pretend it is someone else," Beatrice said. "That makes it more amusing." She covered her face with her hands, bowed down, rocking with laughter at some incongruous recollection. "The most improbable men . . . if they could know!"

"But you might laugh at the time," Muriel said, in an interested voice.

"I do . . . oh, I do."

"Robert would be angry."

"Perhaps husbands sometimes do the same."

Muriel clipped her ear-rings back on. She was herself again. "Oh, no!" she said briskly. "It would be outrageous."

"Marriage-bed" was only one of her many formal phrases. She also thought and talked of "bestowing favours" and "renewed ardours." "To no one else," she told herself firmly. "To no one else." They walked on up the avenue in silence, Beatrice still trembling, dishevelled with laughter. "To no one else?" Muriel thought, in another of those waves of nausea she had felt of late.

As they went upstairs before dinner, she felt an appalling heaviness. She clung to the banisters and Beatrice's voice came to her from afar. Clouded, remote and very cold, she sat down at her dressing-table. Beatrice took up the glass paper-weight, as she always did, and said, as she always said: "These forever fascinate me." She tipped it upside-down and snow began to drift, then whirl, about the little central figure. Muriel watched, the comb too heavy to lift. She watched the figure—a skating lady with raised muff and Regency bonnet—solitary, like herself, blurred, frozen, imprisoned.

"Will she be at dinner?" Beatrice was asking. She flopped down on the marriage-bed itself, still playing with the paper-weight.

Hester, at dinner, did not appear to Beatrice to be a worthy adversary to a woman of Muriel's elegance. She said nothing, except when coaxed by Muriel herself into brief replies; for Muriel had acquired courage and was fluent and vivacious, making such a social occasion of the conversation that they seemed to be characters in a play. "*This* is how experienced people behave," she seemed to imply. "We never embarrass by breaking down. In society, we are impervious."

Robert patronised their conversation in the way of husbands towards wives' women-friends—a rather elaborate but absent-minded show of courtesy. When Hester spilt some wine, he dipped his napkin into the water-jug and sponged the table-cloth without allowing an interruption of what he was saying. He covered her confusion by a rather long speech, and, at its end, Hugh Baseden was ready to take over with an even longer speech of his own. This protectiveness on their part only exposed Hester the more, for Beatrice took the opportunity of not having to listen to observe the girl more closely. She also observed that clumsiness can have a kind of appeal she had never suspected.

She observed technically at first—the fair thick hair which needed drastic shaping: it was bunched up with combs which looked more entangled than controlling. The face was set in an expression which was sulky yet capable of breaking into swift alarm—even terror—as when her hand had knocked against the wine-glass. The hands themselves were huge and helpless, rough, reddened, the nails cropped down. A piece of dirty sticking-plaster covered one knuckle. A thin silver bracelet hung over each wrist.

Then Beatrice next observed that Hugh Baseden's protectiveness was ignored, but that Robert's brought forth a flush and tremor. While he was sponging the table-cloth, the girl watched his hand intently, as if it had a miraculous or terrifying power of its own. Not once did she look at his face.

Beatrice thought that an ominous chivalry hung in the air, and she could see that every victory Muriel had, contributed subtly to her defeat. "She should try less," she decided. She was the only one who enjoyed her dinner.

The boys were all in from the fields and gardens before Robert and Muriel dined, but throughout the meal those in the dining-room were conscious of the school-life continuing behind the baize-covered doors. The sounds of footsteps in the tiled passages and voices calling went on for a long time, and while coffee was being served the first few bars of *"Marche Militaire"* could be heard again and again—the same brisk beginning, and always the same tripping into chaos. Start afresh. Robert beat time with his foot. Muriel sighed. Soon she accompanied Beatrice out to her car, and at once Hester, rather than stay in the room with Robert (for Hugh Baseden had gone off to some duty), went up to her room.

Now, a curious stillness had fallen over the school, a silence drawn down almost by force. The *"Marche Militaire"* was given up and other sounds could be heard—Muriel saying good-bye to Beatrice out on the drive, and an owl crying; for the light was going.

Hester knelt by her window with her elbows on the sill. Evening after evening she thought thunder threatened, and because it did not come she had begun to wonder if the strange atmosphere was a permanent feature of this landscape, and intensified by her own sense of foreboding. The black hillside trees, the grape-coloured light over the church and the bilious green lawns were the after-dinner scene, and she longed for darkness to cover it.

Beatrice's car went down the long drive. A door banged. So Muriel had come in, had returned to the drawing-room to be surprised at Hester's absence. That averted look, which she assumed when she entered rooms where Robert and Hester were alone, would have been wasted.

Hester leant far out of the window. Only the poplars made any sound—a deep sigh and then a shivering and clattering of their leaves. The other trees held out their branches mutely, and she imagined them crowded with sleeping birds, and bright-eyed creatures around their holes, arching their backs, baring their teeth, and swaying their noses to and fro for the first scents of the night's hunting. Her suburban background with its tennis-courts, laburnum trees, golden privet had not taught her how to be brave about the country; she saw only its vice and frightfulness, and remembered the adders in the churchyard and the lizards and grass-snakes which the boys collected. Fear met her at every turn—in her dealings with people, her terror of Muriel, her shrinking from nature, her anxiety about her future—("You are scrupulously untidy," Robert had said. Only a relative would employ her, and she had none but him.)

She made spasmodic efforts to come to terms with these fears; but in trying to face Muriel she fell, she knew, into sullenness. Nature she had not yet braved, had not penetrated the dense woods or the lush meadows by the lake where the frogs were. This evening—as a beginning and because nature was the least of her new terrors, and from loneliness, panic, despair—she moved away from the window, stumbling on her cramped legs, and then went as quietly as she could downstairs and out of doors.

In the garden, at each rustle in the undergrowth, her ankles weakened, but she walked on, treading carefully on the dew-soaked grass. A hedgehog zig-zagged swiftly across her path and checked her. She persisted, hoping thus to restore a little of her self-respect.

She was conscious that each pace was taking her from her safe room, where nothing made her recoil but that phrase of Muriel's that she carried everywhere—"Of course you are in love with Robert." "It was better when we wrote the letters," she thought. "I was happy then. I believe."

As the severest test, she set herself the task of walking through the churchyard where a mist hung over gravestones and nettles. The sound of metal striking flint checked her, and more normal fears than fears of nature came to her almost as a relief; as even burglars might be welcomed in an excessively haunted house. The dusk made it difficult for her to discern what kind of figure it was kneeling beside a headstone under the church walls; but as she stepped softly forwards across the turf she could see it was an old lady, in black flowing clothes and a straw garden-hat swathed with black ribbon. She wore gardening gloves and was planting out salvias and marguerites.

Hester tripped and grazed her arm against some granite. At her cry of pain, the old lady looked up.

"Oh, mercy!" she exclaimed, holding the trowel to her heart. "For pity's sake, girl, what are you doing?"

Her white face was violin-shaped, narrowing under her cheekbones and then widening again, but less, on the level of her wide, thin, lavender-coloured lips. The sagging cords of her throat were drawn in by a black velvet ribbon.

"I was only going for a walk," said Hester.

"I should call it prowling about. Have you an assignation here? With one of those schoolmasters from the house?"

"No."

The old lady drove the trowel into the earth, threw out stones, then, shaking another plant from a pot, wedged it into the hole. The grave resembled a bed in a Public Garden, with a neat pattern of annuals. The salvias bled hideously over a border of lobelias and alyssum. Their red was especially menacing in the dusky light.

"I think a grave should have *formality*," the old lady said, as if she knew Hester's thoughts and was correcting them. "'Keep it neat, and leave it at that,' I warned myself when my father died. I longed to express myself in rather unusual ways; my imagination ran riot with azaleas. A grave is no place for self-expression, though; no place for the indulgence of one's own likings. These flowers are not to my taste at all; they are in *no* taste."

"Is this your father's grave, then?" Hester asked.

"Yes." The old lady pointed with her trowel. "The one you are lolling against is Grandfather's. Mother chained off over there with my sister, Linda. She did not want to go in with Father. I can never remember them sharing a bed, even."

Hester, removing her elbow from the headstone, peered at the name. "Then you lived in the house?" she asked. "This name is carved over the stables."

"Our home since the Dark Ages. Three houses, at least, on this site and brasses in the church going back to the Crusades. Now there are only the graves left. The name going too. For there were only Linda and I. Families decline more suddenly than they can rise. Extraordinarily interesting. The collapse of a family is most dramatic . . . I saw it all happen . . . the money goes, no sons are born—just daughters and sometimes they are not quite the thing . . . my sister Linda was weak in the head. We did have to pinch and scrape, and aunts fastened to us, like barnacles on a wreck. Some of them drank and the servants followed their example. Then trades-people become insolent, although the *nouveaux riches* still fawn." She turned up a green penny with her trowel, rubbed dirt from it and put it in her pocket. "Our disintegration was fairly rapid," she said. "I *can* remember a time before it all overtook us—the scandals and gossip, threadbare carpets, dented silver, *sold* silver, darned linen. Oh, it usually goes the same way for everyone, once it begins. And very fascinating it can be. Dry rot, wood-worm, the walls subsiding. Cracks in plaster and in character. Even the stone-work in the house has some sort of insect in it." She nodded proudly at the school. "Unless they have done something about it."

"Do you come here often?"

"Yes. Yes, I do. I tend the graves. It makes an outing. I once went to the school to have tea with Mrs. Thingummy. A nice little woman." This, Hester supposed, was Muriel. "Interesting to see what they made of it. I liked the school part very much. I went all over, opened every door. I thought the chance might not come again. Into the servants' wing where I had never been before—very nice dormitories and bathrooms. The bathrooms were splendid... little pink, naked boys splashing under showers... a very gay and charming sight... I could hardly drag myself away. They scuttled off as shy as crabs. I expect the look of me startled them. What I did *not* admire was the way she had managed the private part of the house where we had tea... loose-covers, which I abhor... I thought it all showed a cool disregard for the painted ceiling. Never mind, I satisfied my curiosity and no need to be bothered with her again."

Hester, though feeling that Muriel might in fairness be allowed to furnish her drawing-room as she pleased, was none the less delighted to hear this censure, especially over matters of taste. She longed to talk more of Muriel, for she had no other confidante, and this old lady, though strange, was vigorous in her scorn and might, if she were encouraged, say very much more.

"I live there now," she began.

In the darkness, which she had hardly noticed, the old lady had begun to stack up her empty flower-pots.

"Then you will be able to do me a small favour," she said. "In connection with the graves. If it fails to rain tonight I should be obliged if you would water these plants for me in the morning. A good sousing. Before the sun gets strong."

She pulled herself to a standing position with one hand on the gravestone. Her joints snapped with a frail and brittle sound as she moved. Hester faced her across the grave and faced, too, the winey, camphorous smell of her breath and her clothes.

"Only Father's grave. I shall plant Mother's and Linda's tomorrow evening."

She swayed, steadying herself against the stone, and then, with a swinging movement, as if on deck in wild weather, made off through the churchyard, lurching from one gravestone to another, her hands out to balance her, her basket hanging from her arm. She was soon lost to Hester's sight, but the sound of her unsteady progress, as she brushed through branches of yew and scuffled the gravel, continued longer. When she could hear no more, the girl walked back to the house. She had forgotten the snakes and the bats and all the terrors of nature; and she found that for a little while she had forgotten Robert, and Muriel, too; and the sorrows and shame of love.

As she crossed the lawn, Hugh Baseden and Rex Wigmore came round the house from the garages. Stepping out of the darkness into the light shed from upstairs windows, she looked pale-skinned and mysterious, and both men were arrested by a change in her. The breeze blew strands of hair forwards across her face and she turned her head impatiently, so that the hair was whipped back again, lifting up from her ears, around which it hung so untidily by day.

"I thought you were a ghost coming from the churchyard," Hugh said. "Weren't you nervous out there by yourself?"

"No."

But her teeth began to chatter and she drew her elbows tight to her waist to stop herself shivering.

"What *have* you been up to?" Rex asked.

"I went for a walk."

"Alone? How absurd! How wasteful! How unsafe! You never know what might happen to you. If you want to go for a walk, you could always ask me. I like being out with young girls in the dark. I make it even unsafer. And, at least, you could be quite sure what would happen to you then."

"You are cold," Hugh said. He opened the door and, as she stepped past him into the hall, brushed his hand down her bare arm. "You *are* cold."

Rex's remarks, which he deplored, had excited him. He imagined himself—not Rex—walking in the dark with her. He had had so few encounters with women, so few confidings, explorings, and longed to take on some hazards and excitements.

Rex, whose life was full enough of all those things, was bored and wandered off. He found her less attractive—hardly attractive at all—indoors and in the bright light of the hall.

Hester rarely spoke at meal-times, but next morning at breakfast she mentioned the old lady.

"Miss Despenser." Muriel put her hand to her face as she had when speaking of the dead rabbit in the laboratory. She breathed as if she felt faint. "She came to tea once. Once only. I wondered if I should pour whisky in her tea. She is the village drunk. I believe her sister was the village idiot. But now dead."

"You shouldn't go out late at night on your own," Robert said. "You might catch cold," he added, for he could really think of no reason why she should not go—only the vague unease we feel when people venture out late, alone—a guilty sense of having driven them out, or of having proved inadequate to keep them, or still their rest-lessness, or win their confidence.

"It is a wonder she could spare time from the Hand and Flowers," Muriel said. "I am surprised to hear of her tidying the graves in li-censed hours."

"And shall you water the plants?" Robert asked in amusement.

"I have done. She said, before the sun got too strong."

"What impertinence!" Muriel said, and every lash at Miss Despenser was really one at Hester. She felt even more agitated and confused this morning, for Rex's words with their innuendo and suggestion had been spoken beneath her bedroom window the pre-vious night and she, lying in bed, half-reading, had heard him.

Until that moment, she had seen the threat in Hester's youth, defencelessness and pathos; but she had not thought of her as being desirable in any more obvious way. Rex's words—automatic as they were, almost meaningless as they must be from him—proved that the girl might also be desirable in the most obvious way of all. Mu-riel's distaste and hostility were strengthened by what she had over-heard. Still more, a confusion in herself, which she was honest enough to ponder, disquieted her. To be jealous of Hester where

Robert was concerned was legitimate and fitting, she thought; but to be jealous of the girl's least success with other men revealed a harshness from which she turned sickly away. There was nothing now which she could allow Hester, no generosity or praise: grudged words of courtesy which convention forced her to speak seemed to wither on her lips with the enormity of their untruthfulness.

Her jealousy had grown from a fitful nagging to a chronic indisposition, an unreasonableness beyond her control.

She went, after breakfast, to her bedroom without waiting to see Hester follow Robert to his study. The days had often seemed too long for her and now pain had its own way of spinning them out. To go to her kitchen and begin some healing job like baking bread would have appeared to her cook as a derangement and a nuisance. She was childless, kitchenless; without remedy or relief.

Robert, she thought, had not so much become a stranger as revealed himself as the stranger he had for a long time been. The manifestation of this both alarmed her and stirred her conscience. Impossible longings, which had sometimes unsettled her—especially in the half-seasons and at that hour when the light beginning to fade invests garden or darkening room with a romantic languor—had seemed a part of her femininity. The idea that men—or men like Robert—should be beset by the same dangerous sensations would have astonished her by its vulgarity. Their marriage had continued its discreet way. Now, she could see how it had changed its course from those first years, with their anniversaries, secrets, discussions; his hidden disappointment over her abortive pregnancies; the consolation and the bitter tears—all embarrassing now in her memory, but shouldering their way up through layers of discretion to wound and worry her. She had allowed herself to change; but she could tolerate no change in Robert, except for the decline in his ardour, which she had felt herself reasonable in expecting.

In rather the same spirit as Hester's when she had faced the terrors of the churchyard the night before, Muriel now went into Robert's dressing-room and shut the door. She knelt down before a chest, and, pulling out the bottom drawer, found, where she knew she would find them, among his old school photographs, the bundle of letters she had written to him when they were betrothed.

She felt nausea, but a morbid impatience, as if she were about to read letters from his mistress. The first of the pile began: "Dear Mr. Evans..." It was a cool, but artful, invitation. She remembered writing it after their first meeting, thinking he had gone for ever and wanting to draw him back to her. "I am writing for my mother, as she is busy." Not only had he been drawn back, but he had kept the letter. Perhaps he had had his own plans for their meeting again. She might well have let things be and sat at home and waited—so difficult a thing for a young girl to do.

That first letter was the only time he was "Mr. Evans." After that, he progressed from "Dear Robert," through "My Dear Robert," "Dearest Robert," "Robert Dearest," to "Darling." In the middle period of the letters—for he had preserved them chronologically—the style was comradely, witty, undemanding. ("Intolerably affected," Muriel now thought, her neck reddening with indignation. "Arch! Oh, yes!" Did Hester write so to him and could he, at his age, feel no distaste?) The letters, patently snobbish, shallow, worked up, had taken hours to write, she remembered. Everything that happened during the day was embroidered for Robert at night—the books she read were only used as a bridge between their two minds. The style was parenthetic, for she could not take leave even of a sentence. So many brackets scattered about gave the look of her eyelashes having been shed upon the pages. When she had written "Yours, Muriel" or, later, "Your Muriel," there was always more to come, many postscripts to stave off saying good-night. Loneliness, longing broke through again and again despite the overlying insincerity. She had— writing in her room at night—so wanted Robert. Like a miracle, or as a result of intense concentration, she had got what she wanted. Kneeling before the drawer, with the letters in her hand, she was caught up once more in amazement at this fact. "I got what I wanted," she thought over and over again.

His letters to her had often disappointed, especially in the later phase when possessiveness and passion coloured her own. Writing so late at night, she had sometimes given relief to her loneliness. Those were momentary sensations, but his mistake had lain in taking them as such; in writing, in his reply, of quite other things. "But did you get my letter?" Muriel now read—the beginning of a long complaint, which she was never to finish reading; for the door opened and Robert was staring at her with an expression of aloof non-comprehension, as if he had suddenly been forced to close his mind at this intimation of her character.

Muriel said shakily: "I came across our old letters to one another—or rather mine to you . . . I could not resist them."

He still stared, but she would not look at him. Then he blinked, seemed to cast away some unpleasant thoughts, and said coldly, holding up a letter which she still would not glance at: "Lady Bewick is running this dance after the garden party. I came up to ask how many tickets we shall want."

"I thought you were taking Latin," Muriel said naively.

"They are having Break now." And, indeed, if she had had ears to hear it, she would have known by the shouting outside.

"I should let her know today," Robert said. "Whom shall we take?"

Muriel was very still. Warily, she envisaged the prospects—Hester going along, too. Hester's brown, smooth shoulders dramatised by her chalk-white frock. Robert's glance at them. Muriel's pale veined arms incompletely hidden by her lace stole. Perhaps Hester was a good dancer. Muriel herself was too stiff and rather inclined, from panic, to lead her partner.

"Why could we not go alone?" she asked.

"We could; but I thought we should be expected to take a party."

"Whom do you think?"

"I had no thoughts. I came to ask you."

"I see." "He wants it every way," she thought. "For her to go, and for me to suggest it." She tied up the letters and put them away.

"You should take Hester," she said suddenly. She began to tremble with anger and unhappiness. "I can stay at home."

"I had no intention of taking Hester."

"I suppose you are angry with me for reading those letters. I know it was wrong of me to open your drawer. I have never done such a thing in my life before." She still sat on the floor and seemed exhausted, keeping her head bent as she spoke.

"I can believe that. Why did you now?" he asked.

For a moment, gentleness, the possibility of understanding, enveloped them; but she let it go, could think only of her suspicions, her wounded pride.

The tears almost fell, but she breathed steadily and they receded. "I was bored. Not easy not to be. I remembered something... I was talking to Beatrice about it yesterday... I knew I should have written it somewhere in my letters to you. I was sure you wouldn't mind my looking." Her excuses broke off and at last she dared to look at him. She smiled defiantly. "I wrote them, you know. You seem as cross as if they were written by another woman."

"They were," he said.

She was stunned. She slammed the drawer shut and stood up. She thought: "Those are the worst words he ever spoke to me."

"I shall have to go," he said. "I suppose I can leave this till this afternoon." He held up the letter in his hand. "I didn't want to discuss it at lunch, that was all. The point is that Lady Bewick hoped we could take a partner for her niece who is staying there—she thought we could ask one of the staff. I wonder if Hugh..."

"But he's so boring."

"We need not stay together."

"Take Rex."

"Rex?"

"Why not? He dances well."

"But he's so impossible. You have never disguised your scorn for him."

"He would be better than Hugh—not so achingly tedious." Irritability, the wish to sting, underlined her words. "You are achingly tedious, too," she seemed to imply. Her voice was higher pitched than usual, her cheeks flushed. He looked at her in concern, then said: "All right. Three tickets, then." He put the letter in his pocket and turned away.

As soon as he had gone, but too late, she broke into weeping.

They dined at home before the dance. Muriel was intimidating, but uncertain, in too many diamonds. When she brought out her mother's jewels, Robert always felt put in his place, though never before had they all come out at once. Her careless entrance into the drawing-room had astonished him. She was shrugged up in a pink woollen shawl, through which came a frosty glitter. Rex's look of startled admiration confirmed her fear that she was overdressed. "She has never erred in that way before," Robert thought: but she had shown several new faults of late; flaws had appeared which once he could not have suspected. There was, too, something slyly affected about the cosy shawl and the stir and flash of diamonds beneath it.

"It is only a countrified sort of dance," Robert told Rex. His words were chiefly for Muriel, who should have known. "Nothing very exciting. Good of you to turn out."

He hoped that Hester would now feel that she would miss nothing by staying at home, that he could not have gone himself, except as a duty; or asked anyone else to go, except as a favour. His stone, which should have killed two birds, missed both.

Hester, wearing a day-frock and trying to look unconcerned, managed only a stubborn sullenness—a Cinderella performance Muriel thought wrongly, underlined by Rex's greeting to her—"But you are coming with us, surely?"—when her clothes made it quite obvious that she was not.

Robert's shame, Muriel's guilt, Hester's embarrassment, seemed not to reach Rex, although for the other three the air shivered, the wine-glasses trembled, at his tactlessness.

"Too bad," he said easily. "Well, there is no doubt that you are coming." He turned to Muriel, his eyes resting once more upon all her shimmering glitter. ("Ice," he called it, and—later, to Hugh

Baseden—"rocks the size of conkers. Crown jewels. The family coffers scraped to the bottom.")

The glances, which he had meant to appear gallant and flattering, looked so predatory that Muriel put her hand to her necklace in a gesture of protection, and a bracelet fell into the soup. She laughed as Rex leant forward and fished it out with a spoon and fork and dropped it into the napkin she held out. Her laughter was that simulated kind which is difficult to end naturally and her eyes added to all the tremulous glint and shimmer of her. Hester, coldly regarding her, thought that she would cry. A Muriel in tears was a novel, horrifying idea.

The bracelet lay on the stained napkin. "The catch must be loose. I shan't wear it," Muriel said, and pushed it aside.

"That will be one less," Robert thought.

After dinner he had a moment alone with Hester.

"All rather awkward about this dance. I hope you don't mind, my dear. Don't like leaving you—like Cinderella."

Hester could see Muriel, re-powdered, cocooned in tulle, coming downstairs and laughed at this illusion, remembering who did go to the ball in the fairy-tale. "We must go to a real dance another time," Robert said. "Not a country hop, but a proper dance, with buckets of champagne." But Muriel, rustling across the hall, finished this vision for them. "I should sit with Matron," he added.

"Oh, it is quite all right," Hester said, with a brightness covering her extreme woundedness. "I could not have gone with you tonight, or sit with Matron either; because I have another engagement, and now I must hurry." With a glance at their halted expressions she ran upstairs, leaving behind an uneasiness and raised eyebrows.

The cistern in the downstairs cloakroom made a clanking sound and there was a dreadful rush of water. This always embarrassed Muriel, and she turned aside as Rex appeared.

Hester, at the bend of the stairs, called out in a ringing, careless voice: "Oh, do have a lovely time."

In this exhortation she managed to speak to them both in different ways—a difficult thing to do. Muriel felt herself condescended to and dismissed, unenvied, like a child going to a treat. But Robert's guilt was not one scrap appeased, and Hester did not mean it to be. He perceived both her pathos and her gallantry, as she desired. Her apparent lack of interest in their outing and her sudden look of excitement worried him. Even Rex was puzzled by her performance. "Now what's she up to?" he wondered, as they went out to the car.

Yet, when she was in her own room Hester could not imagine where she might go. Recklessness would have led her almost anywhere, but in the end she could only think of the churchyard. As Miss Despenser had said, "to water the graves makes an outing," and perhaps she could borrow a grave—Miss Linda's, for instance—and cherish it in such dull times as these.

When she arrived in the churchyard, she found that Miss Despenser had finished planting and was vigorously scrubbing the headstones. Dirty water ran down over an inscription. "That's better," were her first words to Hester as she came near.

"I watered the plants."

"Yes, I noticed that."

"Can I help you?"

Miss Despenser threw the filthy water out in a great arc over some other graves—not her own family ones, Hester was sure—and handed her the bucket. "Clean water from the tap by the wall."

"Is that where the adders were?"

"Adders?"

"There were some once. I thought they might have come again."

"This is a fine thing—a stranger telling me about my own churchyard. I know nothing of adders. Are you a naturalist?"

"Oh, no! I am really rather afraid of nature."

Miss Despenser threw out her arms and laughed theatrically. "You're a damn witty girl, I know that. When I first met you I thought you were a bit of a nincompoop. You improve on acquaintance." She turned to examine the lettering on the grave, and Hester went to fetch the water.

"Afraid of nature!" Miss Despenser said, when she returned. "I appreciate that."

The water, swinging in the pail, had slopped over into Hester's sandals and her feet moved greasily in them.

"So you're afraid of nature!" Miss Despenser said, and she grasped the bucket and threw the water over the headstones. Some went over her and more into Hester's sandals. "She is drunk," Hester thought, remembering Muriel's words and feeling annoyance that there should be any truth in them.

"The bucket goes back into the shed and the scrubbing-brush into the basket." Miss Despenser shook drops of water off her skirt. "And we will go down to call on Mrs. Brimmer."

"Mrs. Brimmer?"

"A friend of mine. You are quite welcome. I will look in at the house first and leave the scrubbing-brush. Mrs. Brimmer would think me rather eccentric if I went to see her with a scrubbing-brush in my basket."

"Any adders?" she asked, when Hester came back from the tool-shed. The piquancy of her own humour delighted her and she returned to the allusion again and again, puzzling Hester—who expected drunkenness to affect the limbs, but not the wits, and was exasperated as the young so often are at failing to read an extra meaning into the remarks of their elders.

Through a kissing-gate they came into a wood of fir trees. Miss Despenser slid and scuffled down the sloping track which was slippery with pine-needles. Jagged white flints had surfaced the path like the fins of sharks, so that Miss Despenser tripped and stumbled until Hester took her arm. She thought that they must look a strange pair and—such was the creaking darkness and mysterious resinous smell of the wood—half-feared that as the path curved they might see themselves coming towards them through the trees, like a picture of Rossetti's she remembered called *How They Met Themselves*. "I shouldn't care to meet myself," she said aloud, "in this dark place."

"You wouldn't recognise yourself. You are much too young. When at long last you really learn what to look for, you will be too old to be alarmed."

"I didn't mean that I should, or could; just that I'd hate it."

"I meet myself every so often. 'You hideous old baggage,' I say, and I nod. For years I thought it was someone else."

"This wood goes on and on," Hester said nervously.

"Ah, you are frightened of adders." When she had finished laughing, Miss Despenser said: "When I go into the town to get the cat's meat, the chances are that as I go round by the boot shop I see myself walking towards me—in a long panel of mirror at the side of the shop. 'Horrid old character,' I used to think. 'I must change my shopping morning.' So I changed to Fridays, but there she was on Fridays just the same. 'I can't seem to avoid her,' I told myself. And no one can. Go on your holidays. You take yourself along too. Go to the ends of the earth. No escape. And one gets so bored, bored. I've had nearly seventy years of it now. And I wonder if I'd been beautiful or clever I might have been less irritated. Perhaps I am difficult to please. My mother didn't care for *herself*, either. When she died, the Vicar said: 'It is only another life she has gone to, an *everlasting* life.' An extraordinarily trite little man. He hadn't got much up here." She tapped her forehead and stumbled badly. "I said to him: 'Oh dear, oh dear, for pity's sake, hasn't she had enough of herself?' I asked. He couldn't answer that one. He just stared at the glass of sherry I was drinking, as if he were taking comfort in the idea of my being drunk. 'I believe in personality,' I said. 'You believe in souls.' That's the difference between us. Souls are flattened out and one might very well spend an eternity with one's own—though goodness knows what it would be like—as interesting as a great bowl of nourishing soup. I always think of souls as saucers, full of some tepid, transparent liquid. Couldn't haunt anyone. Personalities do the haunting—Papa's for instance. Tiresome, dreadful things. Can't shake them off. Unless under the influence, of course."

"Of drink, I suppose," Hester thought.

"Of drink," the old lady added.

"It *is* a gruesome place. I like trees which shed their leaves."

The bark of the trees was blood-red in the dying light and there were no sounds of birds or of anything but branches creaking and tapping together. Then the pink light thinned, the trees opened out and blueness broke through, and in this new light was a view of a tilted hillside with houses, and a train buffeting along between cornfields.

"And there is my home," Miss Despenser said. She scrambled down the bank into a lane and, as she brushed dust and twigs from her skirt, she crossed the lane and opened a gate.

Laurels almost barred the way to the little house, which was of such dark grey and patchy stucco that it looked sopping wet. The untidy curtains seemed to have rooms of blank darkness behind them. Shepherd's-purse grew round the mossy doorstep where a milk-bottle dribbling curdled milk had been knocked over.

"Welcome!" said Miss Despenser, throwing open the door upon such a smell of dampness and decay, such a chaotic litter, that Hester stepped aside to take a last full breath before going in.

"You were right. He *is* behaving abominably," Muriel said to Robert as they danced.

Rex had reconnoitred, got his bearings, soon left Lady Bewick's niece and now was slipping out through the flap of the marquee with a girl in a green frock. Muriel saw his hand pass down the back of his gleaming hair in an anticipatory gesture as he went.

"He's lost no time in finding the most common-looking little minx in the room," she told Robert. She was unsteady and almost breathless with frustration, not getting her own way. So far she had danced once with the doctor and the rest of the time with Robert.

"It's his duty, if nothing else," she thought. But Rex and his duty made a casual relationship. "Am I so faded, that he would rather be rude?" But Rex was firstly doing what he wanted to do. If rudeness was involved, it was only as a side-issue. "It is because he knows I am inaccessible," she told herself.

They continued to catch brief glimpses of Rex during the evening; at the bar, at the buffet. Someone else took Lady Bewick's niece to supper. As it grew later, the sky deepened its blue behind the black shapes of the garden trees—the monkey-puzzles darkly barbed; the cedars; and the yews clipped into pagodas and peacocks. Voices floated across the lawns; long skirts brushed the grass.

In twos, the dancers strolled in the enclosed warmth of the walled garden, sat on the terrace among the chipped statues, or gazed down at the silvered lily-leaves in the pool.

"A good thing we *didn't* bring Hester," Muriel said. "Rex would have left her stranded."

"Sorry!" said Robert, as they fell out of step. They had never danced well together, yet they went on dancing. There was nothing to walk in the garden *for*, among all that pulsating romance. At their age.

In the end, Muriel's dance with Rex was accidental, during a Paul Jones. Hearing the first romping bars of this, she was all for going to the bar, but Lady Bewick hustled her into the dance—"Now, *every-one*! You must"—and took her by the hand and led her to the circle. They revolved, with absurd smiles, feeling looked-over by the encir-cling men. Robert's expression was one of sudden gaiety, as if he were let off the leash for a moment. "How many years has he had that suit?" Muriel wondered. "Since he was at school, I should think. The sleeves are too short. He looks buttoned-up, spry, like a cock-sparrow. What can a young girl see in him, unless a father?" Yet could not that be a danger, especially if Robert were at the same time looking for a daughter? Rex bowed mockingly as he passed her; but his eyes were instantly elsewhere.

"An absurd game, like a child's," Muriel thought, feeling out-raged and also secretly dismayed at the thought of the music stop-ping as she faced blankness; then to trail disconsolately to a chair, watched by Robert, and by Rex. She had not learnt how to mind less than as a little girl at parties—the panic of not being chosen, the first seeds of self-mistrust.

But when the music stopped she was at once in the doctor's arms again. He came straight forward with his hands outstretched; easy to dance with, he waltzed away with her, bouncy, soft-treading, his rounded paunch doing the guiding. By fate or by manoeuvre, Rex had the green girl. Muriel could not see Robert and was inattentive to the dance as she tried to search him out. Then she saw him at the edge of the room. He had been left without a partner and now was going forward to claim a very plain woman in a pink frock and tortoiseshell-rimmed glasses. Muriel was at peace, until the next round. It was then that she found herself between Rex and another man when the music stopped. Both hesitated; then Rex seemed to master his unwillingness, smiled and stepped forward. Authoritatively he took her over; automatically pressed her to him. She made some remark, and, while his eyes still roved round the room, he smiled again and laid his cheek to her hair. "What did you say?"

"I am his headmaster's wife!" Muriel thought indignantly; but her heart had cantered away.

"She *will* be angry," Robert thought, as he caught sight of her. But it was she who had suggested bringing him. Robert—blame-evading—had known that Rex would behave like a bounder. Then, to his amazement, he saw that Muriel was smiling. She looked up at Rex, who shook his head teasingly, and then sank deftly back to his nestling embrace.

His eyes stopped following the girl in the green dress, for there was fun closer at hand.

"We shouldn't keep Mrs. Brimmer waiting too long," Miss Despenser said. She put the scrubbing-brush down on the hall-table. "I must give the cat his supper before we go. Wander about. Make yourself at home."

A great, gooseberry-eyed, striped cat walked stiffly out of the darkness, stretched, hooped up its back. "Naughty cat, doesn't deserve supper. What is this? Another mess on the Soumak rug?" She took some newspaper from the clutter on the table and bent down to wipe at the clotted fringe. The cat leant against her legs as she did so, staring up at Hester, callously detached.

"Well, that's that!"

But it wasn't and, to escape the smell, Hester followed her to the kitchen, thinking: "Only the graves can she keep clean."

In the kitchen, the richness of litter was as if a great cornucopia of dirty dishes and decaying food had been unloaded over tables, chairs, shelves and stove. Flies had stopped their circling and eating and excreting for the day and now slept on the walls and ceiling. Miss Despenser tipped a cod's head out of a saucepan on to a dish on the floor, and Hester half-faintly wished she had stayed in the hall. The cat sniffed at the boiled, clouded eyes and walked away.

"Have you no help?" Hester asked.

"Not now. Gone are the days, alas! when there was a maid to do my hair. But if a woman of my age cannot dress her own hair she should be quite ashamed."

"But not your hair. I meant all the dishes."

"I have all day."

She picked up a sticky-looking wine-glass and drank something from it. "That was careless of me," she said. "I hate waste. And now for Mrs. Brimmer!"

"How sweet the outside air," Hester thought. As they walked down the lane to the village, warmth flowed between the hedges and she felt a great lassitude and unhappiness.

Miss Despenser struck along beside her, seemed conscious of her mood, and kept glancing up. "Like some nauseating little dog asking for attention," Hester thought, and looked at the hedgerow, ignoring her.

"If they're not good to you at that school, I am not surprised," Miss Despenser said at last. "I didn't like the wife. And he's as poor a nincompoop as ever there was, I think. Nimminy pimminy; but *she's* a thundering dunderhead, as my father used to call the Vicar. There was a beautiful panel in the drawing-room, and she has moved it away and put shelves up for her collection of mediocre china. It was a clever painting with a great deal of work in it. Detail. Rich in detail. Neptune, d'you know, simply smothered in barnacles and sea-weed; sea-serpents; tritons; dolphins. A great painstaking monsterpiece. I suppose she thought it indecent. The boys would've liked it, I am sure. If ever things get too much for you, you know, you must come and tuck in with me—at any time of the day or night. I have a spare room ... Linda's room."

Hester tried not to imagine poor Miss Linda's room (herself tucking into it), where she had lived, "not quite all there"—and probably died.

"They are good to me," she said.

"I thought you seemed rather on the mopy side."

"No."

"Perhaps in love?"

"Not in love. No."

"Linda and I once were. With the same man fortunately. That was nice. We could discuss him at night. We always shared everything. Oh, we used to laugh, comparing notes, d'you know. If we met him . . . he used to ride a grey mare called Mirabella—you see, I remember the name even—he always raised his hat. Once I was hurrying to the post with a letter in my hand and he stopped and offered to take it for me." She paused, reflecting on this long-ago kindness, then said: "Well, you *ought* to be in love, I should say. Now is the time for it. Ah, there is Mrs. Brimmer on the look-out for me."

In the lighted bar-window of the pub a huge, cardiganed woman appeared. She raised her arms and laid a cloth over a bird-cage, then receded. She did not seem to see Miss Despenser.

Over the pub doorway, Hester saw the notice—"Melanie Brimmer, licensed to sell Beer, Wines and Spirits."

"Here I am at last, Mrs. Brimmer," Miss Despenser said, stepping into the flagged passage-way.

Mrs. Brimmer, behind the bar, nodded vaguely at them. She then opened a bottle of Guinness, which seemed to flop into the glass in an exhausted way, and beside this she placed a glass of Madeira.

"Will you have the same?" Miss Despenser asked Hester.

"The same as which?"

"I like to sip at both."

Miss Despenser began to pull at her skirts and pat herself and at last brought out a purse.

"Oh, I should like . . . if I could have a sherry . . ." ("Oh, God! I didn't know it would be a pub!" she thought. "I have no money—nothing.") Again, she felt like running.

The sherry was handed to her by the silent Mrs. Brimmer.

"And you, yourself, Mrs. Brimmer?"

At last Mrs. Brimmer spoke: "No, I won't touch anything to-night if it's the same to you. I had one of my turns after tea." She began to tap her fingers rhythmically between her lower ribs. "Heart-burn. Stew keeps repeating." She belched softly and gravely.

Hester sipped, then moved her eyes slowly round the room. Two old men played dominoes at a trestle-table. By the empty fireplace, Hugh Baseden had risen from his chair and stood waiting awkwardly to be recognised.

After the next absurd circling in the dance, Muriel faced a blank—the chain of men had thinned, broken, just in front of her as the music stopped. Robert, not far away, knowing how she hated to feel conspicuous or unclaimed even in the smallest ways, made a little gesture of frustration to her, as if to say he would have helped her if he could. She smiled and put on an exaggeratedly woebegone expression and moved aside.

"Time to knock-off for the old noggin," Rex said, putting his arm through hers. He had been a fighter-pilot in the war and in certain situations tended to resuscitate the curious *mélange* of archaisms and slang which once had been his everyday language.

"So you were left, too?"

"I didn't go in. I was stooging round the perim as it were, on the lookout."

"Oh, I see."

"I hope you have no objection, ma'am."

"None."

After two whiskies, they went into the garden. The music came to an end with a jarring clash of cymbals, then clapping; but Rex and Muriel walked on down the terrace.

"The landed gentry don't do themselves half badly," Rex said, slapping a statue across the buttocks as they passed it. "Hardly a hot-bed of Bolshevism."

Inside the marquee a man's voice rose above the confusion of sound which then gradually sank. "Forty-nine!" was shouted and repeated. After a moment, clapping broke out again.

"Oh, that is the raffle," Muriel said.

Couples made their way back across the lawns towards the marquee, but she and Rex walked on.

"Do you want to go and see if you have won a bottle of rich old ruby port or something?" he asked. "Let's sit down here, or will it spoil your dress?"

She did not even glance at the stone seat, but sat down at once.

"Are you warm enough?" He rearranged her lace stole round her shoulders. Her diamonds shone in the moonlight, and he put his warm hand to her throat and touched them.

"Heavenly!" he said. "You have some lovely jewels, ma'am."

"Perhaps he is going to steal them," she thought, in a flash of panic and candour with herself. "I must have been deluded to think he just wanted to be with me." But his hand turned over and lay palm down against her beating throat. "Or he will strangle me first," she thought, putting nothing past him.

"Why did you ask me to come tonight?" he asked. "You don't like me, do you?"

She closed her eyes.

"Do you?" he persisted. "So often seen your face go smooth and expressionless at things I've said."

"I don't understand men like you."

"What sort of man am I then?"

She had an impulse to flatter him, though it was strange for her to flatter any man. "Although I'm older than you, you make me feel inexperienced and immature."

"It wasn't that," he said. "You were just plainly looking down your nose at me, ma'am."

"Don't call me 'ma'am,'" she whispered.

"What then?"

For a moment she didn't answer and then murmured, "I don't know."

"Mustn't call you 'Muriel.' Not respectful in one so young, so junior. Mrs. Evans, then?"

He slid his hand down her throat and under her armpit. She began to tremble, and at this he leant forward and kissed her.

"I might call you 'darling,'" he suggested. "I wonder how that would sound."

"This is absurd," she said shakily. "We must go back."

"Back to the marquee, or back to where we were before tonight?"

"Both."

"Just as you say, my dear." He moved away from her, but she did not move. He let the humiliation of this sink into her for a moment, then took her hands. Her fingers twisted restlessly in his, but fastening and not freeing themselves. "Nothing so avid as a married woman," he thought complacently and began to kiss her and embrace her in ways of the most extravagant vulgarity such as she had not encountered outside literature.

In the Hand and Flowers, political discussion, though not really raging, was of enough strength to redden cheeks.

There were two periods of acrimony during the evening, Mrs. Brimmer knew. The first was soon after opening-time, when the regulars came in fresh from the six o'clock news and such disasters as it had announced. Later, some of the contentious went home to their supper: others stayed and played darts. By eight o'clock, a different clientele, more genial, out for the evening, had begun to arrive. Politics, at this stage, were tabu. Towards closing-time, however, geniality might wear thin and argument erupt in one place after another. Mrs. Brimmer, leaning on the bar, or going ponderously down into the cellar to bring up the half-slopped pots of beer, was always brief or silent unless describing her indigestion, but towards ten o'clock she would sometimes say abruptly: "I'm Labour anyway," as in a few minutes she would say "Time now, gentlemen." Mrs. Brimmer held one or two unexpected opinions which were all the same ground inextricably into her personality. Another of her beliefs which she often made clear was that women should not go into public houses. She served them silently and grudgingly and would have horse-whipped every one, she often said. She really did not approve of drinking at all, apart from the gin-and-pep she sometimes took to shift her wind. However, having lived in the pub as a wife, she duly carried on as a widow.

"What they want is to have us all equal," Miss Despenser said, "and the only way to do that is to level everyone *down*. Not to raise everyone *up*. No, it's down, down, down all the time. When we're finally in the gutter, then we shall have true democracy."

"But surely..." said Hugh Baseden.

"When I was young everyone was better off and do you know why?"

"Well..."

"Because we all knew our proper places. No one was ashamed to serve. Why, my mother's maid was like a sister to her. Two sisters. Peas in a pod."

"That's right." Mrs. Brimmer nodded.

"But when she had helped your mother to dress, she didn't go to the dance with her. She stayed and tidied the bedroom," Hester said. She glanced at Hugh, who looked gravely back in agreement. Some of his gravity, however, was his anxiety at Hester's having drunk too much.

"She didn't want to go. That is what I am saying. She didn't want to go. That is why she was so happy."

"My mother was in service," one of the dominoes players said. "Happiest days of her life, she reckoned. No worries. All found."

"There you are, you see," Miss Despenser said.

"It's wrong to be happy like that...not to have your own life," Hester said. At the back of her mind, she felt a great sense of injustice somewhere, of sacrifices which ought not to be asked or made. "Kow-towing," she murmured and, looking flushed and furious, sipped her sherry.

"Kow-towing fiddlededee," Miss Despenser said. "You talk as if the educated classes exist for nothing."

Mrs. Brimmer drew her blouse away from her creased chest, glanced down mysteriously, blowing gently between her breasts, then fanned herself. "I hear Charlie's gone," she said.

"He's gone, has he?" asked the gaitered gamekeeper. His setters stretched by the fire, blinking their bloody eyes, nosing their private parts.

"So Les Salter said when he came with his club money."

"I said to the missus I reckon old Charlie's going at last. I said that only last night when I saw the lamp upstairs."

"That's right."

"When was that?"

"This morning. They sent along for Mrs. Brown about eight o'clock. He'd just gone then."

"Would you like a drink?" Hugh asked Miss Despenser.

"Most kind."

"What may I get you?"

"Mrs. Brimmer knows."

He stood awkwardly before Hester. "The same?" "If I take her back drunk, I take the blame, too, I suppose," he thought. To his relief she shook her head.

"How are you getting home?" he asked quietly.

"I shall look after her," Miss Despenser said, and she laid her hand on Hester's arm. Hester looked down at it with loathing. Under the shiny, loose skin the high veins seemed to writhe and knot themselves as if separately alive. Nothing was said. He turned to the bar and watched Mrs. Brimmer reluctantly pouring out the drinks.

"He is rather familiar," Miss Despenser said. "After all, he is not quite in the same position as you. You could spend the night with me if you are nervous."

To be saved for one night from her dreams would be so very wonderful, she thought. She and Hester could sit up until morning and talk. Her dreams were usually distressing. There was one in which her father kept entering the library, always from the same door, crossing the room, disappearing, only to come in again in the same way, with the dread inevitability of dreams. Then there was the one in which her mother told her to pull down her clothes, but her skirts shrank and shrank. Because of her nightmares, she had tried to sleep in the daytime, for bad dreams come in the dark; but to be awake in the quiet house—especially as it seemed to be only *just* quiet—was frightening, too.

"I will pop a hot-bottle in your bed," she promised. "You are not to think it will be a trouble."

"I must go home. There is no reason why I should not."

Miss Despenser bent her head. "I dare say you think me very frumpish," she said. "Can't be helped. We all come to it. Most kind," she said again to Hugh, but gave Mrs. Brimmer a sharp glance as a Guinness only was placed before her. Mrs. Brimmer was once more glancing nonchalantly inside her blouse.

"Is she cooking something down there?" Hugh muttered, as he sat down beside Hester, and then in an even lower voice asked: "May I walk home with you?"

"But how can I get rid of her?" Hester asked, and felt soiled by her disloyalty.

"Time, gentlemen, if you please." Mrs. Brimmer went to the door and opened it, letting in cool air and moths.

"I will see you home," Miss Despenser told Hester. "But let *him* get on his way first." She slowly drained her Guinness, keeping her eyes shut. When she opened them, Hugh Baseden was still there. "Good-night!" she bade him. Froth was drying on her moustached upper lip, and Hugh looked away from her as he spoke.

"I am taking Hester back to the school. May we see you home first?"

"Good-*night*!" said Mrs. Brimmer, not caring who went with whom, as long as all went without delay.

They set off together, and Miss Despenser was sullen and her course vague and veering. Once she stumbled against the high bank and, hoping to steady herself, put her hand down into a patch of nettles. She righted herself and wandered on, rubbing her inflamed wrist, drawing herself obstinately away from Hugh when he tried to support her. But when they reached her house she allowed him to take her key and open the door. He switched on the light, and she sat down abruptly on a chair in the hall. When Hester said good-night, she just nodded without lifting her head to see her go and stared at the cat who seemed to have waited for her to come home before he squatted in a corner and began to wet the carpet. She did not rebuke him but sat still for a long time, and at last tears began to slant out of her eyes and down the sides of her face. "Not since Linda died!" she thought. For Hester, that stranger to her, had come up out of a mist or a dream to confront her with loneliness. Unsteadily, she stood up and crossed the hall. The looking-glass was filmed with damp and dust, but she could see herself dimly in it. Clutching the back of a chair she rocked to and fro, staring. "It is what I am," she told herself. "It is what I live with." Her vision seemed to slide and slip like colours in a kaleidoscope. "Pussy," she called. "Naughty pussy! Now where are you?" He came swaying out of the kitchen, paw before paw, coat rippling, pupils only a dark slit, tail curved. "I am master here," he seemed to say.

"Who was that tipsy, tittupping little person?" Hugh Baseden asked.

"I met her once when I was wandering around. She is mad, I think."

"The stench in that house! Is she a witch?"

"I expect so."

"I didn't know what to think when you walked in with her."

"I have to go somewhere."

"Do...*they*...know?"

"Neither know nor care."

They climbed the bank and began to cross the field towards the wood.

"You must be very lonely," he said. "I have often thought that. I suppose they're very nice, though so terribly set in their complacent ways. And when they do do something enjoyable...this dance, I mean...they leave you at home."

"I didn't want to go—like Miss Despenser's mother's maid."

"And Robert's a kind chap, but such a very dry old stick. Very fussy to work for."

"Very fussy," Hester panted, breathless from the steep field-path.

"Of course, he's your uncle. I shouldn't have said that..."

"My cousin...my cousin."

"He has some rather old-maidish ways, you know...peering over his glasses, taking pills..."

"And the barometer!" Hester was astonished to hear herself saying. "Tapping it at least three times a day. Why not just take the weather as it comes?"

They entered the warm wood and this time she was not afraid.

"*She* is the dominant one, of course," Hugh said.

Hester thought: "Perhaps I was only scared not to be in love with someone; anybody." She was confused by her sudden sensations of irritability towards Robert. "My head!" she said, and stumbled along over the tree roots, pressing both hands to her temples.

"I will find you some of Rex's famous hangover pills when we get back. It was funny about Rex going tonight."

"Funny?"

"I thought Madam's view of him was very dark indeed." He took Hester's elbow and guided her out of the way of some low branches. "Nearly there," he said.

The air was thinner and cooler outside the wood. They came to the churchyard and the neat Despenser graves.

Muriel had creamed her face and was weeping. Robert was silent with frightening displeasure.

"I don't want to see him again," she cried.

He took the cuff-links out of his shirt and put them back into their velvet-padded box. He said: "That is what you cannot help doing. It is a little awkwardness you have created for us all."

"He might resign."

"But he won't, and there is no reason why he should. You will find he is quite unperturbed. It will have meant nothing to him," Robert added cruelly. "When he remembers, and if it amuses him, he may take advantage of the situation to discomfit us. It is dreadfully late to be crying so," he said fretfully. "I am very tired, and he will see your red eyes in the morning and purr more than ever."

"Robert, you are rather working this up. By the way you are speaking I might have committed adultery."

"I think you might, if you hadn't suddenly heard 'God Save the Queen.' Your patriotism made you stand up—even if it *was* in one another's arms."

"Oh, the brittle wit! How dare you? We had suddenly realised that the dance was over."

"Time had stood still."

She began angrily to splash cold water on her eyes. When she was in bed, she said shakily: "After all, *you* don't make love to me."

He got neatly into bed and lay down as far from her as he could, his back turned.

"Do you?" she wept.

"You know I do not, and you know why I do not."

"If I didn't like it, perhaps that was your fault. Did you ever think of that?"

"Very often. I surveyed every explanation in turn. Then I became rather bored and thought 'so be it.'"

"I know I was wrong tonight . . . though really sillier than wrong."

"You made us both look absurd and started a ridiculous scandal by your behaviour. Everyone missed you. I suppose it was an arranged thing between you . . . I remember your insistence on having him there. How long, if you wouldn't mind telling me, has this romance been flourishing?" He spoke stiffly, lying with his back to her. He was anxious to be reassured, to shake off the insecurity which results from a serious deviation in one we have trusted.

"You shall not say such a thing," she cried.

He had gone too far in his suspicions, and her amazed rejection of them was so genuine that he now went too far in his relief; although he only gravely said: "I apologise." "This dreadful conversation!" he thought. "The cold phrases of hatred—'I apologise.' 'How dare you!' 'You *know* why.'" "If it was just a sudden ill-judged thing," he said, "I can understand better. Anything else—plotting, lying—would not have been like you."

She lay on her back and stared up through the darkness; said "Thank you" in a far-away voice.

"Oh, don't cry again." He turned over and touched her hair.

"We were so happy," she cried.

"I don't think we were very happy."

"I was."

He meant his silence to punish her. To explain—she thought—everything; to simplify everything and press the punishment back upon him, she said: "If Hester had never come here! If we could be as we were!"

"She had no part in this. She was utterly innocent."

"Her innocence has been like a poison to us. It has corrupted us both." In her mind she seemed to step back from the thought of their married life, as if she recoiled physically from an unexpected horror. She said: "It is like the time when I found the adders lying under the ferns."

"What is like that?" he asked. His head lay on his crooked arm, and he stared into the darkness where there was less to see than behind his closed lids.

"To realise my ignorance about you; to discover our estrangement—this tangle of secrets; and to know that I can behave as I did tonight..."

"Don't cry, Muriel."

"Why do you call me 'Muriel'? You have never done so until now, until lately." "Until Hester came," both thought.

"She...Hester, I mean...has made no difference to us. I'm not in love with her, if that is any comfort...if you want to hear such embarrassing things really said aloud." He spoke coldly and angrily and with a sense of treachery to himself, as if she had forced from him some alien oath. "She has changed nothing...only shown us what existed, exists."

"We should be very grateful for that."

Her burst of anger was a relief from tears.

"If I can never love her again," he thought, "why is it Hester's fault? It is she, Muriel, who destroyed it, let it slip from her and then, in trying to have it back again, broke it for ever." Lying so close to her, he let this monstrous treason against her form in the darkness. Then he felt her lift herself up on one elbow. She was wiping her eyes. Crying was over, then? But, more dread to him even than her weeping, she put out her hand and touched his arm and he wondered if she had sensed the fissure widening, separating her from him, in his heart—the hard knowledge of non-love. She began to throw words into this abyss as if to close it before too late. "Robert, forgive me! I will try. I will do everything. I am sorry. I cannot bear it."

The words worked no magic, and continued into unseemliness, he thought. This reserve had changed to cold-heartedness, and he wondered how he could ever change it back again. He turned over and put his arms round her.

"Let us try again!" she begged, and she pressed her burning eyes against his shoulder. He moved his head back a little, for her hair had fallen against his mouth.

"We will both try!" he whispered. "I will try very hard." "But will it be any use?" he wondered.

Robert, in the days that followed, wondered if it were the mildness of his nature which enabled him to find the suppression of love more easy than the suppression of non-love. No concentration could cure him of his lack of feeling towards Muriel, and, to ward off his indifference to her, he began, without knowing it, to catalogue her virtues. In this way, he always had a ready antidote for the irritations she caused him, and quickly smothered thoughts of her coldness with remembrances of her kindness to animals and that servants loved her. Against her sarcasm he recalled her loyalty, and tried to acknowledge her steadfastness when beset by her lack of humour.

At first, as if a true understanding were between them, Muriel went through her days in chastened peace of mind, submissive and forgiving. Emotion had tired her and she seemed weakly convalescent, her mind on such little things, as if she only waited for the time to pass. At night, the resentment she fought during the day poisoned her dreams, so that, lying beside Robert with her heart full of love for him, she dreaded to fall asleep and so out of love again—would wake trembling or tearful at his dream-betrayals, carrying imaginary wrongs beyond the dawn, to discolour all the morning.

Bravely, she set out to enchant him all over again, as she had done so many years ago, but disheartened now, frightened, and lacking the equipment of romanticism, energy, curiosity. "For I did not have him once for all," she thought sadly, arranging her pink dress against the red carpet and her white hands on the tapestry; glancing timidly at him, who did not look in her direction. Her voice lost its edge when she spoke to him, but only Hester noticed the new warmth, and was embarrassed.

"It will soon be Speech Day," Muriel said. "Will last year's hat do, Robert? Or would that look as if the school were going downhill?"

"I should buy a new one—for your sake, not the school's. I can't imagine parents remembering a hat from one year to the next."

"Hester and I can't agree with that."

Hester did not raise her eyes.

For the first time, Muriel was self-conscious at Speech Day, watched the great marquee going up, arranged flowers, and finally pinned on her new cartwheel hat, feeling unusual sensations of flurried dread. "Exquisite!" Rex whispered, passing her as she crossed the hall. Until that moment, the evening of the dance, for him, might never have been. He was as heedless as a bird snatching at berries along a hedgerow.

Muriel stood beside Robert and shook hands with the parents and felt that beneath their admiration these people did not like her;

fathers were over-awed and mothers were doubtful—unsure as to whether she really loved their sons as they deserved. Hester watched her; Rex watched her; Robert looked away from her; tiredness overtook her.

In the evening, she telephoned Beatrice—her only friend, she now felt; though more than a friend: perhaps an extension of her own personality and her own experiences (sometimes sullying) greedily grafted on to the weaker parts of Beatrice's nature. "Oh God, let her not be out!" she prayed, imagining the telephone ringing and ringing in the empty house. But Beatrice, breathless from hurrying, soon answered and lost her mystery in doing so, became accessible, too easily summoned.

"I was in the garden. How did it go, darling? I thought of you. Was the hat right? Did Robert love it?"

"He didn't say he didn't."

"And tea and everything? And Robert's speech?"

"Yes. Beatrice, if I call in, will you come for a drive before dinner? My head aches. The last ones have only just gone away."

"Oh, parents!" she said later. They drove along the lanes, down the hill past the Hand and Flowers, where Mrs. Brimmer stood at the doorway in the sun. "Perhaps I just hate them because they have children," Muriel said.

The car was open and the soft air flowed over them, lifting their hair, but none of the peace of the evening reached Muriel, who drove fast, noticed nothing, frowned at the road ahead. "You've had children, Beatrice, and you cannot *know*..."

"Darling, you are overtired..."

"No. For years it has been so improbable that I should ever have a child that I stopped thinking about it... I might have been shocked, perhaps, to find myself pregnant... but now, just lately, knowing for sure that I never could be, that in *this* lifetime, and for *this* woman, it couldn't ever happen, I feel panicky, want to go back, be different, have another chance. I can't explain." She changed gear badly, was driving carelessly.

"Do slow down," Beatrice said.

"I'm sorry."

"I never think about having children now," Beatrice said. "All the business bores me enormously, like some hobby one has discarded. When I hear of younger women having them, I even feel slightly surprised, for it all seems so finished with and *démodé*. They think they are being so clever and can't know how I lack interest. I just think, 'Goodness me, are people still doing *that*?'"

"But you'll have grandchildren and then you'll be caught up in it again."

"I suppose so." She looked smug.

"Where are we going?" Muriel asked. "I *ought* to be going home."

She drove on, brushing the cow-parsley in the ditch, swerving as a bird flew up suddenly from some horse-droppings on the road.

"Very sorry! Then the holidays will soon come," she said, as if continuing the same plaint, "the three of us left alone together."

"Has nothing been done about her going?"

"There is nowhere for her to go."

"You should go away yourself. I would come with you, if you liked. You need a holiday."

"And leave them together?"

"Oh, no, of course."

They laughed shakily. Muriel said: "It is as well one still has a sense of humour."

"Thank you, Hester, for all your help," Robert said. He handed her a drink and, taking up his own, asked if she had seen Muriel.

"No." She had watched her driving away, but thought that Muriel could explain her own comings and goings.

"And I heard her asking Hugh in for a drink. You look very smart, Hester." But it was too robustly said, not tender. "I suppose it all went off all right. At any rate, it went off. Muriel is splendid at that sort of thing. Never complains, as most women would, although I can see it all seems a great deal of nonsense to her."

Before Hugh came, Robert was called away to the telephone and

Hester was left alone. The day had tired and confused her, for she had never been quite sure of her duties. Ashamed to stand idle, she had tried to attach herself to the other workers, but Matron's campaign of defence had not included her. She had managed to hand a few cups of tea and annoyed the senior boys by doing so. Few things are so fatiguing as standing by to help and not being called upon, and now her feet, her back, even her teeth were aching. She drank her sherry and put the glass on the chimneypiece. Wavering clumsily, her hand touched a china figure and knocked it into the hearth. She gave a quick glance at the door, then stooped down to see what damage was done. Muriel's favourite Dresden girl lay in the fender, an arm carrying a gilt basket of strawberries was broken off at the elbow. Hester prayed for time, as if that could make the figure whole again; but in a school there are so many footsteps and any she could hear above the beating blood in her head might be Robert's or Muriel's coming to this room. She pushed the figure behind a bowl of flowers and put the broken piece in her pocket. If she were ever granted a few undisturbed moments she was sure she could have mended it; but now, although no one came and the waiting was unbearable, she could not be certain of being alone. She tried to find a nonchalant pose, sitting on the window-seat, far from the fireplace: then saw her sherry glass still there, incriminatingly near to and drawing attention to the empty place. She went to fetch it and on her way back to the window-seat thought of refilling it, to give a more natural look to her pose. As she was lifting the decanter, Hugh came in.

Her trembling guilt, the sherry slopped over the table, worried him. "They are turning her into a secret drinker," he thought; but her confusion touched him immeasurably, for he knew similar sensations, and had learnt new refinements of them at Muriel's hands. "We are always mopping up for this girl," he thought, as he dabbed at the table with his handkerchief. Her misery had gone so far beyond accountable bounds that he began to wonder how much she had drunk.

"Where is everyone?" he asked. He passed his handkerchief under the bottom of the glass before he gave it to her.

"Robert is telephoning."

"And … Madam?" For Muriel set up such awkwardnesses in people that they could sometimes not even give her her proper name.

"Went out in the car."

"Who went out in the car?" Robert asked, as he came from the hall.

In Hester's shattered face, her lips moved stiffly, as if from some rigor, and at last formed the name.

"Oh, I wondered where she was. She'll be back. Sherry, Hugh?" Robert's bustling about could not conceal his perplexity. "If people are liars, who makes them be?" he was wondering. "Everything went off well, Hugh," his voice wavered upwards. "Nothing untoward? No one insulted Matron? Mrs. Vallance seemed incensed at something."

"The wretched boy's cricket-boot. She kept saying she would much rather both were lost than only one."

"People often say that—particularly about gloves," Muriel said, hurrying into the room. She went to the mirror and smoothed her hair. "Sorry, Robert! Sorry, Hugh! Oh, and Hester, too! I didn't see you hiding in the window-seat. I went for a little drive with Beatrice. May I have a drink, darling; and, Hugh, your glass is empty. God, what a day! Never mind, another year until the next one. Darling, Hugh's glass! Dinner is cold and can wait for us for once. I went into the Science Room, Hugh, just to see if you had been up to anything sinister, and I was charmed. The heavenly demonstration of cross-pollination. I do think you are to be congratulated."

Hugh gazed intently into his glass as Robert filled it. He looked as if he were parched with thirst, but sherry was a long way from his thoughts. He knew he was being ridiculed but could not sort it out sufficiently to make an answer. "Meaningless innuendo," he decided. "And the very worst kind, too; because it finishes the game."

"I did Botany at school," Muriel said. "That was considered lady-like even in those days—particularly in those days, when we drew no conclusions from it. Purple loosestrife seemed to have nothing in common with us."

"Muriel!" Robert protested. "Your Victorian girlhood doesn't convince us, you know."

She went close to the mirrored over-mantel, leant forward to her reflection and once more smoothed her hair. Hester watched in terror the long white hands moving then from hair to flowers, tidying them, too. Then the room froze. Muriel picked up the Dresden figure, seemed surprised by genuine grief, paused; then turned to face them, looking dazed and puzzled.

"What a beautiful... thing!" Hugh said, stepping forward, as if she were only asking him to admire it. "The dress is just like real lace."

"Robert!" Muriel cried, ignoring Hugh. "Her grief is out of all proportion," Hester thought, remembering the same stunned look of wives in old news-reels, waiting at pit-heads as the stretchers were carried away, or of mothers lifting their babies across the rubble of bombed streets.

Robert asked sharply—as if he foresaw hell for all of them: "How did that happen?" He took the china figure and examined it. Muriel turned back and began to search the chimneypiece.

"Is it broken?" Hugh asked, but no one answered. He was accustomed to that. Hester began to tremble, and clutched the fragment in her pocket as though she might be searched.

"It must be there," Robert said. "One of the maids must have done it without knowing, or they would have told you."

Hester, falsely, went over and looked into the flower-bowl.

"Not there?" Muriel asked. "No."

"Quite a clean break," Robert said. "It could be mended easily."

"If we find the other piece," said Muriel.

"What is it we are looking for?" Hugh asked. "I shall have to question the maids," Muriel said. "It has been hidden purposely. They have never deceived me before." She was proud of her relationship with domestic staff, to whom she was always generous and considerate: they saw a side of her which was hidden from most people and they were loyal to her. She delayed the task of questioning them, refilled her glass with sherry and as she drank it went on searching, lifting cushions and rugs and thrusting her fingers down the sides of stuffed chairs until the backs of her hands looked bruised.

Hugh did not dine with them, and Muriel said nothing during the meal. When dishes were brought in, she helped herself and ate without raising her eyes, feeling awkwardness with the maid and guilt at her own suspicions.

After dinner, Hester went out into the garden and walked in an opposite direction to the church—down an azalea walk to a ferny grotto. The dark, dusty leaves parted and disclosed a little Gothic summer-house, which was locked so that the boys should not damage it. No one came there—the dark rockiness of the place was chilling, the clay paths slippery in wet weather; the creaking trees were clotted with rooks' nests, and the rooks themselves filled the air with commotion, restlessly calling, circling, dropping again and again to the branches.

Robert had brought her here on her first day when he had shown her round; he had taken a key from his pocket and unlocked the door for her. The cave-smell was unpleasant to breathe, but she had marvelled aloud at the interior. The walls and domed roof were encrusted with shells in fan patterns set in cement. Light from the coloured glass in the windows shone in patches.

Now she could only stand on tiptoe at the door and look through the wire-covered glass-panel. The piece of china from her pocket she forced through the wire and broken pane. It struck the stone floor inside.

"Were you trying to get in?" Hugh asked her; shouting rather, above the noise of the rooks.

"No, it is always locked."

"Did I surprise you? I saw you come this way when I was down at the nets with some of the boys. I meant to ask you before dinner if you'd come for a walk, but there was all that rumpus about the ornament—put it out of my mind; I mean I hadn't a chance. Of course, she has some nice things—Madam, Muriel, that is—and she thinks a lot of them: naturally."

"They were her mother's."

"Nice diamonds, too, Rex was saying."

"Yes."

Hugh began to perceive that Hester lacked interest in Muriel's possessions.

"Never having had anything very valuable myself," he said, "it is hard for me to understand anyone being as upset as she was tonight."

"It is because she hasn't anything valuable," Hester said. "And she knows it."

"Children, you mean?"

"Partly."

They walked down the winding path. Two boys were kneeling by some flint steps, looking for lizards under the stones. Hugh had a little patronising chat with them, then he and Hester walked on again. The boys exchanged slow winks.

"Did you ever see that horrible old baggage again?" Hugh asked. "The one with the cat."

"No. Not again."

"Are you happy here?"

"Not very."

This was so promising that he made no answer until they reached the seat in the laurel walk where Muriel and Beatrice had sat and talked; then, when he was sitting at Hester's side, he asked, "Why aren't you happy?" Looking round carefully, he made sure there were no boys about, and took her hand.

"I am in the way, you see," Hester said gravely. "I ought not to be here."

When he took her other hand and drew nearer to her, she seemed not to notice. Although her indifference was in a sense discouraging to him, it allowed him to proceed without hindrance. He kissed her, but still looking rather mopishly before her, she said: "I didn't want to harm anyone. Not even someone I hate."

"You couldn't harm anyone," he said. "You are so entirely gentle."

Some boys shouted in the distance, and he moved promptly aside, leant forward, his elbows on his knees, in an attitude of serious but impersonal discussion. But the voices faded and no one came. A bell rang, and he muttered, "Thank God for that," and turned again to Hester and took her in his arms.

In the morning, Muriel questioned the maids, Lucy and Sylvia. One showed transparent surprise and concern; the other haughty offendedness: and since both reacted in their own ways as their innocence dictated, Muriel said no more. She often boasted that she knew at once when people were lying, not realising how little this endeared her to anyone, least of all to Hester who, never very honest in the easiest of times, was lately finding it almost impossible to tell the truth.

One thing Hester was determined on and it was to avoid being left alone with Muriel. She managed this all morning and was about to manage it after lunch as she followed Robert to his study, when Muriel, letting her reach the door, said: "Oh, Hester! If you wouldn't mind . . . I won't keep you a moment."

Robert walked on as if he had not heard; but by the time he reached his study, his agitation was so great, he was so sure of what Muriel would inflict on the girl, that he went out into the hall again and stood guiltily at the table pretending to read *The Times*.

The voices on the other side of the door were separated by long silences; the blurred murmurings seemed without consequence or meaning. Then he heard Hester crying. The sobs came in a rush towards the door and in a panic he hurried back to his study and sat down at his desk. He heard footsteps in the hall, and was so sure that they were coming to him and felt so anxious to be ready to deal with disaster—fidgeting busily with papers, continually clearing his throat—that he did not listen, and when at last he realised that the house was silent, he could not tell in which direction Hester had gone.

At three o'clock, he gave a Latin lesson. Afterwards, he returned to his study. She was not there, and the typewriter was still covered. He put down his books and went to look for Muriel; but Muriel, he was told, had gone to a meeting in the village. He spent an idle, worried afternoon, and Hester did not appear. "Another man," he thought, "could get away from this, could leave the women and go to work!" He was forced to remain, always morbidly aware of the atmosphere in the house.

Muriel returned in the early evening, said, "Hello, Robert!" very casually, as she took her afternoon's post from the hall-table and walked into the drawing-room.

"Where is Hester?"

She read her letters attentively. "I can't tell you. I went out soon after lunch."

"Not soon enough."

She had to raise her head then.

"What have you done to her? You made her cry."

"From no sense of shame, either, I'm afraid. Only from chagrin at being found out."

"I suppose she *did* break that damned thing."

"Exactly."

"She was afraid to tell you. You shouldn't frighten her so."

"She stood there and listened to me saying that I should question Lucy and Sylvia."

"Did you know then that she had done it?"

"I wasn't sure, although she is so clumsy that one's thoughts naturally fly to her."

"You make her clumsy, you know."

"Yes, I dare say it is my fault."

"I know she doesn't always speak the truth and I worry sometimes that she should be driven to deceit."

"Driven? You choose melodramatic words, Robert. And I can't imagine anyone driving anyone into such fantastic lunatic deceptions as your Hester's."

"You must have upset her very much."

"Yes, as you say, I made her cry. I am glad I did not make Lucy cry. I am glad I took their word at once."

"But where is Hester now?"

Muriel put aside her letters with a sigh of weariness. "I do not know, Robert. I do not know. You have seen her since I."

"But I haven't. I left her here with you."

"The last I saw of her, she was coming to you for the key."

"What key?"

"The key to the Shell House. Where she had hidden the piece of china. I sent her to fetch it and to get the key from you."

"That was her punishment, was it? To have to face me, as she was, and make that pathetic little confession, then go out, humiliated, to pick up the bits? And you can do that to someone just because they have broken some china."

"She has broken more than china for me."

"The deepest destruction is done with finesse, not clumsiness. She couldn't hold a candle to you. I must go to look for her."

"He will find her weeping in her room and console her, take sides against me," Muriel thought. She said: "I am at the end of this marriage, Robert. I cannot bear any more of it."

"I will ask Hugh," he said. "Perhaps he will have seen her."

"Why Hugh?"

"Because I think he is in love with her."

"Is that so? I wouldn't have thought it of him. You need not speak so angrily. Poor young man, I don't suppose he has any idea of how he is trespassing. Anyone else would know; but he's a little extra stupid." Once again, she desired to strike him, did so with words instead. "I expect she is just sulking in her bedroom, so I shouldn't fuss."

But Hester was not in her room, and those who were discreetly questioned had not seen her.

Fortune struck blindingly at Miss Despenser. All fell into place and she saw that, given the right ingredients and patience, heart's desire at last will come, like risen bread, to proving point. She had despaired in loneliness, then conquered her despair, up to that stage of no-feeling, where the mind goes joggety-jog on little errands of the will, each minute measured out in a tiny sip. "For time heals all," she told herself. "At the end of life, we should be quite healed, and so go whole to dissolution."

Mrs. Brimmer, towards two o'clock, had mysteriously run out of both Guinness and Madeira; could only suggest a mild-and-bitter, and then the bitter had given out. The men sniggered. "You know I don't like cold drinks," Miss Despenser complained. "You should write to the brewers!"

"I will," Mrs. Brimmer said, and they laughed again.

"Mother would be shocked," Miss Despenser thought, as she wandered home. "The way they speak nowadays."

It seemed siesta-time in the lanes. Only the bees moved. But the house was buzzing with activity. Green and dark-blue flies were delirious over the plates of cat's food in the kitchen. In sudden disgust with her life, Miss Despenser took them all up and threw them— dishes, too—into the dustbin, and started a furious zigzagging as she lifted the lid.

At that moment, Hester rang the bell.

"What luck!" said Miss Despenser when she opened the door. "You came just at the right time. I was doing a bit of spring-cleaning and I shall be glad to knock off and have a chat. You will cheer me up, I know you."

Hester, trembling, swollen-eyed, entered the house. She bore her nausea for the sake of Muriel's punishment, knowing she could not hope to hurt her without sacrificing herself; had even contemplated, in a brief moment of rage, the supreme sacrifice; for no greater hatred could she show than that.

"I knew it would be a red-letter day," Miss Despenser said and handed Hester a postcard, "when this came this morning. I don't often have anything in the post," she explained simply. It was a printed invitation from a girls' school. "Tennis Match," Hester read. "Past *v.* Present. 2.15 sharp." "What is Asboga?" she asked dully, and pressed her fingers to her burning eyes.

"Abbey School, Brighton, Old Girls' Association," Miss Despenser said. "Linda and I were both Asbogs. Though she could only stand a term there. It was the happiest time I ever had, although at times we pined for one another. The food was so good. I don't think you could better that food anywhere. On Fridays, we had a red jelly with bananas sliced up in it. Every Friday. We looked forward to it, I can tell you. What is the food like where you are? What did you have for luncheon today, for instance?"

Hester thought, then said: "A sort of shepherd's pie."

"My favourite! And after?"

"Oh, dear, I don't know."

"But it can only have been half an hour ago."

"I think it was apple ... something with apple ..." She began to cry again.

"Now, chin up! Surely you don't grizzle over your food, like poor Linda? She once cried over an apple-charlotte. She cried all afternoon without stopping. My father made her sit there till tea-time. She ate it in the end. He had a will of iron. I advise you to eat up in the beginning ..."

"I don't want to answer questions, that's all," Hester said.

"You look peaky. Come along, hop on to the sofa, legs up! I'll make you a cup of tea."

Hester lay down, the dusty plush against her cheek. Misery obliterated her. "Someone take over, take charge, take care!" She wept for a little while, then fell asleep.

Miss Despenser was a long time getting the tea ready. She worked happily, but slowly, in her usual state of afternoon muzziness.

After dinner, Robert found Hugh walking about the grounds and asked if he had seen Hester.

"No, I was looking for her."

"She didn't come to dinner, and I am rather anxious."

"Has there been some upset?" Hugh asked at once.

"Yes. Why do you ask?"

"She seemed fairly miserable last night. We went for a walk, you know. Is she in her room?"

"No. Of course, we looked there first. I'll stroll about and keep my eyes open."

When he had shaken off Hugh, Robert went quickly up the path to the Shell House and unlocked the door. It swung open with a grating sound. The piece of china lay on the dusty floor, proving nothing but what Muriel had said, that Hester had delivered herself into her hands.

He began an aimless search of the grounds, for he could not think where Hester might go, or what she did in her spare time. Some of the boys watched him with excitement, for they were sure he was out on some mysterious investigation and they wondered if school monotony might be enlivened after prayers next day by the announcement of some appalling scandal—some of the lordly ones found smoking in the shrubbery, or the copy of *Lady Chatterley's Lover* unearthed. When he was seen to be walking more quickly towards the churchyard, as if struck by a sudden idea, he was watched intently by one boy, Terence Mooney, who always made his beer in the little shed by the church. His father was a brewer—Mooney's Sunshine Ales—and Terry's school-life was an everlasting misery in consequence. "You must know how to make it," the boys said. "Surely your old man told you. Well, write and ask him, then." He had pretended to write to ask, and the boys gathered round and watched him open his next letter from home—"Darling, I hope you are happy and your earache better. Don't talk after lights out, but get all the rest you can."..."Did he say anything?" "Yes, of course." "Well, what?" "Well, he says I mustn't say. It's a family secret." "Well, you're his family, aren't you? Can't he tell you?" "Yes." "Well, get on, then. We don't want to know how you do it. We just want to drink it." "It takes time. It has to ferment, you see." "All right, we'll give you time." They arranged to give him a week. He studied encyclopaedias. He did not sleep. He stole potatoes and brewed concoctions. These never tasted right to him, or to most of the boys, who made it clear that they would never touch Mooney's beer when they left school and could choose. Terry lived in wretched unpopularity, busy, furtive; he segregated his parents on Speech Day, and now, watching Robert, wondered if he would be expelled.

"Mr. Baseden's prowling about, too," a boy said. "He went through the churchyard a few minutes ago."

"They might be going for walks," poor Mooney said.

"Not them. They keep looking round."

It did not occur to them that masters could have anything but boys in their minds.

Hugh went to the Hand and Flowers, but neither Miss Despenser nor Hester was there. "I'm not breaking my heart, either," Mrs. Brimmer said as she drew his beer. He drank it quickly and hurried back up the lane to the stucco villa.

"No, there's no one there," Miss Despenser told Hester, who had heard the knocking on the door. "I often fancy the same thing; but nobody calls here. Perhaps Pussy jumped down off my bed. It wouldn't be anyone."

But at the second knock, Hester went to the window. Hugh, stepping back from the porch, saw her behind the dusty pane. She had a fan of old photographs in her hand and her face was stained with tears.

"Yes. It is Hugh Baseden," she said, and he could see her lips moving as she still stared at him.

"Then draw the curtains. How dare he trespass here! Peering and prying!"

Hester—dreamy with weakness—moved towards the hall and opened the door. She was at a stage of recovery from grief—the air was vacant, silence enfolded her, and when she put out her hand to the wall to steady herself after the effort of opening the door, the wall seemed to bend, to slope away from her; and it was as if Hugh's hand as she touched it dissolved, vanished.

He lifted her and carried her to a chair in the hall. "Put your head down," he told her. She obeyed. Her hand with the photographs swung against the floor. Pussy came up and walked in a figure-of-eight round her feet. Hugh pushed him aside. "And now, Paul Pry, you can leave my house at once," Miss Despenser said. "I was just coming into the hall when I saw what you did to Pussy. You peer through my windows, force your way in, are cruel to my cat and

goodness knows what you have done to this poor girl. Sit up, Hester!
The blood will run to your head."

Hester sat up and Hugh pushed her head down again.

"You blockhead!" Miss Despenser shouted. "She will faint, you
great dunce, if you are not careful."

He knelt down before Hester and held her head against him.

"She was all right until you came," Miss Despenser said. "I wish
you would go away again."

"What are these?" Hugh asked, gently taking the photographs
from Hester.

"They are mine. I am showing them to her," Miss Despenser said.
"We haven't nearly finished yet." She sprang forward and snatched
up one of the photographs he had dropped. "How dare you throw
my things on the floor, you blundering oaf! That is my sister." She
looked, with a change to tenderness, at the yellowed card, the girl
with the vapid smile, the hand resting on a carved pedestal behind
which a backcloth of roses and pillars met the carpet unevenly.

"Are you well enough to come home?" Hugh asked Hester. "Shall
I get a car?"

"I can't go home."

"No, she can't go home."

"What is wrong?" Hugh asked softly, kneeling by her, rocking
her gently in his arms.

"It is out of the question," Miss Despenser said. "Now you must
run along. I am sorry I cannot invite you to dinner." She fought
bravely, but by now she knew that she was going to lose. He had
forgotten her, as an adversary, while he listened to Hester's story.

"Get up off your knees!" Miss Despenser tried to interrupt them.
"You exhibitionist."

"I don't know why I did," Hester was moaning. "I lost my nerve.
She makes me behave badly. I hate her. Oh, I hate her." Her mouth
squared like a howling child's, then she began to beat her forehead
with her hands.

"There you are, you see," said Miss Despenser.

"If you would only marry me!" said Hugh, and at once began to cloud the proposal with doubts and apologies. "I know so little about girls—no time to learn . . . I had to work so hard, and I've so little money. I'm awfully dull, I know . . ."

"As dull as ditchwater," Miss Despenser said, but her remarks were now automatic. She had covered her retreat with them, and exhausted, with her efforts and her disappointment, could say no more. She took a pace back in the shadowy hall and when at last Hugh stood up and helped Hester to do so, she closed her eyes and could watch no longer.

"Good-bye," Hester said, turning to her. "I'm sorry, and thank you. I had better go back after all."

Miss Despenser kept her eyes shut; a hard tear was under each lid.

Hugh looked away from Hester for the first time and saw the old woman's wedge-shaped face, so angrily grieved, her down-turned mouth. With the palm of her hand she was pressing to her skirt the photograph of her dead sister. From his own timid loneliness, he had knowledge of such a poverty of love. He said: "Thank you for taking care of her." The tragic mask could not move, or the eyes open. When Hester and Hugh had gone, she lifted her lids and two tears dropped out and made tracks down her face to her chin. She picked up the cat and wiped her wet face on his fur, then she gathered up the photographs and crammed them back into the mother-o'-pearl-inlaid box.

Not long after, just as Mrs. Brimmer at the Hand and Flowers was saying: "Well, we choked her off, gentlemen," Miss Despenser entered the bar. "So sorry I am late. Some visitors called," she said cheerily.

"A pleasure, I'm sure," Mrs. Brimmer replied. "And now last orders, if you please."

At the school, Hester was enveloped by tact—Muriel, relieved at her reappearance, seemed unconcerned and talked of trivial things, though lapsing sometimes into sad preoccupation. Robert's lack of allusion was almost imbecilic. Hugh, suddenly masterful, had arranged with him that no words should pass and they did not, although sometimes Hester felt swollen with the rehearsed explanations she was not allowed to make.

As day after day went by, poor little Mooney began at last to wonder if he had escaped expulsion; but Robert's abstracted ways prolonged the boys' uneasiness. Dissociation became the policy under this cloud—the copy of *Lady Chatterley's Lover*, or Latin cribs, lost their value; the shrubbery, or Hell's Kitchen, where the older ones smoked, was deserted.

One day, after lunch, when Robert had said Grace he still stood there, as if he had more to say. They paused and turned their faces towards him, candid, innocent. Only Mooney looked down desperately at his plate—the five prune-stones at its edge: *this* year.

The announcement of Hugh's and Hester's engagement was a tremendous relief. Robert's attempt at joviality brought forth sycophantic cheers and smiles. They were all in a good humour, especially as one wedding present would do for both. "It is better for them not to marry 'outside' people," the head boy explained. "Now what we want is for Matron to marry Mr. Wigmore!"

Hugh's first biology class of the afternoon was in a mood of refreshment and good humour.

"Congratulations, sir."

"Thank you, Palmer."

"Congratulations, sir."

"I will take Palmer as spokesman for all of you," Hugh said firmly. "Page fifty-one." They opened their books.

"So that's the solution," Beatrice said. "You were quite right to be patient and let things work their own way out."

"I don't know that I did that," Muriel said. "And it has taken a long time and she hasn't gone yet."

"She seems too moony, too dull a girl to fall in love, be fallen in love with."

"Is love the prerogative of the bright ones? He is very dull himself, you know, and it is a good thing if two uninteresting people marry and keep their dullness to themselves. Though she has changed a little for the better—looks less *driven*, and doesn't knock things over quite as much as she used; can sometimes drink a glass of water without spilling it."

"Well, if marriage stops her being clumsy it will be something." Then Beatrice asked slyly: "How has Robert taken it?"

"Nobly. He arranged Hugh's new job for him and still has nobody to take his place."

"I meant—about Hester."

"Oh, Hester!" Muriel's voice was light with annoyance. "I think I imagined a great deal of that." If Hester were going, her own agitation would sink; then she wanted her old life again, her picture of serene marriage, of Robert's devotion to her. She regretted having confided in Beatrice, who made past miseries more real by her knowledge of them. To turn the conversation she said: "I will give her a lovely wedding...I suppose that she has some friends she can invite—school-friends if nothing better. I have chosen the dress-material. Just think, Beatrice, when we were married we wore those hideous short frocks. It would be our luck to strike that fashion. I wouldn't let anyone see my wedding photographs for all the world." With tender condescension they recalled the nineteen-twenties and the gay and gentle girlishness of their natures then.

Muriel began to feel energy and optimism, as the holidays and the wedding grew nearer. She worked to bring to life one imagined scene, the beginning of peace for her; foresaw Hester and Hugh going down the steps to the car—"She was married from my house," she would tell people.

"She was like a daughter to me"—and when the car had gone (for ever, for ever) down the drive, she and Robert would turn and go up the confetti-littered steps to begin their new—or, rather, their *old*—life, together and alone.

She worked on the wedding and discussed it incessantly. "Suppose it rains!" Robert said abruptly one night. Muriel was sitting up in bed while he undressed. She was brushing her hair and at his words parted it from her face, looked up at him in perplexity. "Are you angry about it, then?"

"Angry? I only said 'Suppose it rains!'"

"You sounded so sarcastic."

He got into bed and closed his eyes at once. Smoothing her hair back, she dropped the brush to the floor and put out the light. "You do love me, Robert?" she asked in her meekest voice.

"Yes, dear."

"You aren't still angry with me about Hester? It has turned out well in the end for her."

"I hope so."

"He will be very good to her, I am quite sure."

"Yes, I am sure, too. Good-night, Muriel."

"Good-night, Robert."

He turned over and seemed to fall asleep: yet she doubted if he did so, and lay and listened for a long while to his regular, unbroken breathing. Once, to test him, she touched him gently with the back of her hand, but he did not turn to her as years ago he would have done. "I cannot make him come to me," she thought in a panic. "I cannot get my own way." She became wide awake with a longing for him to make love to her; to prove his need for her; so that she could claim his attention; and so dominate him; but at last wished only to contend with her own desires, unusual and humiliating as they were to her. She lay close to him and masked her shame with a pretence of sleep. When he did not, would not, stir, her tenderness hardened to resentment. She raised herself and looked down at him. His profile was stern; his hair ruffled; he breathed steadily. "He cannot be asleep," she thought, as she bent over him, put her cheek to his brow, no longer dissembling or hiding her desire.

His stillness defeated her and after a while, hollowed and exhausted by her experience, she turned away and lay down on her side, listening to her thunderous heart-beat, feeling giddy. "If I could be young again!" she thought. "If I could be young!"

Two thrushes were singing in the garden before she fell asleep.

The night had dishevelled her, her hair was tangled on the creased pillow, her body damp in the hot bed. But in her dreams, a less dis-ordered Muriel took command. She dreamed that she was making Hester's wedding cake—white and glistering it rose before her, a sac-rificial cake, pagoda-shaped in tier on tier, with arcades of sugar pil-lars, garlanded friezes. Delicate as hoar-rimed ferns she made the fronded wreaths of flowers and leaves. It blossomed as she worked her magic on it with the splendid virtuosity of dreams. "Yes, that is how it will be!" she thought. "And no one must ever touch it or break it." She had surprised herself with her own skill, and, standing back to view her work, felt assuaged, triumphant, but bereft, too, as artists are when their work is done and gone for good.

GRAVEMENT ENDOMMAGÉ

THE CAR devoured the road, but the lines of poplars were without end. The shadow of sagging telegraph wires scalloped the middle of the road, the vaguer shadows of the pretty telegraph posts pleased Louise. They were essentially French, she thought—like, perhaps, lilies of the valley: spare, neatly budded.

The poplars dwindled at intervals and gave place to ruined buildings and pock-marked walls; a landscape of broken stone, faded Dubonnet advertisements. Afterwards, the trees began again.

When they came to a town, the cobblestones, laid fan-wise, slowed up the driving. Outside cafés, the chairs were all empty. Plane trees in the squares half-hid the flaking walls of houses with crooked jalousies and frail balconies, like twisted bird-cages. All had slipped, subsided.

"But it is so *dead*!" Louise complained, wanting to get to Paris, to take out from her cases her crumpled frocks, shake them out, hang them up. She dreamt of that; she had clung to the idea across the Channel. Because she was sick before the boat moved, Richard thought she was sick deliberately, as a form of revenge. But seasickness ran in her family. Her mother had always been prostrated immediately—as soon (as she so often had said) as her foot touched the deck. It would have seemed an insult to her mother's memory for Louise not to have worked herself up into a queasy panic at the very beginning. Richard, seeing walls sliding past port-holes and then sky, finished his drink quickly and went up on deck. Hardier women than Louise leant over the rails, their scarves flapping, watching the coast of France come up. The strong air had made him hungry, but when they had driven away from the harbour and had stopped for luncheon, Louise would only sip brandy, looking away from his plate.

"But we can never get to Paris by dinner-time," he said, when they were in the car again. "Especially driving on the wrong side of the road all the way."

"There is nowhere between here and there," she said with authority. "And I want to *settle*."

He knew her "settling." Photographs of the children spread about, champagne sent up, maids running down corridors with her frocks on their arms, powder spilt everywhere, the bathroom full of bottles and jars. He would have to sit down to telephone a list of names. Her friends would come in for drinks. They would have done better, so far as he could see, to have stayed in London.

"But if we are pushed for time... Why kill ourselves?... After all, this is a holiday... I do remember... There is a place I stayed at that time... When I first knew you..." Only parts of what he said reached her. The rest was blown away.

"You are deliberately going slow," she said.

"I think more of my car than to drive it fast along these roads."

"You think more of your car than of your wife."

He had no answer. He could not say that at least his car never betrayed him, let him down, embarrassed him, because it constantly did and might again at any moment.

"You planned this delay without consulting me. You planned to spend this night in some god-forsaken place and sink into your private nostalgia while my frocks crease and crease..." Her voice mounted up like a wave, trembled, broke.

The holiday was really to set things to rights between them. Lately, trivial bickering had hardened into direct animosity. Relatives put this down to, on his part, overwork, and, on hers, fatigue from the war, during which she had lived, after their London house was bombed, in a remote village with the children. She had nothing to say of those years but that they were not funny. She clung to the children and they to her. He was not, as he said—at first indulgently but more lately with irritation—in the picture. She knit them closer and closer to her, and he was quite excluded. He tried to understand that there must be, after the war, much that was new in her, after so long a gap, one that she would not fill up for him, or discuss. A new quirk was her preoccupation with fashion. To her, it was a race in which she must be first, so she looked *outré* always, never normal. If any of her friends struck a new note before her, she by-passed and cancelled out that particular foible. Men never liked her clothes, and women only admired them. She did not dress for men. Years of almost exclusively feminine society had set up cold antagonisms. Yes, hardship had made her superficial, icily frivolous. For one thing, she now must never be alone. She drank too much. In the night, he knew, she turned and turned, sighing in her sleep, dreaming bad dreams, wherein she could no longer choose her company. When he made love to her, she recoiled in astonishment, as if she could not believe such things could happen.

He had once thought she would be so happy to leave the village, that by comparison her life in London after the war would seem wonderful. But boredom had made her carping, fidgety. Instead of being thankful for what she had, she complained at the slightest discomfort. She raised her standards above what they had ever been; drove maids, who needed little driving, to give notice; was harried, piteous, unrelaxed. Although she was known as a wonderful hostess, guests wonderfully enjoying themselves felt—they could not say why—wary, and listened, as if for a creaking of ice beneath their gaiety.

Her doctor, advising the holiday, was only conventional in his optimism. If anyone were benefited by it, it would be the children, stopping at home with their grandmother—for a while, out of the arena. What Richard needed was a holiday away from Louise, and what Louise needed was a holiday from herself, from the very thing she must always take along, the dull carapace of her own dissatisfaction, her chronic unsunniness.

The drive seemed endless, because it was so monotonous. War had exhaled a vapour of despair over all the scene. Grass grew over grief, trying to hide collapse, to cover some of the wounds. One generation hoped to contend with the failure of another.

Late in the afternoon, they came to a town he remembered. The small cathedral stood like torn lacework against the sky. Birds settled in rows on the empty windows. Nettles grew in the aisle, and stone figures, impaled on rusty spikes of wire, were crumbling away.

But it looks too old a piece of wreckage, he thought. That must be the war before last. Two generations, ruined, lay side by side. Among them, people went on bicycles, to and fro, between the improvised shops and scarred dwellings.

"After wars, when there is so little time for patching up before the next explosion, what hope is there?" he began.

She didn't answer, stared out of the window, the car jolting so that her teeth chattered.

When Richard was alone in the hotel bedroom, he tried, by spreading about some of Louise's belongings, to make the place seem less temporary. He felt guilty at having had his own way, at keeping her from Paris until the next day and delaying her in this dismal place. It was destined to be, so far as they were concerned, one of those provincial backgrounds, fleeting, meaningless, that travellers erase from experience—the different hotel rooms run together to form one room, this room, any room.

When he had put the pink jars and bottles out in a row above the hand basin, he became dubious. She would perhaps sweep them all back into her case, saying, "Why unpack before we reach Paris?" and he would find that he had worsened the situation, after all, as he so often did, meaning to better it.

His one piece of selfishness—this halt on the way—she had stubbornly resisted, and now she had gone off to buy picture-postcards for the children, as if no one would think of them if she did not.

Because he often wondered how she looked when he was not there, if her face ever smoothed, he went to the window, hoping to see her coming down the little street. He wanted to catch in advance, to be prepared for, her mood. But she was not moody nowadays. A dreadful consistency discoloured her behaviour.

He pulled the shutters apart and was faced with a waste of fallen masonry, worse now that it was seen from above, and unrecognisable. The humped-up, dark cathedral stood in an untidy space, as if the little shops and cafés he remembered had receded in awe. Dust flowed along the streets, spilling from ruined walls across pavements. Rusty grasses covered debris and everywhere the air was unclean with grit. Dust, he thought, leaning on the iron rail above window-boxes full of shepherd's-purse—dust has the connotation of despair. In the end, shall we go up in a great swirl of it? He imagined something like the moon's surface, pock-marked, cratered, dry, deserted. When he was young, he had not despaired. Then, autumn leaves, not dust, had blown about these streets; chimes dropped like water, uneven, inconsequential, over rooftops; and the lime trees yellowed along neat boulevards. Yet, in the entrancement of nostalgia, he remembered, at best, an imperfect happiness and, for the most part, an agony of conjecture and expectancy. Crossing the vestibule of this very hotel, he had turned; his eyes had always sought the letter-rack. The Channel lay between him and his love, who with her timid smile, her mild grimace, had moaned that she could not put pen to paper, was illiterate, never had news; though loving him inordinately, could not spell, never had postage stamps; her ink dried as it approached the page; her parents interrupted. Yes, she had loved him to excess but had seldom written, and now went off in the dust and squalor for picture-postcards for their children.

At the window, waiting for her to appear, he felt that the dust and destruction had pinned down his courage. Day after day had left its residue, sifting down through him—cynicism and despair. He wondered what damage he had wreaked upon her.

Across the street, which once had been narrow and now was open to the sky, a nun went slowly, carrying bread under her arm. The wind plucked her veil. A thin cat followed her. They picked their way across the rubble. The cat stopped once and lifted a paw, licked it carefully, and put it back into the grit. The faint sound of trowel on stone rang out, desultory, hopeless, a frail weapon against so convincing a destruction. That piteous tap, tap turned him away from the window. He could not bear the futility of the sound, or the thought of the monstrous task ahead, and now feared, more than all he could imagine, the sight of his wife hurrying back down the street, frowning, the picture-postcards in her hand.

Louise was late. Richard sat drinking Pernod at a table in the bar where he could see her come into the hotel. There was only the barman to talk to. Rather clouded with drink, Richard leant on his elbow, describing the town as it had been. The barman, who was Australian, knew only too well. After the '14–'18 war, he had put his savings into a small café across the road. "I knew it," Richard said eagerly, forgetting the lacuna in both years and buildings, the gap over which the nun, the cat had picked their way.

"I'll get the compensation some day," the Australian said, wiping the bar. "Start again. Something different."

When a waiter came for drinks, the barman spoke in slow but confident French, probably different from an Englishman's French, Richard thought, though he could not be sure; a Frenchman would know.

"She gets later and later," he said solemnly.

"Well, if she doesn't come, that's what she's bound to do," the barman agreed.

"It was a shock to me, the damage to this town."

"Twelve months ago, you ought to have seen it," the barman said.

"That's the human characteristic—patience, building up."

"You might say the same of ants."

"Making from something nothing," Richard said. "I'll take another Pernod."

The ringing sound of the trowel was in his ears. He saw plodding humanity piling up the bricks again, hanging sacking over the empty windows, temporising, camping-out in the shadow of even greater disaster, raking ashes, the vision lost. He felt terribly sorry for humanity, as if he did not belong to it. The Pernod shifted him away and made him solitary. Then he thought of Louise and that he must go to look for her. Sometimes she punished him by staying away unaccountably, but knowing that did not lessen his anxiety. He wished that they were at peace together, that the war between them might be over for ever, for if he did not have her, he did not have all he had yearned for; steadied himself with, fighting in the jungle; holding fast, for her, to life; disavowing (with terrible concentration) any danger to her.

He wondered, watching the barman's placid polishing of another man's glasses, if they could begin again, he and Louise, with nothing, from scratch, abandoning the past.

"First I must find her," he thought. His drinking would double her fury if she had been lingering to punish him, punishing herself with enforced idling in those unfestive streets; a little scared, he imagined; hesitantly casual.

She came as he was putting a foot unsteadily to the floor. She stood at the door with an unexpectant look. When he smiled and greeted her, she tried to give two different smiles at once—one for the barman to see (controlled, marital), the other less a smile than a negation of it ("I see nothing to smile about").

"Darling, what will you have?"

She surveyed the row of bottles hesitantly, but her hesitation was for the barman's benefit. Richard knew her pause meant an unwillingness to drink in such company, in such a mood, and that in a minute she would say "A dry Martini," because once he had told her she should not drink gin abroad. She sat down beside him in silence.

"A nice dry Martini?" he suddenly asked, thinking of the man with the trowel, the nun with the bread, the battered cathedral, everybody's poor start. Again she tried to convey two meanings; to the barman that she was casual about her Martini, to her husband that she was casual about him.

Richard's head was swimming. He patted his wife's knee.

"Did you get the postcards all right?"

"Of course." Her glance brushed his hand off her knee.

"Cheers!" She held her glass at half-mast very briefly, spoke in the most annulling way, drank. Those deep lines from her nose to her mouth met the glass.

"Cheers, my darling!" he said, watching her. Her annoyance froze the silence.

Oh, from the most unpromising material, he thought, but he did seem to see some glimmer ahead, if only of his own patience, his own perseverance, which appeared, in this frame of mind, in this place, a small demand upon him.

THE IDEA OF AGE

WHEN I was a child, people's ages did not matter; but age mattered. Against the serious idea of age I did not match the grown-ups I knew—who had all an ageless quality—though time unspun itself from year to year. Christmases lay far apart from one another, birthdays even farther; but that time was running on was shown in many ways. I "shot out" of my frocks, as my mother put it. By the time that I was ten, I had begun to discard things from my heart and to fasten my attention on certain people whose personalities affected me in a heady and delicious way.

Though the years drew me upwards at a great pace, as if they were full of a hurried, *growing* warmth, the seasons still held. Summers netted me in bliss, endlessly. Winter did not promise spring. But when the spring came, I felt that it was there for ever. I had no dread that a few days would filch it from me, and in fact a few days were much when every day was endless.

In the summer holidays, when we went to the country, the spell of the long August days was coloured, intensified, by the fascinations of Mrs. Vivaldi. My first thought when we arrived at the guesthouse in Buckinghamshire was to look for some sign of *her* arrival—a garden hat hanging in the porch, or books from Mudie's. She came there, she made it clear, to rusticate (a word she herself used, which put a little flushed constraint upon the ladies who kept the guest-house, who felt it to be derogatory); she came to rest from the demands of London; and she did seem to be always very tired.

I remember so many of the clothes she wore, for they seemed to me unusual and beautiful. A large hat of coarse hessian sacking was surprisingly lined under the brim with gold lamé, which threw a light over her pale face. In the evenings, panels heavy with steel-bead embroidery swung away from her as she walked. She was not content to appeal only to one's sight, with her floating scarves, her fringes and tassels, but made claims upon the other senses, with scents of carnations and jasmine, with the rustling of moiré petticoats and the more solid sound of heavy amber and ivory bracelets sliding together on her wrists. Once, when we were sitting in the garden on a still afternoon, she narrowed her hand and wriggled it out of the bracelets and tried them on me. They were warm and heavy, alive like flesh. I felt this to be one of the situations I would enjoy in retrospect but find unendurable at the time. Embarrassed, inadequate, I turned the bracelets on my arm; but she had closed her eyes in the sun.

I realise now that she was not very young. Her pretty ash-blond hair had begun to have less blond, more ash; her powdered-over face was lined. Then I did not think of her as being any age. I drifted after her about house and garden, beset by her magic, endeavouring to make my mark on her.

One evening in the drawing-room she recited, for the guests, the Balcony Scene from *Romeo and Juliet*—all three parts—sitting on the end of the sofa, with her pearls laced through her fingers, her bronze shoes with pointed toes neatly together. Another evening, in that same room, she turned on the wireless and fixed the headphones over my ears (pieces of sponge lessened the pressure), and very far off, through a tinkling, scuffling, crackling atmosphere, I heard Edith Sitwell reciting through a megaphone. Mrs. Vivaldi impressed me with the historical nature of the occasion. She made historical occasions seem very rare and to be fastened on to. Since then, life has been one historical occasion after another, but I remember that scene clearly and the lamplight in the room with all the beautiful china. The two ladies who kept the guest-house had come down in the world and brought cupboards full of Crown Derby with them. The wireless-set, with its coils and wires, was on a mosaic-topped table that, one day, my brother stumbled against and broke. It disintegrated almost into powder, and my mother wept. Mrs. Vivaldi walked with her in the garden. I saw them going under the rose-arches—the fair head and the dark—both very tall. I thought they looked like ladies in a book by Miss Braddon.

One afternoon I was alone in the drawing-room when Mrs. Vivaldi came in from the garden with a basketful of sweet-peas. As if the heat were suddenly too much for her, she sat down quite upright, in a chair, with the basket beside her, and closed her eyes.

The room was cool and shadowy, with blinds half-drawn to spare the threadbare carpet. The house seemed like a hollow shell; its sub-fusc life had flowed out into the garden, to the croquet lawn, to the shade of the mulberry tree, where elderly shapes sagged in deck chairs, half-covered with newspapers.

I knew that Mrs. Vivaldi had not seen me. I was reading, sitting in my ungainly way on the floor, with my body slewed round so that my elbows and my book rested on the seat of a chair. Down there among the legs of furniture, I seemed only part of the overcrowded room. As I read, I ate sweets out of a rather grubby paper bag. Nothing could, I felt, have been more peaceful than that afternoon. The clock ticked, sweets dissolved in my cheek. The scent of the flowers Mrs. Vivaldi had brought in began to mix with the clove smell of pinks outside. From the lawn came only an occasional grim word or two—the word "partner" most of all, in tones of exhortation or apology—and the solid sound of the mallet on the ball. The last smells of luncheon had faded, and the last distant clatter of washing-up. Alone in the room with Mrs. Vivaldi, I enjoyed the drowsy after-noon with every sense and also with peaceful feelings of devotion. I liked to be there while she slept. I had her presence without needing to make her love me, which was tiring.

Her presence must have been enough, for I remember that I sat with my back to her and only once or twice turned to glance in her direction. My book was about a large family of motherless children. I did not grudge children in books their mothers, but I did not want them to run the risk, which haunted me, of losing them. It was safer if their mother had already gone before the book began, and the

wound healed, and I always tried to choose stories in which this had happened.

From time to time I glanced a little beyond the book and fell into reverie. I tried to imagine my own mother, who had gone out walking that afternoon, alone in the cherry orchard that ran down from hilltop to valley. Her restlessness often sent her off on long walks, too long for me to enjoy. I always lagged behind, thinking of my book, of the large, motherless family. In the cherry orchard it would be hot and scented, with bees scrambling into flowers, and faded-blue butterflies all over the chicory and heliotrope. But I found that I could not imagine her walking there alone; it seemed an incomplete picture that did not contain me. The reality was in this room, with its half-drawn blinds, its large gros-point picture of a cavalier saying good-bye to his lady. (Behind him, a soldier said good-bye in a less affecting way to a servant.) The plush-covered chairs, the Sèvres urns were so familiar to me, so present, as never to fade. It was one of those stamped scenes, heeled down into my experience, which cannot link up with others, or move forward, or change. Like a dream, it was separate, inviolable, and could be preserved. Then I suddenly thought that I should not have let my mother go out alone. It was a revolutionary thought, suggesting that children have some protection to offer to grown-ups. I did not know from what I should have protected her; perhaps just from her lonely walk that hot afternoon. I felt an unwelcome stir of pity. Until now I had thought that being adult put one beyond the slur of being pitiable.

I tried to return to my book, to draw all those children round me for safety, but in my disturbed mind I began to feel that Mrs. Vivaldi was not asleep. A wasp zigzagged round the room and went abruptly, accidentally, out of the window. It did not leave the same peace behind, but unease. I could see myself—with *her* eyes—hunched up over my book, my frock crumpled under me, as I endlessly sorted out and chose and ate and brooded over my bag of sweets. I felt that had intruded and it was no longer a natural thing to be indoors such a day. If she was awake, I must get up and speak to her.

Her hand supported her head, her white elbow was on the plush arm of the chair. In that dark red chair she seemed very white and fair and I could see long blue veins branching down the inside of her arm.

As I went towards her, I saw, through the slats of her parted fingers, her lashes move. I stood in front of her, holding out the bag of sweets, but she did not stir. Yet so sure was I that she was awake that I did not know how to move away or leave her. Just as my hand wavered uncertainly, her hand fell from her face. She opened her eyes and made a little movement of her mouth, too delicate to be called a yawn. She smiled. "I must have dropped off for a moment," she said. She glanced at the basket of flowers, at the clock, then at my bag of sweets.

"How kind of you!" she murmured, shaking her head, increasing my awkwardness. I took a few steps to one side, feeling I was looming over her.

"So you were here all the time?" she asked. "And I asleep. How dreadful I must have looked." She put her hand to the plaited hair at the nape of her neck. "Only young people should be seen asleep."

She was always underlining my youth, emphasising her own age. I wanted to say, "You looked beautiful," but I felt clumsy and absurd. I smiled foolishly and wandered out into the garden, leaving my book in the room. The painted balls lay over the lawn. The syringa made the paths untidy with dropped blossom. Everyone's afternoon was going forward but mine. Interrupted, I did not know where to take it up. I began to wonder how old Mrs. Vivaldi was. Standing by the buddleia tree, I watched the drunken butterflies clinging to the flowers, staggering about the branches. Why did she pretend? I asked myself. I knew that children were not worth acting for. No one bothered to keep it up before us; the voices changed, the faces yielded. We were a worthless audience. That she should dissemble for me made me feel very sad and responsible. I was burdened with what I had not said to comfort her.

I hid there by the buddleia a long time, until I heard my mother coming up the path, back from her walk. I dreaded now more than

ever that her step would drag, as sometimes it did, or that she would sigh. I came out half-fearfully from behind the buddleia tree.

She was humming to herself, and when she saw me, she handed me a large bunch of wild strawberries, the stalks warm from her hand. She sat down on the grass under the tree, and, lifting her long arms, smoothed her hair, pressing in the hair-pins more firmly. She said: "So you crept out of that stuffy little room after all?"

I ate the warm, gritty strawberries one by one, and my thoughts hovered all over her as the butterflies hovered over the tree. My shadow bent across her, as my love did.

SHADOWS OF THE WORLD

"I DON'T call this the real country," she said. "People only *sleep* here."

From the window, she watched the cars going by from the station. There was almost a stream of traffic, for the London train was in.

"And not always with whom they should," George Eliot agreed. His name was something he had to carry off. He tried to be the first with the jokes and never showed his weariness. His parents were the most unliterary people and had chosen his name because it had somehow sprung to their minds, sounding right, and familiar. Taking that in his stride had originated his flamboyance, his separateness. He made his mark in many dubious ways; but the ways *were* only dubious and sometimes he was given the benefit of the doubt. As a bachelor, he was a standby to dissatisfied wives and only the wives knew—and would not say—how inadequate he turned out to be.

"There go the Fletchers," Ida said. "What a mass of silverware they have on that car! They were sitting bolt upright and not speaking to one another."

"How could you see? She would scarcely have her head on his shoulder just driving back from the station."

"Nor on any other occasion. Nor his on hers."

"Come away from the window and talk to me. What time will Leonard come?"

"Who could know but Leonard? He might have caught that train and stepped aside on the way."

"For a drink?"

"It might be that even," she said, brightly insinuating.

She turned her back to the window, but stayed where she was. The branches of trees with their young leaves came close to the house and threw a greenish shadow over the walls inside. The colours of the spring evening were intense rather than brilliant: the lilac was heaped up against sky of the same purple. A house nearby had a sharp outline, as if before rain; but there had been neither rain nor sun for several days. Swallows flew low so that she could see their pale, neat bellies as they flickered about the eaves. In the wood, cuckoos answered one another, at long intervals, haltingly; one had its summer stammer already; its explosive, broken cry.

"The peonies almost open! How it all hastens by and vanishes!" Ida said, working herself up for a storm of her own.

"Why not have a drink?" George asked. He had come in for that, and because it looked like being a dark and thundery evening. No golf.

"I hate our lives," she cried. "We fritter our time away."

She looked round the room, at the rather grubby roughcast walls, little pictures hanging crooked, the red-brick fireplace with its littered grate, its dusty logs. "Everything goes wrong with what I do," she thought. "This room has simply no character. It looks raw, bleak, dull." Studying pictures in magazines it all seemed easy enough, but her colour schemes became confused, something always obtruded. If she followed elaborate recipes, what resulted was nothing like the photograph in the cookery-book. Her enthusiasms scarcely deserved the name. Her piano-playing, to which she resorted in boredom, remained sketchy and improvised in the bass. Resolutions, too, soon abated. Slimming-exercises, diets, taking the children to church, were all abandoned. Only dull habit remained, she thought. When her daughter wished to learn to play the violin, she refused. "You will want to give it up after a couple of lessons. You will never practise," she said, thinking only of her experience of herself; for Virginia was a tenacious child.

"A drink...?" George began once more. Though they were old friends he did not feel like going to what she called the cocktail cabinet and helping himself.

"I have nothing," she said moodily and dramatically. He looked surprised and alarmed. "The empty days," she continued, to his great relief, "the long, empty days."

"Oh hell, I thought for one moment you meant the drink situation."

"Have what you want," she said ungraciously, impatiently.

"Those damn cuckoos!" He laughed, pausing with the bottle in his hand pointing at her like a gun, his head on one side.

She persisted in her mood, pacing the room, trying to claim his whole attention. Vexed, frustrated, she was baulked by his indifference.

"You have the children," he said. "This nice home." He glanced at the crooked pictures, at some fallen petals lying round a jar of flowers.

As if he were a conjuror, the door opened and Virginia came in. She looked like a Japanese doll, with her white face, her straight black hair with the curved fringe, and her brightly patterned frock. At the back of the house, life was gayer. In the maid's sitting-room she and the nineteen-year-old girl from the village gossiped and giggled. She held the edges of the sheets to the sewing-machine while Nancy turned the handle, putting sides to middle. ("All the sheets are going at once," Ida had said bitterly, as if even household linen conspired against her.) The whir of the sewing-machine interrupted their discussions and they sucked sweets instead. The stuffy room smelt of pear-drops. But at seven, Nancy said: "Hey, you! Go on. Bed. Hop it."

"Where's Laurie?"

"Out in the shed, I dare say, with the cat. You can just run quick and see whether there's any kittens yet, but mind, when I say quick I don't mean your usual hanging about."

Virginia pressed her elbows to her sides. The oppressive evening menaced her with thunder and lightning, now with the horror of birth. Her mother had special feelings of the same kind; could forecast storms by her headaches; was sick at the smell of lilies; could not eat shell-fish, and fainted at the sight of blood. She over-reacted to the common things of life, even in physical ways, with giddiness and rashes on her skin. She taught her family to reverence her allergies and foibles and they were constantly discussed.

"I don't want to go," Virginia had said.

"Then say good-night to your mother," Nancy said, as if she had no better alternative to offer.

Virginia did not want that either, but stood obediently at the door, with her suspicious, upward look at them, at George and Ida.

Out in the shed, Laurie hung over the cat's basket, absorbed, though a little frightened. His cat, Moira, swaying with her weight of kittens, trampled the basket, crying. When Laurie stroked her head, she stopped, turning her golden eyes on him, appeased. She seemed as nervous as he, and as uninstructed. Maternity wrought an immediate, almost a comical change in her. The first kitten was born, silent, still. Laurie feared that it was dead. It looked so un-kittenish —livid, slimed-over, more blue than black. But at once, Moira became definite and authoritative: she licked and cuffed, treating brutally the poor clambering thing with its trailing navel-cord, its mouth pursed up like a flower-bud. Fantastic, at last alive, it tried to lift on its stringy neck the nodding weight of its head. Its paws were more hands than paws, with frail claws out-stretched, and piteously it raked the air with them.

Laurie imagined the edged cold after the warm; the discomforts of breathing. Surely, he thought, the poor creature felt, if not through its sealed eyes, then through its shivering body, the harsh, belabouring light, after such utter darkness.

Moira was arrogant in maternity, no uncertainty beset her now. When the kitten was cleaned, she lay down on her side awaiting the others, purring a little. She seemed contemptuous of Laurie and gave him only an occasional, unseeing glance. At the approach of each birth, she seemed to gather herself up, took on a suspicious look, with eyes narrowed. When she had cleaned them, the kittens were indistinguishable from her own black body, her thrust-out satiny legs. They clambered feebly over the mound of her belly, even before the last was born: their pink hands frailly felt the air: splayed out on dampish legs, they looked old and burdened creatures: they mewed wretchedly, resenting the bitter, cuffing, hard-edged world in which they were—the unrocking, unyielding stubbornness of it. Black, like their mother, they had bare-looking patches which would one day, Laurie thought, be white feet, white bibs. He looked forward for them. They peopled his home. He thought of them opening their eyes at last and playing; putting on mock terror at the sound of a footfall; arching their spines, cavorting, curveting about the legs of the furniture.

The stream of cars had dwindled and run out. The beech-leaves against the sloe-coloured sky looked more lucent; the birdsong which had suddenly increased in urgency and hysteria as suddenly ceased. Only a single thrush went on and its notes echoed in the silence, the intent air vibrated with the sound.

Thirty miles from London, the village had a preponderance of middle-sized houses. They lay at the end of short but curving drives, embowered in flowering trees. At this time of the year, the landscape was clotted with greenish creamy blossom—pear, white lilac, guelder-rose. Later, as it all faded, a faint grubbiness, a litter of petals seemed a total collapse. But there always were a great many birds: green woodpeckers appeared on the suburban-looking lawns; owls cried in the night. When the rain came it fell through layers of leaves, loosening gravel, staining the white roughcast houses and vibrating on sun-porches and greenhouses.

Ida was unusually placed in being able to see the road. Only rather low beech-hedges separated her. The cars reminded her of fish going by in shoals. At the week-ends when there were parties she would stand waiting by the window to be sure that plenty of her friends had gone by, not caring to be early. Like shoals of fish, they all headed one way, arrived at one destination (where there would be plenty to drink); turned homewards at last in unison.

Ida drank little, although sometimes at parties, because of her very indifference, she would accept glasses haphazardly with no knowledge of her mounting foolishness. She scorned and resented the way her acquaintance revolved round, took their pattern from, so much alcohol. For one thing, the cost dismayed her. She loved clothes, or rather new clothes, and her own clothes. It seemed that dozens of bottles of gin stood between her and all the things she wanted. George, who knew her so well, had no idea of her ill-will each time he filled his glass, which he did while she was saying good-night to Virginia.

Sounds of knives and forks being put out came from the dining-room. Virginia, opening the door, had let in a steaminess from the kitchen, a smell of mint.

"Ask Nancy not to *race* the potatoes like that," Ida said. "Good-night, darling one." She drew the child to her as if she were a spring-ing young tree; Virginia leant, but did not move her feet. Her mother used endearments a great deal: sometimes to put an edge to displea-sure. "*Darling*, how *could* you be so stupid!"

"I don't know if I should wait dinner for Leonard," she said to George, who was just raising his replenished glass. "You'll stay, won't you?"

"Well, I will then. Do you mean Leonard just may not come home?"

She had a desire to lay waste something, if only George's compla-cency.

"He may not come home to *me*."

"Then, dear, you are wondrous cool. Where else should he go?"

"To Isabel's, I expect."

"Isabel?"

"Oh, you must know," she said impatiently, surprised at her own tone.

"At the Fletchers' party, you mean? But parties are nothing. Everyone forgets the next day."

"Do they?"

She went to the window again, rapping her finger-nails on the glass. She felt isolated, because she did not forget the next day. Her own romantic hopes remained, and the young man at the party who had said "You don't belong," and pressed his knuckles steadily against her thigh as they stood in the porch waiting for cars, who promised—so falsely—to seek her out again, was real to her, her brooding mood enlarged, improved him. She had taken no heed of Leonard all that evening; given no thoughts to him. But some impression had been formed, as if her mind had photographed, without her knowledge, the picture of Leonard and Isabel intently talking. Now her dissatisfaction printed the negative. What had been to her advantage that evening, suddenly infuriated her.

"I'm sure it's nothing," George assured her. "Your imagination. Just one of those village things."

She had imagined the young man sitting in this room with her. The fire was lit; flames had consumed the cigarette-ends and litter. The house was silent, the walls receded into shadow. They watched the fire...

"I thought I heard thunder," George said, hoping to turn the conversation, and also quietly, one-handedly, filling his glass.

"I feel it in my head," Ida said, putting her hand across her eyes. When she heard footsteps on the road, she could not resist looking out again. She felt like the Lady of Shalott. "Shadows of the world appear," she thought. She imagined the young man, riding down between the hedges. But it was Isabel, going along the road in her old tweed coat with her dejected spaniel on a lead.

Virginia took off her vest and hung it over the mirror. Her nail-scissors and a silver comb she put in a drawer away from the lightning. Naked, she was thin and long-legged, her side marked with a neat appendix-scar. Her spine was silky, downy. She dropped her nightgown over her head and stood, legs apart, elbows up like wings, trying to do up buttons at the back.

Outside, the sky seemed to congeal cruelly, charged with lead. At the first sound of thunder splitting across the roof, she jumped into bed and lay under the thin coverings, quite rigid, as if she were dead.

The birth of the fourth, the last kitten, was a triumph. Creamy and blond tortoiseshell, it was distinguished and mysterious from the beginning, suggesting an elegant grandparent on one side or the other. Larger than the others, longer-haired, somehow complete at once, blind but not helpless, it put the finishing touches to the basket, decorated Moira's maternity.

Laurie shifted from his squatting position, feeling stiff, the pattern of wicker-work dented into one knee. He was relieved and exhilarated. Leaving benign, smug Moira, he went to put his bicycle away, for a few spots of rain had fallen on the path.

"Well, we won't wait," Ida said. The sight of Isabel had strangely frustrated her. "I'll tell Nancy, and Laurie must go to bed." She thought: "Better to dine alone with George than have him drinking all this gin."

"Where *is* Laurie?"

"With his cat. She's having kittens."

She put her hand on the bell and, when Nancy came, gave orders for dinner to be served. "And tell Laurie it's bedtime."

"Four kittens," Nancy said. "Isn't that lovely?"

"Thank you, Nancy," Ida said in her quelling way.

"Whatever will you do with them?" George asked. "Four kittens."

"Do? What do you imagine? Need we go into details?"

The rain, suddenly released, fell like knives into the flower-beds; bounced and danced on the paths. Different scents steamed up from the earth: the drenched lilac looked as if it would topple over with the weight of its saturated blossom.

Just as Nancy announced with her touch of sarcasm that dinner was served, Leonard's car swept into the drive. They heard him slamming the garage-doors together. George drained his glass and put it reluctantly on the table. Leonard came running up from the garage, his head down and his shoulders stained dark with the rain.

OASIS OF GAIETY

AFTER luncheon, Dosie took off her shoes and danced all round the room. Her feet were plump and arched, and the varnish on her toe nails shone through her stockings.

Her mother was sitting on the floor playing roulette with some of her friends. She was always called Auntie except by Dosie, who "darlinged" her in the tetchy manner of two women living in the same house, and by her son, Thomas, who stolidly said "Mother," a *démodé* word, Auntie felt—half insulting.

On Sunday afternoons, most of Auntie's "set" returned to their families when the mid-day champagne was finished. They scattered to the other houses round the golf course, to doze on loggias, snap at their children, and wonder where their gaiety had fled. Only Mrs. Wilson, who was a widow and dreaded her empty house, Ricky Jimpson, and the goatish Fergy Burns stayed on. More intimate than a member of the family, more inside than a friend, Fergy supported Auntie's idea of herself better than anyone else did, and, at times and in ways that he knew she couldn't mind, he sided with Dosie and Thomas against her.

In some of the less remote parts of Surrey, where the nineteen-twenties are perpetuated, such pockets of stale and elderly gaiety remain. They are blank as the surrounding landscape of fir trees and tarnished water.

Sunshine, especially blinding to the players after so much champagne, slanted into the room, which looked preserved, sealed off. Pinkish-grey cretonnes, ruched cushions with tassels, piles of gramophone-records, and a velvet Maurice Chevalier doll recalled the stage-sets of those forgotten comedies about weekends in the country and domestic imbroglio.

Auntie's marmoset sat on the arm of a chair, looking down sadly at the players and eating grapes, which he peeled with delicate, worn fingers and sharp teeth. His name was Rizzio. Auntie loved to name her possessions, everything—her car (called the Bitch, a favourite word of her youth), her fur coat, the rather noisy cistern in the WC. Even some of her old cardigans and shawls had nicknames and personalities. Her friends seemed not to find this tiresome. They played the game strenuously and sometimes sent Christmas presents to the inanimate objects. In exchange for all the fun and champagne they were required only to assist the fantasy and preserve the past. Auntie thought of herself as a "sport" and a "scream." (No one knew how her nickname had originated, for neither niece nor nephew had ever appeared to substantiate it.) "I did have a lovely heyday," she would say in her husky voice. "Girls of Dosie's age have never had anything." But Dosie had had two husbands already, not to count the incidentals, as Thomas said.

Thomas was her much younger brother, something of an incidental flowering himself. "Auntie's last bit of nonsense," people called him. Fifteen years and their different worlds separated brother and sister. He was of a more serious generation and seemed curiously practical, disabused, unemotional. His military service was a life beyond their imagination. They (pitying him, though recoiling from him) vaguely envisaged hutted sites at Aldershot, and boorish figures at football on muddy playing-fields with mists rising. Occasionally, at week-ends, he arrived, wearing sour-smelling khaki, which seemed to rub almost raw his neck and wrists. He would clump into the pub in his great Army boots and drink mild-and-bitter at his mother's expense, cagey about laying down a halfpenny of his own.

He made Fergy feel uneasy. Fergy had, Auntie often said, an impossible conscience. Watching bullocks being driven into a slaughterhouse had once taken him off steak for a month, and now, when he saw Thomas in khaki, he could only remember his own undergraduate days, gilded youth, fun with fireworks and chamber-pots, débutantes arriving in May Week, driving his red MG to the Beetle and Wedge for the Sunday-morning session. But Thomas had no MG. He had only the 7:26 back to Aldershot. If he ever had any gaiety, his mother did not discover it: if he had any friends, he did not bring them forward. Auntie was, Fergy thought, a little mean with him, a little on the tight side. She used endearments to him, but as if in utter consternation. He was an uncouth cuckoo in her nest. His hands made excruciating sounds on the silk cushions. Often, in bars, she would slip him a pound to pay his way, yet here he was, this afternoon, making as neat and secret a little pile as one would wish to see.

He played with florins, doubling them slowly, giving change where required, tucking notes into the breast pocket of his battle-dress, carefully buttoning them away as if no one was to be trusted. He had a rather breathy concentration, as he had had as a child, crouching over snakes-and-ladders; his hands, scooping up the coins, looked, Auntie thought, like great paws.

Only Mrs. Wilson's concentration could match his, but she had none of his stealthy deliberation. She had lost a packet, she proclaimed, but no one listened. She kept putting her hand in her bag and raking about, bringing out only a handkerchief, with which she touched the corners of her mouth. The others seemed to her quite indifferent to the fortunes of the game—Fergy, for instance, who was the banker, pushing Thomas's winnings across to him with no change of expression and no hesitation in his flow of talk.

Auntie gave a tiny glance of dislike at her son as he slipped some coins into his pocket. She could imagine him counting them all up, going back in the train. In her annoyance, she added a brutish look to his face. She sighed, but it was almost imperceptible and quite unperceived, the slightest intake of breath, as she glanced round at her friends, the darlings, who preserved her world, drinking her whisky, switching the radio away from the news to something gayer, and fortifying her against the dreary post-war world her son so typified. Mrs. Wilson, also, was a little dreary. Although trying gallantly, she had no real flair for recklessness and easily became drunk, when she would talk about her late husband and what a nice home they had had.

"Oh, Dosie, do sit down!" Auntie said.

Dosie was another who could not drink. She would become gayer and gayer and more and more taunting to poor Ricky Jimpson. Now she was dancing on his winnings. He smiled wanly. After the game, he would happily give her the lot, but while he was playing, it was sacred.

What Dosie herself gave for all she had from him was something to conjecture. Speculation, beginning with the obviously shameful, had latterly run into a maze of contradictions. Perhaps—and this was even more derogatory—she did only bestow taunts and abuse. She behaved like a very wilful child, as if to underline the fact that Ricky was old enough to be her father. Rather grey-faced (he had, he thought, a duodenal ulcer, and the vast quantity of whisky he drank was agony to him), he would sit and smile at her naughty ways, and sometimes when she clapped her hands, as if she pretended he was her slave, he would show that this was not pretence but very truth, and hurry to carry out her wishes.

Dosie, with one hand on the piano to steady herself, went through some of the *barre* exercises she had learnt as a child at ballet class. Her joints snapped and crackled with a sound like a fire kindling.

"You are a deadly lot," she suddenly said, and yawned out at the garden. "Put ten shillings on *rouge* for me, Ricky. I always win if you do it."

At least she doesn't lose if it isn't her money, Mrs. Wilson thought, wondering if she could ever, in a rallying way, make such a request of Fergy.

The hot afternoon, following the champagne, made them all drowsy. Only Ricky Jimpson sat up trimly. Fergy, looking at Mrs. Wilson's bosom, which her décolleté blouse too generously tendered, thought that in no time it would be all she had to offer. He imagined her placing it on, perhaps *zéro*—her last gesture.

Quite frightful, Auntie thought, the way Thomas's brow furrowed because he had lost two shillings. He was transparently sulky, like a little boy. All those baked beans in canteens made him stodgy and impossible. She hadn't visualised having such a son, or such a world for him to live in. "We can really do nothing for young people," she had once told Mrs. Wilson. "Nothing, nowadays, but try to preserve for them some of the old days, keep up our standards and give them an inkling of what things used to be, make a little oasis of gaiety for them." That had been during what she called "the late war." Thomas was home from school for the Christmas holidays. With tarnished pre-war tinsel Auntie was decorating the Christmas tree, though to this, as to most things, Thomas was quite indifferent. He had spent the holidays bicycling slowly round and round the lawn on the white, rimed grass. In the evenings, when his mother's friends came for drinks, he collected his books and went noticeably to his room. The books, on mathematics, were dull but mercifully concerned with things as they were, and this he preferred to all the talk about the tarnished, pre-war days. He could not feel that the present day was any of his doing. For the grown-ups to scorn what they had bequeathed to him seemed tactless. He ignored those conversations until his face looked mulish and immune. His mother arranged for his adenoids to be removed, but he continued to be closed-up and unresponsive.

Dosie was so different; she might almost be called a ringleader. She made her mother feel younger than ever—"really more like a sister," Auntie said, showing that this was a joke by saying it with a Cockney accent. Oh, Dosie was the liveliest girl, except that sometimes she went too far. The oasis of gaiety her mother provided became obviously too small and she was inclined then to go off into the desert and cry havoc. But Auntie thought her daughter mischievous, not desperate.

"Either play or not," she told her sharply, for sometimes the girl irritated her.

But Dosie, at the French windows, took no notice. She could feel the sun striking through her thin frock, and she seemed to unfold in the warmth, like a flower. In the borders, lilies stood to attention in the shimmering air, their petals glazed and dusty with pollen. The scent was wonderful.

"I shall bathe in the pool," she said, over her shoulder. The pool—a long rectangle of water thick with plants—was deep and Dosie had never learnt to swim, had always floundered wildly.

Only Ricky Jimpson remonstrated.

"She can't swim," Auntie said, dismissing her daughter's nonsense. "Does anyone *want* to go on playing?"

Mrs. Wilson certainly did not. She had never believed in last desperate flings, throwing good money after bad. In games of chance there was no certainty but that she would lose; even the law of averages worked against her. What she wanted now was a cup of tea and aspirins, for champagne agreed with her no better than roulette. She felt lost. Her widowhood undermined her and she no longer felt loved.

But who was loved—in this room, for instance? Mrs. Wilson often thought that her husband would not have dared to die if he had known she would drift into such company. "What *you* need, darling, is a nice, cosy woman friend," Fergy had said years ago when she had reacted in bewilderment to his automatic embrace. He had relinquished her at once, in a weary, bored way, and ignored her coldly ever since. His heartless perception frightened her. Despite her acceptance of—even clinging to—their kind of life, and her acquiescence in every madness, every racket, she had not disguised from him that what she wanted was her dull, good husband back and a nice evening with the wireless; perhaps, too, a middle-aged woman friend to go shopping with, to talk about slimming and recipes. Auntie never discussed those things. She was the kind of woman men liked. She amused them with her scatter-brained chatter and innuendo and the fantasy she wove, the stories she told, about herself. When she was with women, she rested. Mrs. Wilson could not imagine her feeling unsafe, or panicking when the house emptied. She seemed self-reliant and efficient. She and Dosie sometimes quarrelled, or appeared to be quarrelling, with lots of "But, *darling*!" and

"*Must* you be such a fool, sweetie?" Yet only Thomas, the symbol of the post-war world, was really an affront. Him she could not assimilate. He was the grit that nothing turned into a pearl—neither gaiety nor champagne. He remained blank, impervious. He took his life quite seriously, made no jokes about the Army, was silent when his mother said, "Oh, *why* go? Catch the last train or wait until morning. In fact, why don't you desert? Dosie and I could hide you in the attic. It would be the greatest fun. Or be ill. Get some awful soldier's disease."

Dosie was blocking the sunlight from the room, and Mrs. Wilson suddenly felt goose flesh on her arms and cramp in her legs from sitting on the floor.

Ricky Jimpson put his winnings in his pocket without a glance at them. He sat, bent slightly forward, with one hand pressed to his waist. He smiled brilliantly if he caught anybody's eye, but his face soon reassembled itself to its look of static melancholy. The smile was an abrupt disorganisation. His eyes rarely followed Dosie. He seemed rather to be listening to her, even when she was silent. He was conscious of her in some other way than visually. His spirit *attended* to her, caught up in pain though he was.

The roulette cloth was folded and put away. The marmoset was busy tearing one of the cushion tassels. Then, to Mrs. Wilson's relief, the door opened and a maid pushed in a trolley with a jazzy black-and-orange pottery tea-set and some rolled-up bread and butter.

Dosie wandered out across the gravelled path in her stockinged feet. The garden, the golf course beyond it, and all the other wistaria-covered, balconied Edwardian villas at its perimeter seemed to slant and swoon in the heat. Her exasperation weakened and dispersed. She always felt herself leaving other people behind; they lagged after her recklessness. Even in making love, she felt the same isolation—that she was speeding on into a country where no one would pursue her. Each kiss was an act of division. "Follow me!" she willed "them"—a succession of them, all shadowy. They could not follow, or know to what cold distances she withdrew. Her punishment for them was mischief, spite, a little gay cruelty, but nothing drastic. She had no beauty, for there was none to inherit, but she was a bold and noticeable woman.

When Fergy joined her in the garden, he put his arm across her shoulders and they walked down the path towards the pool. Water-lilies lay picturesquely on the green surface. The oblong of water was bordered by ornamental grasses in which dragonflies glinted. A concrete gnome was fishing at the edge.

They stood looking at the water, lulled by the heat and the beauty of the afternoon. When he slipped his arm closer round her, she felt herself preparing, as of old, for flight. Waywardly, she moved from him. She stripped seeds off a tall grass, viciously, and scattered them on the water. Goldfish rose, then sank away dejectedly.

"Let us throw in this bloody little dwarf," Dosie said, "and you can cry for help. They will think I am drowning." She began to rock the gnome from side to side. Small brown frogs like crumpled leaves leapt away into the grass.

"Auntie dotes on the little creature," Fergy said. "She has a special nickname for him."

"So have I."

Together they lifted the gnome and threw him out towards the centre of the pool.

"I always loathed the little beast," Dosie said.

"Help!" Fergy cried. "For *God's* sake, help!"

Dosie watched the house, her face alight, her eyebrows lifted in anticipation. Rings widened and faded on the water.

Ricky Jimpson dashed through the French windows and ran towards the pool, his face whiter than ever, his hand to his side. When he saw them both standing there, he stopped. His look of desperation vanished. He smiled his brilliant, dutiful smile, but, receiving one of his rare glances, Dosie saw in his eyes utter affliction, forlornness.

That evening, Thomas, on his way back to Aldershot, met Syd at the top of the station subway; as per usual arrangement, Syd had said when they parted the day before. Their greeting was brief and they went in silence towards the restaurant, shouldering their way along the crowded platform. In the bar, they ordered two halves of mild-and-bitter and two pieces of pork-pie.

Syd pushed back his greasy beret and scratched his head. Then he broke open the pie to examine the inside—the pink gristle and tough grey jelly.

"What they been up to this time?" he asked.

"The usual capering about. My mother was rather lit up last night and kept doing the Charleston."

"Go on!"

"But I suppose that's better than the Highland fling," Thomas said. "Pass the mustard."

Syd, whose own mother rarely moved more than, very ponderously, from sink to gas stove, was fascinated. "Like to've seen it," he said. "From a distance."

"What did you do?" Thomas asked.

"Went to the Palais Saturday night along with Viv. Never got up till twelve this morning, then went round the local. Bit of a read this afternoon, then went for a stroll along with Viv. You know, up by the allotments. Had a nice lie-down in the long grass. She put her elbow in a cow-pat. Laugh!" He threw back his head and laughed there and then.

"Same again," Thomas said to the barmaid. "Want some more pie, Syd?"

"No, ta. I had me tea."

"I made thirty-four bob," Thomas said, tapping his breast pocket.

"You can make mine a pint then," Syd said. But Thomas didn't say anything. They always drank halves. He looked at Syd and wondered what his mother would say of him. He often wondered that. But she would never have the chance. He looked quite fiercely round the ugly restaurant room, with its chromium tables, ringed and sticky, thick china, glass domes over the museum-pieces of pork pie. The look of the place calmed him, as Syd's company did—something he could grasp, *his* world.

"Don't know how they stick that life, week after week," Thomas said. "My sister threw a garden ornament in the pond—pretended she'd fallen in herself. A sort of dwarf," he added vaguely.

"What for?" Syd asked.

"I think she was fed up," Thomas said, trying to understand. But he lived in two irreconcilable worlds.

Syd only said, "Rum. Could they fish it out again?"

"No one tried. We had tea then." He gave up trying to explain what he did not comprehend, and finished his beer.

"Better get a move on," Syd said, using as few consonants as possible.

"Yes, I suppose so." Thomas looked at the clock.

"The old familiar faces."

"You're right," Thomas agreed contentedly.

PLENTY GOOD FIESTA

LONG, long ago, during the Spanish Civil War, Fernando came to live with us for a short time. Nowadays, refugees are part of the world's landscape, but he was much less a refugee than an ambassador. He had come to England with other children from the bombed cities of Spain. They lived in a camp near our home, and were always about the country lanes—graceful, swarthy children. Young as they were, fear had come closer to them than to us, and they seemed like our futures walking towards us. Fernando was the one my husband and I knew most intimately. Because of his nervous habits, which shock had caused, the other children teased him; and the camp doctor asked us if we would take him into our home until he recovered. I knew nothing about him except what the doctor told me—that his father, a schoolmaster, was in hiding, his mother in prison, and his one brother, grown-up, had been killed by the Fascists. Nine years old, forlorn, speaking no word of English, he had achieved a jaunty gaiety to cover up his naturally clinging disposition. I imagined him a "spoilt" child (though kindness could no more spoil him than evil had)—much petted, the baby of the family, born to his mother in her middle age.

Although he found himself among strangers in a strange country, he gave no measuring glances, showed no surprise or hesitancy; he walked into our house purposefully, carrying in a paper bag some girls' underwear he had been given, a cherished Fair Isle jersey, and a handful of glass marbles. Pride was in each step he took.

Neither my husband nor I can speak Spanish, but the dictionary on the dinner table was unnecessary. Fernando reached for what he needed. He pushed back his chair and went round the table, spearing with his fork whatever took his fancy. Never over everyday things did we feel lack of language a barrier; only over subtler things, emotional nuances or matters of reassurance.

He was a robust child with beautiful ways of walking and moving. His dark cheeks were always suffused with rose, an unusual warmth in such a dusky skin. His black hair was curly and untidy, but on formal occasions he combed it under the bath tap in a great rush of cold water. His appearance was then quite changed. The long damp fringe level above his eyes gave him a sinister look.

Along with the girls' underwear, he had been given a pair of heavy boots. It was summer, but he would not discard these for the sandals we gave him.

He was never timid or ingratiating, as, in his strange position, he might have been. Only once was he disobedient. I found him striking a box of matches, one by one. Because he always dropped the matches as soon as they flared, he had been told not to touch them. This time, he had used up the whole box. He threw down the last match as I arrived, and smiled. "Is quite all right," he said in one breath. It was his first English phrase. He did not know the meaning but took it to be reassuring, as it was what I said when he dropped a plate, or, once, when he wet his bed. For his pidgin English we must have been to blame, as he knew no word when he first came to us. He began to talk like a stage Chinaman. "Plenty bad," he explained when he was discovered stoning the sign of the Cyclists' Touring Club, which, with its whirling arrangement of legs, he took to be the Fascist swastika.

He sometimes had a male swagger, hands in pockets, his trousers tight across his buttocks. He would whistle, shrug his shoulders, behave in a precociously cheeky manner to me. He had, especially, a startlingly adult wink, with his finger to the side of his nose. Slowly, laden with meaning, his lid would drop. He would do this in company, across a room at me, suggesting a dubious complicity. I wondered if he had watched his grown-up brother in his conquering days, as he had later watched him killed.

His male arrogance was mingled with a strong maternal tenderness. He loved to push our baby in the pram along the lanes, the blond baby sitting up smiling at him as Fernando strode along singing the songs of Republican Spain. For he never forgot that he was Spanish. He accepted our life with grace and courtesy, but he did not become English. He admired the best we had to offer—the Fair Isle jersey, the boots, our babies, the English countryside—but he was always the proud and formal Catalan. He was for the Republic, against the Fascists, politically conscious, loyal. He also spat as he passed the church; in his country the *iglesia* had often concealed machine-guns. He even cleaned his mouth at the sight of the Baptist Chapel.

Fernando's anger, when it occurred, was a ceremonious anger. His gaiety, which was the gayest gaiety I ever encountered, had some of the same formality. In England, gaiety is informal, spasmodic. We do not reserve it for special occasions, and at Christmas it is sometimes a dogged duty. We did not have Fernando with us for Christmas. But we did have him for the *fiesta*.

One afternoon, we took Fernando and the baby for a drive. Not far from home we came to a village where a little fair was set out on the green—a few caravans, a roundabout, sideshows, swing boats. Fernando, in the back seat, began to wave his arms, and cried, "*Fiesta! Fiesta!*" As we had to get back for the baby's six-o'clock feeding (and even that seemed un-Spanish, dogged), we could only promise to return to the fair next day. "*Mañana.*" He nodded with satisfaction.

Late that night, as my husband and I were thinking of going to bed, we heard Fernando's boots on the landing, then the sound of water running from the bathroom tap. We ran upstairs to see what he was doing. He was dressed in the Fair Isle jersey, his wet hair flattened to his brow. "For the *fiesta*," he said. Dismayed by memories of Ernest Hemingway, of bulls charging through the streets at dawn, and wine running in the gutters, I wondered how to explain. In England, I said, the fiesta does not begin until daytime. Dazed, a little scornful, he was led back to his bed.

Very early in the morning, I awoke to the sound of the boots and the rushing water. Again I explained. Puzzled, Fernando watched my husband go to work. ("In England, we do not stop work for the *fiesta*.") Because he spent such a disconsolate morning, and from a kind of national guilt, I let him strike match after match. Thoughts of the modest village fair lowered me.

As it was Saturday, my husband came home at noon, and we all got into the car and drove off after lunch. I was as flattened and subdued as Fernando's hair. Over my shoulder, the baby bobbed its head at him. Long strings of dribble festooned me. Fernando spoke Catalan baby talk, winked, whistled, sang. He was lifted to a pitch of excitement that filled us with gloom and despair. We drove into the village, and the fair was gone.

There were no words to cover our horror. We thanked God for His arrangements about the Tower of Babel, which seemed now a piece of long-term wisdom. We smiled reassuringly and said, "Is quite all right." As if he knew where we were going, my husband drove confidently down the lanes, made enquiries at village shops. No one could help. After a long time, we found a few caravans on a dirty fairground, outside a market town. Drearily set amid mud and cinders, they looked shabby and unclean compared with those we had seen the day before.

Fernando put a hand apprehensively to his fringe, as if about to enter Windsor Castle. I wished I had not read that book by Hemingway. It was so full of local colour, of which Britain seemed to have none (save the Fair Isle jersey).

The baby's eyes stretched in terror at the panic of music forced by steam out of the roundabout. Fernando, with his hand still on his fringe, burst from the car. Utterly dejected, my husband and I made our way down the cinder path.

I think that one of the most touching things I have read about a war was by Gertrude Stein, who remarked how the look of her French village altered in 1939. The elder brothers and the fathers went off to the front, and suddenly the lanes were full of little boys riding bicycles too big for them, standing on the pedals, their elbows in the air. I do not know if Fernando's brother had a bicycle and there was the same brief period of riding it, but it was now revealed to us that the great force and passion of Fernando's life was to own one—or at least to ride one for a while, pretending ownership. Ignoring the rest of the fair, he made for the children's roundabout, where, among peacocks, racing cars, airplanes, and gilded horses, he could see a stationary bicycle with movable pedals.

Excitement exploded in him. His hair, beginning to curl again, bounded on his forehead. The few people who were about glanced from the blond baby to the impassioned Spaniard with amusement. Self-consciously, we led him to the bicycle. The other children, used to their fairy-cycles and tricycles, preferred the more exotic birds or the airplanes.

The rides—in those days—were a penny, and lasted perhaps for three minutes. Two shillings' worth covered about an hour and a half, for there were gaps while the man waited for more customers. My husband and I stood watching, taking turns holding the baby. At first Fernando waved as he passed us, but later forgot. He gazed into the distance, pedalling rapidly, grave, absorbed. His eyes narrowed, and he leant to an imagined camber of the road.

What distances in Catalonia, we wondered, did he cover? What goal achieve? Sometimes, impatiently, because of fool drivers, he rang the bell, sometimes seemed to stiffen his whole body, bear down on the pedals, braking for unseen obstacles, though the roundabout took him merrily on.

He became a character to the man in charge and to some of the onlookers, but he was oblivious of them. Each time the roundabout ran down, the bronchial music wheezed off into a trailing sigh, he would hand in another penny in a peremptory, irritable way, checked in his dream, and sit steady, tense, waiting. Once, catching my eye, he looked quickly aside, as if the sight of me violated his privacy.

At the end, when his money was spent, he climbed down. He stumbled towards us, seeming drunk. He did not speak.

We drove off through the drab town, with its queue already outside the cinema, and then into the quiet, lovely countryside. The fields were tented with cornstooks. A picture of peace. The baby slept now. Fernando, gorged with pleasure, replete, dulled, sat with his head jogging against the side of the car. Awkwardly, I was silent, too, thinking of the bullfights, the *corrida*, a mounting, vinous excitement.

When we reached home, I turned to look at Fernando. He seemed drowsy and blissful. He smiled his fine smile. "Plenty good *bicicleta*," he said, nodding. "Plenty good *fiesta*."

THE BLUSH

THEY WERE the same age—Mrs. Allen and the woman who came every day to do the housework. "I shall never have children now," Mrs. Allen had begun to tell herself. Something had not come true; the essential part of her life. She had always imagined her children in fleeting scenes and intimations; that was how they had come to her, like snatches of a film. She had seen them plainly, their chins tilted up as she tied on their bibs at meal-times; their naked bodies had darted in and out of the water-sprinkler on the lawn; and she had listened to their voices in the garden and in the mornings from their beds. She had even cried a little dreaming of the day when the eldest boy would go off to boarding-school; she pictured the train going out of the station; she raised her hand and her throat contracted and her lips trembled as she smiled. The years passing by had slowly filched from her the reality of these scenes—the gay sounds; the grave peace she had longed for; even the pride of grief.

She listened—as they worked together in the kitchen—to Mrs. Lacey's troubles with her family, her grumblings about her grown-up son who would not get up till dinner-time on Sundays and then expected his mother to have cleaned his shoes for him; about the girl of eighteen who was a hairdresser and too full of dainty ways which she picked up from the women's magazines, and the adolescent girl who moped and glowered and answered back.

"My children wouldn't have turned out like that," Mrs. Allen thought, as she made her murmured replies. "The more you do for some, the more you may," said Mrs. Lacey. But from gossip in the village which Mrs. Allen heard, she had done all too little. The children, one night after another, for years and years, had had to run out for parcels of fish and chips while their mother sat in the Horse and Jockey drinking brown ale. On summer evenings, when they were younger, they had hung about outside the pub: when they were bored they pressed their foreheads to the window and looked in at the dark little bar, hearing the jolly laughter, their mother's the loudest of all. Seeing their faces, she would swing at once from the violence of hilarity to that of extreme annoyance and, although ginger-beer and packets of potato crisps would be handed out through the window, her anger went out with them and threatened the children as they ate and drank.

"And she doesn't always care who she goes there *with*," Mrs. Allen's gardener told her.

"She works hard and deserves a little pleasure—she has her anxieties," said Mrs. Allen, who, alas, had none.

She had never been inside the Horse and Jockey, although it was nearer to her house than the Chequers at the other end of the village where she and her husband went sometimes for a glass of sherry on Sunday mornings. The Horse and Jockey attracted a different set of customers—for instance, people who sat down and drank, at tables all round the wall. At the Chequers no one ever sat down, but stood and sipped and chatted as at a cocktail party, and luncheons and dinners were served, which made it so much more respectable: no children hung about outside, because they were all at home with their nannies.

Sometimes in the evenings—so many of them—when her husband was kept late in London, Mrs. Allen wished that she could go down to the Chequers and drink a glass of sherry and exchange a little conversation with someone; but she was too shy to open the door and go in alone: she imagined heads turning, a surprised welcome from her friends, who would all be safely in married pairs; and then, when she left, eyes meeting with unspoken messages and conjecture in the air.

Mrs. Lacey left her at midday and then there was gardening to do and the dog to be taken for a walk. After six o'clock, she began to pace restlessly about the house, glancing at the clocks in one room after another, listening for her husband's car—the sound she knew so well because she had awaited it for such a large part of her married life. She would hear, at last, the tyres turning on the soft gravel, the door being slammed, then his footsteps hurrying towards the porch. She knew that it was a wasteful way of spending her years—and, looking back, she was unable to tell one of them from another—but she could not think what else she might do. Humphrey went on earning more and more money and there was no stopping him now. Her acquaintances, in wretched quandaries about where the next term's school-fees were to come from, would turn to her and say cruelly: "Oh, *you're* all right, Ruth. You've no idea what you are spared."

And Mrs. Lacey would be glad when Maureen could leave school and "get out earning." "'I've got my geometry to do,' she says, when it's time to wash up the tea-things. 'I'll geometry you, my girl,' I said. 'When I was your age, I was out earning.'"

Mrs. Allen was fascinated by the life going on in that house and the children seemed real to her, although she had never seen them. Only Mr. Lacey remained blurred and unimaginable. No one knew him. He worked in the town in the valley, six miles away, and he kept himself to himself; had never been known to show his face in the Horse and Jockey. "I've got my own set," Mrs. Lacey said airily. "After all, he's nearly twenty years older than me. I'll make sure neither of my girls follow my mistake. 'I'd rather see you dead at my feet,' I said to Vera." Ron's young lady was lucky; having Ron, she added. Mrs. Allen found this strange, for Ron had always been painted so black; was, she had been led to believe, oafish, ungrateful, greedy and slow to put his hands in his pockets if there was any paying out to do. There was also the matter of his shoe-cleaning, for no young woman would do what his mother did for him—or said she did. Always, Mrs. Lacey would sigh and say: "Goodness me, if only I was their age and knew what I know now."

She was an envious woman: she envied Mrs. Allen her pretty house and her clothes and she envied her own daughters their youth. "If I had your figure," she would say to Mrs. Allen. Her own had gone: what else could be expected, she asked, when she had had three children? Mrs. Allen thought, too, of all the brown ale she drank at the Horse and Jockey and of the reminiscences of meals past which came so much into her conversations. Whatever the cause was, her flesh, slackly corseted, shook as she trod heavily about the kitchen. In summer, with bare arms and legs she looked larger than ever. Although her skin was very white, the impression she gave was at once colourful—from her orange hair and bright lips and the floral patterns that she always wore. Her red-painted toe-nails poked through the straps of her fancy sandals; turquoise-blue beads were wound round her throat.

Humphrey Allen had never seen her; he had always left for the station before she arrived, and that was a good thing, his wife thought. When she spoke of Mrs. Lacey, she wondered if he visualised a neat, homely woman in a clean white overall. She did not deliberately mislead him, but she took advantage of his indifference. Her relationship with Mrs. Lacey and the intimacy of their conversations in the kitchen he would not have approved, and the sight of those calloused feet with their chipped nail-varnish and yellowing heels would have sickened him.

One Monday morning, Mrs. Lacey was later than usual. She was never very punctual and had many excuses about flat bicycle-tyres or Maureen being poorly. Mrs. Allen, waiting for her, sorted out all the washing. When she took another look at the clock, she decided that it was far too late for her to be expected at all. For some time lately Mrs. Lacey had seemed ill and depressed; her eyelids, which were chronically rather inflamed, had been more angrily red than ever and, at the sink or ironing-board, she would fall into unusual silences, was absent-minded and full of sighs. She had always liked to talk about the "change" and did so more than ever as if with a desperate hopefulness.

"I'm sorry, but I was ever so sick," she told Mrs. Allen, when she arrived the next morning. "I still feel queerish. Such heartburn. I don't like the signs, I can tell you. All I crave is pickled walnuts, just the same as I did with Maureen. I don't like the signs one bit. I feel I'll throw myself into the river if I'm taken that way again."

Mrs. Allen felt stunned and antagonistic. "Surely not at your age," she said crossly.

"You can't be more astonished than me," Mrs. Lacey said, belching loudly. "Oh, pardon. I'm afraid I can't help myself."

Not being able to help herself, she continued to belch and hiccough as she turned on taps and shook soap-powder into the washing-up bowl. It was because of this that Mrs. Allen decided to take the dog for a walk. Feeling consciously fastidious and aloof she made her way across the fields, trying to disengage her thoughts from Mrs. Lacey and her troubles; but unable to. "Poor woman," she thought again and again with bitter animosity.

She turned back when she noticed how the sky had darkened with racing, sharp-edged clouds. Before she could reach home, the rain began. Her hair, soaking wet, shrank into tight curls against her head; her woollen suit smelt like a damp animal. "Oh, I am drenched," she called out, as she threw open the kitchen door.

She knew at once that Mrs. Lacey had gone, that she must have put on her coat and left almost as soon as Mrs. Allen had started out on her walk, for nothing was done; the washing-up was hardly started and the floor was unswept. Among the stacked-up crockery a note was propped; she had come over funny, felt dizzy and, leaving her apologies and respects, had gone.

Angrily, but methodically, Mrs. Allen set about making good the wasted morning. By afternoon, the grim look was fixed upon her face. "How dare she?" she found herself whispering, without allowing herself to wonder what it was the woman had dared.

She had her own little ways of cosseting herself through the lonely hours, comforts which were growing more important to her as she grew older, so that the time would come when not to have her cup of tea at four-thirty would seem a prelude to disaster. This afternoon, disorganised as it already was, she fell out of her usual habit and instead of carrying the tray to the low table by the fire, she poured out her tea in the kitchen and drank it there, leaning tiredly against the dresser. Then she went upstairs to make herself tidy. She was trying to brush her frizzed hair smooth again when she heard the door bell ringing.

When she opened the door, she saw quite plainly a look of astonishment take the place of anxiety on the man's face. Something about herself surprised him, was not what he had expected. "Mrs. Allen?" he asked uncertainly and the astonishment remained when she had answered him.

"Well, I'm calling about the wife," he said. "Mrs. Lacey that works here."

"I was worried about her," said Mrs. Allen.

She knew that she must face the embarrassment of hearing about Mrs. Lacey's condition and invited the man into her husband's study, where she thought he might look less out-of-place than in her brocade-smothered drawing-room. He looked about him resentfully and glared down at the floor which his wife had polished. With this thought in his mind, he said abruptly: "It's all taken its toll."

He sat down on a leather couch with his cap and his bicycle-clips beside him.

"I came home to my tea and found her in bed, crying," he said. This was true. Mrs. Lacey had succumbed to despair and gone to lie down. Feeling better at four o'clock, she went downstairs to find some food to comfort herself with; but the slice of dough-cake was ill-chosen and brought on more heartburn and floods of bitter tears.

"If she carries on here for a while, it's all got to be very different," Mr. Lacey said threateningly. He was nervous at saying what he must and could only bring out the words with the impetus of anger. "You may or may not know that she's expecting."

"Yes," said Mrs. Allen humbly. "This morning she told me that she thought . . ."

"There's no 'thought' about it. It's as plain as a pikestaff." Yet in his eyes she could see disbelief and bafflement and he frowned and looked down again at the polished floor.

Twenty years older than his wife—or so his wife had said—he

really, to Mrs. Allen, looked quite ageless, a crooked, bow-legged little man who might have been a jockey once. The expression about his blue eyes was like a child's: he was both stubborn and pathetic.

Mrs. Allen's fat spaniel came into the room and went straight to the stranger's chair and began to sniff at his corduroy trousers.

"It's too much for her," Mr. Lacey said. "It's too much to expect."

To Mrs. Allen's horror she saw the blue eyes filling with tears. Hoping to hide his emotion, he bent down and fondled the dog, making playful thrusts at it with his fist closed.

He was a man utterly, bewilderedly at sea. His married life had been too much for him, with so much in it that he could not understand.

"Now I know, I will do what I can," Mrs. Allen told him. "I will try to get someone else in to do the rough."

"It's the late nights that are the trouble," he said. "She comes in dog-tired. Night after night. It's not good enough. 'Let them stay at home and mind their own children once in a while,' I told her. 'We don't need the money.'"

"I can't understand," Mrs. Allen began. She was at sea herself now, but felt perilously near a barbarous, unknown shore and was afraid to make any movement towards it.

"I earn good money. For her to come out at all was only for extras. She likes new clothes. In the daytimes I never had any objection. Then all these cocktail parties begin. It beats me how people can drink like it night after night and pay out for someone else to mind their kids. Perhaps you're thinking that it's not my business, but I'm the one who has to sit at home alone till all hours and get my own supper and see next to nothing of my wife. I'm boiling over some nights. Once I nearly rushed out when I heard the car stop down the road. I wanted to tell your husband what I thought of you both."

"My husband?" murmured Mrs. Allen.

"'What am *I* supposed to have?' I would have asked him. 'Is she my wife or your sitter-in? Bringing her back at this time of night.' And it's no use saying she could have refused. She never would."

Mrs. Allen's quietness at last defeated him and dispelled the anger he had tried to rouse in himself. The look of her, too, filled him with doubts, her grave, uncertain demeanour and the shock her age had been to him. He had imagined someone so much younger and—because of the cocktail parties—flighty. Instead, he recognised something of himself in her, a yearning disappointment. He picked up his cap and his bicycle-clips and sat looking down at them, turning them round in his hands. "I had to come," he said.

"Yes," said Mrs. Allen.

"So you won't ask her again?" he pleaded. "It isn't right for her. Not now."

"No, I won't," Mrs. Allen promised and she stood up as he did and walked over to the door. He stooped and gave the spaniel a final pat. "You'll excuse my coming, I hope."

"Of course."

"It was no use saying any more to her. Whatever she's asked, she won't refuse. It's her way."

Mrs. Allen shut the front door after him and stood in the hall, listening to him wheeling his bicycle across the gravel. Then she felt herself beginning to blush. She was glad that she was alone, for she could feel her face, her throat, even the tops of her arms burning, and she went over to a looking-glass and studied with great interest this strange phenomenon.

THE LETTER-WRITERS

AT ELEVEN o'clock, Emily went down to the village to fetch the lobsters. The heat unsteadied the air, light shimmered and glanced off leaves and telegraph wires and the flag on the church tower spreading out in a small breeze, then dropping, wavered against the sky, as if it were flapping under water.

She wore an old cotton frock, and meant to change it at the last moment, when the food was all ready and the table laid. Over her bare arms, the warm air flowed, her skirt seemed to divide as she walked, pressed in a hollow between her legs, like drapery on a statue. The sun seemed to touch her bones—her spine, her shoulder-blades, her skull. In her thoughts, she walked nakedly, picking her way, over dry-as-dust cow-dung, along the lane. All over the hedges, trumpets of large white convolvulus were turned upwards towards the sky—the first flowers she could remember; something about them had, in her early childhood, surprised her with astonishment and awe, a sense of magic that had lasted, like so little else, repeating itself again and again, most of the summers of her forty years.

From the wide-open windows of the village school came the sound of a tinny piano. "We'll rant, and we'll roar, like true British sailors," sang all the little girls.

Emily, smiling to herself as she passed by, had thoughts so delightful that she began to tidy them into sentences to put in a letter to Edmund. Her days were not full or busy and the gathering in of little things to write to him about took up a large part of her time. She would have made a paragraph or two about the children singing, the hot weather—so rare in England—the scent of the lime and privet blossom, the pieces of tin glinting among the branches of the cherry trees. But the instinctive thought was at once checked by the truth that there would be no letter-writing that evening after all. She stood before an alarming crisis, one that she had hoped to avoid for as long as ever she lived; the crisis of meeting for the first time the person whom she knew best in the world.

"What will he be like?" did not worry her. She knew what he was like. If he turned out differently, it would be a mistake. She would be getting a false impression of him and she would know that it was temporary and would fade. She was more afraid of herself, and wondered if he would know how to discount the temporary, and false, in her. Too much was at stake and, for herself, she would not have taken the risk. "I agree that we have gone beyond meeting now. It would be retracing our steps," he had once written to her. "Although, perhaps if we were ever in the same country, it would be absurd to make a point of *not* meeting." This, however, was what she had done when she went to Italy the next year.

In Rome, some instinct of self-preservation kept her from giving him her aunt's address there. She would telephone, she thought; but each time she tried to—her heart banging erratically within a suddenly hollow breast—she was checked by thoughts of the booby-trap lying before her. In the end, she skirted it. She discovered the little street where he lived, and felt the strangeness of reading its name, which she had written hundreds of times on envelopes. Walking past his house on the opposite pavement, she had glanced timidly at the peeling apricot-coloured plaster. The truth of the situation made her feel quite faint. It was frightening, like seeing a ghost in reverse—the insubstantial suddenly solidifying into a patchy and shabby reality. At the window on the first floor, one of the shutters was open; there was the darkness of the room beyond, an edge of yellow curtain and, hanging over the back of a chair set near the window, what looked like a white skirt. Even if Edmund himself threw open the other shutter and came out on to the balcony, he would never have known that the woman across the road was one of his dearest friends, but, all the same, she hastened away from the neighbourhood. At dinner, her aunt thought she might be ill. Her visitors from England so often were—from the heat and sight-seeing and the change of diet.

The odd thing to Emily about the escapade was its vanishing from her mind—the house became its own ghost again, the house of her imagination, lying on the other side of the road, where she had always pictured it, with its plaster unspoilt and Edmund inside in his tidied-up room, writing to her.

He had not chided her when she sent a letter from a safer place, explaining her lack of courage—and explain it she could, so fluently, half-touchingly yet wholly amusingly—on paper. He teased her gently, understanding her decision. In him, curiosity and adventurousness would have overcome his hesitation. Disillusionment would have deprived him of less than it might have deprived her; her letters were a relaxation to him; to her, his were an excitement, and her fingers often trembled as she tore open their envelopes.

They had written to one another for ten years. She had admired his novels since she was a young woman, but would not have thought of writing to tell him so; that he could conceivably be interested in the opinion of a complete stranger did not occur to her. Yet, sometimes, she felt that without her as their reader the novels could not have had a fair existence. She was so sensitive to what he wrote, that she felt her own reading half-created it. Her triumph at the end of each book had something added of a sense of accomplishment on her part. She felt it, to a lesser degree, with some other writers, but they were dead; if they had been living, she would not have written to them, either.

Then one day she read in a magazine an essay he had written about the boyhood of Tennyson. His conjecture on some point she could confirm, for she had letters from one of the poet's brothers. She looked for them among her grandfather's papers and (she was never impulsive save when the impulse was generosity) sent them to Edmund, with a little note to tell him that they were a present to repay some of the pleasure his books had given her.

Edmund, who loved old letters and papers of every kind, found these especially delightful. So the first of many letters from him came to her, beginning, "Dear Miss Fairchild." His handwriting was very large and untidy and difficult to decipher, and this always pleased her, because his letters took longer to read; the enjoyment was drawn out, and often a word or two had to be puzzled over for days. Back, again and again, she would go to the letter, trying to take the problem by surprise—and that was usually how she solved it.

Sometimes, she wondered why he wrote to her—and was flattered when he asked for a letter to cheer him up when he was depressed, or to calm him when he was unhappy. Although he could not any longer work well in England—for a dullness came over him, from the climate and old, vexatious associations—he still liked to have some foothold there, and Emily's letters refreshed his memories.

At first, he thought her a novelist manqué, then he realised that letter-writing is an art by itself, a different kind of skill, though with perhaps a similar motive—and one at which Englishwomen have excelled.

As she wrote, the landscape, flowers, children, cats and dogs, sprang to life memorably. He knew her neighbours and her relation to them, and also knew people, who were dead now, whom she had loved. He called them by their Christian names when he wrote to her and re-evoked them for her, so that, being allowed at last to mention them, she felt that they became light and free again in her mind, and not an intolerable suppression, as they had been for years.

Coming to the village, on this hot morning, she was more agitated than she could ever remember being, and she began to blame Edmund for creating such an ordeal. She was angry with herself for acquiescing, when he had suggested that he, being at last in England for a week or two, should come to see her. "For an hour, or three at most. I want to look at the flowers in the *very* garden, and stroke the cat, and peep between the curtains at Mrs. Waterlow going by."

"He knows too much about me, so where can we begin?" she

wondered. She had confided such intimacies in him. At that distance, he was as safe as the confessional, with the added freedom from hearing any words said aloud. She had written to his mind only. He seemed to have no face, and certainly no voice. Although photographs had once passed between them, they had seemed meaningless.

She had been so safe with him. They could not have wounded one another, but now they might. In ten years, there had been no inadvertent hurts, of rivalry, jealousy, or neglect. It had not occurred to either to wonder if the other would sometime cease to write; the letters would come, as surely as the sun.

"But will they now?" Emily was wondering.

She turned the familiar bend of the road and the sea lay glittering below—its wrinkled surface looking solid and without movement, like a great sheet of metal. Now and then a light breeze came off the water and rasped together the dried grasses on the banks; when it dropped, the late morning silence held, drugging the brain and slowing the limbs.

For years, Emily had looked into mirrors only to see if her hair were tidy or her petticoat showing below her dress. This morning, she tried to take herself by surprise, to see herself as a stranger might, but failed.

He would expect a younger woman from the photograph of some years back. Since that was taken, wings of white hair at her temples had given her a different appearance. The photograph would not, in any case, show how poor her complexion was, unevenly pitted, from an illness when she was a child. As a girl, she had looked at her reflection and thought "No one will ever want to marry me" and no one had.

When she went back to the living-room, the cat was walking about, smelling lobster in the air; baulked, troubled by desire, he went restlessly about the little room, the pupils of his eyes two thin lines of suspicion and contempt. But the lobster was high up on the dresser, above the Rockingham cups, and covered with a piece of muslin.

Emily went over to the table and touched the knives and forks, shook the salt in the cellar nicely level, lifted a wine-glass to the light. She poured out a glass of sherry and stood, well back from the window—looking out between hollyhocks at the lane.

Unless the train was late, he should be there. At any moment, the station taxi would come slowly along the lane and stop, with terrible inevitability, outside the cottage. She wondered how tall he was—how would he measure against the hollyhocks? Would he be obliged to stoop under the low oak beams?

The sherry heartened her a little—at least, her hands stopped shaking—and she filled her glass again. The wine was cooling in a bucket down the well and she thought that perhaps it was time to fetch it in, or it might be too cold to taste.

The well had pretty little ferns of a very bright green growing out of the bricks at its sides, and when she lifted the cover, the ice-cold air struck her. She was unused to drinking much, and the glasses of sherry had, first, steadied her; then, almost numbed her. With difficulty, she drew up the bucket; but her movements were clumsy and uncertain, and greenish slime came off the rope on to her clean dress. Her hair fell forward untidily. Far, far below, as if at the wrong end of a telescope, she saw her own tiny face looking back at her. As she was taking the bottle of wine from the bucket, she heard a crash inside the cottage.

She knew what must have happened, but she felt too muddled to act quickly. When she opened the door of the living-room she saw, as she expected, the cat and the lobster and the Rockingham cups spread in disorder about the floor.

She grabbed the cat first—though the damage was done now—and ran to the front door to throw him out into the garden; but, opening the door, was confronted by Edmund, whose arm was raised, just about to pull on the old iron bell. At the sight of the distraught woman with untidy hair and her eyes full of tears, he took a pace back.

"There's no lunch," she said quickly. "Nothing." The cat struggled against her shoulder, frantic for the remains of the lobster, and a long scratch slowly ripened across her cheek; then the cat bounded from her and sat down behind the hollyhocks to wash his paws.

"How do you do," Emily said. She took her hand away from his almost as soon as she touched him and put it up to her cheek, brushing blood across her face.

"Let us go in and bathe you," he suggested.

"Oh, no, please don't bother. It is nothing at all. But, yes, of course, come in. I'm afraid . . ." She was incoherent and he could not follow what she was saying.

At the sight of the lobster and the china on the floor, he understood a little. All the same, she seemed to him to be rather drunk.

"Such wonderful cups and saucers," he said, going down on his knees and filling his hands with fragments. "I don't know how you can bear it."

"It's nothing. It doesn't matter. It's the lobster that matters. There is nothing else in the house."

"Eggs?" he suggested.

"I don't get the eggs till Friday," she said wildly.

"Well, cheese."

"It's gone hard and sweaty. The weather's so . . ."

"Not that it isn't too hot to eat anything," he said quickly. "Hotter than Rome. And I was longing for an English drizzle."

"We had a little shower on Monday evening. Did you get that in London?"

"Monday? No, Sunday we had a few spots."

"It was Monday here, I remember. The gardens needed it, but it didn't do much good."

He looked round for somewhere to put the broken china. "No, I suppose not."

"It hardly penetrated. Do put that in the waste-paper basket."

"This cup is fairly neatly broken in half, it could be riveted. I can take it back to London with me."

"I won't hear of it. But it is so kind . . . I suppose the cat may as well have the remains of this—though not straight away. He must be shown that I am cross with him. Oh, dear, and I fetched it last thing from the village so that it should be fresh. But that's not much use to you, as it's turned out."

She disappeared into the kitchen with her hands full of lobster shells.

He looked round the room and so much of it seemed familiar to him. A stout woman passing by in the lane and trying to see in through the window might be Mrs. Waterlow herself, who came so amusingly into Emily's letters.

He hoped things were soon going to get better, for he had never seen anyone so distracted as Emily when he arrived. He had been prepared for shyness, and had thought he could deal with that, but her frenzied look, with the blood on her face and the bits of lobster in her hands, made him feel that he had done some damage which, like the china, was quite beyond his repairing.

She was a long time gone, but shouted from the kitchen that he must take a glass of sherry, as he was glad to do.

"May I bring some out to you?" he asked.

"No, no thank you. Just pour it out and I will come."

When she returned at last, he saw that she had washed her face and combed her hair. What the great stain all across her skirt was, he could not guess. She was carrying a little dish of sardines, all neatly wedged together as they had been lying in their tin.

"It is so dreadful," she began. "You will never forget being given a tin of sardines, but they will go better with the wine than the baked beans, which is the only other thing I can find."

"I am *very* fond of sardines," he said.

She put the dish on the table and then, for the first time, looked at him. He was of medium height after all, with broader shoulders than she had imagined. His hair was a surprise to her. From his photograph, she had imagined it white—he was, after all, ten years older than she—but instead, it was blond and bleached by the sun. "And I always thought I was writing to a white-haired man," she thought.

Her look lasted only a second or two and then she drank her sherry quickly, with her eyes cast down.

"I hope you forgive me for coming here," he said gravely. Only by seriousness could he hope to bring them back to the relationship in which they really stood. He approached her so fearfully, but she shied away.

"Of course," she said. "It is *so* nice. After all these years. But I am sure you must be starving. Will you sit here?"

"How are we to continue?" he wondered.

She was garrulous with small talk through lunch, pausing only to take up her wine-glass. Then, at the end, when she had handed him his coffee, she failed. There was no more to say, not a word more to be wrung out of the weather, or the restaurant in Rome they had found they had in common, or the annoyances of travel—the train that was late and the cabin that was stuffy. Worn-out, she still cast about for a subject to embark on. The silence was unendurable. If it continued, might he not suddenly say, "You are so different from all I had imagined," or their eyes might meet and they would see in one another's nakedness and total loss.

"I *did* say Wednesday," said Mrs. Waterlow.

"No, Thursday," Emily insisted. If she could not bar the doorway with forbidding arms, she did so with malevolent thoughts. Gentle and patient neighbour she had always been and Mrs. Waterlow, who had the sharp nose of the total abstainer and could smell alcohol on Emily's breath, was quite astonished.

The front door of the cottage opened straight into the living-room and Edmund was exposed to Mrs. Waterlow, sitting forward in his chair, staring into a coffee-cup.

"I'll just leave the poster for the Jumble Sale then," said Mrs. Waterlow. "We shall have to talk about the refreshments another time. I think, don't you, that half a pound of tea does fifty people. Mrs. Harris will see to the slab cake. But if you're busy, I mustn't keep you.

Though since I am here, I wonder if I could look up something in your Encyclopaedia. I won't interrupt. I promise."

"May I introduce Mr. Fabry?" Emily said, for Mrs. Waterlow was somehow or other in the room.

"Not Mr. *Edmund* Fabry?"

Edmund, still holding his coffee-cup and saucer, managed to stand up quickly and shake hands.

"The author? I could recognise you from your photo. Oh, my daughter will be so interested. I must write at once to tell her. I'm afraid I've never read any of your books."

Edmund found this, as he always found it, unanswerable. He gave an apologetic murmur, and smiled ingratiatingly.

"But I always read the reviews of them in the Sunday papers." Mrs. Waterlow went on, "I'm afraid we're rather a booky family."

So far, she had said nothing to which he could find any reply. Emily stood helplessly beside him, saying nothing. She was not wringing her hands, but he thought that if they had not been clasped so tightly together, that was what would have happened.

"You've *really* kept Mr. Fabry in the dark, Emily," said Mrs. Waterlow.

"Not so *you* to *me*," Edmund thought. He had met her many times before in Emily's letters, already knew that her family was "booky" and had had her preposterous opinions on many things.

She was a woman of fifty-five, whose children had grown up and gone thankfully away. They left their mother almost permanently, it seemed to them, behind the tea-urn at the village hall—and a good watching-place it was. She had, as Emily once put it, the over-alert look of a ventriloquist's dummy. Her head, cocked slightly, turned to and fro between Emily and Edmund. "Dyed hair," she thought, glancing away from him. She was often wrong about people.

"Now, don't let me interrupt you. You get on with your coffee. I'll just sit quiet in my corner and bury myself in the Encyclopaedia."

"Would you like some coffee?" Emily asked. "I'm afraid it may be rather cold."

"If there *is* some going begging, nothing would be nicer. 'Shuva to Tom-Tom,' that's the one I want." She pulled out the Encyclopaedia and rather ostentatiously pretended to wipe dust from her fingers.

She has presence of mind, Edmund decided, watching her turn the pages with speed, and authority. She has really thought of something to look up. He was sure that he could not have done so as quickly himself. He wondered what it was that she had hit upon. She had come to a page of photographs of Tapestry and began to study them intently. There appeared to be pages of close print on the subject. So clever, Edmund thought.

She knew that he was staring at her and looked up and smiled; her finger marking the place. "To settle an argument," she said. "I'm afraid we are a very argumentative family."

Edmund bowed.

A silence fell. He and Emily looked at one another, but she looked away first. She sat on the arm of a chair, as if she were waiting to spring up to see Mrs. Waterlow out—as indeed she was.

The hot afternoon was a spell they had fallen under. A bluebottle zig-zagged about the room, hit the window-pane, then went suddenly out of the door. A petal dropped off a geranium on the window-sill; occasionally—but not often enough for Edmund—a page was turned, the thin paper rustling silkily over. Edmund drew his wrist out of his sleeve and glanced secretly at his watch, and Emily saw him do it. It was a long journey he had made to see her, and soon he must be returning.

Mrs. Waterlow looked up again. She had an amused smile, as if they were a couple of shy children whom she had just introduced to one another. "Oh, dear, why the silence? I'm not listening, you know. You will make me feel that I am in the way."

You preposterous old trollop, Edmund thought viciously. He leant back, put his finger-tips together and said, looking across at Emily, "Did I tell you that cousin Joseph had a nasty accident? Out bicycling. *Both* of them, you know. Such a deprivation. No heir, either. But Constance very soon consoled herself. With one of the Army padres out there. They were discovered by Joseph's batman in the most unusual circumstances. The Orient's insidious influence, I suppose. So strangely exotic for Constance, though." He guessed—though he did not look—that Mrs. Waterlow had flushed and, pretending not to be listening, was struggling hard *not* to flush.

"Cousin Constance's Thousand and One Nights," he said. "The padre had courage. Like engaging with a boa-constrictor, I'd have thought."

If only Emily had not looked so alarmed. He began to warm to his inventions, which grew more macabre and outrageous—and, as he did so, he could hear the pages turning quickly and at last the book was closed with a loud thump. "That's clinched *that* argument," said Mrs. Waterlow. "Hubert is so often inaccurate, but won't have it that he can ever be wrong." She tried to sound unconcerned, but her face was set in lines of disapproval.

"You are triumphant, then?" Edmund asked and he stood up and held out his hand.

When she had gone, Emily closed the door and leant against it. She looked exhausted.

"Thank you," she said. "She would never have gone otherwise. And now it is nearly time for *you* to go."

"I am sorry about Cousin Joseph. I could think of no other way."

In Emily's letters, Mrs. Waterlow had been funny; but she was not in real life and he wondered how Emily could suffer so much, before transforming it.

"My dear, if you are sorry I came, then I am sorry, too."

"Don't say anything. Don't talk of it," she begged him, standing with her hands pressed hard against the door behind her. She shrank from words, thinking of the scars they leave, which she would be left to tend when he had gone. If he spoke the truth, she could not bear it; if he tried to muffle it with tenderness, she would look upon it as pity. He had made such efforts, she knew; but he could never have protected her from herself.

He, facing her, turned his eyes for a moment towards the window; then he looked back at her. He said nothing; but she knew that he had seen the station-car drawing to a standstill beyond the hollyhocks.

"You have to go?" she asked.

He nodded.

Perhaps the worst has happened, she thought. I have fallen in love with him—the one thing from which I felt I was completely safe.

Before she moved aside from the door, she said quickly, as if the words were red-hot coals over which she must pick her way—"If you write to me again, will you leave out today, and let it be as if you had not moved out of Rome?"

"Perhaps I didn't," he said.

At the door, he took her hand and held it against his cheek for a second—a gesture both consoling and conciliatory.

When he had gone, she carried her grief decently upstairs to her little bedroom and there allowed herself some tears.

When they were dried and over, she sat down by the open window.

She had not noticed how clouds had been crowding into the sky. A wind had sprung up and bushes and branches were jigging and swaying.

The hollyhocks nodded together. A spot of rain as big as a half-penny dropped on to the stone sill, others fell over leaves down below, and a sharp cool smell began to rise at once from the earth.

She put her head out of the window, her elbows on the outside sill. The soft rain, falling steadily now, calmed her. Down below in the garden the cat wove its way through a flower-bed. At the door, he began to cry piteously to be let in and she shut the window a little and went downstairs. It was dark in the living-room; the two windows were fringed with dripping leaves; there were shadows and silence.

While she was washing up, the cat, turning a figure-of-eight round her feet, brushed her legs with his wet fur. She began to talk to him, as she often did, for they were alone so much together. "If you were a dog," she said, "we could go for a nice walk in the rain."

As it was, she gave him his supper and took an apple for herself. Walking about, eating it, she tidied the room. The sound of the rain in the garden was very peaceful. She carried her writing things to the table by the window and there, in the last of the light, dipped her goose-quill pen in the ink, and wrote, in her fine and flowing hand, her address, and then, "Dear Edmund."

A TROUBLED STATE OF MIND

IN THE old part of the town, between the castle and the cathedral, were some steep and cobbled streets whose pavements were broken open by the roots of plane trees. The tall and narrow houses stood back, beyond the walls of gardens and courtyards, but there were glimpses of them through wrought-iron gates. The quiet here was something that country people found unbelievable. Except for the times when the cathedral bells were ringing, the silence was broken only by the rooks in the castle trees or, as on this afternoon, by the sound of rain.

Lalage left the car in the garage at the foot of the hill and the two girls—Lalage herself and her step-daughter, Sophy—walked as quickly as they could towards home, carrying the smaller pieces of Sophy's luggage, Lalage, already hostess-like (Sophy thought), bowed over to one side with the weight of the bigger suitcase, and the other arm thrust out shoulder-high to right her balance.

The road narrowed gradually to less than a car's width and rain ran fast down the cobbles, swirling into drains. Reaching the gate in the wall, Sophy swung her skis off her back and turned the iron handle. The scraping, rusty sound of it was suddenly remembered and was as strange to her as anything else in a world where every familiar thing had moved into a pattern too fantastic ever—she was sure—to be dealt with or understood. She and Lalla, for instance, going in through this gate as they had done so often before; but Sophy now at a loss to guess what might be waiting for her inside, in her own home.

Her father, Colonel Vellacott, had always loved Italy and everything Italian and had tried to make a Venetian courtyard in wet

England. Its sadness was appalling, Sophy thought. The paving-stones were dark with rain and drops fell heavily from the vine and the magnolia, off statues and urns and, in a sudden gust of wind, rattled like bullets on the broad fig-leaves by the wall. In the seats of some iron chairs puddles reflected the cloudy sky.

"John will be back for dinner," Lalage said, as they picked their way across the wet stones—"He had to go because he was in the chair."

Ah yes, "John," of course, Sophy thought.

The front door opened and Miss Sully came out to take the case from Lalage, primly eager to wring all she could from the peculiar situation. "It is just like old times," she said to Sophy, "when Madam used to come to stay with you in the holidays and I used to listen to hear the gate so that I could run out with a welcome."

"Madam" had been a shock and a calculated one, Sophy thought. She smiled and shook hands. "In the old days, you always said we had grown. Not any more, I hope."

"Grown *up*, I should say."

"Isn't she brown?" said Lalla.

"As brown as a berry."

They went into the dark hall where the Italian influence contin-ued in glass and marble, trailing leaves and a wrought-iron screen which served no purpose. Nothing visible had been altered since So-phy was here last, a year ago, but everything invisible had been. At Sophy's bedroom door, Miss Sully turned away, with promises of tea in five minutes and a fire in the drawing-room. Sophy, standing in the middle of the room, looking about her, but not at Lalla, asked: "How do you get on with *her*?"

"As I always did, trying to be as nice as pie, wearing myself out, really, but not getting anywhere. She is, as we always found her, a mystery woman."

"Kind..." Sophy began.

"Kindness itself. Thoughtful, considerate, efficient. But what lies underneath, who knows? Something does. She's learning Italian now."

"Perhaps that's what's underneath. Not enough goes on here for her. She's too intelligent to be a housekeeper, and too ambitious."

"Then why go on?"

Sophy could not now say "I think because she hoped to marry my father." She had sometimes thought it in the past and suddenly wondered if she had ever told Lalla. She felt that she must have done, for she had told her everything, though she no longer could.

"What was Switzerland *like*?" Lalla asked. "I mean really."

"It went on too long."

Sophy put her fingers to the locks of her suitcase, about to spring them open, and then could not be bothered, and straightened her back, thinking, "She will wonder why, if I found it too long, I did not come back earlier, as I could have done, and should have done and would have done, if it had not been for *that*." It was always "that" in her mind—the marriage of her father and her dearest friend. The other questions—Sophy's questions—that hovered between them were too unseemly to be spoken—for instance "why?" and "how?" and "where did it begin?" The only question in the least possible Sophy was turning over in her mind and beginning to make a shape of it in words, when Lalla, before it could be spoken, answered it. Since early girlhood, they had often found their thoughts arriving at the same point without the promptings of speech.

"I am so happy, you know," Lalla said. "It is all so lovely in this house and now to have you in it with me at last! Though," she added quickly, "it is you who have always been here and I who has at last arrived."

"But, Lalla dear, you always seemed *part* of the house to me. We never called the spare room anything but 'Lalla's room.' When other people came to stay, it seemed wrong to me that they should hang their clothes in your cupboard."

Then she suddenly bent down and unclicked her suitcase after all, to have something to do with her trembling fingers, and wondered, "What is the spare room called now? I have made another booby-trap for us, where there already were too many."

"Did you notice," Lalage asked, as if she had not heard, "how eagerly Miss Sully ran out to greet you? She has been quite excited all the week."

"I can understand that." Sophy lifted the lid of the suitcase and looked gloomily at her creased and folded clothes. "She loves situations and she wanted to see how I was facing this one."

"Yes, to see if you were jealous of me, hoping perhaps that life here from now on would be full of interesting little scenes between us, something to sustain and nourish her while she chops the parsley—which she does—doesn't she?—with not just *kitchen* venom?"

"She will analyse everything we say and fit it into her conception of our relationship."

"She has already tried to haunt me with your mother—so beautiful she was and you are growing up to be her image."

Sophy lifted her head from the unpacking and could not help giving a quick look into the mirror before her. "How absurd!" she said. "If she could throw up a woman so long dead, how impatiently she must have waited for *me* to throw *myself* up."

"She longs for incidents. I am sure she will hover to see who pours out the tea and whether, from habit, you will go to your old place at the table."

This was brave of Lalage and seemed to clear the air.

"It is a good thing," Sophy said, "that you and I have read so many novels. The hackneyed dangers we should be safe from."

"We shall be safe *together*," Lalla said. "Loving one another," she added, so quietly that she seemed to be talking to herself.

"Demurrings and deprecations will not escape notice either," said Sophy. "Saying '*you* do it, please,' or 'you go first.' We must beware of every one of those. I will be a straightforward daughter to you, I think. It may be ageing for you, but I think it will be safer than for us to try to be like sisters. I thought of that in Switzerland, and I decided that a daughter has privileges and a rôle to play, which a younger or inferior sister has not."

"As long as I am never called 'Mamma.'"

Miss Sully, hovering at the foot of the stairs, heard laughter as the bedroom door opened and Lalage's voice saying with great gaiety, "Who—a year ago—would have believed that we could come to this?"

They were on the stairs now, and Miss Sully hurried back to the kitchen for the hot scones. She wanted to watch the approach to the tea table.

This turned out to be disappointing. Sophy went straight to the drawing-room window and, with her back turned to the room, said, "Since last I saw you, Lalla, I've given up milk and sugar. What Father used to call 'puppy-fat' turned out just to be fat."

"Then I must do the same," said Lalla and sat down before the tray and took up the tea-pot. "And every time John goes out, we will have those slimming meals I am always reading about at the hair-dresser's—meagre things like tomato jellies and stuffed cucumbers and lettuce juice. Meanwhile, you could have a scone, couldn't you?"

Sophy turned from the window and sat down in a chair, opposite the one where she had always sat before.

"Only this time," she said.

Miss Sully, having very slowly put a log on the fire and rearranged the tongs, was now obliged to go. At the door, she heard Sophy say, "Just to celebrate the occasion."

By the time Colonel Vellacott returned from his meeting, a mode of behaviour was established between the two girls. It had often been tried out in their minds during their separation, suggested and explored with nervous tact in their letters to one another.

He found them by the drawing-room fire, Lalage winding wool from Sophy's outstretched hands. Kneeling on the rug, Sophy rocked from side to side, and swayed her arms, turning her wrists deftly as the wool slipped off them. So often, bemused and patient, she had held Lalla's wool for her: the knitting craze came and went, jerseys were seldom finished and, if they were, were sorry things. From past experience, neither had high hopes for this new skein.

"A charming sight," Colonel Vellacott said. They had settled down together already, he was relieved to see. It was like bringing a new dog into a house where another had reigned alone for a long time. The scene might have been prearranged—the girls were so tangled up in wool that they could not extricate themselves and the kisses he gave each on the top of her head were almost simultaneous, Lalla hardly first at all.

"That's *that* over," he thought, and for no reason felt self-congratulatory. "That," for him, was his embarrassment. Now, it was as easy as could be to talk about Switzerland and Sophy most brilliantly took the lead with her descriptions of the school and the lunacy of its inhabitants.

"Don't!" Lalage half-sobbed, gasping with laughter, and wiped her eyes on the ball of wool.

"Ah, you are going into fits," her husband said. He remembered all the holiday laughter in this house, Lalla's cries of "Don't" and her collapsed state, his teasing of them both and his mocking echoes of their girlish phrases. He had felt in those days wonderfully indulgent. "Bring Lalla back with you," he always told Sophy. "It is sad for you to be alone—and sad for her, too." Lalla—the poor orphan child—lived with an aunt, but was more often, in school holidays, at Ancaster, with Sophy.

"Now, Lalla!" he said, in a severe voice. He leant back in his chair and folded his arms with a show of excessive patience. "If you snort again, you must be sent away."

"Oh, please, I *ache*," she implored Sophy, holding the ball of wool tight to her ribs, her beautiful eyes glittering with tears.

"Oh, please, I *ache*, Sophy," said Colonel Vellacott.

"I am only telling you what happened," Sophy said, with what Lalla called her straight face.

"The experience seems to have been worth every penny," her father said.

"Yes, I am truly finished."

The end of the wool slipped from her fingers, she sank back on her heels and looked up at her father, at last returning his gaze, smiling with love and delight, but with a reserve of mischief, too, and that pleased him most of all, it was what gave reality to her warm-

droom, above her father's, overlooked the courtyard and
heard footsteps out there, she went across to the window
d out. It was almost dark. Lalage and her father were going
 in the rain. He opened the courtyard door into the street
lage passed through it, put his hand on her shoulder.
es, and bedtime, too," Sophy thought, turning away. "Be-
's imagination, thank God. I hope I can hide my revulsion
 I dare say there's nothing to stop her having a baby even. It
ly possible."
footsteps and voices faded away down the street. The driz-
nued, and downstairs Miss Sully was singing "Oh, what a
 Morning."
st get a job," Sophy thought. "Without a day's delay."

 job" was soon a great topic of conversation.
nel Vellacott was full of facetious suggestions. At every meal
w one came to mind, and Sophy grinned, and wondered if
 would crack in two, as her heart must.
 hush, I can't hear of it," Lalage would beg her husband, and
 fingers in her ears. "Sophy, please! You will make me think
running away from *me* and it will be as Miss Sully predicted."
t her hands pressed to her cheekbones, ready to make herself
in, if necessary. Her bracelets slid down her thin arms to her
 Her eyes were full of pleading.
ected," Sophy thought. "She used not to be. Father loves it."
ways meant to get a job," she said. "I couldn't have just stayed
d looked after the house—which Miss Sully does much bet-
how." But this was dangerous ground and she stepped from it
. "I should have taken the Secretarial course with you, Lalla,
er hadn't made me go to Switzerland first."
ade?" said Colonel Vellacott.
rsuaded, then."
ur French was horrible."
ell, 'made' me, then."

heartedness. If she were dissembling her gaiety and friendliness, she
would not have dissembled *that*, he thought. It would not have occurred to her as a necessary ingredient of mirth.

Sophy kept up her spirits throughout dinner and then flagged. It
was her long journey, the other two said and she agreed. "And you
miss the clarity of that air," her father added.

But there were other exhaustions she could less easily endure and
the chief was, she saw, that she had cast herself in a rôle that would
take too much from her.

She remembered—and this was after she had said good-night and
gone to her room—long ago and when her mother was alive, she herself perhaps five or six years old, being taken on a train journey, from
Edinburgh, her mother's old home it may have been. Kneeling in her
corner seat, breathing on the window, breathing and wiping, in stu-
pefying boredom, she had begun suddenly to talk in baby talk, demanding, for no reason she could now recall, in a lispy, whiny voice
that had never been her own, a "chocky bikky." Her mother, gently
remonstrating, had made publicly clear that this odd voice was to be
regarded as a game. "Icky chocky bikky," Sophy had insisted, pout-
ing. It was then that she had first realised her own power of mim-
icry; power it was and went to her head. She had become the
nauseating infant she impersonated. Other people in the compartment took the lead from her mother and laughed. Sophy herself had
pretended not to hear this and turned her back and breathed on the
window again, but soon she could not help herself. "Pitty gee-gees,"
she said, pointing. When she had tired of talking, she let her eyelids
droop and began to suck her thumb as she had scornfully watched
other children doing. Her mother, who knew that things were going
too far, but was never brisk with her in public, tried to distract her
attention, but could not. The performance had been tiring, like playing Lady Macbeth with heart and soul and, in the end, Sophy had
become sickened by her own creation, caught in its tentacles and
quite unable to escape. Everyone else was tired, too; she knew that

her mother was desperate and that glances were exchanged; but she seemed powerless to end the misery. It was too late to speak suddenly in her own voice. What voice was it, and what things did it say? She could remember putting her forehead to the cool window-pane and counting to herself, "One, two, then three and then I'll speak again as I used and they will all know the other voice has gone." But her shyness was too great, she was too committed to the other character and had no way of breaking loose from it. Badgered, exhausted and embarrassed, she had at last burst into tears, taking refuge, as she wept, against her mother's arm. "Over-tired," the grown-ups said. "Such a long journey. She's stood up to it very well."

Lalla and her father had said good-night and used the same words, though now the climate was to blame as well. They were no more true than when she was a child. The acting had exhausted her, and nothing else. She could have cried, as she had when a young girl, "Oh, my darling Mamma, why did you have to die?" The words were so loud in her head and her breast that she might have said them aloud. They returned with the aching familiarity of a long time ago, when she had lain in bed after lights-out at boarding-school, or on their first Christmas Eve alone, with her father trying to remember everything her mother had always done, so that Sophy should not be deprived of one sprig of holly or Christmas-tree candle. In the end, unbelievably, the words had become a habit and lost their pain. Her life without her mother was different from before, but it was, after all, the same life. If Mamma had been here, she sometimes thought, accepting that she could not be.

This evening the phrase sprang at her with a sudden freshness, the first time for years. She sat down on the edge of her bed and her hands dropped into her lap, palms upwards in a gesture of hopeless inertia. "If she were alive," she thought, "she would be downstairs with Father, and Lalla here with me, as she ought to be. Or not under this roof at all. And I should be relieved of this tiring pretence, that won't end with the end of the train journey, as it did before. It will be there waiting for me in the morning and all the mornings after—having to be gay and unselfconscious—as if it were a per-

fectly normal thing for one's father to 1 fifty-three and eighteen and all plotted out of the way in a foreign country," sh must be gracious and hand over my ho have, day in, day out, my constant compa

Sometimes, at school, Lalla had stolen remember well the case of the borrowe promise, the forgotten appointment, the l instances came to her mind from the dark ago been thrust impatiently away.

"I must get away," she thought, and he were clenched tight, drumming on her kne my own home, as soon as I have come back had longed for it so much, in that clear air h faced for months at a time with the monot dark trees that never shed their leaves, as t "Write to me about England," she had begg "Describe a nice drizzle, a beautiful muggy leaves sticking to the pavements. *You* descri I to you."

Instead, they had written to say that the They had met several times in London, for missing Sophy. In their loneliness they ha clung, and wished to remain so for ever. Th much stressed—orphan and widower, as they themselves. Companionship (and Sophy wa and common interests (both liked going to pl were enlarged upon. Love itself was not once was glad that it was not. She was to fly home f quiet, just the three of them and Lalage's aunt. go. She was on her way up to a chalet for the v made arrangements which she could not con they were glad to have her stay in Switzerland a so, although she was sure that if she had not g place, she could have prevented things from rea

Her b
when she
and looke
for a walk
and as La
"Ah, y
yond one
from her
is perfec
Their
zle conti
Beautifu
"I mu

"Sophy'
Col
some n
her face
"Oh
stuff he
you are
She kep
deaf ag
elbows
"Af
"I a
here a
ter any
quickl
if Fath
"M
"P
"Y
"W

"You'd have loathed the Secretarial School," Lalla said complacently. "I hated every moment."

"And was glad to leave it and get married," Sophy thought. "So it was typing and shorthand that drove you to it. He hasn't, after all, a spectacular enough amount of money to be married for. And love? If you love him, you show none of it. Perhaps I inhibit you and force you to keep it for when you are alone. In which case, the sooner I go, the better."

She felt absurdly in the way, but also shut out that they should turn to secrecy because of her.

It was not easy to slip away from Lalage, her too-constant companion, but, one morning, she managed to, and set out, as if on an illicit errand, through wet alleyways towards the Market Place. It had rained for all of the fortnight she had been at home, but had this morning stopped. The clouds had lifted and broken open and bright light, though not yet quite sunshine, poured down over the puddles and dripping eaves. Slate roofs dried rapidly and pavements steamed. It was the end of April.

"We begin the second of May," said the Principal of the Secretarial School in Market Street. She underlined this date on the application form. "Your father will complete this for you." She thought it strange for the girl to come there on her own, making enquiries. Sophy stared at her hands, which were a dark plum colour, scarred from broken chilblains. Clumsy as they were, she used them affectedly, drawing attention to them with hooked fingers as she wrote, and then by twisting round an engagement ring of dull little diamonds.

"I know your father very well," Miss Priestley said. "Although I don't suppose he would be able to place *me*. I was a reporter once upon a time on the *Ancaster Herald* and used to cover some of the Court cases when he was on the bench. And my late fiancé was in his regiment in the war. He didn't come back," she added, in an affectedly casual voice she had learnt at the cinema.

"I'm so sorry," Sophy murmured.

"Yes, we had been engaged for eleven years. But you don't want to listen to all my sad affairs."

Although this was true, Sophy felt obliged to make a sound which she hoped suggested denial as well as a certain amount of discouragement. "If only there were something amusing in this," she thought. "Something with which to decorate the plain statement when I tell them at lunch." But there was not: the bereaved Miss Priestley with her chilblains was saddening and unattractive and the office was stuffy and untidy, not a good example to the pupils.

The sun was shining when Sophy stood, dazed by its brightness, on the steps in Market Street. The Town Hall clock struck twelve. She hurried back home and was there before Lalla returned from the hairdresser's.

"Just *see* what they've done," was Lalla's piteous cry at luncheon. They had always done the same thing and Sophy only briefly glanced.

"Why don't you tell them?" asked Colonel Vellacott and seemed to have an edge of exasperation to his voice.

"I tell them and tell them. As smooth as smooth, I always say. Not a kink or a curl or I shall be so cross."

"It will settle down," Sophy said. "It always does."

They had just finished what Miss Sully called "chicken and all the trimmings."

"They've caught that man," Miss Sully said, as she lifted the dishes off the table. "They gave it out on the one o'clock news."

"What man?" asked Lalla, still fidgeting with her hair.

"The one that assaulted that little boy and then smothered him."

"Oh dear!" Lalage frowned.

"I shouldn't have mentioned it, only I thought you'd like to know. It isn't very nice at meal-times, I'm afraid." She stacked the plates and carried them away.

"This is a very rum Baba," said Colonel Vellacott, as he always did when given this pudding, and Sophy felt the usual embarrassment, wondering—as she was also used to wondering—just how tedious her friend found this heavy jocularity. Then she remembered that her father was much more Lalage's responsibility. The old situation was reversed. It should be Lalla's task to try to prevent the inevitable phrases, to turn the conversations as deftly as she could as the stale quip rose ominously before them.

"And I shall enjoy seeing how she does it, as time goes on," she thought. At present, Lalla was merely smiling her bright, usual smile, a guest's smile, vaguely willing.

"I met someone this morning who knows you, Father," Sophy suddenly told him, deciding that as any kind of approach to her embarrassment would lead to it, this would do as well as any. "In fact, I did not so much meet her as go to see her."

Colonel Vellacott waited—with the calm of a man who has nothing to fear—for the mystery to unfold, but Lalla stopped eating, put her fork down on her plate and glanced anxiously at Sophy, who went on: "Though she says you would never be able to place *her*. *Can* you place someone called Miss Priestley, who has a secretarial school—no, college, so sorry—in Market Street?"

"No. She is right. I can't."

"Is she from your past?" Lalla asked. "Poor Miss Priestley! I am glad that I am in your present."

"No, she simply wrote down in shorthand things you said in Court," Sophy explained. "And her fiancé was in the regiment and was killed, but I don't think she blamed you for it."

"It was generous of her. Especially as I survived. I should have thought she would have resented that."

"Why did you go to see her?" Lalla asked, taking up her fork again.

"She is going to teach me to be a secretary."

"Oh no! Then I shall come too, I won't be left here on my own. May I go, too, John?"

"You know that we agreed not to be sisters," Sophy told her. "You have to learn to be my mamma and stay at home while I go off to school."

"I shall be lonely."

"Mothers are. Though perhaps they get used to it, and even rather like it in the end."

"Why did you go about the business in so odd a way?" her father asked. "There was no necessity to be secretive. If you wanted to do it at all, you should have said so."

"I said, and said."

"We thought you were joking."

"Yes, I knew you thought that."

"And I might have been consulted, I should have thought. I could have done much better for you than this Miss Whatshername, of whom I certainly have never heard."

"Then why did you do nothing?"

"Now, Sophy, don't try to be cool with me. You are only just home from Switzerland and there was all the time in the world to make arrangements."

"I never like to do things at a leisurely pace," Sophy said, looking calmly at him. "One may as well get on with life." As you did, her voice implied.

"But we know nothing of this Miss Thingummy. She seems a strange end to your education."

"It is what I want, Father."

Lalla, murmuring "coffee," left the room.

"I was bringing it," said Miss Sully, who was never caught out. The tray was in her hands.

Instead of going ahead to the drawing-room, Lalla ran upstairs murmuring "handkerchief."

In the dining-room Colonel Vellacott and his daughter were arguing. "Unlike you, Sophy," Miss Sully heard.

"I've put the coffee in the drawing-room," she said, then hurried forward to rearrange the fire. But there was nothing for her to listen to but the sound of their chairs being pushed back. "Madam will be down directly," she added.

This was unanswerable and unanswered. Sophy crossed the hall to the drawing-room and without sitting down, carelessly poured out her father's coffee and her own. She took hers over to the window-seat and began to sip it, lifting the cup only a little from its brimming saucer. She supposed that Lalla was upstairs, waiting for them to finish their quarrel.

Displeased and austere Colonel Vellacott remained for days, wearing what Sophy called his Doge's face. With Lalage, too, and in private, he was reserved. Rebellion was in the air—a youthful contagion that he intended should not spread. Don't *you* go running to some Miss Thingummy, or even worse, his mood seemed to warn her.

That Sophy's action was hardly drastic he constantly reminded himself, but her way of taking it had been cold and secretive. For her to earn her own living was nothing other than he intended and desired, but it seemed to him that there was no desperate need and that for a month or two she might have helped him out with Lalla. "Helped me out" was his own phrase. He had seen what he called "Bride's despondency" in Lalage's eyes, in spite of her bright smiles and her laughter. He did not know how to cheer her up; his time was so much given over to public work and there was no theatre here in Ancaster. She was lonely and suffering reaction from the sudden adventure of their courtship and wedding. He could not hide his anxiety that the house was dull and silent and—with all his Italian décor long ago perfected—too completed. She had simply taken over what was there and had had nothing to contribute. Although he was pleased with what he had done, he began to wonder if it was what a bride would hope for. "One day, we will have a change," he had promised, but could not bring himself to move one fern or sconce. She had insisted—not knowing what was good for her—that nothing should be touched and that she loved it exactly as it was.

Sophy's home-coming had raised her spirits and he himself had felt freer and happier and less anxious. He looked forward to entering the house when he returned from his meetings. People who have had the best of both worlds are the crossest of all when the best in one is lost, and he knew this and scolded himself, but the Doge's face remained and, inhibited by his new habit of sternness, he found himself unable to make love to Lalage. The marriage, Miss Sully thought, was crumbling even more quickly than she had predicted.

At Miss Priestley's, Sophy was by far the eldest girl and the slowest one at learning, too. Miserably, she bowed her head over the abominable hooks and dots of her shorthand, or touch-typed rows of percentage signs or fractions where should have been "Dear Sirs, We beg to confirm receipt of your esteemed order."

The other girls had left school at sixteen and seemed as quick as birds with their taking down and reading back, always put their carbon paper in the right way round and never typed addresses on upside-down envelopes.

The class-rooms were on the first floor of the old house, a building now given over to offices. The boards were bare and the long tables were ribbed and splintered and ink-stained. Miss Priestley felt the cold and even in May the windows were kept shut, so that the air was chalk-laden and smelt of lead pencils and glue and india-rubber and girls. The windows faced south, over the top branches of budding lilac trees. Below was a tangled garden into which Sophy found herself more and more inclined to stare. At twelve and four, the heavy notes of the Town Hall clock descended on the roof tops in the most gracious—Sophy thought—signal of release. She was the first to have her books closed, knowing before the chimes began that they were imminent; she could feel the air growing tense and the clock gathering itself to strike, and her face would put on its bright, good-bye look, turned expectantly towards Miss Priestley for dismissal.

Then, being free, she was suddenly loth to go home to Lalla's "I knew you'd hate it!" The other girls clustered together and showed one another their work, but Sophy took down her jacket from its peg. She knew that the others exchanged looks when she left them and when she called out "good-bye" only one or two answered her, and then in a surprised tone as if it were strange of her to address them.

Sometimes, instead of going home to tea, she would buy an evening paper and read it in a little café in Market Street. The idea of punishment being in the air, it suited her to think of her teacup on the tray at home, unfilled. There, in the Oak Beams Tea Shop, she met Graham Dennis again. He was working in a solicitor's office nearby and had so grown up that she had not recognised him.

The Dennises' parties were famous in Ancaster, and Sophy had been going to them for as long as she could remember. Mrs. Dennis always described herself as putting herself out for her young people and was not content with Christmas and birthday parties. There were Hallowe'en parties and garden parties, and parties at the New Year and on Guy Fawkes' Day. Her husband could find no escape. If there were not children bobbing for apples in the hall, they were playing charades in several rooms, or hunting for treasure all over the house. "I shall rope Herbert in," Mrs. Dennis told her friends, who, rather aggrieved because she put themselves so much to shame, wondered how she could manage it. Herbert had been roped in to let off fireworks or be Father Christmas. Lately, as Denise and Graham were no longer children, he was roped in to make claret cup or dance with an odd girl out.

Sophy remembered even the first parties, when she was a little girl. After the exquisite orderliness of her own home, the great, shabby, untidy house with its lighted windows and its noise infected her with delicious excitement.

Mrs. Dennis was always kindness itself. "You are only young once," she often told her children and their friends and made sure that, as well as youth, they had as many other delights lavished on them as she could find time and money to bestow. At the back of her mind, she knew that the two most important parties of all would come at the end: even in nursery days, watching the little ones departing with their balloons and presents, she felt that she was only rehearsing for the culmination of it all—Denise's wedding and Graham's twenty-first birthday. Now, both were looming in the same year and "loom" was her own word for their approach. She was confident that she would surpass herself—the Dennis wedding would be talked about for years; but, for the last time of many, Denise would say, as she drove away: "Thank you for doing it all." Beyond, lay a blank future for her mother. But first would come Graham's twenty-first birthday and any champagne left over from that would come in later for the wedding. Only one thing perplexed her, as they went over the list of invitations. Lalage, when staying with Sophy, as she so often was, had always been invited too. For years and years, she had attended the Dennis parties.

"We couldn't leave her out now," Mrs. Dennis said.

"And how possibly ask her?" Graham said. "Husbands and wives go to parties together. You'd have to ask that old man."

"He is only your father's age," Mrs. Dennis said, but she knew that that was what Graham meant. It was an awkward situation. She realised that she and Herbert were only at the parties themselves in order to see that the food and drink were plentiful and available. Herbert knew his place and preferring it, made off to his study as soon as he was able, and Mrs. Dennis was always in and out of the kitchen.

"How sad to leave her out, after all these years, poor girl," she said.

Lalage felt both sad and embarrassed when Sophy's invitation came. Her husband, watching her show of unconcern, realised for the first time the consequences of their romance. The marriage, surviving important hazards, seemed now as likely as not to founder upon trivial matters, on this invitation, for instance, and others that would follow. Lalage had been ardent and generous in her love, to come first in someone's life exalted her and, radiant and incredulous, she had given herself in gratitude. Yet, at the sight of an invitation to a party, she appeared to falter, she glanced away and was confused and could not hide her feeling that she had placed herself in a special position with her contemporaries, was being markedly pushed by them into the ranks of the middle-aged.

Sophy, her father realised, was no longer making things easier, but worsening them. The sooner she could go away and leave them, the better for them all. He could perfectly see this now and wondered how he could hasten what he had so lately tried to prevent.

"As you seem so sure about your typing and shorthand," he said one day, with a great show of tolerance, "and are really settled to it, I am quite willing for you to do the thing properly, to go up to London and train at some reputable place."

But Sophy had not settled to her shorthand and typing; every day she fell back, as the other girls progressed; and now she no longer wanted to go away from Ancaster, having at the twenty-first birthday party fallen in love with Graham Dennis.

Graham and Sophy had rediscovered one another, as young people do who have lived in the same neighbourhood for years and then been separated by school, so that, meeting in the holidays, they seem almost total strangers. Violent changes of height and voice and manner were bewildering and shyness descended. Now, with all the changes made—as they thought—quite grown-up and likely to remain the same for ever, they could sum one another up, and come to a conclusion. Sophy and Graham concluded that they were in love, that they must always have loved, though first immaturity and then separation had hindered their acceptance of the fact.

To Colonel Vellacott, Graham's National Service had not made the man of him it should. Nonchalant and without ambition, he had spent the two years cheerfully peeling potatoes or drinking in the Naafi. Promotion had seemed to him quite as undesirable as it was unlikely. To Colonel Vellacott's questions, on their first meeting after some years, he gave unsatisfactory answers. Nor did Colonel Vellacott like his clothes—his dirty cord trousers and suede shoes and vivid pullovers. Particularly he disliked—and in a cathedral city it was out of place, as Graham himself was—the car he drove. It was an old London taxi painted yellow, with window-boxes and lace curtains. Once, Graham had had written across the back, "Do not laugh, madam, your daughter may be inside." In love, and serious at last, he had painted this over.

Even so, that *his* daughter should be inside annoyed Colonel Vellacott considerably.

"Lots of young men have cars like it," Sophy told him. "It isn't smart to have a new one. The older and funnier the better."

"Not in a place like this."

"We can't *help* living in a place like this. And I think it's amusing. You were young once yourself, remember."

Lalage, who could not easily escape these much dreaded discussions, turned aside.

Sophy and Lalla found their so gallantly planned relationship beginning to wear threadbare. It was difficult to keep up, especially as it was so unproductive of incredulity in others—its primary aim. Their affection for one another was too easily taken for granted and few of their friends or acquaintances seemed to find it at all remarkable. Their laughter about the hackneyed jealousies that might have threatened them was joined in by their guests, who—so infectious was the gaiety—did not realise how much of relief it contained.

Sophy was the first to find the ordeal going on too long. It had become a mere routine of good behaviour, with no congratulation in it for herself. Miss Sully thought, observing the minute omens, that soon the situation would have more piquancy. Lalla seemed dull and puzzled, with nothing to do but mend her clothes, change her library books and water all the ferns—too often, for they began to droop and rot away.

One morning, when Colonel Vellacott was in Court and Sophy at her Typing School, Lalage, feeling more restless than ever, wandered into the kitchen, where Miss Sully was making stuffing for green peppers. Lalla sat on a corner of the table and watched, picking up bits of parsley and chewing them, holding pepper-seeds on the tip of her tongue until it tingled.

Miss Sully, mixing raisins and rice, was talking of the days when she was companion to an old lady whose footman had interfered with one of the gardener's boys. She brought in many a Freudian phrase along with those of the cheapest newspapers and her voice dropped to its cathedral hush as it did when she talked of sex. One side of her neck was a bright red. Deftly her fingers worked and when she took up a large knife and began to chop some mushrooms, she abandoned herself almost obscenely to the job. "What's for pudding?" Lalla asked, like a little girl, as soon as there was quiet again. It had never occurred to her that she might order meals herself. She had once timidly put forward a suggestion that Colonel Vellacott would like jugged hare, but had been told that hare was out of season.

"Well, what *shall* we have?" Miss Sully asked, suddenly indulgent. The names of puddings at once went from Lalla's head, although Miss Sully had such a repertoire of them—there was Cabinet Pudding and High Church Pudding and Guardsman's Pudding and even Railway Pudding—they were mostly sponge mixtures, differing with a dash of spice or jam, or a handful of candied peel. Lalla could never remember which was which.

"What about rice pudding?" she asked. "I haven't had that since I was at school."

"Well, we can't very well have rice two courses running, can we?" Miss Sully asked, laughing gently and pointing at the dish of peppers, now ready for the oven. "And you will have to give me plenty of warning for rice pudding, because the grain must soak at least an hour, you know."

Lalage hadn't known.

"Is there anything I can do?" she asked, jumping down from the table. It was only eleven o'clock.

"Well, now, you could run the ribbon through the hem of Miss Sophy's petticoat. I know she'll be wanting it this evening. Then I can get on with some scones for tea." ("Without you under my feet," she seemed to imply.) By the time she had told Lalla where to find the petticoat and then the ribbon and the bodkin, she thought that she could have done the job herself.

"The shiny side of the ribbon facing you, mind," she warned her, thinking, "Really, she's as useless as a little doll."

When Lalla had finished that small task, she carried the petticoat to Sophy's room and laid it carefully on the bed, hoping she would be touched and grateful when she discovered it there. "And I would do anything for her," she thought, "if there were anything else to do."

She went over to the window and looked down into the courtyard—so still and full of heat and the scent of honeysuckle this sunny morning. On the wall below her was the starry jasmine that framed her own bedroom window. She leant out, resting her elbows on the rough stone sill, feeling insecurely attached to space and time—the seconds would never tick on till luncheon, or the silence be broken, or the sun ever again go in.

It was the room behind her that overcame, at last, her sense of unreality—though she had turned her back upon it, she felt it awaiting her attention—Sophy's room, where Sophy shut the door on all that she pretended downstairs and where she was confronted by her own thoughts, which she kept imprisoned in this place. They were almost palpably imprisoned, Lalla suddenly felt, and she spun round quickly from the window as if to catch them unawares.

The room was menacing to her now and laden with treachery, its air heavy with secrets. The clock ticked slyly and a curtain lifted slowly and sank back full of warning. It was an alien territory and one where Lalla knew she had no right to be. Even the way the towels hung by the basin expressed hostility, she thought, and so did the truculent angle of the looking-glass. It did not seem too fanciful to imagine mute things infected by Sophy's own antagonism.

A letter addressed to Graham lay on the writing-table, the envelope unsealed and the pages sticking out from it as if as a reminder that they were to be added to, or something else enclosed.

In terror, Lalla thought, I could find out if I cared to, just where I stand with her and why, for weeks, she has shrugged me aside in that bright, cold way.

She recoiled and then, almost immediately, stepped quickly forward and drew the pages from the envelope, very careful to make no sound, lest Miss Sully, far below in the kitchen, would prick up her ears and sense the treachery.

"It is the worst thing people can do to one another," she told herself, "and I knew nothing about myself, when I believed that I could not."

The first lines—Sophy's lament at Graham's absence for five whole days—Lalla passed over. She was looking only for her own name and, sure that she would find it, turned to the second page.

"Father, of course, will disapprove and say that I should not go, for he gets more stuffy and morose each day. Anyone young is what he can't bear nowadays, and all that we two do is vulgar and absurd. I wish that Lalla would try to be a wife to him and not a romping schoolgirl still. I should think he would like to be quiet for a while and serious, and so should I. To see him all the time exposed to her high spirits—that gather *me* in, but exclude him—and in any case they are far beyond his powers—is quite painful. He is less and less in the house, and when he is, is so sour and gruff. But he can't—so far—be gruff with *her*, so is with me instead. Where can it end? But all the same, I'll brave his wrath and tell him that I'll go away with you."

There was no more. Very gently, Lalla folded the pages and put them inside the envelope. Then she tiptoed from the room. Her heart beat so loudly that she thought it would betray her. Her hands were icy-cold, and hurt, as if they had touched poison.

She tried to eat luncheon, but failed. The sight of the dish of peppers reminded her of how short a time ago she had been sitting in the kitchen, bored and restless, but still innocent and loving.

Perhaps it is a baby already, Sophy thought, when Lalla, too sick to stay, had left the room. She now had her father to herself and in a nonchalant voice said: "Graham and I think of going to France in August, as soon as Denise's wedding is over!"

"You couldn't choose a worse month," said Colonel Vellacott and threw down his napkin and stood up. "I'm worried about Lalla. I think I'll go up to her." Sophy sat alone. Her eyebrows were raised and she looked down at her plate with an air of surprise and curiosity.

Afterwards she went to her bedroom. The petticoat threaded with its scarlet ribbon lay on the bed, and she wondered if Lalla had done it. She could imagine her trying to while away her mornings with one trivial task after another, spending as long upon them as she could. She pictured her standing in this sunny room, with the petticoat over her arm, feeling lonely and out-of-place. Then a fearful intuition sprang upon Sophy and she swung round and looked for the letter she had so carelessly left on the table. It lay there, just as she expected, and with a trembling hand she picked it up and stared at it. "I have been read," it seemed to say.

Miss Sully could now watch things worsening daily. The laughter had worn off: it was strange to her that it had lasted so long.

Lalla recovered from her sickness, but was dispirited. Her attitude towards her husband changed, was appealing and conciliatory and over-anxious. With Sophy she was reserved. They had drawn a long way apart and the distance was clouded with suspicions and mistrust.

Colonel Vellacott, as the letter had stated, was less and less in the house, and when she was alone, Lalla paced up and down, clasping her hands tight to her breast, and then the other words of the letter echoed over and over in her mind, with burning emphasis—"Where can it end? Where can it end?"

"You are run down," her husband told her. He was wonderfully solicitous, yet bored. She seemed unreal to him, but he would do his best for her. This summer he was feeling his age; marriage had drawn too much attention to it, and so much youth in the house underlined it. Once, he had thought it would have the opposite effect.

"You need a holiday, poor Lalla. And you shall have one. In September I should be able to get away for a couple of weeks. How would you like to go to Florence?"

Yes, she would like to go to Florence and she smiled and nodded; but she thought, "I am not really used to him *here*, and now I must try to get used to him in a foreign country."

She tried hard to be more wifely to him, but when she made attempts at serious discussion, he smiled so fondly, so indulgently, that she was aggravated. Sophy watched her attempts with grim understanding. "I know what *this* is all about," she thought.

So they were all going abroad—Lalla and her husband sedately to Florence, and Sophy and Graham, full of secrecy and excitement, to France. There was a great difference, Lalla thought.

"I neglect you shamefully," said Colonel Vellacott. "I promise I will mend my ways after our holiday. I will come off some of my committees."

"But couldn't I go with you?" Lalla asked. "I should be so interested to hear you speak. Just this once?"

"You would be bored to death and, in any case, I'm afraid tonight's meeting is in camera."

To her own distress, her eyes filled with tears. She was most dreadfully sorry for herself and grieved that no one else was.

She knew that the tears were a pity and that he would think her more childish than ever. "Where will it end?" she wondered, as he patted her cheek, saying "good-bye."

Sophy was out with Graham, Miss Sully listening to a Murder play on the wireless in her sitting-room. "I could teach myself Italian, perhaps," Lalla thought, and she went to the study and looked along the shelves, but, though there were many books written in Italian, she could find none to teach the language to her. One was expected to know it already.

"In Florence, they will all gabble away and leave me out of it," she thought, growing sorrier and sorrier for herself. "It really is too bad." Now, they were to be joined in Italy by Major and Mrs. Mallett, old friends of the Colonel's, a pleasant elderly couple, who still regarded the Colonel as of a younger generation.

"They are only going because he would be so bored with just me," Lalla thought, crossly. "Oh, I have been complaisant for too long," she decided. "I have tried hard and given in and got nowhere."

She thought that, instead of meekly waiting up for him, she would go up to bed, without telling Miss Sully even. She would turn out the lights and if she were not asleep when he came home, she would pretend to be.

A long drawn-out scream came from Miss Sully's wireless-set as Lalla crossed the hall and went softly upstairs.

When she awoke it was dark and she was still alone. She got out of bed and went to the window. Lamplight shone over leaves in the street beyond the wall and fell over the courtyard. The statues and urns looked blanched. In the centre was an ornamental stand for plants. Its wrought-iron lilies threw slanting shadows across the paving-stones; she could even see the shadows of the fuchsia blossoms—real flowers, these—swinging upon the ground.

It was a romantic place in this light, and she knelt by the window looking down at it, quite awake now and refreshed by her sleep. Then she saw that Sophy and Graham found the place romantic too. She had not noticed them at first, under the dark wall, clasped close together, as still as the tree beyond them. But before Lalla could turn away, she saw them move—they swayed lightly, like the fuchsia blossoms, as if rocked by the same faint air, of which they were so heedless.

She went back to bed and lay down and drew the covers over her, her eyes wide open to the darkness. "Defend me from envy, God," she prayed. But the poison of it gathered in her against her will and when it had filled her and she was overflowing with despair, tears broke in her like waves. Even Miss Sully, coming upstairs when the play was over, could hear her.

THE ROSE, THE MAUVE,
THE WHITE

IN THE morning, Charles went down the garden to practise calling for three cheers. When he came to the place farthest of all from the house and near to the lake, he paused among clumps of rhubarb and mounds of lawn-clippings, and glanced about him. His voice had broken years before, but was still uncertain in volume; sometimes it wavered, and lost its way and he could never predict if it would follow his intention or not. If his voice was to come out in a great bellow or perhaps frenziedly high-pitched, people would turn towards him in surprise, even astonishment, but how, if it sank too low, would he claim anyone's attention after the boisterous confusions of "Auld Lang Syne"? He could hardly be held responsible for it, he felt, and had often wished that he might climb to the top of a mountain and there, alone, make its acquaintance and come to terms with it. As he could not, this morning in the garden at home, he put on what he hoped was an expression of exultant gaiety, snatched off his spectacles and, waving them in the air, cried out: "And now three cheers for Mrs. Frensham-Bowater." He was about to begin "Hip, hip, hooray," when a bush nearby was filled with laughter; all the branches were disturbed with mirth. Then there were two splashes as his little sisters leapt into the lake for safety. "And now three cheers for Charles," they called, as they swam as fast as they could away from the bank.

If he went after them, he could only stand at the edge of the water and shake his fist or make some other ineffectual protest, so he put his spectacles on again and walked slowly back to the house. It was a set-back to the day, with Natalie arriving that afternoon and likely to hear at once from the twins how foolishly he had behaved.

"Mother, could you make them be quiet?" he asked desperately, finding her at work in the rose-garden. When he told her the story, she threw back her head and laughed for what seemed to him to be about five minutes. "Oh, poor old Charles. I wish I'd been in hiding, too." He had known he would have to bear this or something like it, but was obliged to pay the price; and at long last she said: "I will see to it that their lips are sealed; their cunning chops shut up."

"But are you sure you can?"

"I think I know how to manage my own children. See how obedient you yourself have grown. I cross my heart they shall not breathe a word of it in front of Natalie."

He thanked her coldly and walked away. In spite of his gratitude, he thought: "She is so dreadfully chummy and slangy. I wish she wouldn't be. And why say just 'Natalie' when there are two girls coming? I think she tries to be 'knowing' as well," he decided.

Two girls were coming. His sister, Katie, was picking sweet-peas for the room these school-friends were to share with her.

"You are supposed to cut those with scissors," Charles said. The ones she couldn't strip off, she was breaking with her teeth. "What time are they coming?"

"In the station-taxi at half-past three."

"Shall I come with you to meet them?"

"No, of course not. Why should you?"

Katie was sixteen and a year younger than Charles. It is a very feminine age and she wanted her friends to herself. At school they slept in the same bedroom, as they would here. They were used to closing the door upon a bower of secrets and intrigue and diary-writing; knew how to keep their jokes to themselves and their conversations as incomprehensible as possible to other people. When Charles's friends came to stay, Katie did not encroach on them, and now she had no intention of letting him spoil that delightful drive back from the station: she could not imagine what her friends would think of her if she did.

So after luncheon she went down alone in the big, musty-smelling taxi. The platform of the country station was quite deserted: a porter was whistling in the office, keeping out of the hot sun. She walked up and down, reading the notices of Estate Agents posted along the fence and all the advertisements of auction-sales. She imagined the train coming nearer to her with every passing second; yet it seemed unbelievable that it would really soon materialise out of the distance, bringing Frances and Natalie.

They would have the compartment to themselves at this time of the day on the branch line and she felt a little wistful thinking that they were together and having fun and she was all alone, waiting for them. They would be trying out dance-steps, swaying and staggering as the train rocked; dropping at last, weak with laughter, full-length on the seats. Then, having been here to stay with Katie on other occasions, as they came near to the end of their journey they would begin to point out landmarks and haul down their luggage from the rack—carefully, because in the suitcases were the dresses for this evening's dance.

The signal fell with a sharp clatter making Katie jump. "Now where shall I be standing when the train stops?" she wondered, feeling self-conscious suddenly and full of responsibility. "Not here, right on top of the gents' lavatory of all places. Perhaps by the entrance." Nonchalantly, she strolled away.

The porter came out of the office, still whistling, and stared up the line. Smoke, bowing and nodding like a plume on a horse's head, came round a bend in the distance and Katie, watching it, felt sick and anxious. "They won't enjoy themselves at all," she thought. "I wish I hadn't asked them. They will find it dreadfully dull at home and the dance is bound to be a failure. It will be babyish with awful things like 'The Dashing White Sergeant' and 'The Gay Gordons.' They will think Charles is a bore and the twins a bloody nuisance."

But the moment they stepped out of the train all her constraint vanished. They caught her up into the midst of their laughter. "You can't think what happened," they said. "You'll never believe what happened at Paddington." The ridiculous story never did quite come clear, they were so incoherent with giggling. Katie smiled in a grown-up way. She was just out of it for the moment, but would soon be in the swim again.

As they drove up the station-slope towards the village, they were full of anticipation and excitement. "And where is Charles?" asked Natalie, smoothing her dark hair.

Tea was such great fun, their mother, Myra Pollard, told herself: though one moment she felt rejuvenated; the next minute, as old as the world. She had a habit of talking to herself, as to another person who was deeply interested in all her reactions: and the gist of these conversations was often apparent on her face.

"They keep one young oneself—all these young people," she thought as she was pouring out the tea. Yet the next second, her cheek resting on her hand as she watched them putting away great swags and wadges and gobbets of starch, she sighed; for she had not felt as they all felt, eager and full of nonsense, for years and years. To them, though they were polite, she was of no account, the tea pourer-out, the starch-provider, simply. It was people of her own generation who said that Charles and she were like brother and sister—not those of Charles's generation, to whom the idea would have seemed absurd.

Frances and Natalie were as considerate as could be and even strove to be a little woman-to-womanly with her. "Did you ever find your bracelet, Mrs. Pollard? Do you remember you'd lost it when we were here last time? At a . . . a dance, wasn't it?" Natalie faltered. Of course, Katie's mother went to dances, too. Indeed, why not? Grotesque though they must be. She was glad that her own parents were more sedate and did not try to ape the young.

"I wish *we* could go to a ball," said Lucy, one of the twins.

"Your time will come," their mother said. She laid her hand to the side of the silver tea-pot as if to warm and comfort herself.

"Oh, do you remember that boy, Sandy, in the elimination dance?" Katie suddenly exploded.

Frances, who was all beaky and spectacly, Mrs. Pollard thought, exploded with her.

"The one who was wearing a kilt?" Natalie asked, with more composure. She wondered if Charles was thinking that she must be older than the other girls and indeed she was, by two and a half months.

"Will Mrs. Frensham-Bowater be there?" Lucy asked.

Her sly glance, with eyelids half-lowered, was for Caroline's—her twin's—benefit.

"Of course, Mrs. Frensham-Bowater always organises the dance," their mother said briskly, and changed the subject.

Charles was grateful to her for keeping her promise; but all the same he had had an irritating afternoon. The twins, baulked in one direction, found other ways of exasperating him. When he came out of the house with his gun under his arm, they had clapped their hands over their ears and fled shrieking to the house. "Charles is pointing his gun at us," they shouted. "Don't be bloody silly," he shouted back. "Charles swore," they cried.

"What an unholy gap between Katie and me and those little perishers," he thought. "Whatever did Mother and Father imagine they were up to? What can the neighbours have thought of them—at their time of life?" He shied away from the idea of sexual love between the middle-aged; though it was ludicrous, evidence of it was constantly to be seen.

"Did you shoot anything?" his mother asked him.

"There wasn't anything to shoot." He had known there wouldn't be and had only walked about in the woods with his gun for something to do until the taxi came.

"And the girl next door?" Frances asked. "I have forgotten her name. Will she be going to the dance tonight?"

"Oh, Deirdre," said Caroline to Lucy.

"Yes, Deirdre," Lucy said, staring across the table at Charles.

"No, she has gone to school in Switzerland," said Katie.

"Poor Charles!" the twins said softly.

"Why not try to be your age?" he asked them in a voice which would, he hoped, sound intimidating to them, but nonchalant to everybody else.

"Have you had nice holidays?" Mrs. Pollard asked, looking from Frances to Natalie, then thinking that she was being far too hostessy and middle-aged, she said without waiting for their answer, "I do adore your sweater, Natalie."

"Jesus bids us shine, with a pure, clear light," Caroline began to sing, as she spread honey on her bread.

"Not at the table," said her mother.

"What shall we do now?" Katie asked after tea. She was beginning to feel her responsibility again. There was no doubt that everything was very different from school; there were Frances and Natalie drawn very close together from sharing the same situation; and she, apart, in the predicament of hostess. It was now that she began to see her home through their eyes—the purple-brick house looked heavy and ugly now that the sun had gone behind a cloud; the south wall was covered by a magnolia tree; there were one or two big, cream flowers among the dark leaves: doves were walking about on the slate roof; some of the windows reflected the blue sky and moving clouds. To Katie, it was like being shown a photograph which she did not immediately recognise—unevocative, as were the photographs of their mothers in the dormitory at school—they seldom glanced at them from the beginning of term to the end.

They sat down on the grass at the edge of the orchard and began to search for four-leaf clovers. Their conversation consisted mostly of derogatory remarks about themselves—they were hopeless at dancing, each one said; could never think what to say to their partners; and they had all washed their hair that morning and now could do simply nothing with it.

"So lucky having red hair, Katie. How I envy you."

"But it's horrible. I hate it."

"It's so striking. Isn't it, Frances?"

"Well, yours is, too, in a different way. It's this awful mousiness of mine I can't abide."

"You can't call it mousy: it's chestnut."

It was just a game they played and when they had finished with their hair they began on the shape of their hands. There was never any unkindness in anything they said. They were exploring themselves more than each other.

The twins wandered about the garden, shaking milk in jars to make butter: every few minutes they stopped to compare the curd they had collected. They had been doing this tirelessly for days, but were near the time when that game would seem dull and done with and they would never play it again. This evening, they marched about the lawn, chanting a meaningless song.

The older girls were discussing whether they would rather be deaf or blind. Frances lay on her stomach watching the children and wondering if they were not lucky to be so free of care and without the great ordeal of the dance ahead of them.

"Deaf any day," said Katie.

"Oh, no!" said Natalie. "Only think how cut off you'd be from other people; and no one is ever as nice to the deaf or has much patience with them. Everyone is kinder to the blind."

"But imagine never seeing any of this ever again," said Frances. Tears came up painfully in Katie's eyes. "This garden, that lovely magnolia tree, sunsets. Never to be able to read *Jane Eyre* again."

"You could read it in Braille," Katie said.

"It wouldn't be the same. You know it wouldn't be. Oh, it would be appalling...I can't contemplate it...I really can't."

Anyone who reminded them that the choice might not arise would have been deeply resented.

"I suppose we had better go in and iron our frocks," Katie said. No one had found a four-leaf clover.

"Where is Charles?" Natalie asked.

"The Lord knows," said Katie.

Frances was silent as they went towards the house. She could feel the dance coming nearer to her.

"The house is full of girls," Charles told his father. George Pollard left the car in the drive and went indoors. "And steam," he said.

Natalie, Frances and Katie had been in the bathroom for nearly an hour and could hardly see one another across the room. Bath-salts, hoarded from Christmas, scented the steam and now, still wearing their shower-caps, they were standing on damp towels and shaking their Christmas talcum powder over their stomachs and shoulders.

"Will you do my back and under my arms?" asked Katie, handing to Frances the tin of Rose Geranium. "And then I will do yours."

"What a lovely smell. It's so much nicer than mine," said Frances, dredging Katie as thoroughly as if she were a fillet of fish being prepared for the frying-pan.

"Don't be too long, girls!" Mrs. Pollard called, tapping at the door. She tried to make her voice sound gay and indulgent. "The twins are waiting to come in and it's rather past their bedtime." She wondered crossly if Katie's friends were allowed to monopolise bathrooms like that in their own homes. Katie was plainly showing off and would have to be taken aside and told so.

"Just coming," they shouted.

At last they opened the door and thundered along the passage to their bedroom where they began to make the kind of untidiness they had left behind them in the bathroom.

Yvette, the French mother's-help, whose unenviable task it now was to supervise the twins' going to bed, flung open the bathroom window and kicked all the wet towels to one side. "They will be clean, certainly," she was thinking. "But they will not be chic." She had seen before the net frocks, the strings of coral, the shining faces.

She rinsed the dregs of mauve crystals from the bath and called out to the twins. The worst part of her day was about to begin.

"This is the best part of the day," George said. He shut the bedroom door and took his drink over to the window. Myra was sitting at her dressing-table. She had taken off her ear-rings to give her ears a little rest and was gently massaging the reddened lobes. She said: "It doesn't seem a year since that other dance, when we quarrelled about letting Katie go to it."

"She was too young. And still is."

"There were girls of thirteen there."

"Well, that's no affair of mine, thank God."

"I wonder if Ronnie what's-his-name will be sober. For the MC of a young people's dance I consider he was pretty high last time. He always has drunk unmercifully."

"What the devil's this?" George asked. He had gone into his dressing-room and now came back with his safety-razor in his hand.

"Oh, the girls must have borrowed it."

"Very hospitable guests they are, to be sure. They manage to make me feel quite at home."

"Don't fuss. You were young yourself once."

She dotted lipstick over her cheekbones and he watched her through the looking-glass, arrested by the strange sight. The incredulous expression made her smile, eyebrows raised, she was ready to tease. He tilted her face back towards him and kissed her quickly on the mouth.

"You look absurd," he said.

As soon as she was released, she leant to the mirror again and began to smooth the dots of colour over her cheeks until they were merged into the most delicate flush. "A clever girl," he said, finishing his drink.

The girls were still not dressed when a boy called Benedict Nightingale arrived in his father's car—and dinner-jacket, George decided. "Katie's first beau," he told himself, "come calling for her." He felt quite irritable as he took the boy into the drawing-room.

"They won't be long," he said, without conviction.

"Don't be too long, girls," Myra called again in her low, controlled and unexasperated voice. She stopped to tap on their bedroom door before she went downstairs; then, knowing that Charles would be having trouble with his tie, she went in to his rescue.

"What about a drink?" George asked Benedict reluctantly.

"No thank you, sir."

"Cigarette?"

"No thank you, sir."

"I don't know what they can be doing all this time. Now what the hell's happening up there?"

The twins were trying to get into Katie's bedroom to pry into adolescent secrets, and the girls, still in their petticoats, held the door against them. From the other side of it Lucy and Caroline banged with their fists and kicked until dragged away at last by Yvette.

"Now we shall be late," said Katie.

They lifted their frocks and dropped them over their heads, their talcumed armpits showed white as they raised their elbows to hook themselves at the back. Frances tied Natalie's sash, Natalie fastened Katie's bracelet.

"Is this all right? Does it hang down? You're sure? Am I done up?" they asked.

"Oh, yes, yes, yes, I mean no," they all answered at once, not one of them attending.

"*This* is what *I'm* allowed," said Katie, smudging on lipstick, stretching her mouth as she had seen her mother do. "So pale, I'm wasting my time."

Natalie twisted her bracelet, shook back her hair: she hummed; did a glissade across the clothes-strewn floor, her skirts floating about her. She was away, gone, in Charles's arms already. She held her scented arm to her face and breathed deeply and smiled.

Frances stood uncertainly in the middle of the room. "I am the one who will be asked to dance last of all," she thought, cold with the certainty of her failure. "Katie and Natalie will go flying away and I shall be left there on my own, knowing nobody. The time will go slowly and I shall wish that I were dead." She turned to the long looking-glass and smoothed her frock. "I hate my bosoms," she suddenly said. "They are too wide apart."

"Nonsense, that's how they're supposed to be," Katie said, as brisk as any nanny.

"Give those girls a shout, Charles," George said and helped himself to another drink.

But they were coming downstairs. They had left the room with its beds covered with clothes, its floor strewn with tissue-paper. They descended; the rose, the mauve, the white. Like a bunch of sweet-peas they looked, George thought.

"What a pretty frock, Frances," Myra said, beginning with the worst. "Poor pet," she thought, and Frances guessed the thought, smiling primly and saying thank you.

"And such a lovely colour, Natalie," Myra went on.

"But is it, though?" Natalie asked anxiously. "And don't my shoes clash terribly? I think I look quite bleak in it, and it is last year's, really."

Myra had scarcely wanted to go into all that. "Now, Katie," she began to say, as soon as she could. "I don't think your friends know Benedict. And when you have introduced them we must be on our way. Your father and I have to go out to dinner after we've taken you to the dance. So who's to go with whom?"

That was what Frances had wondered. The worst part of being a guest was not being told enough about arrangements. One was left in a shifting haze of conjecture.

Benedict had come to attention as the girls came in and now he stepped forward and said with admirable firmness: "I will take Katie in my car." Then he was forced to add: "I would have room for some-one else in the back."

"That's me," thought Frances.

"Good! Now don't crush your dresses, girls," said Myra. "Gather them up—so—from the back of the skirt. Have you got every-thing?"

"Of course, Mother," said Katie. "We aren't children," she thought.

Four hours later, Charles let go of Natalie's hand and took a pace forward from the circle of "Auld Lang Syne." "Three cheers for Mrs. Frensham-Bowater," he shouted. "Hip, hip, hooray!"

Myra, standing in the entrance hall with the other parents, tried to look unconcerned. She knew that Charles had been nervous all along of doing that little duty and she was thankful that it was safely over. And that meant that the dance was over, too.

With the first bars of "God Save the Queen," they all became rigid, pained-looking, arms to their sides and heads erect; but the moment it was over, the laughter and excitement enlived their faces again. They began to drift reluctantly towards the hall.

"How pretty the girls are," the mothers said to one another. "Goodness, how they grow up. That isn't Madge's girl, surely, in the yellow organza? They change from day to day at this age."

"Was it lovely?" Myra asked Katie.

"So lovely! Oh and someone spilt fruit-cup all down poor Natalie's front."

"Oh, no!" said Myra.

"She doesn't care though."

"But her mother . . . I feel so responsible."

"Oh, her mother's awfully understanding. She won't give a damn." ("Unlike you," Katie's voice seemed to imply.) "It was last year's, anyway."

Benedict was hovering at Katie's shoulder.

"Charles had torn the hem already, anyway," Katie said.

"But how on earth?"

"They won a prize in the River Dance."

Myra had not the faintest idea what a River Dance was and said so.

"The boys have to run across some chalk lines carrying their partners and he tore her skirt when he picked her up. She's no light weight, I can assure you."

"I hope it hasn't been rowdy," Myra said, but this remark was far too silly to receive an answer.

Frances had attached herself to Charles and Natalie, so that she would not seem to leave the floor alone; but she knew that Mrs. Pollard had seen her standing there by the door, without a partner, and for the last waltz of all things. To be seen by her hostess in such a predicament underlined her failure.

"Did you enjoy it, Frances?" Myra asked. And wasn't that the only way to put her question, Frances thought, the one she was so very anxious to know—"Did you dance much?"

"We had better go back as we came," Myra said. "Have you all got everything? Well then, you go on, Benedict dear, with Frances and Katie, and we will follow."

"I wish she wouldn't say 'dear' to boys," Katie thought. "And she doesn't trust us, I suppose, to come on after. I hope that Benedict hasn't noticed that she doesn't trust him: he will think it is his driving, or worse, that she is thoroughly evil-minded. Goodness knows what she got up to in her young days to have such dreadful ideas in her head."

The untidy room was waiting for them. Five hours earlier, they had not looked beyond the dance or imagined a time after it.

"Well, I don't think that poor boy, Roland, will thank you much for asking him in your party," Frances said. "He was wondering how he would ever get away from me."

She thought, as many grown-up women think, that by saying a thing herself she prevented people from thinking it. She had also read a great many nostalgic novels about girls of long ago spending hours in the cloak-room at dances and in her usual spirit of defiance she had refused to go there at all, had stuck the humiliation out and even when she might have taken her chance with the others in the Paul Jones had stuck that out, too.

"He told me he thought you danced very well," Katie said.

This made matters worse for Frances. So it wasn't just the dancing, but something very much more important—her personality, or lack of it; her plainness—what she was burdened with for the rest of her life, in fact.

Natalie seemed loth to take off her frock, stained and torn though it now was. She floated about the room, spreading the skirt about her as she hummed and swayed and shook her hair. She would not be back on earth again until morning.

"Here is your safety-pin, Katie," said Frances.

"And here, with many thanks, your necklace safe and sound."

The trinkets they had borrowed from one another were handed back; they unhooked one another; examined their stockings for ladders. Katie took a pair of socks out of her brassiere.

One by one, they got into bed. Natalie sat up writing her diary and Katie thought hers could wait till morning. Benedict's amusing sayings would be quite safe till then and by tomorrow the cloud that had been over the evening might have dispersed. The next day, when they were swimming in the lake, or cleaning out the rabbits or making walnut fudge, surely Frances would be re-established among them, not cut off by her lack of success as she now was, taking the edge off Benedict's remembered wit, making Katie's heart ache just when it was beginning to behave as she had always believed a heart should.

Turning in Benedict's arms as they danced she had sometimes caught Frances's eyes as she stood there alone or with some other forlorn and unclaimed girl. Katie had felt treachery in the smile she had been bound to give—the most difficult of smiles, for it had to contain so much, the assurance that the dance was only a dance and nothing very much to miss, a suggestion of regret at her—Katie's—foolishness in taking part in it and surprise that she of all people had been chosen. "It is soon over," she tried to signal to Frances. "You are yourself. I love you. I will soon come back."

And Frances had received the smiles and nodded. "There are other things in the world," she tried to believe.

"Shall we have a picnic tomorrow?" Katie asked. She snuggled down into bed and stared up at the ceiling.

"Let's have one day at a time," said Natalie. She had filled in the space in her diary and now locked the book up with a little key that hung on a chain round her neck.

"Do put out the light before the moths come in," said Frances.

They could hear Katie's parents talking quietly in the next room. Frances thought: "I expect she is saying, 'Poor Frances. I'm afraid she didn't get many dances; but I am sure that Katie did what she could

for her. It would really have been kinder not to have invited her.'"
The unbroken murmuring continued on the other side of the wall
and Frances longed for it to stop. She thought: "She is forever working things out in her mind, and cruelly lets people guess what they
are. It would be no worse if she said them out loud." She had prayed
that before Myra came to fetch them from the dance it would all be
over; "God Save the Queen" safely sung and her own shame at last
behind her. As the last waltz began, she had longed for someone to
claim her—any spotty, clammy-handed boy would do. Benedict and
Katie had hovered by her, Benedict impatient to be away, but Katie
reluctant to leave her friend alone at such a crucial moment. "Please
go," Frances had told them and just as they danced away, Myra had
appeared in the doorway, looking tired but watchful, her eyes everywhere—Katie accounted for, Charles, Natalie, then a little encouraging smile and nod to Frances herself, trying to shrink out of sight
on the perimeter of the gaiety. "As I expected," her eyes said.

Gradually, the murmurings from the other room petered out and
the house became silent. Then, in Charles's room across the landing,
Natalie heard a shoe drop with a thud on the floor and presently
another. "Sitting on the edge of the bed, dreaming," she thought.
She lay awake, smiling in the darkness and stroking her smooth
arms long after the other two had fallen asleep.

SUMMER SCHOOLS

SITTING outside on the sill, the cat watched Melanie through the window. The shallow arc between the tips of his ears, his baleful stare, and his hunched-up body blown feathery by the wind, gave him the look of a barn-owl. Sometimes, a strong gust nearly knocked him off balance and bent his whiskers crooked. Catching Melanie's eye, he opened his mouth wide in his furious, striped face, showed his fangs and let out a piteous mew instead of a roar.

Melanie put a finger in her book and padded across the room in her stockinged feet. When she opened the French windows, the gale swept into the room and the fire began to smoke. Now that he was allowed to come in, the cat began a show caprice; half in, he arched his back and rubbed against the step, purring loudly. Some leaves blew across the floor.

"Either in or out, you fool," Melanie said impatiently. Still holding the door, she put her foot under the cat's belly and half-pushed, half-lifted him into the room.

The French windows had warped, like all the other wooden parts of the house. There were altogether too many causes for irritation, Melanie thought. When she had managed to slam the door shut, she stood there for a moment, looking out at the garden, until she had felt the full abhorrence of the scene. Her revulsion was so complete as to be almost unbelievable; the sensation became ecstatic.

On the veranda, a piece of newspaper had wrapped itself, quivering frenziedly, round a post. A macrocarpa-hedge tossed about in the wind; the giant hydrangea by the gate was full of bus-tickets, for here was the terminus, the very end of the esplanade. The butt and end, Melanie thought, of all the long-drawn-out tedium of the English holiday resort. Across the road a broken bank covered with spiky grass hid most of the sands, but she could imagine them clearly, brown and ribbed, littered with bits of cuttle-fish and mussel-shells. The sea—far out—was staved with white.

Melanie waited as a bowed-over, mufflered man, exercising a dog, then a duffel-coated woman with a brace of poodles on leads completed the scene. Satisfied, she turned back to the fire. It was all as bad as could be and on a bright day it was hardly better, for the hard glitter of the sun seemed unable to lift the spirits. It was usually windy.

The creaking sound of the rain, its fitful and exasperated drumming on the window, she listened to carefully. In one place at the end of the veranda, it dropped more heavily and steadily: she could hear it as if the noise were in her own breast. The cat—Ursula's— rubbed its cold fur against her legs and she pushed him away crossly, but he always returned.

"A day for indoors," Ursula said gaily. She carried in the tea-tray, and set down a covered dish on the hearth with the smug triumph of one giving a great treat.

"I am to be won over with buttered scones," Melanie thought sulkily. The sulky expression was one that her face, with its heavy brows and full mouth, fell into easily. "One of Miss Rogers's nasty looks," her pupils called it, finding it not alarming, but depressing. Ursula, two years younger, was plumper, brighter, more alert. Neither was beautiful.

"Oh, sod that cat of yours," Melanie said. He was now mewing at the French windows to be let out. Melanie's swearing was something new since their father had died—an act of desperation, such as a child might make. Father would turn in his grave, Ursula often said. Let him turn, said Melanie. "Who will look after him while you're away?" she asked, nodding at the cat. Ursula put him outside again and came back to pour out the tea. "How do you mean, look after him? Surely you don't mind. I'll order the fish. You'll only have to cook it and give it to him."

"I shan't be here."

The idea had suddenly occurred, born of vindictiveness and envy. For Pamela had no right to invite Ursula to stay there on her own. Melanie was only two years their senior; they had all been at the same school. Apart from all that, the two sisters always spent their holidays together; in fact, had never been separated. To Melanie, the invitation seemed staggering, insolent, and Ursula's decision to accept it could hardly be believed. She had read out the letter at breakfast one morning and Melanie, on her way out of the room to fetch more milk, had simply said, "How extraordinary," her light, scornful voice dismissing the subject. Only a sense of time passing and middle-age approaching had given Ursula the courage (or effrontery) to renew the subject. For the first time that either she or Melanie could remember, her energy and enthusiasm overcame the smothering effect of her sister's lethargy.

"She means to go," Melanie told herself. Her sensation of impotence was poison to her. She had a bitter taste in her mouth, and chafed her hands as if they were frozen. If Ursula were truly going, though, Melanie determined that the departure should be made as difficult as possible. Long before she could set out for the station she should be worn out with the obstacles she had had to overcome.

"You can't expect me to stay here on my own just in order to look after your cat."

And lest Ursula should ask where she was going before she had had time to make her plans, she got up quickly and went upstairs.

The cat was to stay in kennels and Ursula grieved about it. Her grief Melanie brushed aside as absurd, although she was at the same time inclined to allow Ursula a sense of guilt. "A dog one can at least take with one," she told her. She had decided that the cat reflected something of Ursula's own nature—too feminine (although it was a tom); it might be driven, though not led, and the refusal to co-operate mixed, as it was, with cowardice resulted in slyness.

The weather had not improved. They could remember the holidays beginning in this way so often, with everything—rain, flowers, bushes—aslant in the wind. "It will be pretty miserable at Pamela's," Melanie thought. She could imagine that house and its surroundings—a parade of new shops nearby, a tennis club, enormous suburban pubs at the corners of roads. She was forever adding something derogatory to the list. "Dentists' houses always depress me," she said. "I don't think I could stay in one—with all that going on under the same roof."

What awaited herself was much vaguer.

"It will be like being at school—though having to run to the bell instead of ringing it," Ursula said, when she had picked up the prospectus for the Summer Lecture Course. "A pity you can't just go to the discussions and not stay there. Breakfast 8:15," she read. "Oh, Lord. The Victorian Novel. Trollope, 9:30."

Melanie, in silence, held out her hand for the prospectus and Ursula gave it to her. She did not see it again.

"Will you want Mother's fur?" she asked, when she began to pack. "I just thought . . . evenings, you know, it might be useful . . ."

"I shall have evenings, too," Melanie reminded her.

Their mother could not have guessed what a matter of contention her ermine wrap would turn out to be when she was dead.

"How is Melanie?" Pamela asked.

"Oh, she's well. She's gone on a little holiday, too."

"I'm so glad. I should have liked to have asked her to come with you," Pamela lied. "But there's only this single bed."

Ursula went over to the window. The spare room was at the back of the house and looked across some recreation grounds—a wooden pavilion, a bowling-green; and tennis courts—just as Melanie had said there would be.

That evening, there was the pub.

All afternoon the front-door bell had rung, and Pamela and Ursula, sitting in the drawing-room upstairs, could hear the crackle of

Miss Potter's starched overall as she crossed the hall to answer it. Patients murmured nervously when they entered, but shouted cheerful good-byes as they left, going full tilt down the gravelled drive and slamming the gate after them.

"I'm sorry about the bell," Pamela said. "At first, I thought it would send me out of my mind, but now it's no worse than a clock striking."

Ursula thought it extraordinary that she had changed so much since their schooldays. It was difficult to find anything to talk about. The books they had once so passionately discussed were at the very bottom of the glass-fronted case, beneath text-books on dentistry and Book Club editions, and Ursula, finding Katherine Mansfield's Journal covered with dust, felt estranged. Perhaps Pamela had become a good cook instead, she thought, for there were plenty of books on that.

Melanie would have scorned the room, with its radiogram and cocktail cabinet and the matching sofa and chairs. The ash-trays were painted with bright sayings in foreign languages; there were piles of fashion magazines that later—much later, Ursula guessed—would be put in the waiting-room downstairs. The parchment lamp-shades were stuck over with wine labels and the lamps were made out of Chianti bottles. The motif of drinking was prevalent, from a rueful yet humorous viewpoint. When Pamela opened the cigarette-box it played "The More We Are Together," and Ursula wondered if the clock would call "Prosit" when it struck six.

"That's the last patient," Pamela said. "Mike will come up panting for a drink."

Her full skirt, printed with a jumble of luggage-labels, flew out wide as she made a dash to the cocktail cabinet. She was as eager to be ready with everything as if she were opening a pub.

Panic now mingled with the feeling of estrangement, as Ursula listened to the footsteps on the stairs. "Hello, there, Ursula," said Mike as he threw open the door. "And how are you? Long time, no see, indeed."

"Not since our wedding," Pamela reminded him.

"Well, what will you be after taking?" Mike asked. He slapped his hands together, ready for action, took up a bottle and held it to the light.

"I suppose he feels uneasy because I am a schoolmistress," Ursula thought; "And perhaps also—lest I shall think Pam married beneath her."

Pamela put out the glasses and some amusing bottle-openers and corkscrews. Ursula remembered staying with her as a girl, had a clear picture of the gloomy dining-room: a dusty, cut-glass decanter, containing the dregs of some dark, unidentified liquid had stood in the centre of the great sideboard, its position never shifting an inch to the right or left. From that imprisoning house and those oppressive parents, Mike had rescued his betrothed and, though she had shed Katherine Mansfield somewhere on the way, she seemed as gay as could be that she had escaped.

Now she kissed her husband, took her drink and went downstairs—to turn the waiting-room back into a dining-room, she said. Mike's uneasiness increased. He was clearly longing for her to return.

"You must be a brave man," Ursula said suddenly. "I remember Pam's mother and father and how nervous I was when I stayed there. Even when we were quite well on in our teens, we were made to lie down after luncheon, in a darkened room for ages and ages. 'And no reading, dears,' her mother always said as we went upstairs. At home, we never rested—or only when we were little children, but I pretended that we did, in case Pam's mother should think badly of mine. They seemed so very stern. To snatch away their only daughter must have needed courage."

For the first time, he looked directly at her. In his eyes was a timid expression. He may have been conscious of this and anxious to hide it, for almost immediately he glanced away.

"I girded on my armour," he said, "and rode up to the portcullis and demanded her. That was all there was to it."

She smiled, thinking, "So this room is the end of a fairy tale."

"Astonishing good health, my dear," Mike said, lifting his glass.

Melanie took her coffee and, summoning all her courage, went to sit down beside Mrs. Rybeck, who gave her a staving-off smile, a slight shake of her head as she knitted, her lips moving silently. When she came to the end of the row, she apologised, and jotted down on her knitting-pattern whatever it was she had been counting.

"What a stimulating evening," Melanie said.

"Have you not heard George Barnes lecture before?" Mrs. Rybeck was obviously going to be condescending again, but Melanie was determined to endure it. Then—what she had hoped—Professor Rybeck came in. She felt breathless and self-conscious as he approached.

"Darling!" he murmured, touching his wife's hair, then bowed to Melanie.

"Miss Rogers," his wife reminded him quickly. "At St. Winifred's, you know, where Ethel's girls were."

"Yes, of course I know Miss Rogers," he said.

His dark hair receded from a forehead that seemed always moist, as were his dark and mournful eyes. As soon as they heard his voice—low, catarrhal and with such gentle inflections—some of the women, who had been sitting in a group by the window, got up and came over to him.

"Professor Rybeck," one said. "We are beside ourselves with excitement about your lecture tomorrow."

"Miss Rogers was just saying that she thought highly of George's talk this evening," said Mrs. Rybeck.

"Ah, George!" her husband said softly. "I think George likes to think he has us all by the ears. Young men do. But we mustn't let him sharpen his wits on us till we ourselves are blunt. None the less, he knows his Thackeray."

Melanie considered herself less esteemed for having mentioned him.

"How I love *Middlemarch*," some woman said. "I think it is my favourite novel."

"Then I only hope I do it justice tomorrow," Professor Rybeck said. Although he seemed full of confidence, he smiled humbly. Nothing was too much trouble.

Pamela had insisted that the three of them should squeeze into the front of the car and Ursula, squashed up in the middle, sat with rounded shoulders and her legs tucked to one side. She was worried about the creases in her skirt. The wireless was on very loud and both Pamela and Mike joined in the Prize Song from *Die Meistersinger*. Ursula was glad when they reached the Swan.

The car-park was full. This pub was where everybody went, Pamela explained; "at the moment," she added. In the garden, the striped umbrellas above the tables had been furled; the baskets of geraniums over the porch were swinging in the wind.

"Astonishingly horrid evening," Mike said, when some of his acquaintances greeted him. "This is Pam's friend, Ursula. Ursie, this is Jock"—or Jean or Eve or Bill. Ursula lost track. They all knew one another and Mike and Pam seemed popular. "Don't look now, the worst has happened," someone had said in a loud voice when Mike opened the door of the saloon bar.

Ursula was made much of. From time to time, most of them were obliged to bring out some dull relation or duty-guest. ("Not really one of us"), and it was a mark of friendliness to do one's best to help with other people's problems—even the most tiresome of old crones would be attended to; and Ursula, although plump and prematurely grey, was only too ready to smile and join in the fun.

"You're one of us, I can see," someone complimented her.

"Cheers!" said Ursula before she drank. Melanie would have shivered with distaste.

"We are all going on to Hilly's," Pam called to Mike across the bar at closing-time.

This moving-on was the occasion for a little change-round of passengers and, instead of being squeezed in between Pamela and Mike, Ursula was taken across the car-park by a man called Guy.

"Daddy will give you a scarf for your head," he promised, opening the door of his open car. The scarf tucked inside his shirt was yellow, patterned with horses and when he took it off and tied it round Ursula's head, the silk was warm to her cheeks.

They drove very fast along the darkening roads and were the first to arrive.

"Poor frozen girl," said Guy when he had swung the car round on the gravelled sweep in front of the house and brought it up within an inch of the grass verge. With the driving off his mind, he could turn his attention to Ursula and he took one of her goosefleshy arms between his hands and began to chafe it. "What we need is a drink," he said. "Where the hell have they all got to?"

She guessed that to drive fast and to arrive first was something he had to do and, for his sake and to help on the amiability of the evening, she was glad that he had managed it.

"You're sure it's the right house?" she asked.

"Dead sure, my darling."

She had never been called "darling" by a man and, however meaningless the endearment, it added something to her self-esteem, as their arriving first had added something to his.

She untied the scarf and gave it back to him. He had flicked on his cigarette lighter and was looking for something in the dash-pocket. For a moment, while the small glow lasted, she could study his face. It was like a ventriloquist's dummy's—small, alert, yet blank; the features gave the appearance of having been neatly painted.

He found the packet of cigarettes; then he put the scarf round his neck and tied it carefully. "Someone's coming," he said. "They must have double-crossed us and had one somewhere on the way."

"You drove fastest, that's all," she said, playing her part in the game.

"Sorry if it alarmed you, sweetheart." He leant over and kissed her quickly, just before the first of the cars came round the curve of the drive.

"That's the first evening gone," Ursula thought, when later, she lay in bed, rather muzzily going over what had happened. She could remember the drawing-room at Hilly's. She had sat on a cushion on the floor and music from a gramophone above her had spilled over her head, so that she had seen people's mouths opening and shutting but had not been able to hear the matching conversations. In many ways the room—though it was larger—had seemed like Pamela's, with pub signs instead of bottle labels on the lamp-shades. Her sense of time had soon left her and her sense of place grew vaguer, but some details irritated her because she could not evade them—particularly a warming-pan hanging by the fireplace in which she confronted her distorted reflection.

There had seemed no reason why the evening should ever end and no way of setting going all the complications of departure. Although she was tired, she had neither wanted to leave or to stay. She was living a tiny life within herself, sitting there on the cushion; sipping and smiling and glancing about her. Mike had come across the room to her. She turned to tilt back her head to look up into his face but at once felt giddy and had to be content with staring at his knees, at the pin stripes curving baggily, a thin stripe, then a wider, more feathery one. She began to count them, but Mike had come to take her home to bye-byes he said, stretching out a hand. "If I can only do this, I can do anything," Ursula thought, trying to rise and keep her balance. "I was silly to sit so low down in the first place," she decided. "I think my foot has gone to sleep," she explained and smiled confidingly at his knees. His grip on her arm was strong; although appearing to be extending a hand in gallantry, he was really taking her weight and steadying her, too. She had realised this, even at the time and later, lying safe in bed at last, she felt wonderfully grateful for his kindness, and did not at all mind sharing such a secret with him.

Pamela had put a large jug of water by her bed. An hour earlier, it had seemed unnecessary, but now water was all she wanted in the world. She sat up and drank, with a steady, relentless rhythm, as animals drink. Then she slid back into the warm bedclothes and tried to reconstruct in her mind that drive with Guy and became, in doing so, two people, the story teller and the listener; belittling his endearments, only to reassure herself about them. The sports car, the young man (he was not very old, she told herself), the summer darkness, in spite of its being so windy, were all things that other young girls she had known had taken for granted, at Oxford and elsewhere, and she herself had been denied. They seemed all the more miraculous for having been done without for so long.

Of recent years she had often tried to escape the memory of two maiden-ladies who had lived near her home when she and Melanie were girls. So sharp-tongued and cross-looking, they had seemed then as old as could be, yet may have been no more than in their fifties, she now thought. Frumpish and eccentric, at war with one another as well as all their neighbours, they were to be seen tramping the lanes, single-file and in silence, with their dogs. To the girls, they were the most appalling and unenviable creatures, smelling of vinegar, Melanie had said. The recollection of them so long after they were dead disturbed Ursula and depressed her, for she could see how she and Melanie had taken a turning in their direction, yet scarcely anything as definite as this, for there had been no action, no decision; simply, the road they had been on had always, it seemed, been bending in that direction. In no time at all, would they not be copies of those other old ladies? The Misses Rogers, the neighbours would think of them, feeling pity and nervousness. The elder Miss Rogers would be alarmingly abrupt, with her sarcastic voice and old-fashioned swear-words. "They won't be afraid of me," Ursula decided; but had no comfort from the thought. People would think her bullied and would be sorry. She, the plumper one, with her cat and timid smiles, would give biscuits to children when Melanie's back was turned. Inseparable, yet alien to one another, they would become. Forewarned as she was, she felt herself drifting towards that fate and was afraid when she woke at night and thought of it.

Her first drowsiness had worn off and her thirst kept her wakeful. She lay and wondered about the details of Pamela's escape from her parents' sad house and all that had threatened her there—watchfulness, suspicion, envy and capricious humours; much of the kind of thing she herself suffered from Melanie. Pamela's life now was bright and silly, and perhaps she had run away from the best part of herself; but there was nothing in the future to menace her as Ursula was menaced by her own picture of the elderly Misses Rogers.

"But *surely*," insisted the strained and domineering voice. The woman gripped the back of the chair in front of her and stared up at Professor Rybeck on the platform.

At the end of his lecture, he had asked for questions or discussions. To begin with, everyone had seemed too stunned with admiration to make an effort; there were flutterings and murmurings, but for some time no one stood up. Calmly, he waited, sitting there smiling, eyes half-closed and his head cocked a little as if he were listening to secret music, or applause. His arms were crossed over his chest and his legs were crossed too, and one foot swayed back and forth rhythmically.

The minute Mr. Brundle stood up, other people wanted to. He was an elderly, earnest man, who had been doggedly on the track of culture since his youth. His vanity hid from him the half-stifled yawns he evoked, the glassy look of those who, though caught, refused to listen and also his way of melting away to one victim any group of people he approached. Even Professor Rybeck looked restless, as Mr. Brundle began now to pound away at his theory. Then others, in disagreement or exasperation, began to jump to their feet, or made sharp comments, interrupting; even shot their arms into the air, like schoolchildren. World Peace they might have been arguing about, not George Eliot's Dorothea Casaubon.

"Please, please," said Professor Rybeck, in his melodious protesting voice. "Now, Mrs. Thomas, let us hear you."

"But *surely*," Mrs. Thomas said again.

"Wouldn't it be time to say?" asked Mrs. Wetherby—she sounded diffident and had blushed; she had never spoken in the presence of so many people before, but wanted badly to make her mark on the Professor. She was too shy to stand upright and leant forward, lifting her bottom a couple of inches from the chair. Doing so, she dropped her notebook and pencil, her stole slipped off and when she bent down to pick it up she also snatched at some large, tortoise-shell pins that had fallen out of her hair. By the time she had done all this, her chance was gone and she had made her mark in the wrong way. The one and only clergyman in the room had sprung to his feet and, knowing all the tricks needed to command, had snatched off his spectacles and held them high in the air while, for some reason no one was clear about, he denounced Samuel Butler.

"I think, Comrade . . . Professor, I should say," Mr. Brundle interrupted. "If we might return but briefly to the subject . . ."

Melanie closed her eyes and thought how insufferable people became about what has cost them too much to possess—education, money, or even good health.

"Lightly come or not at all, is what I like," she told herself crossly and, when she opened her eyes, glanced up at Professor Rybeck, who smiled with such placid condescension as the ding-dong argument went on between clergyman and atheist (for literature—Victorian or otherwise—had been discarded) and then she looked for Mrs. Rybeck and found her sitting at the end of the second row, still knitting. She gave, somehow, an impression of not being one of the audience, seemed apart from them, preoccupied with her own thoughts, lending her presence only, like a baby-sitter or the invigilator at an examination—well accustomed to the admiration her husband had from other women of her own age, she made it clear that she was one with him in all he did and thought; their agreement, she implied, had come about many years ago and needed no more discussion, and if the women cared to ask her any of the questions he had no time to answer, then she could give the authorised replies. With all this settled, her placidity, like his, was almost startling to other people, their smiling lips (not eyes), their capacity for waiting for others to finish speaking (and it was far removed from the act of listening), is often to be found in the mothers of large families. Yet she was childless. She had only the Professor, and the socks she knitted were for him. She is more goddessy than motherly, Melanie thought.

"We are summoned to the banqueting-hall," said the Professor, raising his hand in the air, as a bell began to ring. This was the warning that lunch would be ready in ten minutes, the Secretary had told them all when they arrived, and "warning" was a word she had chosen well. The smell of minced beef and cabbage came along passages towards them. To Melanie it was unnoticeable, part of daily life, like other tedious affairs; one disposed of the food, as of any other small annoyance, there were jugs of water to wash it down and slices of bread cut hours before that one could crumble as one listened to one's neighbour.

One of Melanie's neighbours was an elementary school-teacher to whom she tried not to be patronising. On her other side was a Belgian woman whose vivacity was intolerable. She was like a bad caricature of a foreigner, primly sporty and full of gay phrases. "Mon Dieu, we have had it, chums," she said, lifting the water-jug and finding it empty. The machine-gun rattle of consonants vibrated in Melanie's head long after she was alone. "Oh, là, là!" the woman sometimes cried, as if she were a cheeky French maid in an old-fashioned farce.

"You think 'Meedlemahtch' is a good book?" she asked Melanie. They all discussed novels at meal-times too; for they were what they had in common.

Melanie was startled, for Professor Rybeck had spent most of the morning explaining its greatness. "It is one of the great English novels," she said.

"As great as Charles Morgan, you think? In the same class?"

Melanie looked suspicious and would not answer.

"It is such a funny book. I read it last night and laughed so much."

"And will read *War and Peace* between tea and dinner, I suppose," the elementary school-teacher murmured. "Oh dear, how disgusting!" She pushed a very pale, boiled caterpillar to the side of her plate. "If that happened to one of our little darlings at school dinner, the mother would write at once to her M.P."

At Melanie's school, the girls would have hidden the creature under a fork in order not to spoil anyone else's appetite, but she did not say so.

"A *funny* book?" she repeated, turning back to the Belgian woman.

"Yes, I like it so much when she thinks that the really delightful marriage must be that where your husband was a sort of father, and could teach you Hebrew if you wished it. Oh, là, là! For heaven's sake."

"Then she did read a page or two," said the woman on Melanie's other side.

A dreadful sadness and sense of loss had settled over Melanie when she herself had read those words. They had not seemed absurd to her; she had felt tears pressing at the back of her eyes. So often, she had longed for protection and compassion, to be instructed and concentrated upon; as if she were a girl again, yet with a new excitement in the air.

As they made their way towards the door, when lunch was over, she could see Professor Rybeck standing there talking to one or two of his admirers. Long before she drew near to him, Melanie found another direction to glance in. What she intended for unconcern, he took for deliberate hostility and wondered at what point of his lecture he had managed to offend her so.

In a purposeless way, she wandered into the garden. The Georgian house—a boys' preparatory-school in the term-time—stood among dark rhododendron bushes and silver birches. Paths led in many directions through the shrubberies, yet all converged upon the lake—a depressing stretch of water, as bleary as an old looking-glass, shadowed by trees and broken by clumps of reeds.

The pain of loneliness was a worse burden to her here than it had ever been at home and she knew—her behaviour as she was leaving the dining-room had reminded her—that the fault was in herself.

"Don't think that I will make excuses to speak to you," she had wanted to imply. "I am not so easily dazzled as these other women." "But I wanted him to speak to me," she thought, "and perhaps I only feared that he would not."

She sat down on the bank above the water and thought about the Professor. She could even imagine his lustrous eyes turned upon her, as he listened.

"I give false impressions," she struggled to explain to him. "In my heart...I am..."

"I know what you are," he said gently. "I knew at once."

The relief would be enormous. She was sure of that. She could live the rest of her life on the memory of that moment.

"But he is a fraud," the other, destructive voice in her insisted, the voice that had ruined so much for her. "He is not a fraud," she said firmly; her lips moved; she needed to be so definite with herself. "Perhaps he cannot find the balance between integrity and priggishness."

"Is that all?" asked the other voice.

The dialogue faded out and she sighed, thinking: "I wish I hadn't come. I feel so much worse here than I do at home."

Coming round the lake's edge towards her was the atrocious little Mr. Brundle. She pretended not to have seen him and got to her feet and went off in the other direction.

By the afternoon post came a letter from Ursula, saying how dull she was and that Melanie had been so right about it all—and that comforted her a little.

Ursula was polishing a glass on a cloth printed with a chart of vintage years for champagne. Although she was drunk, she wondered at the usefulness of this as a reference. It would be strange to go home again to a black telephone, white sheets and drying-up cloths on which there was nothing at all to read, not a recipe for a cocktail or a cheerful slogan.

On the draining-board two white tablets fizzed, as they rose and fell in a glass of water. The noise seemed very loud to her and she was glad when the tablets dissolved and there was silence.

"There you are," Guy said, handing the glass to her. The water still spat and sparkled and she drank it slowly, gasping between sips.

"Pamela will wonder where I am," she said. She put the glass on the draining-board and sat down with a bump on one of the kitchen chairs. She had insisted on washing the two glasses before she went home, and had devoted herself to doing so with single-mindedness; but Guy had been right, and she gave in. Everything she had to do had become difficult—going home, climbing the stairs, undressing. "I shall just have to sit on this chair and let time pass," she decided. "It will pass," she promised herself, "and it mends all in the end."

"Where did we go after that Club?" she suddenly asked frowning.

"Nowhere," said Guy. "On our way back to Pamela's we stopped here for a drink. That's all."

"Ah, yes!"

She remembered the outside of this bungalow and a wooden gate with the name "Hereiam." It had been quite dark when they walked up the stony path to the front door. Now, it seemed the middle of the night. "I think you gave me too much whisky," she said, with a faint, reproachful smile.

"As a matter of fact, I gave you none. It was ginger-ale you were drinking."

She considered this and then lifted her eyes to look at him and asked anxiously: "Then had I had ... was I ... ?"

"You were very sweet."

She accepted this gravely. He put his hands under her arms and brought her to her feet and she rested the side of her face against his waistcoat and stayed very still, as if she were counting his heart-beats. These, like the fizzing drink, also sounded much too loud.

"I didn't wash the other glass," she said.

"Mrs. Lamb can do it in the morning."

She went from one tremulous attempt at defence to another, wanting to blow her nose, or light a cigarette or put something tidy. In the sitting-room, earlier, when he had sat down beside her on the sofa, she had sprung up and gone rapidly across the room to look for an ash-tray. "Who is this?" she had asked, picking up a framed photograph and holding it at arm's length, as if to ward him off. "Girl friend," he said briefly, drinking his whisky and watching her manoeuvres with amusement.

"Haven't you ever wanted to get married?" she had asked.

"Sometimes. Have you?"

"Oh, sometimes . . . I dare say," she answered vaguely.

Now, in the kitchen, he had caught her at last, she was clasped in his arms and feeling odd, she told him.

"I know. There's some coffee nearly ready in the other room. That will do untold good."

What a dreadful man he is, really, in spite of his tenderness, she thought. So hollow and vulgar that I don't know what Melanie would say.

She was startled for a moment, wondering if she had murmured this aloud; for, suddenly, his heartbeat had become noisier—from anger, she was afraid.

"You are very kind," she said appeasingly. "I am not really used to drinking as much as people do here—not used to drinking at all."

"What *are* you used to?"

"Just being rather dull, you know—my sister and I."

His way of lifting her chin up and kissing her was too accomplished and she was reminded of the way in which he drove the car. She was sure that there was something here she should resent. Perhaps he was patronising her; for the kiss had come too soon after her remark about the dullness of her life. I can bring *some* excitement into it, he may have thought.

Without releasing her, he managed to stretch an arm and put out the light. "I can't bear to see you frowning," he explained. "Why frown anyway?"

"That coffee . . . but then I mustn't stay for it, after all. Pamela will be wondering . . ."

"Pam will understand."

"Oh, I hope not."

She frowned more than ever and shut her eyes tightly although the room was completely dark.

Melanie sat on the edge of the bed, coughing. She was wondering if she had suddenly got T.B. and kept looking anxiously at her handkerchief.

The sun was shining, though not into her room. From the window, she could see Professor Rybeck sitting underneath the Wellingtonia with an assortment of his worshippers. From his gestures, Melanie could tell that it was he who was talking, and talking continuously. The hand rose and fell and made languid spirals as he unfolded his theme, or else cut the air decisively into slices. Mrs. Rybeck was, of course, knitting. By her very presence, sitting a little apart from her husband, like a woman minding a stall on a fairground, she attracted passers-by. Melanie watched the Belgian woman now approaching, to say her few words about the knitting, then having paid her fee, to pass on to listen to the Professor.

Desperately, Melanie wished to be down there listening, too; but she had no knowledge of how to join them. Crossing the grass, she would attract too much attention. Ah, *she* cannot keep away, people would think, turning to watch her. She must be in love with the Professor after all, like the other women; but perhaps more secretly, more devouringly.

She had stopped coughing and forgotten tuberculosis for the moment, as she tried to work out some more casual way than crossing the lawn. She might emerge less noticeably from the shrubbery behind the Wellingtonia, if only she could be there in the first place.

She took a clean handkerchief from a drawer and smoothed her hair before the looking-glass; and then a bell rang for tea and, when she went back to the window, the group under the tree was breaking up. Mrs. Rybeck was rolling up her knitting and they were all laughing.

"I shall see him at tea," Melanie thought. She could picture him bowing to her, coldly, and with the suggestion that it was she who disliked him rather than he who disliked her. "I could never put things right now," she decided.

She wondered what Ursula would be doing at this minute. Perhaps sitting in Pamela's little back garden having tea, while, at the front of the house, the patients came and went. She had said that she would be glad to be at home again, for Pamela had changed and they had nothing left in common. "And coming here hasn't been a success, either," Melanie thought, as she went downstairs to tea. She blamed Ursula very much for having made things so dull for them both. There must be ways of showing her how mistaken she had been, ways of preventing anything of the kind happening again.

"Miss Rogers," said the Professor with unusual gaiety. They had almost collided at the drawing-room door. "Have you been out enjoying the sun?" She blushed and was so angry that she should that she said quite curtly, "No, I was writing letters in my room."

He stood quickly aside to let her pass and she did so without a glance at him.

Their holiday was over. On her way back from the station, Ursula called at the kennels for the cat and Melanie, watching her come up the garden path, could see the creature clawing frantically at her shoulder, trying to hoist himself out of her grasp. The taxi-driver followed with the suitcase.

Melanie had intended to be the last home and had even caught a later train than was convenient, in order not to have to be waiting there for her sister. After all her planning, she was angry to have found the house empty.

"Have you been home long?" Ursula asked rather breathlessly. She put the cat down and looked round. Obviously Melanie had not, for her suitcase still stood in the hall and not a letter had been opened.

"Only a minute or two," said Melanie.

"That cat's in a huff with me. Trying to punish me for going away,

I suppose. He's quite plump though. He looks well, doesn't he? Oh, it's so lovely to be home."

She went to the hall-table and shuffled the letters, then threw them on one side. Melanie had said nothing.

"Aren't *you* glad to be home?" Ursula asked her.

"No, I don't think so."

"Well I'm glad you had a good time. It was a change for you."

"Yes."

"And now let's have some tea."

She went into the kitchen and, still wearing her hat, began to get out the cups and saucers. "They didn't leave any bread," she called out. "Oh, yes, it's all right, I've found it." She began to sing, then stopped to chatter to the cat, then sang again.

Melanie had been in the house over an hour and had done nothing.

"I'm so glad you had a good time," Ursula said again, when they were having tea.

"I'm sorry you didn't."

"It was a mistake going there, trying to renew an old friendship. You'd have hated the house."

"You'd have liked *mine*. Grey stone, Georgian, trees and a lake."

"Romantic," Ursula said and did not notice that Melanie locked her hands together in rather a theatrical gesture.

"Pam seems complacent. She's scored over me, having a husband. Perhaps that's why she invited me."

"What did you do all the time?"

"Just nothing. Shopped in the morning—every morning—the house-wife's round—butcher, baker, candlestick maker. 'I'm afraid the piece of skirt was rather gristly, Mr. Bones.' That sort of thing. She would fetch half a pound of butter one day and go back for another half-pound the next morning—just for the fun of it. One day, she said, 'I think we'll have some hock for supper.' I thought she was talking about wine, but it turned out to be some bacon—not very nice. Not very nice of me to talk like this, either."

However dull it had been, she seemed quite excited as she described it; her cheeks were bright and her hands restless.

"We went to the cinema once, to see a Western," she added. "Mike is very fond of Westerns."

"How dreadful for you."

Ursula nodded.

"Well, that's their life," she said. "I was glad all the time that you were not there. Darling puss, so now you've forgiven me."

To show his forgiveness, the cat jumped on to her lap and began dough-punching, his extended claws catching the threads of her skirt.

"Tell me about *you*," Ursula said. She poured out some more tea to sip while Melanie had her turn; but to her surprise Melanie frowned and looked away.

"Is something the matter?"

"I can't talk about it yet, or get used to not being there. This still seems unreal to me. You must give me time."

She got up, knocked over the cream jug and went out of the room. Ursula mopped up the milk with her napkin and then leant back and closed her eyes. Her moment's consternation at Melanie's behaviour had passed; she even forgot it. The cat relaxed, too, and, curled up against her, slept.

Melanie was a long time unpacking and did nothing towards getting supper. She went for a walk along the sea road and watched the sunset on the water. The tide was out and the wet sands were covered with a pink light. She dramatised her solitary walk and was in a worse turmoil when she reached home.

"Your cough is bad," Ursula said when they had finished supper.

"Is it?" Melanie said absent-mindedly.

"Something has happened, hasn't it?" Ursula asked her, and then looked down quickly, as if she were confused.

"The end of the world," said Melanie.

"You've fallen in love?" Ursula lifted her head and stared at her.

"To have to go back to school next week and face those bloody children—and go on facing them, for ever and for ever—or other ones exactly like them . . . the idea suddenly appals me."

Her bitterness was so true, and Ursula could hear her own doom in her sister's words. She had never allowed herself to have thoughts of that kind.

"But can't you . . . can't he?" she began.

"We can't meet again. We never shall. So it *is* the end of the world, you see," said Melanie. The scene gave her both relief and anguish. Her true parting with Professor Rybeck (he had looked up from *The Times* and nodded as she crossed the hall) was obliterated for ever. She could more easily bear the agonised account she now gave to Ursula and she would bear it—their noble resolve, their last illicit embrace.

"He's married, you mean?" Ursula asked bluntly.

"Yes, married."

Mrs. Rybeck, insensitively knitting at the execution of their hopes, appeared as an evil creature, tenacious and sinister.

"But to say good-bye for ever . . ." Ursula protested. "We only have one life . . . would it be wicked, after all?"

"What could there be . . . clandestine meetings and sordid arrangements?"

Ursula looked ashamed.

"I should ruin his career," said Melanie.

"Yes, I see. You could write to one another, though."

"Write!" Melanie repeated in a voice as light as air. "I think I will go to bed now. I feel exhausted."

"Yes, do, and I will bring you a hot drink." As Melanie began to go upstairs, Ursula said, "I am very sorry, you know."

While she was waiting for the milk to rise in the pan, she tried to rearrange her thoughts, especially to exclude (now that there was so much nobility in the house) her own squalid—though hazily recollected—escapade. Hers was a more optimistic nature than Melanie's and she was confident of soon putting such memories out of her mind.

When she took the hot milk upstairs, her sister was sitting up in bed reading a volume of Keats' letters. "He gave it to me as I came away," she explained, laying the book on the bedside table, where it was always to remain.

"We have got this to live with now," Ursula thought, "and it will be with us for ever, I can see—the reason and the excuse for everything. It will even grow; there will be more and more of it, as time goes on. When we are those two elderly Misses Rogers we are growing into it will still be there. 'Miss Melanie, who has such a sharp tongue,' people will say. 'Poor thing . . . a tragic love-affair a long way back.' I shall forget there was a time when we did not have it with us."

Melanie drank her milk and put out the light; then she lay down calmly and closed her eyes and prepared herself for her dreams. Until they came, she imagined walking by the lake, as she had done, that afternoon, only a few days ago; but instead of Mr. Brundle coming into the scene, Professor Rybeck appeared. He walked towards her swiftly, as if by assignation. Then they sat down and looked at the tarnished water—and she added a few swans for them to watch. After a long delicious silence, she began to speak. Yet words were not really necessary. She had hardly begun the attempt; her lips shaped the beginning of a sentence—"I am . . ." and then he took her hand and held it to his cheek. "I know what you are," he said. "I knew at the very beginning."

Although they had parted for ever, she realised that she was now at peace—she felt ennobled and enriched, and saw herself thus, reflected from her sister's eyes, and she was conscious of Ursula's solemn wonder and assured by it.

PERHAPS A FAMILY FAILING

OF COURSE, Mrs. Cotterell cried. Watery-eyed, on the arm of the bride-groom's father, she smiled in a bewildered way to left and right, coming down the aisle. Outside, on the church steps, she quickly dashed the tears away as she faced the camera, still arm-in-arm with Mr. Midwinter, a man she detested.

He turned towards her and gave a great meaningless laugh just as the camera clicked and Mrs. Cotterell had his ginny breath blown full in her face. Even in church he had to smell like that, she thought, and the grim words, "Like father, like son," disturbed her mind once more.

Below them, at the kerb's edge, Geoff was already helping his bride into the car. The solemnity of the service had not touched him. In the vestry, he had been as jaunty as ever, made his wife blush and was hushed by his mother, a frail, pensive creature, who had much, Mrs. Cotterell thought, to be frail and pensive about.

It was Saturday morning and the bridal car moved off slowly among the other traffic. Mrs. Cotterell watched until the white-ribboned motor disappeared.

The bridesmaids, one pink, one apple-green, were getting into the next car. Lissport was a busy place on Saturdays and to many of the women it was part of the morning's shopping-outing to be able to stand for a minute or two to watch a bride coming out of the church. Feeling nervous and self-conscious, Mrs. Cotterell, who had often herself stood and watched and criticised, crossed the pavement to the car. She was anxious to be home and wondered if everything was all right there. She had come away in a flurry of confused directions, leaving two of her neighbours slicing beetroot and sticking blanched almonds into the trifles. She was relieved that the reception was her own affair, that she could be sure that there would be no drunkenness, no rowdy behaviour and suggestive speeches, as there had been at Geoff's sister's wedding last year. One glass of port to drink a toast to the bride and bridegroom she had agreed to. For the rest she hoped that by now her kindly neighbours had mixed the orange cordial.

Mrs. Cotterell cried again, much harder, when Beryl came downstairs in her going-away suit, and kissed her and thanked her (as if her mother were a hostess, not her own flesh and blood, Mrs. Cotterell thought sorrowfully) and with composure got into Geoff's little car, to which Mr. Midwinter had tied an empty sardine-tin.

Then everyone else turned to Mrs. Cotterell and thanked her and praised the food and Beryl's looks and dress. It had all gone off all right, they said, making a great hazard of it. "You'll miss her," the women told her. "I know what it's like," some added.

The bridesmaids took off their flower wreaths and put on their coats. Geoff's brothers, Les and Ron, were taking them out for the evening. "Not long till opening-time," they said.

Mrs. Cotterell went back into the house, to survey the wedding presents, and the broken wedding cake, with the trellis work icing she had done so lovingly, crumbled all over the table. Beryl's bouquet was stuck in a vase, waiting to be taken tomorrow to poor Grandma in hospital.

In the kitchen, the faithful neighbours were still hard at work, washing up the piles of plates stained with beetroot and mustard and tomato sauce.

"She's gone," Mrs. Cotterell whispered into her crumpled handkerchief as her husband came in and put his arm round her.

"Soon be opening-time," Geoff said, driving along the busy road to Seaferry. He had long ago stopped the car, taken the sardine-tin off the back axle and thrown it over a hedge. "Silly old fool, Dad," he had said fondly. "Won't ever act his age."

Beryl thought so, too, but decided not to reopen that old discussion at such a time. For weeks, she had thought and talked and dreamt of the wedding, studied the advice to brides in women's magazines, on make-up, etiquette and Geoff's marital rights—which he must, she learnt, not be allowed to anticipate. "Stop it, Geoff!" she had often said firmly. "I happen to want you to respect me, thank you very much." Unfortunately for her, Geoff was not the respectful kind, although, in his easy-going way, he consented to the celibacy—one of her girlish whims—and had even allowed the gratifying of his desires to be postponed from Easter until early summer, because she had suddenly decided she wanted sweet-peas in the bridesmaids' bouquets.

To the women's magazines Beryl now felt she owed everything; she had had faith in their advice and seen it justified. I expect Geoff's getting excited, she thought. She was really quite excited herself.

"Now where are you going?" she asked, as he swerved suddenly off the road. It was perfectly plain that he was going into a public house, whose front door he had seen flung open just as he was about to pass it by.

"Well, here it is," he said. "The White Horse. The very first pub to have the privilege of serving a drink to Mr. and Mrs. Geoffrey Midwinter."

This pleased her, although she wanted to get to the hotel as quickly as she could, to unpack her trousseau, before it creased too badly.

It was a dull little bar, smelling frowsty. The landlord was glumly watchful, as if they might suddenly get out of hand, or steal one of his cracked ash-trays.

Geoff, however, was in high spirits, and raised his pint pot and winked at his wife. "Well, here's in anticipation," he said. She looked demurely at her gin and orange, but she smiled. She loved him dearly. She was quite convinced of this, for she had filled in a questionnaire on the subject of love in one of her magazines, and had scored eighteen out of twenty, with a rating of "You and Cleopatra share the honours." Only his obsession with public houses worried her, but she was sure that—once she had him away from the influence of his father and brothers—she would be able to break the habit.

At six o'clock Mr. Midwinter took his thirst and his derogatory opinions about the wedding down to the saloon bar of the Starter's Orders. His rueful face, as he described the jugs of orangeade, convulsed his friends. "Poor Geoff, what's he thinking of, marrying into a lot like that?" asked the barmaid.

"Won't make no difference to Geoff," said his father. "Geoff's like his dad. Not given to asking anybody's by-your-leave when he feels like a pint."

Mrs. Midwinter had stayed at home alone. It had not occurred to her husband that she might be feeling flat after the day's excitement. She would not have remarked on it herself, knowing the problem was insoluble. He could not have taken her to a cinema, because Saturday evening was sacred to drinking, and although she would have liked to go with him for a glass of stout, she knew why she could not. He always drank in the Men Only bar at the Starter's Orders. "Well, you don't want me drinking with a lot of prostitutes, do you?" he often asked, and left her no choice, as was his habit.

Beryl had never stayed in an hotel before, and she was full of admiration at the commanding tone Geoff adopted as they entered the hall of the Seaferry Arms.

"Just one before we go up?" he enquired, looking towards the bar.

"Later, dear," she said firmly. "Let's unpack and tidy ourselves first; then we can have a drink before dinner." The word "dinner" depressed him. It threatened to waste a great deal of Saturday evening drinking time.

From their bedroom window they could see a bleak stretch of promenade, grey and gritty. The few people down there either fought their way against the gale, with their heads bowed and coats clutched to their breasts, or seemed tumbled along with the wind at their heels. The sun, having shone on the bride, had long ago gone in and it seemed inconceivable that it would ever come out again.

"No strolling along the prom tonight," said Geoff.

"Isn't it a shame? It's the only thing that's gone wrong."

Beryl began to hang up and spread about the filmy, lacy, ribboned lingerie with which she had for long planned to tease and entice her husband.

"The time you take," he said. He had soon tipped everything out of his own case into a drawer. "What's this?" he asked, picking up something of mauve chiffon.

"My nightgown," she said primly.

"What ever for?"

"Don't be common." She always affected disapproval when he teased her.

"What about a little anticipation here and now?" he suggested.

"Oh, don't be so silly. It's broad daylight."

"Right. Well, I'm just going to spy out the lie of the land. Back in a minute," he said.

She was quite content to potter about the bedroom, laying traps for his seduction; but when she was ready at last, she realised that he had been away a long time. She stood by the window, wondering what to do, knowing that it was time for them to go in to dinner. After a while, she decided that she would have to find him and, feeling nervous and self-conscious, she went along the quiet landing and down the stairs. Her common sense took her towards the sound of voices and laughter and, as soon as she opened the door of the bar, she was given a wonderful welcome from all the new friends Geoff had suddenly made.

"It seems ever so flat, doesn't it?" Mrs. Cotterell said. All of the washing-up was done, but she was too tired to make a start on packing up the presents.

"It's the reaction," her husband said solemnly.

Voices from a play on the wireless mingled with their own, but were ignored. Mrs. Cotterell had her feet in a bowl of hot water. New shoes had given her agony. Beryl, better informed, had practised wearing hers about the house for days before.

"Haven't done my corns any good," Mrs. Cotterell mourned. Her feet ached and throbbed, and so did her heart.

"It all went off well, though, didn't it?" she asked, as she had asked him a dozen times before.

"Thanks to you," he said dutifully. He was clearing out the budgerigar's cage and the bird was sitting on his bald head, blinking and chattering.

Mrs. Cotterell stared at her husband. She suddenly saw him as a completely absurd figure, and she trembled with anger and self-pity. Something ought to have been done for her on such an evening, she thought, some effort should have been made to console and reward her. Instead, she was left to soak her feet and listen to a lot of North Country accents on the radio. She stretched out her hand and switched them off.

"What ever's wrong, Mother?"

"I can't stand any more of that 'By goom' and 'Nowt' and 'Eee, lad.' It reminds me of that nasty cousin Rose of yours."

"But we always listen to the play on a Saturday."

"This Saturday isn't like other Saturdays." She snatched her handkerchief out of her cuff and dabbed her eyes.

Mr. Cotterell leant forward and patted her knee and the budgerigar flew from his head and perched on her shoulder.

"That's right, Joey, you go to Mother. She wants a bit of cheering-up."

"I'm not his mother, if you don't mind, and I don't want cheering-up from a bird."

"One thing I know is you're overtired. I've seen it coming. You wouldn't care to put on your coat and stroll down to the Public for a glass of port, would you?"

"Don't be ridiculous," she said.

After dinner, they drank their coffee, all alone in the dreary lounge of the Seaferry Arms, and then Beryl went to bed. She had secret things to do to her hair and her face. "I'll just pour you out another cup," she said. "Then, when you've drunk it, you can come up."

"Right," he said solemnly, nodding his head.

"Don't be long, darling."

When she had gone, he sat and stared at the cupful of black coffee and then got up and made his way back to the bar.

All of his before-dinner cronies had left and a completely different set of people stood round the bar. He ordered some beer and looked about him.

"Turned chilly," said the man next to him.

"Yes. Disappointing," he agreed. To make friends was the easiest thing in the world. In no time, he was at the heart of it all again.

At ten o'clock, Beryl, provocative in chiffon, as the magazines would have described her, burst into tears of rage. She could hear the laughter—so much louder now, towards closing-time—downstairs in the bar and knew that the sound of it had drawn Geoff back. She was powerless—so transparently tricked out to tempt him—to do anything but lie and wait until, at bar's emptying, he should remember her and stumble upstairs to bed.

It was not the first happy evening Geoff had spent in the bar of the Seaferry Arms. He had called there with the team, after cricket-matches in the nearby villages. Seaferry was only twenty miles from home. Those summer evenings had all merged into one another, as drinking evenings should—and this one was merging with them. "I'm glad I came," he thought, rocking slightly as he stood by the bar with two of his new friends. He couldn't remember having met nicer people. They were a very gay married couple. The wife had a miniature poodle who had already wetted three times on the carpet. "She can't help it, can you, angel?" her mistress protested. "She's quite neurotic; aren't you, precious thing?"

Doris—as Geoff had been told to call her—was a heavy jolly woman. The bones of her stays showed through her frock, her necklace of jet beads was powdered with cigarette ash. She clutched a large, shiny handbag and had snatched from it a pound note, which she began to wave in the air, trying to catch the barmaid's eye. "I say, miss! What's her name, Ted? Oh, yes. I say, Maisie! Same again, there's a dear girl."

It was nearly closing-time, and a frenzied reordering was going on. The street door was pushed open and a man and woman with a murderous-looking bull terrier came in. "You stay there," the man said to the woman and the dog, and he left them and began to force his way towards the bar.

"Miss! Maisie!" Doris called frantically. Her poodle, venturing between people's legs, made another puddle under a table and approached the bull terrier.

"I say, Doris, call Zoë back," said her husband. "And put that money away. I told you I'll get these."

"I insist. They're on me."

"Could you call your dog back?" the owner of the bull terrier asked them. "We don't want any trouble."

"Come, Zoë, pet!" Doris called. "He wouldn't hurt her, though. She's a bitch. Maisie! Oh, there's a dear. Same again, love. Large ones."

Suddenly, a dreadful commotion broke out. Doris was nearly knocked off her stool as Zoë came flying back to her for protection, with the bull terrier at her throat. She screamed and knocked over somebody's gin.

Geoff, who had been standing by the bar in a pleasurable haze, watching the barmaid, was, in spite of his feeling of unreality, the first to spring to life and pounce upon the bull terrier and grab his collar. The dog bit his hand, but he was too drunk to feel much pain. Before anyone could snatch Zoë out of danger, the barmaid lifted the jug of water and meaning to pour it over the bull terrier, flung it instead over Geoff. The shock made him loosen his grip and the fight began again. A second time he grabbed at the collar and had his hand bitten once more; but now—belatedly, everyone else thought—the two dog-owners came to his help. Zoë, with every likelihood of being even more neurotic in the future, was put, shivering, in her mistress's arms, the bull terrier was secured to his lead in disgrace, and Maisie called Time.

After some recriminations between themselves, the dog-owners thanked and congratulated Geoff. "Couldn't get near them," they said. "The bar was so crowded. Couldn't make head or tail of what was going on."

"Sorry you got so wet," said Doris.

The bull terrier's owner felt rather ashamed of himself when he saw how pale Geoff was. "You all right?" he asked. "You look a bit shaken up."

Geoff examined his hand. There was very little blood, but he was beginning to be aware of the pain and felt giddy. He shook his head, but could not answer. Something dripped from his hair on to his forehead, and when he dabbed it with his handkerchief, he was astonished to see water and not blood.

"You got far to go?" the man asked him. "Where's your home?"

"Lissport."

"That's our way, too, if you want a lift." Whether Geoff had a car or not, the man thought he was in no condition to drive it; although, whether from shock or alcohol or both, it was difficult to decide.

"I'd *like* a lift," Geoff murmured drowsily. "Many thanks."

"No, any thanks are due to *you*."

"Doesn't it seem strange without Geoff?" Mrs. Midwinter asked her husband. He was back from the Starter's Orders, had taken off his collar and tie and was staring gloomily at the dying fire.

"Les and Ron home yet?" he asked.

"No, they won't be till half-past twelve. They've gone to the dance at the Town Hall."

"Half-past twelve! It's scandalous the way they carry on. Drinking themselves silly, I've no doubt at all. Getting decent girls into trouble."

"It's only a dance, Dad."

"*And* their last one. I'm not having it. Coming home drunk on a Sunday morning and lying in bed till all hours to get over it. When was either of them last at Chapel? Will you tell me that?"

Mrs. Midwinter sighed and folded up her knitting.

"I can't picture why Geoff turned from Chapel like that." Mr. Midwinter seemed utterly depressed about his sons, as he often was at this time on a Saturday night.

"Well, he was courting..."

"First time I've been in a church was today, and I was not impressed."

"I thought it was lovely, and you looked your part just as if you did it every day."

"I wasn't worried about *my* part. Sort of thing like that makes no demands on *me*. What I didn't like was the service, to which I took exception, and that namby-pamby parson's voice. To me, the whole thing was—insincere."

Mrs. Midwinter held up her hand to silence him. "There's a car stopping outside. It can't be the boys yet."

From the street, they both heard Geoff's voice shouting goodbye, then a car door was slammed, and the iron gate opened with a whining sound.

"Dad, it's Geoff!" Mrs. Midwinter whispered. "There must have been an accident. Something's happened to Beryl."

"Well, he sounded cheerful enough about it."

They could hear Geoff coming unsteadily up the garden path. When Mrs. Midwinter threw open the door, he stood blinking at the sudden light, and swaying.

"Geoff! What ever's wrong?"

"I've got wet, Mum, and I've hurt my hand," Geoff said.

YOU'LL ENJOY IT
WHEN YOU GET THERE

"SHYNESS is *common*," Rhoda's mother insisted. "I was never *allowed* to be shy when I was a girl. Your grandparents would soon have put a stop to *that*."

The stressed words sounded so peevish. Between each sentence she refreshed herself with a sip of invalid's drink, touched her lips with her handkerchief, and then continued.

"Self-consciousness it was always called when I was young, and that is what it is. To imagine that it shows a sense of modesty is absurd. *Modesty*. Why, I have never known a *truly* modest person to be the least bit shy."

The jaundice, which had discoloured her face and her eyes, seemed as well to wash all her words in poison.

"It's all right for you, Mother," Rhoda said. "You can drink. Then anyone can talk."

Mrs. Hobart did not like to be reminded that she drank at all: that she drank immoderately, no one—she herself least of all—would ever have dared to remind her.

Rhoda, who was sitting by the window, nursing her cat, stared down at the gardens in the square and waited huffily for an indignant rebuke. Instead, her mother said wearily: "Well, you will have a drink, too, before the banquet, and no nonsense. A 'girl of eighteen.'"

"I hate the taste."

"I, I, I. I hate this; I loathe that. What do you think would have happened if *I* had considered what *I* liked through all these years. Or the Queen," she added. "The poor girl! The rubbish she's been forced to eat and drink in foreign countries. And never jibbed."

"You and the Queen are different kettles of fish from me," Rhoda said calmly. Then she threw up the window from the bottom and leant out and waved to her father, who was crossing the road below.

"Please shut that window," Mrs. Hobart said. "Leaning out and waving, like a housemaid. I despair." She put the glass of barley-water on one side and said again: "I despair."

"There is no need. I will do my best," said Rhoda. "Though no one likes to be frightened in quite such a boring way."

She sat in the train opposite her father and wedged in by businessmen. In books and films, she thought, people who go on train journeys always get a corner seat.

In a corner, she could have withdrawn into her day-dreaming so much more completely; but she was cramped by the fat men on either side, whose thighs moved against hers when they uncrossed and recrossed their legs, whose newspapers distracted her with their puzzling headlines—for instance "Bishop Exorcises £5,000 Ghost," she read. Her father, with his arms folded neatly across his chest, dozed and nodded, and sometimes his lips moved as if he were rehearsing his speech for that evening. They seemed to have been in the train for a long time, and the phlegmy fog, which had pressed to the windows as they left London, was darkening quickly. The dreadful moment of going in to dinner was coming nearer. Her father suddenly woke up and lifted his head. He yawned and winked a watery eye at her, and yawned and yawned again. She sensed that to be taking his daughter instead of his wife to what her mother called the Trade Banquet made it seem rather a spree to him and she wished that she could share his light-heartedness.

Like sleepwalkers, the other people in the compartment, still silent and drowsy, began now to fold their newspapers, look for their tickets, lift down their luggage from the racks. The train's rhythm changed and the lights of the station came running past the windows. All that Rhoda was to see of this Midlands town was the dark, windy space between the station entrance and the great station hotel as they followed a porter across the greasy paving-stones and later, a glimpse from her bedroom window of a timber-yard beside a canal.

When she was alone in the hotel bedroom, she felt more uncertain than ever, oppressed by the null effect of raspberry-coloured damask, the large intolerable pieces of furniture and the silence, which only sounds of far-away plumbing broke, or of distant lifts rising and falling.

She shook out her frock and was hanging it in a cavernous wardrobe when somebody in the corridor outside tapped on the door. "Is that you, Father?" she called out anxiously. A waiter came in, carrying a tray high in the air. He swirled it round on his fingers and put down a glass of sherry.

"The gentleman in number forty-five ordered it," he explained.

"Thank you," Rhoda said timidly, peeping at him round the wardrobe door, "very much," she added effusively.

The waiter said, "Thank *you*, madam," in a quelling voice, and went away.

Rhoda sniffed at the sherry, and then tipped it into the wash-basin. "I suppose Father's so used to Mamma," she thought. She knew the bedroom imbibing that went on, as her mother moved heavily about, getting dressed: every time she came back to her mirror, she would take a drink from the glass beside it.

The hotel room was a vacuum in which even time had no reality to Rhoda. With no watch to tell her, she began to wonder if she had been there alone for ten minutes or an hour and in sudden alarm she ran to the bathroom and turned on taps and hurriedly unpacked.

She put on a little confidence with her pretty frock; but, practising radiant smiles in the looking-glass, she was sure that they were only grimaces. She smoothed on her long white gloves and took up her satin bag, then heard a distant clock, somewhere across the roofs of high buildings, strike the half-hour and knew that she must wait all through the next, matching half-hour for her father to come to fetch her.

As she waited, shivering as she paced about the room, growing more and more goose-fleshed, she saw the reasonableness in her father's thought about the sherry and wished that she had not wasted it and, even more, that she had lain twenty minutes longer in her warm bath.

He came as the clock struck out the hours and, when she ran and opened the door to him, said: "Heavens, ma'am, how exquisite you look!"

They descended the stairs.

In the reception-room, another waiter circled with a tray of filled glasses. Four people stood drinking by the fire—two middle-aged men, one wearing a mayoral chain, the other a bosomful of medals; and two middle-aged women, stiffly corseted, their hair set in tight curls and ridges. Diamonds shone on their freckled chests and pink carnations slanted heads downwards across their bodices. They look as if they know the ropes, thought Rhoda, paralysed with shyness. They received her kindly, but in surprise. "Why, where is Ethel?" they asked her father, and they murmured in concern over the jaundice and said how dreary it must be to be on the waggon. "Especially for her," the tone of their voices seemed to Rhoda to suggest.

A bouquet was taken from a little side table and handed to Rhoda, who held it stiffly at her waist where it contended fiercely with the colour of her dress.

The six of them were, in their importance, shut off from a crowded bar where other guests were drinking cocktails: on this side of the door there was an air of confidence and expectation, of being ahead of the swim, Rhoda thought. She wished passionately, trying to sip away her sherry, that she might spend the entire evening shut away from the hordes of strangers in the bigger room but, only too soon, a huge toast-master, fussing with his white gloves, brought the three couples into line and then threw wide the doors; inclining his head patronisingly to guest after guest, he bawled out some semblance of the names they proffered. As the first ones came reluctantly forward from the gaiety of the bar, Mr. Hobart leant towards Rhoda and took the glass from her hand and put it on the tray with the others. "How do you do," she whispered, shaking hands with an old gentleman, who was surprised to see that her eyes were filled with tears.

"You are deputising for your dear mother?" he asked. "And very charmingly you do it, my dear," he added, and passed on quickly, so that she could brush her wet lashes with her gloved hand.

"Good-evening, Rhoda." The bracing mockery of this new voice jolted her, the voice of Digby Lycett Senior, as she always called him in her mind—the mind which for months had been conquered and occupied by Digby Lycett Junior. This unexpected appearance was disastrous to her. She felt indignantly that he had no right to be there, so remotely connected was he with the trade the others had in common. "Nice of you to come," her father was now telling him. They were old business friends. It was Digby Lycett who sold her father the machinery for making Hobart's Home-made Cookies. It was *loathsome* of you to come, Rhoda thought, unhappily.

She took one gloved hand after another, endlessly—it seemed—confronted by pink carnations and strings of pearls. But the procession dwindled at last—the stragglers, who had lingered over their drinks till the last moment, were rounded up by the toast-master and sent resignedly on their way to the banqueting-hall, where an orchestra was playing "Some Enchanted Evening" above the noise of chairs being scraped and voices mounting in volume like a gathering wave.

In the reception-room, the Mayor straightened the chain on his breast. One duty done, he now prepared to go on to the next. All of his movements were certain and automatic; every evening of his life, they implied, he had a hall full of people waiting for him to take his seat.

As she moved towards the door a sense of vertigo and nausea overcame Rhoda, confronted by the long walk to her place and the ranks of pink faces turned towards her. With bag and bouquet and skirt to manage, she felt that she was bundling along with downcast eyes. Before a great heap of flowers on the table, they stopped. The Mayor was humming very softly to the music. He put on his spectacles, peered at the table and then laid his hand on the back of a gilt chair, indicating that here, next to him, Rhoda was to be privileged to sit.

At the doors, waitresses crowded ready to rush forward with *hors d'oeuvres.* The music faded. Without raising her eyes, instinctively, wishing to sink out of sight, Rhoda slid round her chair and sat upon it.

Down crashed the toast-master's gavel as the Mayor, in a challenging voice, began to intone Grace. Mr. Hobart put his hand under Rhoda's elbow and brought her, lurching, as she could not help doing, to her feet again. The gilt chair tipped, but he saved it from going over, the bouquet shot under the table and Rhoda prayed that she might follow it.

"Please God, let me faint. Let me never have to look up again and meet anybody's glance."

"*Now* you can, young lady," the Mayor said, helping her down again. Then he turned quickly to the woman on his other side and began a conversation. Rhoda's father had done the same. Sitting between them, she swallowed sardines and olives and her bitter, bitter tears. After a time, her isolation made her defiant. She lifted her head and looked boldly and crossly in front of her, and caught the eye of Digby Lycett Senior, just as he raised a fork to his mouth, and smiled at her, sitting not far across the room, at right angles to her table, where he could perfectly observe her humiliation and record it for his son's interest and amusement later. "Poor old Rhoda"—she could hear the words, overlaid with laughter.

She ate quickly, as if she had not touched food for weeks. Once, her father, fingering a wine-glass restlessly, caught and held as he was in conversation by the relentless woman at his side, managed to turn his head for a moment and smile at Rhoda. "All right?" he asked, and nodded his own answer, for it was a great treat for a young girl, he implied—the music, the flowers, the pretty dress, the wine.

Someone *must* talk to me, she thought, for it seemed to her that, through lack of conversation, her expression was growing sullen. She tried to reorganise her features into a look of animation or calm pleasure. She drank a plate of acid-tasting, red soup to its dregs. Chicken followed turbot, as her mother had assured her was inevitable. The Mayor, who went through the same menu nearly every evening, left a great deal on his plate; he scattered it about for a while and then tidied it up: not so Rhoda, who, against a great discomfort of fullness, plodded painstakingly on.

At last, as she was eating some cauliflower, the Mayor turned his moist, purple face towards her. She lifted her eyes to the level of the chain on his breast and agreed with him that she was enjoying herself enormously.

"It is my first visit to Norley," she said gaily, conscious of Digby Lycett Senior's eyes upon her. She hoped that he would think from her expression that some delicious pleasantry was in progress. To keep the Mayor in conversation she was determined. He should not turn away again and Digby Lycett, Senior or Junior, should not have the impression that she sat in silence and disgrace from the beginning to the end.

"But I have a cat who came from here," she added.

The Mayor looked startled.

"A Burmese cat. A man in Norley—a Doctor Fisher—breeds them. Do you know Doctor Fisher?"

"I can't say that I do."

He was plainly unwilling for her to go on. On his other side was feminine flattery and cajolery and he wished to turn back for more, and Rhoda and her cat were of no interest to him.

"Have you ever seen a Burmese cat?" she asked.

He crumbled some bread and looked cross and said that as far as he knew he never had.

"He came to London on the train all by himself in a little basket," Rhoda said. "The cat, I mean, of course. Minkie, I call him. Such a darling, you can't imagine."

She smiled vivaciously for Digby Lycett Senior's benefit; but, try as she might, she could not summon the courage to lift her eyes any higher than the splendid chain on the Mayor's breast, for she shrank from the look of contempt she was afraid he might be wearing.

"They are rather like Siamese cats," she went on. "Though they are brown all over and have golden eyes, not blue."

"Oh?" said the Mayor. He had to lean a little nearer to her as a waitress put a dish of pistachio ice-cream over his left shoulder.

"But rather the same natures, if you know what I mean," said Rhoda.

"I'm afraid I don't care for cats," said the Mayor, in the voice of simple pride in which this remark is always made.

"On all your many social commitments," the woman on his other side said loudly, rescuing him, "which flavour of ice-cream crops up most often?"

He laughed and turned to her with relief. "Vanilla," he said jovially. "In a ratio of eight to one."

"Enjoying yourself?" Rhoda's father asked her later, as they danced a foxtrot together. "I dare say this is the part of the evening that appeals to you—not all those long-winded speeches."

It appealed to Rhoda because it was nearer to the end, and for no other reason.

"You seemed to be getting on well with the Mayor," Mr. Hobart added.

The Mayor had disappeared. Rhoda could see no sign of his glittering chain and she supposed that he disliked dancing as much as he disliked cats. She prayed that Digby Lycett Senior might not ask her to do the Old Fashioned Waltz which followed. She was afraid of his mocking smile and, ostrich-like, opened her bag and looked inside it as he approached.

Another middle-aged man stepped forward first and asked to have the pleasure in a voice which denied the possibility of there being any. Rhoda guessed that what he meant was "May I get this duty over and done with, pursued as it is as a mark of the esteem in which I hold your father." And Rhoda smiled as if she were enchanted, and rose and put herself into his arms, as if he were her lover.

He made the waltz more old-fashioned than she had ever known it, dancing stiffly, keeping his stomach well out of her way, humming, but not saying a word to her. She was up against a great silence this evening: to her it was the measure of her failure. Sorting through her mind for something to say, she rejected remarks about the floor and the band and said instead that she had never been to Norley before. The observation should have led somewhere, she thought; but it did not: it was quite ignored.

"But I have a cat who came from here," she added. "A little Burmese cat."

When he did not answer this, either, she thought that he must be deaf and raised her voice. "There is a doctor here who breeds them. Perhaps you have come across him—a Doctor Fisher."

"No, I can't say that I have."

"He sent the kitten to London by train, in a little basket. So pretty and gay. Minkie, I call him. Have you ever seen a Burmese cat?" She could not wait for his answers, lest they never came. "They are not a usual sort of cat at all. Rather like a Siamese in many ways, but brown all over and with golden eyes instead of blue. They are similar in nature though, if you can understand what I mean."

He either could not, or was not prepared to try and at last, mercifully, the music quickened and finally snapped off altogether. Flushed and smiling, she was escorted back to her father who was standing by the bar, looking genial and indulgent.

Her partner's silence seemed precautionary now. He handed her over with a scared look, as if she were some dangerous lunatic. Her father, not noticing this, said: "You are having quite a success with your Mayor, my dear."

"My Mayor?"

She turned quickly and looked after the man who had just left her. He was talking to a little group of people; they all had their heads together and were laughing.

"He took that chain off then?" she said, feeling sick and dazed. It was all she had had to distinguish him from the rest of the bald-headed and obese middle-aged men.

"You couldn't expect him to dance with that hanging round his neck—not even in your honour," her father said. "And now, I shall fetch you a long, cool drink, for you look as if the dancing has exhausted you."

GIRL READING

ETTA's desire was to belong. Sometimes she felt on the fringe of the family, at other times drawn headily into its very centre. At meal-times—those occasions of argument and hilarity, of thrust and counterstroke, bewildering to her at first—she was especially on her mettle, turning her head alertly from one to another as if watching a fast tennis match. She hoped soon to learn the art of riposte and already used, sometimes unthinkingly, family words and phrases; and had one or two privately treasured memories of even having made them laugh. They delighted in laughing and often did so scoffingly—"at the expense of those less fortunate" as Etta's mother would sententiously have put it.

Etta and Sarah were school-friends. It was not the first time that Etta had stayed with the Lippmanns in the holidays. Everyone understood that the hospitality would not be returned, for Etta's mother, who was widowed, went out to work each day. Sarah had seen only the outside of the drab terrace house where her friend lived. She had persuaded her elder brother, David, to take her spying there one evening. They drove fifteen miles to Market Swanford and Sarah, with great curiosity, studied the street names until at last she discovered the house itself. No one was about. The street was quite deserted and the two rows of houses facing one another were blank and silent as if waiting for a hearse to appear. "Do hurry!" Sarah urged her brother. It had been a most dangerous outing and she was thoroughly depressed by it. Curiosity now seemed a trivial sensation compared with the pity she was feeling for her friend's drab life and her shame at having confirmed her own suspicions of it. She was threatened by tears. "Aren't you going in?" her brother asked in great surprise. "Hurry, hurry," she begged him. There had never been any question of her calling at that house.

"She must be very lonely there all through the holidays, poor Etta," she thought, and could imagine hour after hour in the dark house. Bickerings with the daily help she had already heard of and—Etta trying to put on a brave face and make much of nothing—trips to the public library the highlight of the day, it seemed. No wonder that her holiday reading was always so carefully done, thought Sarah, whereas she herself could never snatch a moment for it except at night in bed.

Sarah had a lively conscience about the seriousness of her friend's private world. Having led her more than once into trouble, at school, she had always afterwards felt a disturbing sense of shame; for Etta's work was more important than her own could ever be, too important to be interrupted by escapades. Sacrifices had been made and scholarships must be won. Once—it was a year ago when they were fifteen and had less sense—Sarah had thought up some rough tomfoolery and Etta's blazer had been torn. She was still haunted by her friend's look of consternation. She had remembered too late, as always—the sacrifices that had been made, the widowed mother sitting year after year at her office desk, the holidays that were never taken and the contriving that had to be done.

Her own mother was so warm and worldly. If she had anxieties she kept them to herself, setting the pace of gaiety, up to date and party-loving. She was popular with her friends' husbands who, in their English way, thought of her comfortably as nearly as good company as a man and full of bright ways as well. Etta felt safer with her than with Mr. Lippmann, whose enquiries were often too probing; he touched nerves, his jocularity could be an embarrassment. The boys—Sarah's elder brothers—had their own means of communication which their mother unflaggingly strove to interpret and, on Etta's first visit, she had tried to do so for her, too.

She *was* motherly, although she looked otherwise, the girl decided. Lying in bed at night, in the room she shared with Sarah, Etta would listen to guests driving noisily away or to the Lippmanns returning, full of laughter, from some neighbour's house. Late night door-slamming in the country disturbed only the house's occupants, who all contributed to it. Etta imagined them pottering about downstairs—husband and wife, would hear bottles clinking, laughter, voices raised from room to room, good-night endearments to cats and dogs and at last Mrs. Lippmann's running footsteps on the stairs and the sound of her jingling bracelets coming nearer. Outside their door she would pause, listening, wondering if they were asleep already. They never were. "Come in!" Sarah would shout, hoisting herself up out of the bed clothes on one elbow, her face turned expectantly towards the door, ready for laughter—for something amusing would surely have happened. Mrs. Lippmann, sitting on one of the beds, never failed them. When they were children, Sarah said, she brought back *petits fours* from parties; now she brought back *faux pas*. She specialised in little stories against herself—Mummy's Humiliations, Sarah named them—tactless things she had said, never-to-be-remedied remarks which sprang fatally from her lips. Mistakes in identity was her particular line, for she never remembered a face, she declared. Having kissed Sarah, she would bend over Etta to do the same. She smelt of scent and gin and cigarette smoke. After this they would go to sleep. The house would be completely quiet for several hours.

Etta's mother had always had doubts about the suitability of this *ménage*. She knew it only at second hand from her daughter, and Etta said very little about her visits and that little was only in reply to obviously resented questions. But she had a way of looking about her with boredom when she returned, as if she had made the transition unwillingly and incompletely. She hurt her mother—who wished only to do everything in the world for her, having no one else to please or protect.

"I should feel differently if we were able to return the hospitality," she told Etta. The Lippmanns' generosity depressed her. She knew that it was despicable to feel jealous, left out, kept in the dark, but she tried to rationalise her feelings before Etta. "I could take a few days off and invite Sarah here," she suggested.

Etta was unable to hide her consternation and her expression deeply wounded her mother. "I shouldn't know what to do with her," she said.

"Couldn't you go for walks? There are the Public Gardens. And take her to the cinema one evening. What do you do at *her* home?"

"Oh, just fool about. Nothing much." Some afternoons they just lay on their beds and ate sweets, keeping all the windows shut and the wireless on loud, and no one ever disturbed them or told them they ought to be out in the fresh air. Then they had to plan parties and make walnut fudge and de-flea the dogs. Making fudge was the only one of these things she could imagine them doing in her own home and they could not do it all the time. As for the dreary Public Gardens, she could not herself endure the asphalt paths and the bandstand and the beds of salvias. She could imagine vividly how dejected Sarah would feel.

Early in these summer holidays, the usual letter had come from Mrs. Lippmann. Etta, returning from the library, found that the charwoman had gone early and locked her out. She rang the bell, but the sound died away and left an even more forbidding silence. All the street, where elderly people dozed in stuffy rooms, was quiet. She lifted the flap of the letter-box and called through it. No one stirred or came. She could just glimpse an envelope, lying face up on the doormat, addressed in Mrs. Lippmann's large, loopy, confident handwriting. The house-stuffiness wafted through the letter-box. She imagined the kitchen floor slowly drying, for there was a smell of soapy water. A tap was steadily dripping.

She leant against the door, waiting for her mother's return, in a sickness of impatience at the thought of the letter lying there inside. Once or twice, she lifted the flap and had another look at it.

Her mother came home at last, very tired. With an anxious air, she set about cooking supper, which Etta had promised to have ready. The letter was left among her parcels on the kitchen table, and not until they had finished their stewed rhubarb did she send Etta to fetch it. She opened it carefully with the bread knife and deepened the frown on her forehead in preparation for reading it. When she had, she gave Etta a summary of its contents and put forward her objections, her unnerving proposal.

"She wouldn't come," Etta said. "She wouldn't leave her dog."

"But, my dear, she has to leave him when she goes back to school."

"I know. That's the trouble. In the holidays she likes to be with him as much as possible, to make up for it."

Mrs. Salkeld, who had similar wishes about her daughter, looked sad. "It is too one-sided," she gently explained. "You must try to understand how I feel about it."

"They're only too glad to have me. I keep Sarah company when they go out."

They obviously went out a great deal and Mrs. Salkeld suspected that they were frivolous. She did not condemn them for that—they must lead their own lives, but those were in a world which Etta would never be able to afford the time or money to inhabit. "Very well, Musetta," she said, removing the girl further from her by using her full name—used only on formal and usually menacing occasions.

That night she wept a little from tiredness and depression—from disappointment, too, at the thought of returning in the evenings to the dark and empty house, just as she usually did, but when she had hoped for company. They were not healing tears she shed and they did nothing but add self-contempt to her other distresses.

A week later, Etta went the short distance by train to stay with the Lippmanns. Her happiness soon lost its edge of guilt, and once the train had rattled over the iron bridge that spanned the broad river, she felt safe in a different country. There seemed to be even a different weather, coming from a wider sky, and a riverside glare—for the curves of the railway line brought it close to the even more winding course of the river, whose silver loops could be glimpsed through the trees. There were islands and backwaters and a pale heron standing on a patch of mud.

Sarah was waiting at the little station and Etta stepped down on to the platform as if taking a footing into promised land. Over the station and the gravelly lane outside hung a noonday quiet. On one side were grazing meadows, on the other side the drive gateways of expensive houses. The Gables was indeed gabled and so was its boat-house. It was also turreted and balconied. There was a great deal of woodwork painted glossy white, and a huge-leaved Virginia creeper covered much of the red-brick walls—in the front beds were the sal-vias and lobelias Etta had thought she hated. Towels and swim-suits hung over balcony rails and a pair of tennis-shoes had been put out on a window-sill to dry. Even though Mr. Lippmann and his son, David, went to London every day, the house always had—for Etta—a holiday atmosphere.

The hall door stood open and on the big round table were the stacks of new magazines which seemed to her the symbol of extrava-gance and luxury. At the back of the house, on the terrace overlook-ing the river, Mrs. Lippmann, wearing tight, lavender pants and a purple shirt, was drinking vodka with a neighbour who had called for a subscription to some charity. Etta was briefly enfolded in scented silk and tinkling bracelets and then released and introduced. Sarah gave her a red, syrupy drink and they sat down on the warm steps among the faded clumps of aubretia and rocked the ice cubes to and fro in their glasses, keeping their eyes narrowed to the sun.

Mrs. Lippmann gossiped, leaning back under a fringed chair-umbrella. She enjoyed exposing the frailties of her friends and family, although she would have been the first to hurry to their aid in trou-ble. Roger, who was seventeen, had been worse for drink the previous evening, she was saying. Faced with breakfast, his face had been a study of disgust which she now tried to mimic. And David could not eat, either; but from being in love. She raised her eyes to heaven most dramatically, to convey that great patience was demanded of her.

"He eats like a horse," said Sarah. "Etta, let's go upstairs." She took Etta's empty glass and led her back across the lawn, seeming not to care that her mother would without doubt begin to talk about her the moment she had gone.

Rich and vinegary smells of food came from the kitchen as they crossed the hall. (There was a Hungarian cook to whom Mrs. Lippmann spoke in German and a Portuguese "temporary" to whom she spoke in Spanish.) The food was an important part of the holiday to Etta, who had nowhere else eaten *Sauerkraut* or *Apfelstrudel* or cold fried fish, and she went into the dining-room each day with a sense of adventure and anticipation.

On this visit she was also looking forward to the opportunity of making a study of people in love—an opportunity she had not had before. While she unpacked, she questioned Sarah about David's Nora, as she thought of her; but Sarah would only say that she was quite a good sort with dark eyes and an enormous bust, and that as she was coming to dinner that evening, as she nearly always did, Etta would be able to judge for herself.

While they were out on the river all the afternoon—Sarah rowing her in a dinghy along the reedy backwater—Etta's head was full of love in books, even in those holiday set books Sarah never had time for—*Sense and Sensibility* this summer. She felt that she knew what to expect, and her perceptions were sharpened by the change of air and scene, and the disturbing smell of the river, which she snuffed up deeply as if she might be able to store it up in her lungs. "Mother thinks it is polluted," Sarah said when Etta lifted a streaming hand from trailing in the water and brought up some slippery weeds and held them to her nose. They laughed at the idea.

Etta, for dinner, put on the liberty silk they wore on Sunday evenings at school and Sarah at once brought out her own hated garment from the back of the cupboard where she had pushed it out of sight on the first day of the holidays. When they appeared downstairs, they looked unbelievably dowdy, Mrs. Lippmann thought, turning away for a moment because her eyes had suddenly pricked with tears at the sight of her kind daughter.

Mr. Lippmann and David returned from Lloyd's at half-past six and with them brought Nora—a large, calm girl with an air of brittle indifference towards her fiancé which disappointed but did not deceive Etta, who knew enough to remain undeceived by banter. To interpret from it the private tendernesses it hid was part of the mental exercise she was to be engaged in. After all, David would know better than to have his heart on his sleeve, especially in this *dégagé* family where nothing seemed half so funny as falling in love.

After dinner, Etta telephoned her mother, who had perhaps been waiting for the call, as the receiver was lifted immediately. Etta imagined her standing in the dark and narrow hall with its smell of umbrellas and furniture polish.

"I thought you would like to know I arrived safely."

"What have you been doing?"

"Sarah and I went to the river. We have just finished dinner." Spicy smells still hung about the house. Etta guessed that her mother would have had half a tin of sardines and put the other half by for her breakfast. She felt sad for her and guilty herself. Most of her thoughts about her mother were deformed by guilt.

"What have you been doing?" she asked.

"Oh, the usual," her mother said brightly. "I am just turning the collars and cuffs of your winter blouses. By the way, don't forget to pay Mrs. Lippmann for the telephone call."

"No. I shall have to go now. I just thought . . ."

"Yes, of course, dear. Well, have a lovely time."

"We are going for a swim when our dinner has gone down."

"Be careful of cramp, won't you? But I mustn't fuss from this distance. I know you are in good hands. Give my kind regards to Mrs. Lippmann and Sarah, will you, please. I must get back to your blouses."

"I wish you wouldn't bother. You must be tired."

"I am perfectly happy doing it," Mrs. Salkeld said. But if that were so, it was unnecessary, Etta thought, for her to add, as she did: "And someone has to do it."

She went dully back to the others. Roger was strumming on a guitar, but he blushed and put it away when Etta came into the room.

As the days went quickly by, Etta thought that she was belonging more this time than ever before. Mr. Lippmann, a genial patriarch, often patted her head when passing, in confirmation of her existence, and Mrs. Lippmann let her run errands. Roger almost wistfully sought her company, while Sarah disdainfully discouraged him; for they had their own employments, she implied; her friend—"my best friend," as she introduced Etta to lesser ones or adults—could hardly be expected to want the society of schoolboys. Although he was a year older than themselves, being a boy he was less sophisticated, she explained. She and Etta considered themselves to be rather worldly-wise—Etta having learnt from literature and Sarah from putting two and two together, her favourite pastime. Her parents seemed to her to behave with the innocence of children, unconscious of their motives, so continually betraying themselves to her experienced eye, when knowing more would have made them guarded. She had similarly put two and two together about Roger's behaviour to Etta, but she kept these conclusions to herself—partly from not wanting to make her friend feel self-conscious and partly—for she scorned self-deception—from what she recognised to be jealousy. She and Etta were very well as they were, she thought.

Etta herself was too much absorbed by the idea of love to ever think of being loved. In this house, she had her first chance of seeing it at first hand and she studied David and Nora with such passionate speculation that their loving seemed less their own than hers. At first, she admitted to herself that she was disappointed. Their behaviour fell short of what she required of them; they lacked a romantic attitude to one another and Nora was neither touching nor glorious—neither Viola nor Rosalind. In Etta's mind to be either was satisfactory; to be boisterous and complacent was not. Nora was simply a plump and genial girl with a large bust and a faint moustache. She could not be expected to inspire David with much gallantry and, in spite of all the red roses he brought her from London, he was not above telling her that she was getting fat. Gaily retaliatory, she would threaten him with the bouquet, waving it about his head, her huge engagement ring catching the light, flashing with different colours, her eyes flashing too.

Sometimes, there was what Etta's mother would have called

"horseplay," and Etta herself deplored the noise, the dishevelled romping. "We know quite well what it's instead of," said Sarah. "But I sometimes wonder if *they* do. They would surely cut it out if they did."

As intent as a bird-watcher, Etta observed them, but was puzzled that they behaved like birds, making such a display of their courtship, an absurd-looking frolic out of a serious matter. She waited in vain for a sigh or secret glance. At night, in the room she shared with Sarah, she wanted to talk about them more than Sarah, who felt that her own family was the last possible source of glamour or enlightenment. Discussing her bridesmaid's dress was the most she would be drawn into and that subject Etta felt was devoid of romance. She was not much interested in mere weddings and thought them rather banal and public celebrations. "With an overskirt of embroidered net," said Sarah in her decisive voice. "How nice if you could be a bridesmaid, too; but she has all those awful Greenbaum cousins. As ugly as sin, but not to be left out." Etta was inattentive to her. With all her studious nature she had set herself to study love and study it she would. She made the most of what the holiday offered and when the exponents were absent she fell back on the textbooks—*Tess of the D'Urbervilles* and *Wuthering Heights* at that time.

To Roger she seemed to fall constantly into the same pose, as she sat on the river bank, bare feet tucked sideways, one arm cradling a book, the other outstretched to pluck—as if to aid her concentration—at blades of grass. Her face remained pale, for it was always in shadow, bent over her book. Beside her, glistening with oil, Sarah spread out her body to the sun. She was content to lie for hour after hour with no object but to change the colour of her skin and with thoughts crossing her mind as seldom as clouds passed overhead— and in as desultory a way when they did so. Sometimes, she took a book out with her, but nothing happened to it except that it became smothered with oil. Etta, who found sunbathing boring and enervating, read steadily on—her straight, pale hair hanging forward as if to seclude her, to screen her from the curious eyes of passers-by— shaken by passions of the imagination as she was. Voices from boats came clearly across the water, but she did not heed them. People going languidly by in punts shaded their eyes and admired the scarlet geraniums and the greenness of the grass. When motor cruisers passed, their wash jogged against the mooring stage and swayed into the boat-house, whose lacy fretwork trimmings had just been repainted glossy white.

Sitting there, alone by the boat-house at the end of the grass bank, Roger read, too; but less diligently than Etta. Each time a boat went by, he looked up and watched it out of sight. A swan borne towards him on a wake, sitting neatly on top of its reflection, held his attention. Then his place on the page was lost. Anyhow, the sun fell too blindingly upon it. He would glance again at Etta and briefly, with distaste, at his indolent, spread-eagled sister, who had rolled over on to her stomach to give her shiny back, criss-crossed from the grass, its share of sunlight. So the afternoons passed, and they would never have such long ones in their lives again.

Evenings were more social. The terrace with its fringed umbrellas —symbols of gaiety to Etta—became the gathering place. Etta, listening intently, continued her study of love, and as intently Roger studied her and the very emotion which in those others so engrossed her.

"You look still too pale," Mr. Lippmann told her one evening. He put his hands to her face and tilted it to the sun.

"You shan't leave us until there are roses in those cheeks." He implied that only in his garden did sun and air give their full benefit. The thought was there and Etta shared it. "Too much of a bookworm, I'm afraid," he added and took one of her textbooks which she carried everywhere for safety, lest she should be left on her own for a few moments. "*Tess of the D'Urbervilles*," read out Mr. Lippmann. "Isn't it deep? Isn't it on the morbid side?" Roger was kicking rhythmically at a table leg in glum embarrassment. "This won't do you any good at all, my dear little girl. This won't put the roses in your cheeks."

"You are doing that," his daughter told him—for Etta was blushing as she always did when Mr. Lippmann spoke to her.

"What's a nice book, Babs?" he asked his wife, as she came out on to the terrace. "Can't you find a nice story for this child?" The house must be full, he was sure, of wonderfully therapeutic novels if only he knew where to lay hands on them. "Roger, you're our bookworm. Look out a nice story-book for your guest. This one won't do her eyes any good." Buying books with small print was a false economy, he thought, and bound to land one in large bills from an eye specialist before long. "A very short-sighted policy," he explained genially when he had given them a little lecture to which no one listened.

His wife was trying to separate some slippery cubes of ice and Sarah sprawled in a cane chair with her eyes shut. She was making the most of the setting sun, as Etta was making the most of romance.

"We like the same books," Roger said to his father. "So she can choose as well as I could."

Etta was just beginning to feel a sense of surprised gratitude, had half turned to look in his direction when the betrothed came through the French windows and claimed her attention.

"In time for a lovely drink," Mrs. Lippmann said to Nora.

"She is too fat already," said David.

Nora swung round and caught his wrists and held them threateningly. "If you say that once more, I'll...I'll just..." He freed himself and pulled her close. She gasped and panted, but leant heavily against him. "Promise!" she said.

"Promise what?"

"You won't ever say it again?"

He laughed at her mockingly.

They were less the centre of attention than they thought—Mr. Lippmann was smiling, but rather at the lovely evening and that the day in London was over; Mrs. Lippmann, impeded by the cardigan hanging over her shoulders, was mixing something in a glass jug and Sarah had her eyes closed against the evening sun. Only Etta, in some bewilderment, heeded them. Roger, who had his own ideas about love, turned his head scornfully.

Sarah opened her eyes for a moment and stared at Nora, in her mind measuring against her the wedding dress she had been designing. She is too fat for satin, she decided, shutting her eyes again and disregarding the bridal gown for the time being. She returned to thoughts of her own dress, adding a little of what she called "back interest" (though lesser bridesmaids would no doubt obscure it from the congregation—or audience) in the form of long velvet ribbons in turquoise ... or rose? She drew her brows together and with her eyes still shut said, "All the colours of the rainbow aren't very many, are they?"

"Now, Etta dear, what will you have to drink?" asked Mrs. Lippmann.

Just as she was beginning to ask for some tomato juice, Mr. Lippmann interrupted. He interrupted a great deal, for there were a great many things to be put right, it seemed to him. "Now, Mommy, you should give her a glass of sherry with an egg beaten up in it. Roger, run and fetch a nice egg and a whisk, too ... all right, Babsie dear, I shall do it myself ... don't worry, child," he said, turning to Etta and seeing her look of alarm. "It is no trouble to me. I shall do this for you every evening that you are here. We shall watch the roses growing in your cheeks, shan't we, Mommy?"

He prepared the drink with a great deal of clumsy fuss and sat back to watch her drinking it, smiling to himself, as if the roses were already blossoming. "Good, good!" he murmured, nodding at her as she drained the glass. Every evening, she thought, hoping that he would forget; but horrible though the drink had been, it was also reassuring; their concern for her was reassuring. She preferred it to the cold anxiety of her mother hovering with pills and thermometer.

"Yes," said Mr. Lippmann, "we shall see. We shall see. I think your parents won't know you." He puffed out his cheeks and sketched with a curving gesture the bosom she would soon have. He always forgot that her father was dead. It was quite fixed in his mind that he was simply a fellow who had obviously not made the grade; not everybody could. Roger bit his tongue hard, as if by doing so he could curb his father's. "I must remind him again," Sarah and her mother were both thinking.

The last day of the visit had an unexpected hazard as well as its own sadness, for Mrs. Salkeld had written to say that her employer would lend her his car for the afternoon. When she had made a business call for him in the neighbourhood she would arrive to fetch Etta at about four o'clock.

"She is really to leave us, Mommy?" asked Mr. Lippmann at breakfast, folding his newspaper and turning his attention on his family before hurrying to the station. He examined Etta's face and nodded. "Next time you stay longer and we make rosy apples of these." He patted her cheeks and ruffled her hair. "You tell your Mommy and Dadda next time you stay a whole week."

"She *has* stayed a whole week," said Sarah.

"Then a fortnight, a month."

He kissed his wife, made a gesture as if blessing them all, with his newspaper raised above his head, and went from the room at a trot. "Thank goodness," thought Sarah, "that he won't be here this afternoon to make kind enquiries about *her* husband."

When she was alone with Etta, she said, "I'm sorry about that mistake he keeps making."

"I don't mind," Etta said truthfully, "I am only embarrassed because I know that you are." That's *nothing*, she thought; but the day ahead was a different matter.

As time passed, Mrs. Lippmann also appeared to be suffering from tension. She went upstairs and changed her matador pants for a linen skirt. She tidied up the terrace and told Roger to take his bathing things off his window-sill. As soon as she had stubbed out a cigarette, she emptied and dusted the ash-tray. She was conscious that Sarah was trying to see her with another's eyes.

"Oh, do stop taking photographs," Sarah said tetchily to Roger, who had been clicking away with his camera all morning. He obeyed her only because he feared to draw attention to his activities. He had just taken what he hoped would be a very beautiful study of Etta in a typical pose—sitting on the river bank with a book in her lap. She had lifted her eyes and was gazing across the water as if she were pondering whatever she had been reading. In fact, she had been arrested by thoughts of David and Nora and, although her eyes followed the print, the scene she saw did not correspond with the lines she read. She turned her head and looked at the willow trees on the far bank, the clumps of borage from which moorhens launched themselves. "Perhaps next time that I see them, they'll be married and it will all be over," she thought. The evening before, there had been a great deal of high-spirited sparring about between them. Offence meant and offence taken they assured one another. "If you do that once more . . . I am absolutely serious," cried Nora. "You are trying not to laugh," David said. "I'm not. I am absolutely serious." "It will end in tears," Roger had muttered contemptuously. Even good-tempered Mrs. Lippmann had looked down her long nose disapprovingly. And that was the last, Etta supposed, that she would see of love for a long time. She was left once again with books. She returned to the one she was reading.

Roger had flung himself on to the grass nearby, appearing to trip over a tussock of grass and collapse. He tried to think of some opening remark which might lead to a discussion of the book. In the end, he asked abruptly, "Do you like that?" She sat brooding over it, chewing the side of her finger. She nodded without looking up and, with a similar automatic gesture, she waved away a persistent wasp. He leant forward and clapped his hands together smartly and was relieved to see the wasp drop dead into the grass, although he would rather it had stung him first. Etta, however, had not noticed this brave deed.

The day passed wretchedly for him; each hour was more filled with the doom of her departure than the last. He worked hard to conceal his feelings, in which no one took an interest. He knew that it was all he could do, although no good could come from his succeeding. He took a few more secret photographs from his bedroom window, and then he sat down and wrote a short letter to her, explaining his love.

At four o'clock, her mother came. He saw at once that Etta was nervous and he guessed that she tried to conceal her nervousness behind a much jauntier manner to her mother than was customary. It would be a bad hour, Roger decided.

His own mother, in spite of her linen skirt, was gawdy and exotic beside Mrs. Salkeld, who wore a navy-blue suit which looked as if it had been sponged and pressed a hundred times—a depressing process unknown to Mrs. Lippmann. The pink-rimmed spectacles that Mrs. Salkeld wore seemed to reflect a little colour on to her cheekbones, with the result that she looked slightly indignant about something or other. However, she smiled a great deal, and only Etta guessed what an effort it was to her to do so. Mrs. Lippmann gave her a chair where she might have a view of the river and she sat down, making a point of not looking round the room, and smoothed her gloves. Her jewellery was real but very small.

"If we have tea in the garden, the wasps get into Anna's rose-petal jam," said Mrs. Lippmann. Etta was not at her best, she felt—not helping at all. She was aligning herself too staunchly with the Lippmanns, so that her mother seemed a stranger to her, as well. "You see, I am at home here," she implied, as she jumped up to fetch things or hand things round. She was a little daring in her familiarity.

Mrs. Salkeld had contrived the visit because she wanted to understand and hoped to approve of her daughter's friends. Seeing the lawns, the light reflected from the water, later this large, bright room, and the beautiful poppy-seed cake the Hungarian cook had made for tea, she understood completely and felt pained. She could see then, with Etta's eyes, their own dark, narrow house, and she thought of the lonely hours she spent there reading on days of imprisoning rain. The Lippmanns would even have better weather, she thought bitterly. The bitterness affected her enjoyment of the poppyseed cake. She had, as puritanical people often have, a sweet tooth. She ate the cake with a casual air, determined not to praise.

"You are so kind to spare Etta to us," said Mrs. Lippmann.

"*You* are kind to invite her," Mrs. Salkeld replied, and then for Etta's sake, added: "She loves to come to you."

Etta looked self-consciously down at her feet.

"No, I don't smoke," her mother said primly. "Thank you."

Mrs. Lippmann seemed to decide not to, either, but very soon her hand stole out and took a cigarette—while she was not looking, thought Roger, who was having some amusement from watching his mother on her best behaviour. Wherever she was, the shagreen cigarette case and the gold lighter were nearby. Ash-trays never were. He got up and fetched one before Etta could do so.

The girls' school was being discussed—one of the few topics the two mothers had in common. Mrs. Lippmann had never taken it seriously. She laughed at the uniform and despised the staff—an attitude she might at least have hidden from her daughter, Mrs. Salkeld felt. The tea-trolley was being wheeled away and her eyes followed the remains of the poppy-seed cake. She had planned a special supper for Etta to return to, but she felt now that it was no use. The things of the mind had left room for an echo. It sounded with every footstep or spoken word in that house where not enough was going on. She began to wonder if there were things of the heart and not the mind that Etta fastened upon so desperately when she was reading. Or was her desire to be in a different place? Lowood was a worse one—she could raise her eyes and look round her own room in relief; Pemberley was better and she would benefit from the change. "But how can I help her?" she asked herself in anguish. "What possible change—and radical it must be—can I ever find the strength to effect?" People had thought her wonderful to have made her own life and brought up her child alone. She had kept their heads above water and it had taken all her resources to do so.

Her lips began to refuse the sherry Mrs. Lippmann suggested and then, to her surprise and Etta's astonishment, she said "yes" instead.

It was very early to have suggested it, Mrs. Lippmann thought, but it would seem to put an end to the afternoon. Conversation had been as hard work as she had anticipated and she longed for a dry martini to stop her from yawning, as she was sure it would; but something about Mrs. Salkeld seemed to discourage gin drinking.

"Mother, it isn't half-past five yet," said Sarah.

"Darling, don't be rude to your mummy. I know perfectly well what the time is." ("Who better?" she wondered.) "And this isn't a public house, you know."

She had flushed a little and was lighting another cigarette. Her bracelets jangled against the decanter as she handed Mrs. Salkeld her glass of sherry, saying, "Young people are so stuffy," with an air of complicity.

Etta, who had never seen her mother drinking sherry before, watched nervously, as if she might not know how to do it. Mrs. Salkeld—remembering the flavour from Christmas mornings many years ago and—more faintly—from her mother's party trifle— sipped cautiously. In an obscure way she was doing this for Etta's sake. "It may speed her on her way," thought Mrs. Lippmann, playing idly with her charm bracelet, having run out of conversation.

When Mrs. Salkeld rose to go, she looked round the room once more as if to fix it in her memory—the setting where she would imagine her daughter on future occasions.

"And come again soon, there's a darling girl," said Mrs. Lippmann, putting her arm round Etta's shoulder as they walked towards the car. Etta, unused to but not ungrateful for embraces, leant awkwardly against her. Roger, staring at the gravel, came behind carrying the suitcase.

"I have wasted my return ticket," Etta said.

"Well, that's not the end of the world," her mother said briskly. She thought, but did not say, that perhaps they could claim the amount if they wrote to British Railways and explained.

Mrs. Lippmann's easy affection meant so much less than her own stiff endearments, but she resented it all the same and when she was begged, with enormous warmth, to visit them all again soon her smile was a prim twisting of her lips.

The air was bright with summer sounds, voices across the water and rooks up in the elm trees. Roger stood back listening in a dream to the good-byes and thank yous. Nor was *this* the end of the world, he told himself. Etta would come again and, better than that, they would also grow older and so be less at the mercy of circumstances. He would be in a position to command his life and turn occasions to his own advantage. Meanwhile, he had done what he could. None the less, he felt such dejection, such an overwhelming conviction that it was the end of the world after all, that he could not watch the car go down the drive, and he turned and walked quickly—rudely, off-handedly, his mother thought—back to the house.

Mrs. Salkeld, driving homewards in the lowering sun, knew that Etta had tears in her eyes. "I'm glad you enjoyed yourself," she said. Without waiting for an answer, she added: "They are very charming people." She had always suspected charm and rarely spoke of it, but in this case the adjective seemed called for.

Mr. Lippmann would be coming back from London about now, Etta was thinking. "And David will bring Nora. They will all be on the terrace having drinks—dry martinis, not sherry."

She was grateful to her mother about the sherry and understood that it had been an effort towards meeting Mrs. Lippmann's world half-way, and on the way back, she had not murmured one word of criticism—for their worldliness or extravagance or the vulgar opulence of their furnishings. She had even made a kind remark about them.

I might buy her a new dress, Mrs. Salkeld thought—something like the one Sarah was wearing. Though it does seem a criminal waste when she has all her good school clothes to wear out.

They had come on to the main road, and evening traffic streamed by. In the distance the gas holder looked pearl grey and the smoke from factories was pink in the sunset. They were nearly home. Etta, who had blinked her tears back from her eyes, took a sharp breath, almost a sigh.

Their own street with its tall houses was in shadow. "I wish we had a cat," said Etta, as she got out of the car and saw the next door tabby looking through the garden railings. She imagined burying her face in its warm fur, it loving only her. To her surprise, her mother said: "Why not?" Briskly, she went up the steps and turned the key with its familiar grating sound in the lock. The house, with its smell—familiar, too—of floor polish and stuffiness, looked secretive. Mrs. Salkeld, hardly noticing this, hurried to the kitchen to put the casserole of chicken in the oven.

Etta carried her suitcase upstairs. On the dressing-table was a jar of marigolds. She was touched by this—just when she did not want to be touched. She turned her back on them and opened her case. On the top was the book she had left on the terrace. Roger had brought it to her at the last moment. Taking it now, she found a letter inside. Simply "Etta" was written on the envelope.

Roger had felt that he had done all he was capable of and that was to write in the letter those things he could not have brought himself to say, even if he had had an opportunity. No love letter could have been less anticipated and Etta read it twice before she could realise that it was neither a joke nor a mistake. It was the most extraordinary happening of her life, the most incredible.

Her breathing grew slower and deeper as she sat staring before her, pondering her mounting sense of power. It was as if the whole Lippmann family—Nora as well—had proposed to her. To marry Roger—a long, long time ahead though she must wait to do so—would be the best possible way of belonging.

She got up stiffly—for her limbs now seemed too clumsy a part of her body with its fly-away heart and giddy head—she went over to the dressing-table and stared at herself in the glass. "I am I," she thought, but she could not believe it. She stared and stared, but could not take in the tantalising idea.

After a while, she began to unpack. The room was a place of transit, her temporary residence. When she had made it tidy, she went downstairs to thank her mother for the marigolds.

THE THAMES SPREAD OUT

NOTHING could have been lovelier, Rose thought. For most of the day she stayed on the little balcony, looking out over the flooded fields. Although it was Friday, Gilbert had not come and she was sure now that he would not come, and was shaken with laughter at the idea of him rowing out to her from the railway station, across the river and meadows, bowler-hatted and red with exasperation.

This day was usually her busiest of the week, when she stopped pottering and worked methodically to make the ramshackle villa and herself clean and tidy. By four o'clock she would be ready, and Gilbert, who was punctual over his illicit escapades as with everything else, would soon after drive down the lane. Perhaps escapade was altogether too exciting a word for the homely ways they had drifted into. She fussed over his little ailments far more than his wife had ever done, not because she loved him more, or indeed at all, but because her position was more precarious.

On Saturday mornings he left her, having broken his long journey from the North, as he told his wife. He often thought how furious she would have been if she had known that the break was only twenty miles from London, where they lived.

As soon as he left her on Saturdays, Rose went down to the shops by the station, cashed the cheque he had given her, and bought some little treats for herself to while away the weekend—a few slices of smoked salmon, chocolate peppermint-creams, and magazines. She loved the rest of that day. Gilbert had gone—she could shut herself in and be cosy till he came again.

Only the faintest of regrets ruffled her comfort—little faults in herself that depressed her slightly but could easily be rectified later on. She was shamefully lazy, she knew, and self-indulgent. All the time she meant to save money, but never did. Gilbert was not very generous. His Friday nights were expensive and he knew it and very rarely gave Rose a present. She really had nothing.

Her fur coat, which she had worn all day as she leant over the balcony rail watching the seagulls on the floodwater, was shabby and baggy; he had given it to her years ago at the beginning of their liaison when she was still working for him. It was squirrel, and his wife would not have been seen dead in it.

He certainly won't come now, Rose decided, looking at the forsaken water. There had really never been the slightest likelihood of it, and that was just as well, she thought, catching sight of herself in a glass as she was making a cup of tea. A dark band showed at the parting of her golden hair and she had run out of peroxide.

Some young boy had come in a rowing-boat that morning—a Boy Scout, perhaps—and had offered to do her shopping. She had wrapped some money in the shopping-list and let it down in a basket from the bedroom window. Later he had brought back a loaf of bread and some milk, a pound of sausages and cigarettes, a dozen candles. She would have liked a half-bottle of gin, but had not liked to write it down. The peroxide she had quite forgotten.

She made tea on the primus stove Gilbert had bought for their river picnics. These were in July always, when his wife went to stay with her mother in the Channel Islands. Then he moved in with Rose for a whole fortnight; from niggardly motives made love to her excessively, became irritable, felt cramped in the uncomfortable little house and exasperated by the way it was falling to pieces. The primus stove was hardly ever used. It was too often raining, or they were in bed, or both. Rose was afraid it would blow up, but now, with the floodwater in the downstairs rooms, she had to overcome her fears or go without tea.

The sun was beginning to set and she knew how soon it got dark these winter days. She took her cup of tea and went out on to the balcony to watch. Every ten years or so, the Thames in that place would rise too high, brim over its banks and cover the fields for miles, changing the landscape utterly. The course of the river itself she could trace here and there from lines of willow trees or other landmarks she knew.

Beyond, on what before had been the other bank, a little train was crossing the floods. The raised track was still a foot or two above river level. Puffing along, reflected in the water, it curved away into the distance and disappeared among the poplar trees by the church. There, all the gravestones were submerged, and the inn had the river flowing in through the front door and out of the back.

"Thames-side Venice," a newspaper reporter had called it. The children loved it, and now Rose saw two young boys rowing by on the pink water. The sun had slipped down through the mist, was very low, behind some grey trees blobbed with mistletoe; but the light on the water was very beautiful. The white seabirds scarcely moved and a row of swans went in single file down a footpath whose high railing-tops on either side broke the surface of the water.

Rose sipped her tea and watched, intent on having the most of every second of the fading loveliness—the silence and the reflections and the light, and then the silence broken by a cat crying far away or a shout coming thinly across the cold air.

"I'm glad he didn't come," she said aloud.

At this hour, other men, husbands, those who had not sent their families away, would be returning. The train was at the station and they would take to their boats and row homewards, right up to their staircases, tying up to the newel-post and greeted from above by their children. Rose imagined them all as lake dwellers and hoped that they were enjoying the adventure.

She was curious about her neighbours—the few of them scattered along the river bank. She wondered about them when she passed by on her way to the shops, but she had never spoken to them or been inside their houses, and she had never wished to do so. Her solitariness suited her and her position was too informal. She would not embarrass other people by her situation.

But she made up stories to herself about some of them, especially about the people at the white house nearby who came only at week-ends. They seemed very gay, and laughter and music went on till late on Saturday nights. From where she was, she could just see the eaves of their boat-house sticking out of the river, but the house itself lay farther back and out of sight.

It was growing dark very fast, and the water, a moment or two earlier rosy, whitened as the sun went down. Under the high woods, out of the wind, the fields were frozen, their black and glassy surface littered with broken ice that boys had thrown.

Suddenly, at last, Rose could bear no more. The strangeness over-came her and she went inside and washed her cup and saucer in the bathroom basin and emptied the tea-pot over the banisters into the flooded passageway.

A swan had come in through the front door. Looking austere and suspicious, he turned his head about, circled aloofly, and returned to the garden. It was weird, Rose thought. This was a word she often used. So many things were to her either weird or intriguing.

The sunset, for instance, had been intriguing, but the sudden be-ginning of the long evening, the swan coming indoors, the smell of the water lying down there was very weird. She drew the curtains across the balcony doors. They would not meet and she clipped them together with a clothes-peg to keep the darkness hidden.

The bedroom was crowded with furniture and rolled-up matting rescued from downstairs, and looked like a corner of a junk shop. Nothing was new or matched another thing. It had all no doubt been bought off old barrows or hunted for in attics, so that the house could be called furnished when it was let. Wicker uncurled from the legs of an armchair and caught Rose's stockings as she passed by, and in the mornings when she made the bed she picked up dozens of blond feathers from the eiderdown.

It was the first time she had ever had a house to herself. After years of living with her married sister, it had seemed wonderful to put the frying-pan on her own stove and fry her own sausages in it, and she had felt a little self-conscious, as if she were playing at keeping house and did so before an audience, as in the imaginary games of her childhood.

For a time she could not be quite natural on her own. Look at me all the way round, from any angle, I really am a housewife. You won't catch me out, she often thought. But no one was ever there but Gilbert, and he, indifferent to the intriguing notion of her keeping house, sat with his back to her and read his pink newspaper.

In the end the magic had gone, she tired of her rôle, and the home was not one, she saw, that anyone could take a pride in, especially this evening, with candlelight making the crowded room macabre.

"I shall never get the place straight afterwards," she said. She talked to herself a great deal nowadays.

She had forgotten the beauty of the flooded landscape and was overcome by wretchedness. The woman at the post office had warned her of the filth the receding water would leave behind, the smell that lingered, the stained walls and woodwork, and doors half twisted off their hinges.

Earlier that week, as she watched the rockery slowly going under, then the lower boughs of shrubs and very soon the higher ones, Rose had felt apprehensive. She had never had any experience in the least like it. Yet, when the worst happened and the house was invaded, perched up above it, enisled, as if she were hibernating in these unusual surroundings, she had begun to feel elated instead.

Her sister, worried to death from reading about the Thames-side Venice in the newspapers, wrote to ask her to stay. The letter had come by boat and was taken up in a basket through the bedroom window. "Roy and I wish you would come back for good, you know that," Beryl had written. The children missed her. They had been told that she had gone away to work, and the same story did for the neighbours, but they were less likely to think it true.

Roy said that his sister-in-law was wasting herself and ruining her chances. Once a girl takes up with married men, he had told his wife, she will find herself drifting from one to the other and she'll never get married herself. This Beryl left out of the letter.

Rose had been frank about her plans but, wary from long practice of secret affairs, had kept Gilbert's name to herself. "The man I'm going out with," she had called him at the beginning, and so she still wrote of him. She would have made someone a good wife, her brother-in-law often said, knowing what men liked. The house was pleasanter when she was there and the children were easier to manage.

A letter must be written to still her sister's fears. All day, Rose had put it off, but now began to look for some writing-paper. The wardrobe door swung open as she crossed the room and she saw her reflection in the blurred glass front. "My hair!" she thought. She had a suspicion that she might be beginning to let herself go, a serious mistake for one in her position.

When she had found the paper and a bottle of green ink, she cleared a corner of the table and began to write. "Dear B, you'd laugh if you could see me at this minute."

She glanced round the room and then, smiling to herself, began to describe it. She was a born letter-writer, Beryl said, and she tried consciously to display her talent.

The church clock struck seven. The chimes had a different sound, coming across water instead of grassy meadows. She paused, listened, her chin on her hand and her eyes straying to the curtained door. She thought now that she could hear something moving on the water outside and went to the window and parted the curtains.

Below her, she could see two figures in a punt, one standing and using the pole, the other sitting down and fanning torchlight back and forth across the darkness.

"Going next door," she thought, as she sat down again and dipped her pen into the ink. "It's up to the second stair now," she wrote, and then had to jump up, to go and see. Last thing at night, first thing in the morning, and a dozen times a day she would go out to the landing to see if the water had risen or fallen.

The house was open to anyone and the keys of the upstairs rooms had long ago been lost. The swan had come in and so might rats. Nervously, she peered over the banisters.

The water was disturbed and was slapping the threshold and swaying against the staircase. She could hear laughter and then a man's voice echoing up the well of the staircase, calling out to ask if she were safe. "Quite safe and well?" the voice persisted. Torchlight ran up the walls and vanished, and a boat grated against some steps outside.

"Yes, I'm all right," she called. "Who is it?"

"Next door."

The light came bobbing back across the threshold. Holding the torch was a young man, wading carefully through the water, his trousers rolled up above his pale knees. He came to the bottom of the stairs and looked up at her. His smile was the beginning of laughter, and he seemed to be deeply enjoying the novelties of the situation.

"Are you all alone?" he asked. Then he hurried over the indiscretion and, giving her no time to reply, said, "Don't you mind being up there? We saw the light."

She was tempted to say that she did mind. Then perhaps he would come up the stairs and talk to her for a little while. "No, I don't mind," she replied.

"We saw your light," he said again. "I just wondered if you were all right. 'She might be lying there ill for all we know,' I said to Tony." ("Dead," he had really said.) "'We'd better make sure,' I said."

They were both a little drunk. So endearing, Rose found this. It was a long time since she had been with anyone who was in the least intoxicated; Gilbert dully carried his drink and often remarked upon the fact.

"We went to get some whisky."

He seemed not to notice the cold, standing there in the icy water.

"What fun," she said. She smiled back at him. As she leant over the banisters, he spotlighted her with the torch and could see the top of her breasts, white against the green of her jersey as she bent towards him.

A jolly nice bosom, he thought. She seemed to be what he and Tony called a proper auntie. I shall bring out the maternal in her, he thought, and between the banister slats examined her pretty legs. So many plump women have slim ankles. He had often noticed this.

"Why don't you come with us?" he said. "I can carry you to the boat."

"Don't be silly. More like I'd have to carry you."

"Well, paddle, then. It's not cold. It's lovely in."

She had put her hand up to her hair, so he knew that she would come; but, before, would go through all the feminine excuses about her appearance.

"There's only us," he said. "You look very nice to me. What my brother thinks is of no importance. I can't stand in this water much longer, though." He held out his arms.

"I'll take off my stockings, then."

She went quickly back to her room. When she had rolled off her stockings and put them into her coat pocket, screwed up the top of the ink-bottle, she took up her shoes and blew out the candles. The hardly started letter was left lying on the table.

"I *could* do with a drink," she said. "I didn't like to ask that errand-boy to fetch some gin. Breaking the law, I suppose."

The torchlight led her down the stairs, and there the young man took her shoes from her and put them in his pockets. He steadied her with his arm as she hitched up her skirt and stepped down into the icy water.

"Oh, my God," she gasped and began to giggle, wading on tiptoe towards the doorway.

"Got her?" Tony shouted. He was sitting in the boat, holding on to the rustic-work porch.

If it all comes away in his hands, Gilbert will go mad, Rose thought, smiling in the darkness.

They helped her into the boat, and Tony, letting go of the porch, gave her a cigarette, lighting it first and putting it into her mouth with the intimacy which comes easily in time of peril or exultation.

"You can put your stockings on now," said the young man whom Tony called Roger. "No more paddling. We row straight in through the French windows to the landing-stage at the foot of the stairs."

Tony gave a final push at the rustic-work porch and swung the punt towards the next-door garden. Bottles jingled against one another under the seat, and when Roger had wiped Rose's feet with a damp handkerchief, he reached for a whisky bottle, took off the wrapping-paper, and let it blow away across the water.

"Keep the cold out," he urged Rose, trying to hold the bottle to her lips. "Your teeth are chattering. Never mind, nearly there, and we've a wonderful oilstove going upstairs."

As the boat swayed, whisky trickled over her chin; then she put her hands over his and, steadying them, took a long drink.

"I'll bet she's been a barmaid," thought Roger.

"Jolly boating weather," Tony sang, and the punt slipped over the still water, and the white house next door came into sight.

"Isn't it lovely?" Rose murmured.

"Not to be missed," said Roger.

The next morning she slept late. It was nearly noon before she was properly awake, and any errand-boys who might have called her from below had gone away unanswered. Even when she was wide awake at last, she lay in bed staring at the curtains pinned across the window, striving to remember all she could of the evening before.

In bright moonlight they had brought her home in the boat and their singing must have carried a long way across the water. I don't care if the boat capsizes, she had thought.

When she waded indoors they called good-night; and she went upstairs and, still with wet bare feet, watched from the window until they were out of sight.

Quite clearly across the water, she heard Roger say, "Well, that worked out all right, didn't it?"

A moment later, a gust of laughter came back to her, and she had wondered uneasily if they were laughing at her. But they were high-spirited boys, she reminded herself. They would laugh at anything. Perhaps Tony had let go of the punt pole.

Before her return home, there must have been hours and hours of sitting on the floor and drinking in what they called "Mamma's bedroom." An oil-stove threw a shifting daisy pattern on the ceiling, and two pink candles had been burning on the dressing-table—must surely have burnt themselves out.

"How long was I there?" she wondered. "And how did we pass the time?" While it was happening it had seemed one of the loveliest evenings of her life and she was sorry to have forgotten a moment of it.

The peach-coloured bedroom was draped with satin, and a trail of wet foot-prints went back and forth across the white carpet. Mamma's wedding photograph was on a little table, and Rose had at one point suddenly asked, "Whatever would your mother say about this?" By "this" she meant herself being there, not the empty bottles and the cigarette smoke and the dirty glasses.

"We'll clear up afterwards," Roger said. The other bedrooms were full of furniture from downstairs. They had been sent from London to rescue it.

Now it was Saturday morning and she could not walk down to the shops to buy her little week-end treats. Today there was no cheque to cash, and for the first time she realised how much she was at Gilbert's mercy.

She got out of bed and began to search the room for money, found thirty shillings in one bag, some pennies dusty with face powder in another, half a crown in her mackintosh pocket, and a florin in a broken cup on the chest of drawers. She could survive the week until he came again, just as she could survive until Monday on stale bread and the rest of the sausages.

Yes, I can survive all right, she told herself briskly, and pulled off her nightgown and began to dress.

A glimpse in the wardrobe mirror as she crossed the room depressed her. She was getting too fat and her sister would see a difference in her.

"But when?" she wondered. There was the unfinished letter on the table. When she had made herself a cup of tea she would make an effort to write it. I shall go on surviving and surviving, and growing fatter and fatter, she thought, and her lips were pressed together and her eyes flickered because she was frightened.

She lit the primus stove and then unpegged the curtains and opened the balcony windows. Outside, a great change had taken place while she slept. The floods were subsiding. Along the bank of the railway tracks she could see grass, and in the garden the tops of shrubs and bushes had come up for a breath of air and were steaming in the sunshine. She remembered that last night, as the two young men punted away, she had heard one of them say, "The water's going down," and she had felt regret, as if a party were nearing its end.

It was going down more rapidly than it had risen, draining away into the earth, evaporating into the air, hastening down gratings. The adventure was nearly over and in its diminuendo had become an exasperation. What had been so beautiful yesterday was now an inconvenience, and Rose, on her island, would have to drink her tea without milk.

Surely those two dear boys will come, she thought. They had concerned themselves about her last night when they did not know her; it seemed more likely that they would do so today. She so convinced herself of this that, in the middle of sipping her tea, she went into the bathroom to make something of her face.

But they did not come and the day went slowly. She watched from the window and it was a dull, watery world she saw. The crisis was over and the seabirds beginning to fly away. She finished writing her letter and propped it up against the clock, which had stopped.

When it was dark she pinned the curtains together again and sat down at the table, simply staring in front of her; at the back of her mind, listening. In the warm living-room of her sister's house, the children in dressing-gowns would be eating their supper by the fire; Roy, home from a football match, would be lying back in his chair. Their faces would be turned intently to the blue-white shifting screen of the television.

Rose's was another world, candlelit, silent, lifeless. The church clock chimed seven and she got up and wound up her own clock and set it right; then sat down again, stiffly, with her hand laid palm downwards on the table like an old woman.

They asked me for fun, she told herself. It was just a boyish lark—quite understandable; a joke they wouldn't dream of repeating. If I ever see them again, other week-ends, they'll nod, maybe, and smile; that's all; not that, if their mother's with them. At their age, they never look back or do the same thing twice.

As she had come towards middle-age, she had developed a sentimental fondness for young men—especially those she called the undergraduate type, spoilt, reckless, gay, with long scarves twisted round their necks. Roger had, as he predicted, brought out the maternal in her. Humbly, with great enjoyment, she had listened to their banter, the family jokes, a language hardly understood by her, whom they had briskly teased but gallantly drawn in. So the hours must have passed.

Their mother won't be best pleased about that carpet, she thought, and she got up and took the last cigarette from the packet.

All of Sunday the waters receded. Morning and evening the church bells rang across the meadows in which ridges and hillocks of sodden grass stood up. One or two cars splashed down the lane during the afternoon, keeping to the crown of the road and making a great wash.

By Monday morning the garden path was high and nearly dry. Rose looked over the banisters at the wet, muddy entrance and found it difficult to believe that the swan had ever swum about down there. It was all over.

She could go out now and post her letter and fetch what she wanted from the shops; and on Friday Gilbert would come, and on all the Fridays after, she supposed, though she could never be quite sure. So she would survive from year to year, and one day soon would begin a diet and perhaps save some money for her old age.

It was like being in prison, she thought of the last few days. Sunday had been endless and she had cried a little and gone to bed early, but remained awake, yet on other Sundays she most often stayed indoors all day or pottered about the garden, and had always been contented.

Now she was set free and she put on her coat, took the letter from the shelf, and looked out of the window once more to make sure that it was really safe to go out and walk on the earth again. And that really was the sum of her freedom—for the first time the truth of it dawned in her. She could go out and walk to the shops, like a prisoner on parole, and spend the money Gilbert had given her, or save it if she could, and then she would turn back and return, for there was nothing else to do.

The clock ticked—a sound she knew too well. There were other sounds which were driven into her existence—the church bells and the milkman's rattle—and they no longer sufficed and had begun to torment her. Her contentment with them had come to an end.

The exciting thought occurred to her that it was in her power to fly away from them for ever. Nothing could stop her.

For a moment she stood quite still, her head tilted as if she were listening, and then she suddenly turned her handbag upside down and tipped the money on to the table. "What will Gilbert do?" she wondered, as she counted the coins. He would never have visualised her doing anything impulsive, would stand in the porch bewildered, amazed that she did not open the door at once and, when he had sorted out his own key and let himself in, his face would be a picture, she thought.

"I'd like to see it," she said aloud, and scooped up the money and dropped it back into her bag. Where would he break his journey that night? she wondered. Or would he perhaps go petulantly home to his wife?

She was smiling as she quickly packed her suitcase, almost shook with laughter when she slammed the door and set off down the muddy path. Such a dreadful mess she had left behind her.

She felt warm in her fur coat as she picked her way down the lane. The floods had shifted the gravel about and made deep ruts, the hedgerows were laced with scum; but the valley was recovering, cows were being driven back to the pastures and hundreds of birds were out scavenging.

The letter was still in Rose's hand but, as she stopped for a moment by a stile to rest, she suddenly screwed it up and tossed it over the hedge, knowing she would reach Beryl first.

THE PREROGATIVE OF LOVE

WHERE the lawn was in shadow from the house, the watering-spray flung dazzling aigrettes into the air. The scent of the wet earth, the sound of dripping rose-leaves was delicious.

The round marble table was abandoned in the sun, a butterfly hovered above it, both blindingly white. Too hot, Lillah had decided, and had taken her chair and her sewing into the shade; but the damage was done, and she began to feel giddy. Mrs. Hatton made her go upstairs and drink salt water and lie on her bed.

"It's a swine, isn't it?" the gardener said, meaning the weather. He was speaking to the postman, who crunched by on the gravel drive with letters in his hand.

"Too sudden," the postman agreed, stopping for a moment, watching the other man work, the brown hand moving slow as a toad among the geraniums, tweaking up tiny weeds. "A criminal colour, that bright red," he said. "Hurts my eyes to look at it. I always preferred the white ones."

He continued slowly up the drive, hoping to be seen from the house by Mrs. Hatton the cook, and offered tea.

No one saw him, for the curtains, hardly stirring, were drawn across the open windows. He stepped into the hall and laid the letters on the brass tray on the table. He suffered a fit of noisy coughing, stood with bowed head after it, listening, but heard not a sound and made off down the drive again.

The letters—what Lillah would call a tradesman's lot—stayed there until Richard came home. It was six o'clock then and hardly any cooler. The cats lay on the stone floor like cast-off furs. One of them got up and stretched and came towards him, its sides hanging, very thin, for it did not fancy its food in this weather. Listlessly, it rubbed its head against his leg, smelt the streets of London on his shoes and wandered, repelled, back to its place and flopped again.

Mrs. Hatton, neat as a new pin, came down the back stairs to the kitchen, having napped and tidied up and now, ready for the fray, pinned a clean, folded napkin round her head, as if it were a Stilton cheese. She took the grey and white fish off the ice and, looking grim, began to fillet. All her movements were slow, so that she should not get hot. She even sang under her breath; although yearningly— for a Wiltshire woman—about Galway Bay.

"I'm afraid you'll have to hold the fort," Lillah told her husband. "I'll try again later, but at the moment I can't put my feet to the ground."

She lay on the bed, wrapped in a white kimono. The bedroom was cool to Richard, after the hot pavements and the asphyxiating train. His clothes clung to him, he felt that this room was no place for him and longed to plunge into the river, a long dive between the silken, trailing weeds. But Lillah said there would not be time.

She had nothing to do all day but keep herself cool, he thought, and she had not even managed that. He held the curtain aside, so that at least he could look at the river. It flowed by at the foot of the garden, beyond the urns of geraniums where the lawn sloped down to the mooring-stage. On the evenings when there was dinghy-racing from the club, white sails clustered there, tipping and rocking, caught in the sheltered curve of river without wind. There was none tonight. There was no breath of air.

"Too late to put the Foresters off," Lillah said. "I suppose."

Although actressy in so many other ways, she lacked the old trouper's temperament, and her audiences—even such a loyal one as the Foresters—were not considered first if she were out of humour.

"Do you mean you won't come down at all?" he asked in consternation.

"Of course, I'll try. I did a little while ago. You must leave me as long as you can, please, darling. Every minute I think it must get cooler, that the dizziness will go."

She sighed and stirred, then stretched her arm towards him. It looked imploring, but as he moved towards her was withdrawn. She crooked it under her head, and stared up at the ceiling.

"A quick wash, then," he said, turning to the door.

"Did Mrs. Hatton put the wine on ice, I wonder," Lillah said, not exactly giving him instructions to go and find out, but getting that effect.

Richard went to the kitchen as soon as he could, and found that Mrs. Hatton had remembered the wine. She was well forward, she said. And it was certainly hot, she agreed, but nothing to the climate in some parts of the world.

Once upon a time, she had made what she called "the round trip," on a legacy from an employer, and travel had changed her life. She had returned to another kitchen, but so enriched that her mind was forever roaming, as she stirred and whisked and sieved. "Bermuda, you'd like, sir," she once told Richard, as he was setting off for a short holiday in Suffolk.

"The heat's knocked Madam," she remarked, and took up some steak and began to knock that. "I got her to drink some salt water. We always did that in India, I told her. 'It will put back what you've perspired,' I said." She had indeed told Lillah this and Lillah had disdained to listen, drinking quickly to prevent more of such homely hints. "You learn to respect the sun when you've been in the tropics," Mrs. Hatton informed Richard.

"No doubt you do," he said. "I never was east of Biarritz in all my life."

"If Madam wants help dressing, I can spare a minute. I'm quite nicely forward."

"We can always rely on you," he said hurriedly, looking about him in a flustered manner, forgetting what on earth it was that had suddenly come into his mind while she was talking.

"The ice is in the drawing-room on the tray," she said.

She could even recapture and read thoughts that had flown from him. She was always more attuned to the master of the house than to the mistress. "I laid it all out ready."

"Yes, you think of everything."

"It's simple enough when you're on your own. It's when there are two of you that things get overlooked."

"I could have swum, after all," Richard thought.

But that moment he heard a car coming up the drive, and went out to the hall door to greet the Foresters, relieved to know that at last Lillah had decided to get up again and dress.

A small, open car swung round the circle of gravel in front of the house and, alone in it, bare-shouldered, with hair knotted up on top, Lillah's niece, Arabella, looked as if she were naked, she might have been sitting up in her bath.

"I won't stop a second if you would rather not," she said, as the car pulled up.

"I thought you were stark naked," Richard said, opening the door and looking with interest at her small, white frock—which was sparsely patterned with strawberries—and at her shining, tanned legs.

"I'll only come in for a minute," she said, when she had jumped out of the car. She put her thin arms round his neck and kissed him. They were very long arms, he thought, and seemed to have been flung over his head like a lasso. Then she stepped back and hauled out of the car a large wicker hamper.

"Are you picnicking?" he asked.

She looked surprised. "This is only my make-up," she explained. "Don't worry, darling. I shan't stay the night. But I must have it with me. My cigarettes are in it."

"And your shoes?" he asked, for she was crossing the gravel barefoot.

"Maybe," she said, nodding. "Oh, it's cool!" She stood in the hall and let out a deep breath. "I've been in some bogus-looking pub all day long wearing a chinchilla coat—one of those snobbish photographs; playing darts with the locals, draped in fur and choked with pearls and all the mates grinning and enjoying the joke. So hot."

"Lillah's not been well all day."

"Oh, poor old thing. I'll tell you what, Richard—though I promise not to stay one moment—can I just slake my thirst before I go? Oh, you've got people coming," she said, passing the open dining-room door, seeing the table. "That settles it. I'll run out the back way with my empty glass the minute they arrive."

Richard wished that Lillah had been down to answer for him and he poured out the drink quickly and handed it to Arabella.

She picked up ice with her fingers and dropped it into her glass and took another piece and ran it round the nape of her neck and up and down the insides of her arms. "What's wrong with her?" she asked.

"The heat, you know."

"Oh, I *know*. A chinchilla coat, if you please. Oh, I told you. I'll just dash up and say good-bye to her. Who's coming?"

"The Foresters. John and Helen."

"Well, do give them my love."

She ran upstairs, still holding the lump of ice in her fist, and Richard stood staring in a disturbed way at her wicker basket lying on a chair.

Lillah, whose bedroom, at the back of the house, overlooked the river, had not heard the car and answered rather suspiciously when Arabella knocked on the door.

She was at the dressing-table powdering her white shoulders, and turned, looking far from welcoming, to be kissed and then leant towards the glass again and wiped the lipstick off her cheek.

"What are you up to, Arabella?"

"I've been at Henley all day long, playing darts in a pub and wearing fur coats. I was just going home, when I thought that being in striking distance, I would look in for a drink."

She sat down on a brocade-covered chair and sucked her ice cube. "I'm not staying a minute, though."

"How is your mother?"

"Oh, you're not well, Richard was saying. I'm so sorry. I was quite forgetting. I expect it's the heat. I know *I've* sweltered all day long. Guess what I had for lunch. A cheese sandwich. But not to worry, I'll be home in an hour and a half with any luck. You look so wonderfully cool, Lillah. It's the most elegant dress. The Poor Man's Lady Diana Duff Cooper, Mother and I always call you. Don't let me hinder you, but I must shake out my hair."

She wandered round the room, looking for somewhere to put the piece of melting ice and at last threw it out of the window. Then she took the pins from her bright hair and shook it against her bare shoulders.

"I like the colour of your hair today," Lillah said.

"Oh, thank you. And I simply dote on yours."

"Well, mine is always the same."

Lillah leant close to the looking-glass, fixing on some ear-rings.

"Yes, of course, darling," her niece murmured, face hidden now under a tent of hair, rubbing her scalp. Before Lillah had put on the second ear-ring, she saw Arabella stretch out a hand and take up one of her hair-brushes.

"You don't mind, do you?" she asked, and began to brush with great energy.

"Well, as a matter of fact, I do rather," Lillah replied.

Back under her hair and brushing until it crackled, the girl seemed not to hear.

"Haven't you one of your own?" Lillah asked, making an impatient movement to gain the girl's attention. "I thought that models carried the lot wherever they went."

She felt giddy again—rage hitting her, as the sun had.

Arabella swept the hair back from her face and smiled at her aunt. "I left the lot downstairs with Uncle Richard," she replied.

"But you should have put us off," Helen Forester protested.

"Of course you should," her husband added.

"For goodness' sake, we're old enough friends by now..." his wife went on.

"Lillah wouldn't hear of it. She says she feels so much better now and I shall be in trouble for ever having mentioned it. She'll be down in a moment. This is Arabella's, her niece's," he explained, as he moved the wicker basket from a chair so that Helen Forester could sit down. "She's a model in London and just looked in on her way home from some job."

He thought that John Forester seemed to brace himself, and that well he might.

"Forgive me, please," Lillah said, coming across the hall to the open door of the drawing-room. She stretched out her arms to them and put her cheek first to Helen's then John's, a heavy ear-ring swung against each face in turn. "I've felt so stupid all day long. I couldn't lift my silly head."

"You should have put us off," said Helen. "I was telling Richard..."

"But I had looked forward to seeing you so much, and now I have seen you I'm myself again. Mrs. Hatton"—she lowered her voice— "insisted on my going to bed. She's a very strict disciplinarian."

She saw John looking towards the door and turned round.

"This is my niece, Arabella, who's just dropped in," she said, staring down at the girl's bare feet.

Arabella's hair was now looped smoothly against her cheeks, like the youthful Queen Victoria's. She had also, her aunt noticed, helped herself very liberally to Lillah's scent.

"We met when I was a little girl," Arabella said demurely. "I know you can't remember me, because I was fat and had pigtails and a great brace on my teeth. I must look different now."

"You must indeed," John Forester said.

She smiled and came farther into the room. "You're the Labrador breeders, aren't you?" she asked.

"Where are your shoes, dear girl?" asked Lillah, trying to get a tone of asperity across to Arabella, but so that the Foresters would not detect it.

"It's hardly worth putting them on now when I'm just going. I don't care to drive with shoes on."

"You left your drink," said Richard, handing it to her.

"Thank you, darling, I'll thrust it down and be off. I promised to be out of the back door before you arrived," she told John Forester.

"You silly girl," said Lillah lightly. She took the drink that Richard had poured out quickly, before, he hoped, she could put them all in the wrong, as she often did, by asking for something without gin. She laid her hand on his shoulder for a moment, where it looked very pale against the dark cloth, and Richard covered it quickly with his own. He smiled questioningly and she nodded.

"Isn't that a beautiful dress of Lillah's?" Helen asked, slightly embarrassed to find herself caught staring at them.

"It's my beautiful wife in it," Richard said.

"But I meant that, too," Helen said, too willing for words to agree, not to seem restrained by hearing another woman praised.

Arabella was telling John Forester about the chinchilla coat and the game of darts, and he seemed entranced. "And guess what I had for lunch," she asked.

"Isn't it a heavenly frock Lillah's wearing?" Helen asked him. "Doesn't it suit her wonderfully?" To bring Lillah's beauty to the notice of her husband was even greater generosity, she thought, and she looked almost transfigured with the pleasure of finding her friend so lovely.

John's attention was turned from Arabella rather slowly, his eyes moved almost unseeingly to where they were directed. "Perfect," he said.

"A cheese sandwich," said Arabella. "Just imagine."

"I suppose you live on air," he said, his glance, enlivened, returning quickly to her. He was much taken by the rounded thinness of her arms, slim even where they joined the shoulders. If they had been alone, he would have made some excuse to touch them, perhaps patting her in a fatherly way as he begged her not to starve herself or, more youthfully, wondering if he could circle them between finger and thumb.

"I eat like a horse," she said. "Worse—for I'm carnivorous. And the bloodier the better."

"What a gigantic cineraria," Helen said in an admiring voice.

"It is rather ghastly, but dear Mrs. Hatton gave it to me on my birthday and I have to have it about, not to hurt her feelings. It's just the sort of thing she adores."

Helen decided not to like cinerarias in future.

John was looking at Arabella's diminishing drink with anguish. Evenings alone with Richard and Lillah were never so entrancing to him as they were to his wife. Admiration was such a large ingredient of Helen's simple good-nature. She did not feel, as he did, that some attempt should be made on their own behalf. She basks in the shade, he thought. The tops of her arms, he suddenly noticed, were very freckled and their flabbiness flattened against her sides.

What would happen to them all if the girl didn't soon go, Richard wondered. Especially, he wondered, what would happen to him.

Then Lillah—not to be put in the wrong by this ravenous girl, warmly said, "Arabella, may I ask Mrs. Hatton to do a little concocting? You *will* stay?"

"I simply *couldn't*. I know only too well how it is in kitchens. Sometimes I take a man home to dinner without warning and there may be only two cutlets." John seemed to have drawn her eyes back to his, and to his devouring attention she addressed herself. "Mother and I hiss over them all the time they are cooking. 'Let *me* be the vegetarian this time. You were yesterday.' But Mother's so noble. She usually manages to get the poached egg for herself and makes long, long apologies for never eating meat. She goes into it rather too much. She went on and on to one man, and a lot later he came again and this time I had managed to get the egg, and Mother ate her cutlet with great enjoyment. 'You've changed over, you two,' he said."

For some reason, John burst into sycophantic laughter, then he tilted his glass and finished his gin.

"You will think we live on cutlets," Arabella said a few seconds later, and after that there was silence.

"Well, nothing is settled," Richard thought. "She hasn't answered one way or another." He felt that their evening was nearly on the rocks. Adoration cleft the conversation in two—John's of Arabella, Helen's of Lillah—and he began to pour out more drinks, since the continuing silence and John's empty glass made it impossible not to. Lillah, thinking of Mrs. Hatton and even more, no doubt, of social patterns she despised, would be impatient. "Everyone drunk before dinner," she had said so often, driving home from other people's houses. "I have never known a claret so thrown away," or "That poor withered old soufflé."

"I'll tell you what, Lillah," Arabella said in her most childish voice, "let me go and reconnoitre. I'll see how things are with Mrs. Hatton. It's for me to bear the brunt."

Lillah moved quickly to prevent her, tried to say something to detain her, but the girl had sped across the hall. John was touched to see that the soles of her feet were dirty.

"Oh dear," Lillah said. "I'm so sorry."

"Such a beautiful girl," said Helen.

"That family has more than its fair share of looks, I always think," Richard said, smiling at his wife. John looked at her, too, almost for the first time that evening—and saw resemblances between the two faces—the niece's, the aunt's. He had not known Lillah in the early years of her marriage, and he wondered if Richard had had such luck long ago—an Arabella-like bride, whom time had changed and paled and quietened, but whose erstwhile beauty still quite clearly bewitched him.

"Oh, dear," Lillah said again. "I hope she is not lifting the lids off the saucepans and asking questions."

Richard, seeing Mrs. Hatton crossing the hall with a grim stride, going to rearrange her table, closed the door.

"How are the roses this year, John?" he asked.

Having upset all but one of them under that roof, hindered dinner, made an awkward number at the table and talked too much, Arabella, towards the end of the meal, suddenly shivered. Leaning forward, chafing the tops of her arms, she studied the centrepiece of fruit and took out an apple from underneath, so that the pyramid collapsed, a peach rolled across the table and cherries were scattered.

"It will be a chilly run back," she said. "Perhaps I should make a start." For at last the day was cool.

The others were still eating a kirsch-flavoured confection that Mrs. Hatton had sampled in California. Much praised it had been by Helen, who spooned it up lovingly. She would describe it later to her humbler friends and would expect them to listen spellbound.

Arabella was up now and darted round the table with a kiss for each of them. Lillah, receiving hers last, kept her head bent, and John pushed back his chair, dropped his napkin, knocked a spoon and some cherries on the floor. Richard went to the door and opened it.

"Don't stir, anybody," Arabella said.

"It's true that we haven't finished dinner," Lillah said. ("And I consider she had every right to say it," Helen told John afterwards.)

"Don't come out, Richard. Please not to. Lillah, may I borrow a sweater? I'll be frozen driving home."

"There's a cardigan on the hall settle," her aunt said, and seemed with the most delicate gesture to draw Richard's attention to his place at the table. He returned to it and passing Lillah's chair, patted her shoulder—with such a touch of understanding, Helen thought.

"There's lipstick on your face," she told her husband.

"On all your faces, if I may say so," Lillah said, having removed it from her own.

"Such a lively girl," Helen said uncertainly. After all, it was Lillah's own sister's child and so had every claim to praise.

"Delightful," John said in a more definite tone. "She reminds me how scatter-brained I was myself when I was young." He listened to the car being started, then throwing up gravel as it tore away.

"We envy the young, that's what it is," Richard thought sadly. "It is natural for us to harden against them."

"My poor sister was widowed at twenty-three," Lillah said; as if this could be the explanation of her niece's behaviour. She gazed at the scattered cherries on the white cloth, then added: "Her life was haphazard, at the best of times."

"My aunt is a perfectionist," Arabella had said a little while ago. She had spoken to Helen, and as if Lillah herself were not present.

This had often been said of her before, but now she would have liked to disclaim the label, seeing herself, in Arabella's eyes, too much absorbed by trifles, restricted and neurotic. "It must be Mrs. Hatton who is the perfectionist," she had said. "It was all left to her." Helen had once more, boringly, been praising something.

Haphazard though her sister's life was, she had this daughter in it, and close enough they seemed to Lillah whenever she saw them together. And the Foresters had children, too, though grown-up now and gone away.

"Rather a disrupted evening," Lillah said apologetically as her guests were going, and had hardly the patience to listen to their protestations, their expressions of delight. She and Richard went down the steps with them on to the dark drive and stood together as the car drove away, each lifting a hand briefly in farewell, then turning back towards the house, which still threw out from its walls the stored warmth of the day. He took her arm as they went up the steps.

"You were wonderful," he said.

"Well, it is over."

"You must feel exhausted."

"That dreadful girl," she said.

Helen looked back as the car turned into the lane, and saw Richard and Lillah at the top of the steps, in the light from the hall. Until they were out of the drive, she had said nothing, and even now kept her voice low, as if the still air might waft it back towards the house.

"How in love they are," she said. "Every time I see them they seem more so." Which touched her most she hardly knew—Richard's gallantry, or Lillah, who inspired it. "I loved the stuffed vine-leaves. I've so often read about them in books. I suppose Mrs. Hatton picked that up in the Middle East. What a pretty touch—those tiny flowers in the finger-bowls. What were they? I meant to ask. I don't think the niece was welcome. I'm sure I shouldn't have been so smooth about it as Lillah was. If Mrs. Hatton complained, you couldn't blame her. I must try that with the vine-leaves. See what I can do. I suppose you would need to blanch them first. I was longing to ask, but didn't quite like to."

She was really talking to herself.

Those treasure-hunts we used to go on, all about these very lanes, John suddenly remembered. Lovely summer evenings just like this one, tearing like demented things about the countryside, diving into the river in the early hours, parking cars at the edges of woods.

He kept his thoughts to himself, as if they were secrets of his own, and then he remembered that Helen had been there too. She had once swum across the river fully dressed, for a bet. It was difficult to believe.

"A really beautiful frock," she was saying.

"Unusual," he replied. "Not much of it." He suddenly laughed.

"I meant Lillah's."

Presently she sighed and said: "He's so wonderful to her always."

John knew the pattern—the excited admiration invariably turned to dissatisfaction in the end—one of the reasons why these evenings ruffled him.

"I'm sure that to him she's as beautiful as on the day they married," she went on.

"Still a very fine woman," he replied.

"Is it because they've never had children, I wonder? The glamour wasn't worn off by all those nursery troubles. All their love kept for one another."

"It is better to have children," John said.

"Well, of course. Who ever'd deny it? You know I didn't think that. But I wondered if it had drawn them closer together, *not* having them. They never seem to take one another for granted." "As we do," she left unspoken, though her sigh was explicit.

"Well, we mustn't compare ourselves with *them*," he said rather smartly. "And who are we to be talking about love? They're the ones. They're famous for it, after all. It's their prerogative."

THE BENEFACTRESS

FOUR WIDOWS lived in the almshouses beside the church. On the other side of the wall, their husbands' graves were handy. "I've just seen to Charlie's," Mrs. Swan called out to Mrs. Rippon, who was going down the garden path carrying a bunch of phlox.

They were four robust old ladies, and their relationship with one another was cordial, but formal. Living at close quarters, they kept to themselves, drank their own tea in their own kitchens, used surnames, passed a few remarks, perhaps, when they met by chance in the graveyard or weeding their garden plots or, dressed in their best, waiting for the bus to go to the village and draw their pensions.

The almshouses were Elizabethan, with pretentious high chimneys whose bricks were set in a twist. In an alcove above the two middle front doors was a stone bust of the benefactor who had built the cottages and endowed them for the use of four old people of the parish. He wore a high ruff and a pointed beard, and rain had washed deep sockets to his eyes and pitted his cheeks so that he looked as if he were ravaged by some horrible disease. His name was carved in Latin below the alcove—a foreigner, the old ladies had always supposed.

Outside each front door was a wooden bench where they could have sat in the sun to warm their ageing bones, but this they never did. In fine weather it was much too public, with sightseers in and out of the old church taking photographs. They photographed the almshouses without asking permission, and once Mrs. Swan, going down the garden to pick a few gooseberries, had been requested to pose within her porch wearing an old black apron. "Saucy monkeys," she had said to her niece's daughter, who was indoors visiting.

She was there again this afternoon, sitting in the greenish light that came through heavily leaded panes and slanted in from the open, leaf-fringed doorway. The path outside was shaded by a yew tree, and Mrs. Rippon had passed by it carrying her bunch of phlox.

"That grave's a novelty to her," Mrs. Swan said to her grand-niece when her neighbour was out of hearing. "It's only human, after all. I know I was over there every day when Charlie had just died."

The niece, Evie, seemed to stiffen with disdain.

"I wish I could bring her down to earth," Mrs. Swan thought. "What's wrong with going to the graveyard, I should like to know."

"I couldn't bring myself to grieve," she went on. "Poor man, he did suffer. From here to here they opened him." She measured off more than a foot of her own stomach, holding her hands there.

"Yes, you've told me," Evie said, refusing to look.

"'It's a fifty-fifty chance,' the doctor said, before he operated."

As if he would have, Evie thought.

Her mother had told her to take a present to her aunt, and on the way from work she had bought some purple grapes. They were reduced in price, being past their prime, and they lay now on the table in a dish shaped like a cabbage leaf. Dull, and softly dented, they gave a sweet, beery smell to the room. Tiny flies had already gathered round them. They rose for a moment when Mrs. Swan waved her hand over the dish, but soon settled again. Grapes were for the dying, she had always believed, and "deathbed grapes" she called the purple kind. She would rather have had a quarter of a pound of tea.

It was no use Evie glancing up at the clock every few seconds, she thought. The bus would come along no sooner than it was due, if then. It was a wasted afternoon for them both. Mrs. Swan could imagine the argument at her niece's house. "You really ought to go, Evie. No one's been near her for months." "Why pick on me?" Evie would ask, and be told that the others had their families to occupy their time. So Evie—as if being so far unmarried and having to live at home were not enough—was made to do the duty visits, give up her free afternoon. No wonder, Mrs. Swan thought, that she looked as morose as a hen.

She herself had planned a busy afternoon and had brought from the garden a large striped marrow to be made into jam. It matched the white-and-amber cat who had settled beside it on the sofa, as if for company or camouflage. The cat slept most of its life—at night from custom and by day from boredom. On the sofa now he drowsed, had not quite dropped off, for his eyelids wavered. His front legs were folded under him, like a cow's, his whiskers curled down over his alderman's chains—the bib of white rings on his breast.

Mrs. Swan, glancing regretfully at the marrow, noticed him and said mechanically, "Isn't he a lovely ginger, then?"

The cat at once feigned a deep sleep.

"He must be company," Evie said.

Mrs. Swan was often told this, and, although it was not true, she never disagreed. She was not a person who could make a friend of a cat, and had never found the necessity. They bored one another. She had had him to keep away the mice. Instead, he brought them in and played evil games with them on the hearthrug.

"He's no trouble," she said.

Mrs. Rippon passed the open door without glancing in, on her way back from the churchyard. The clock made a sudden rustling noise and struck four with an old-fashioned chime, and Mrs. Swan got up and put the tea-pot by the kitchen range to warm. Evie racked her brains for something to say, and began a tedious description of the bridesmaids' dresses at a wedding she had been to. She thought her aunt could not fail to be grateful for this glimpse of the outside world.

While she waited for the kettle to boil, Mrs. Swan took up her knitting. She was making a blanket from little squares sewn together, and there was already a carrier-bag full of them knitted from oddments of drab-coloured wool—a great deal of khaki left over from the war. The needles clicked steadily and she let her eyes move about the room as her thoughts settled like moths on her possessions. She might wash the muslin curtains tomorrow if the weather held. Evie was dropping cigarette ash on to the rag hearthrug, she noticed. She would put it on the clothes-line in the morning, and give it the devil's own beating.

"The two grown-up bridesmaids were in a sort of figured nylon organza," Evie said. She tried hard to give an accurate picture, but her aunt did not understand the words. The water in the kettle had begun to stir, so she put aside the knitting and finished laying the table. She had some stewed raspberries to eat with the bread and butter. This was her last meal of the day and she always enjoyed it, but she knew that Evie would say "Nothing for me, Auntie," and light another cigarette.

"In a mauvy-pinky shade, lovely with the sweet-peas," she was saying.

"The girl's clothes-mad, though it's only natural," her aunt thought as she poured out the tea and suffered boredom.

Evie lit another cigarette to stop herself yawning, remembering the freedom of stepping on to the bus after these visits, the wonderful release, and the glow of self-righteousness—duty done, sunshine bestowed, vistas widened.

Mrs. Swan stood by the wall of her front garden, knitting, as Evie's bus drove off. It was a summer's evening, with a scent of blossom from the trees in the churchyard. The vicarage doves were strutting about the roof, making peaceful sounds, over the tiles white-splashed with their droppings.

Mrs. Butcher from the Plough Inn had got off the bus before it turned to go back to the town, taking Evie on it. She walked slowly—looking angrily hot, as red-haired people often do—carrying a cardboard dressbox. It was an awkward shape, and the string cut into her fingers. She had hoped to get into the pub without her husband, Eric, noticing it and, seeing him crossing the yard, she stopped to have a chat with Mrs. Swan until he should have disappeared again.

"Lovely evening," she said.

"Yes, very nice," Mrs. Swan responded cheerfully, although usually the woman passed by without speaking, intent on her own business, full of dissatisfactions and impatience. She drank too much at night and laughed for no reason, Charlie used to say when he returned from his evening glass of bitter. But all day long she was morose.

"You're busy." Phyllis Butcher nodded at Mrs. Swan's knitting, determined not to move on until Eric was back in the bar. She would leave the dress-box in the outside Ladies, until after opening-time. Her husband was more observant about parcels than about clothes. Once a dress was unwrapped, she was safe, and if a customer praised a new one and he glanced at it suspiciously, she would look quite surprised and say, "Why, it's been hanging in my wardrobe for at least three years."

"I've got lots of odd wool," she said, when Mrs. Swan explained about the blanket she was making. "The sweaters and things I've started in my time. I'll bring it round tomorrow."

"It's very good of you," said Mrs. Swan. "A different colour makes a change." "I'll believe in it when I see it," she thought, knowing the sort of woman Mrs. Butcher was.

Yet she was wrong, for the very next afternoon Mrs. Butcher came to the cottage with a great assortment of brightly coloured wool. She sat down in the kitchen and drank a cup of tea. She had been crying, Mrs. Swan thought, and presently she began to explain why, stretching her damp handkerchief from corner to corner, and sometimes dabbing her eyes with it.

Mrs. Swan sorted the wool and untangled it. The colours excited her, particularly a turquoise blue with a strand of silver twisted in it, and her fingers itched to begin knitting a new square—an adventure she must put off until she had finished one of mottled grey.

Phyllis Butcher's mother was poorly. Listening, Mrs. Swan thought it did the woman credit that she should weep.

"I'll have to go up there," Mrs. Butcher said. "Up north. Real Geordie country," she added scornfully. "I hate it there."

"I was in service in Scotland once," said Mrs. Swan. "Nice scenery and all, but I was happier when I moved down south. I shouldn't care to go back." The very thought was tiring. She visualised the road to

Scotland, climbing steeply all the way, a long pull uphill, ending in a cold bedroom under the slated turret roof of a castle. "I saw an eagle once," she said. "A wicked great bird. There were stags, too, and cattle with great horns. Five o'clock us girls got up, and some days I could have cried, my hands were so cold."

"Oh, Consett's not romantic," Phyllis Butcher said, "It's all mining round there. I can't stand it, that's a fact, and never could. I know I ought to go more often, but you can't think how it depresses me."

Eric had put it more strongly—hence the tears. "Your own mother," he had said. "You'll be old and lonely one day yourself, perhaps."

"I'd rather be taken!" she had cried.

"Mother's not easy," she told Mrs. Swan. When she had drunk her tea, from habit she turned the cup upside down in the saucer and then lifted it up again and examined the tea leaves. There were always birds flying, and she had forgotten what they meant.

"What's her complaint?" Mrs. Swan enquired, for she was interested in sickness, and when younger had longed to be a nurse.

"Oh, I don't know. If it's not one thing it's another. The house is full of bottles of medicine. Illness gives me the creeps. She's always been chesty, of course." She was still studying the cup and, turning it in her hands, had found the promise of a letter and what she thought was a threatened journey. "I'll go tomorrow," she said. "Get things straightened up here and set off in the morning. 'Hello, stranger,' she'll say when I walk in. That's enough for a start to make me want to turn round and go back the way I came. If she wasn't so catty, I'd go more often. I couldn't do enough for her, if she was only pleasant."

"Why not go straight away?" Eric had said when she received the letter. "She might be worse than she makes out."

"I can't just walk out of the house like that," she had told him. "There are all the things I have to do here—arrangements to make."

To escape his critical eye, she had slipped round with the wool— anything to get out of the house—and had sat in the peaceful little room for over half an hour, trying to improve her self-esteem.

"I should go and get it over with," Mrs. Swan advised, thinking of her niece, Evie, and her bright face when she said good-bye, and her quick, light step going towards the bus-stop. ·

Phyllis did not see Mrs. Swan again until she had returned from the funeral. She had delayed her journey too long, and, as she opened her mother's front gate, bracing herself for the usual sarcastic greeting, she had looked up and seen one of the neighbours drawing the blind over the bedroom window.

She went to stay in a small hotel rather than remain in the house. Eric came up to join her for the funeral, at which she knew the neighbours were watching her and whispering. Their eyes were lowered, their lips set together whenever she turned to look at them, but she guessed what they were saying. They had known her when she was a child, but she had forgotten all of them and their names meant nothing.

She had not pretended to grieve, not even in order to shelter herself from Eric's words of blame. "You could just as easily have gone the day before," he told her. "I don't know what these people think of us."

"And I'm sure I don't care," she said. But she cared very much, and her face burned as she walked out of the chapel after the coffin, feeling the hostility of the other women, the neighbours who had sat with her mother and taken in her meals.

"You'll have to thank them properly," Eric said. "Do something to show your gratitude."

She refused to speak to them. "I know what they're like," she said. "They lean over one another's fences all day long and wag their wicked tongues. Wild horses wouldn't drag me to this place again."

All the unspoken words had hurt her and those spoken ones of Eric's, too. She had such a different picture of herself from the one other people seemed to see, and she was frightened and astounded by glimpses of how she appeared to them, for they perceived traits she was sure she had never possessed—or only under the most serious provocation. She thought so much about herself that it was important to have the thoughts comfortable, and many desolate hours had been made more bearable by gazing at her own reflection. Warm-hearted, impulsive, she was sure she was—herself hardly considered, and then always last, as she bustled about the country-side doing good. "No one knows what people in this village owe her." The words were clear, though the person who said them was only dimly imagined. "She herself would never tell, but I doubt if there's a cottage in the parish where there isn't someone with cause to be grateful. In this village, it's a funny thing, if anyone is in trouble, it's the pub they go to for help, not the vicarage." From her bedroom window, she could look across at the churchyard and would imagine the procession of villagers winding up the pathway under the chestnut trees, in black for her own funeral. "There wasn't a dry eye," she told herself.

Then Eric's sharp phrases splintered the image—"Your own mother." "You think only of yourself and what you are going to put on your back."

She tried not to listen, and could soon comfort herself, just as when she looked in a mirror and the freckled skin and sandy hair were transfigured into alabaster and Titian red.

Sitting at lunch in the train, flying past dreary canals and grey fields, she endured her husband's sullen silence, and buttered bread rolls; buttering and nibbling, to comfort herself, she stared out at the sour-looking pastures.

She was glad to be back in her own picturesque village. The Thames valley consoled her, but uncertainty still hovered about her and she wondered if, after all, she had failed her own image of herself. She had not yet dared to unpack her new dress. It was too bright a colour and she dreaded Eric's comments. She kept it hidden on top of the wardrobe, although she knew that the pleasure of putting it on for the first time was perhaps the only way there was of dispelling her sadness.

To escape the atmosphere of disapproval, she unravelled one of her old sweaters and took the wool to Mrs. Swan, not admitting to herself that, because of past aloofness, there was no other house in the village where she could drop in and exchange a word or two. In the past, an afternoon's shopping had always cured despondency, and, in the evenings, beer and backchat were even better distractions. However, deference to her bereavement seemed to have sobered customers for the time being—the last sort of behaviour to raise her spirits.

Mrs. Swan was not alone. She had called Mrs. Rippon in from the garden to give her a present of a pot of blackberry jelly, and they were sitting at the table, drinking tea.

Phyllis joined them, nervously praising the look of the jelly and everything else she could see.

"I was sorry to hear of your loss," said Mrs. Swan, whose neighbour kept her eyes averted and suddenly took up the pot of jelly and said good-bye.

"I brought some more wool." Phyllis saw the half-finished blanket spread over the back of a horsehair sofa, and began to praise that, too, and got up to study it—the uneven stitches and the cobbled-together squares, the drabness already beginning to break into gaudiness since her last visit. She returned to her chair, feeling that the brightness she had brought was symbolic. "Yes, poor Mother," she said. She bowed her head and sighed and looked resigned. "It sounds a dreadful thing to say, but I can't be sorry, for *her* sake. It really was a merciful release."

That's what young Evie will say about me when I go, Mrs. Swan thought. And so it will be, too, for her.

"It's peaceful here," said Phyllis.

The cat lay asleep by the fender, moving his ears and beating the end of his tail rhythmically against the rug, as if he were in the midst of a dream that bored and angered him. Above the fireplace hung a strip of sticky paper, black with flies, some dead and some dying a wretched death. Others had evaded it, and circled the room slowly and warily.

Phyllis leant forward and sniffed at a vase full of nasturtiums edged with their little round leaves. The smell tantalised her, reminding her of something. Was it mustard, she wondered, or some medicine—or just nasturtiums? They had grown in Consett. Those and dusty, insect-bitten hollyhocks were all she could remember in the shabby strip of garden where her father had kept rabbits.

"Aren't they pretty?" she said, sniffing the flowers again, and then she determined not to praise another thing, lest she should sound condescending. "That's your husband, isn't it?" she asked, nodding at an old photograph in a frame made of sea shells.

"He had that taken the day he joined up, when he was twenty-five. And he wore a moustache like that till he was fifty. Then he began to go bald, and that great bush looked silly then, he thought, so he shaved it off. He hadn't a hair between his head and Heaven by the time he was sixty."

"Yes, I remember," Phyllis said. She supposed she did remember seeing him in the public bar, but she had never bothered to give him a name.

"It's a pity having to leave your mother all that long way away," Mrs. Swan said. "My own mother's buried down in Bristol and the train fare's out of the question. I'd dearly like to go." After a pause, she said, "I expect the flowers were lovely, though it's not an easy time of the year. I find plenty of garden flowers for Charlie, but they're no use for a burial. Gladioli don't make up well and shop roses are exorbitant."

"We sent carnations, Eric and I."

She got up to go and stood looking down at the cat, whose dream seemed to have taken a better turn, for he lay relaxed now, with crossed paws and a smile on his face. Phyllis felt peaceful, too.

"Well, come again," Mrs. Swan said, from politeness.

"I really will," Phyllis promised.

Enlivening Mrs. Swan's life became an absorbing pastime and something of which, for once, Eric could not disapprove. Phyllis was always dropping in to the cottage, and found ingenious ways of giving presents tactfully, not knowing that the tact was wasted, since Mrs. Swan had grace enough to be pleased with the gifts and to accept them simply, unbothered by motives. She thought of them as charity, and had no objection to that. She only wondered why there was so little of it about nowadays.

"The hens are laying like wildfire," Phyllis would say. If she met anyone she knew on the way home, she always explained her outing. "I was just taking a few eggs to poor old Mrs. Swan."

One day she asked her to go back to the Plough for a glass of sherry, but Mrs. Swan thought it a mistake for widows to drink. "I haven't taken any since Charlie died," she said.

"You're very good to that old lady," one of the customers told Phyllis.

"I'm not at all. I just like being with her. And she's got no one else. It means a lot to her and costs me nothing."

"Most people wouldn't bother, all the same."

"It's a terrible thing, loneliness."

"There's no need to tell *me* that."

The bar had only just opened for the evening, and he was the only customer so far. He was always the first to arrive, and although he came so regularly, Phyllis knew very little about him. He was middle-aged and not very talkative, and never stayed drinking for long. "Very genuine," she said, when other people mentioned him. It was an easy label and she made it sound utterly dull.

This evening, instead of opening his newspaper, he seemed inclined to talk. "Living in lodgings palls in the end," he said. "I never married, and it gets lonely, the evenings and weekends. I sometimes think what I'd give to have some nice family where I could drop in when I wanted, and be one of them—remember the children's birthdays, give a hand with the gardening, that sort of thing. Everyone ought to have some family like that where they're just accepted and taken for granted, given pot luck, not a lot of fuss. It's tiring always being a guest. Well, I find it so."

"It sounds to me as if there's a fairy godfather being wasted," Phyllis said.

He smiled. "You feel you'd like to have your stake in someone else's family if you haven't got one of your own. Will you have a drink with me?"

"Thank you very much," she said brightly. "I'd like a lager."

"Well, please do."

"What a lovely rose," she said. "I've always noticed what lovely roses you wear in your buttonhole, Mr...." Her voice trailed off, as she couldn't remember his name. "Well, here's all you wish yourself," she said, and sipped the lager, then wiped her lips on her scented handkerchief.

He had taken the rose from his buttonhole and handed it to her across the bar. "Out of my landlady's garden," he said. "I always look after them for her."

"Oh, you are sweet!" She twirled the rose in her fingers and then turned to the mirrored panelling behind the bar and, standing on tiptoe to see her reflection above the shelf of bottles, tucked the rose into her blouse.

"That reminds me of that picture—*The Bar at the Folies-Bergère*—one of my favourites," he said. "All the bottles, and your reflection, and the rose."

"Well, how funny you should say that. We had it for our Christmas card one year. Everyone liked it. 'Well, we didn't realise they had Bass in those days'—that's what everyone said. 'In Paris, too!' There's those bottles on the bar, if you remember. It makes the picture look a bit like an advertisement. Look at my lovely rose, Eric."

"Good evening, Mr. Willis," Eric said, carrying in a crate of light ale. "Yes, it's quite a perfect bloom, isn't it? I suppose she cadged it off you."

"It's a pleasure to give Mrs. Butcher something," Mr. Willis replied. "As far as I have seen, it's usually *she* who does it all."

Phyllis was happier, gentler than she had been for years. In Mr. Willis's eyes she saw her ideal self reflected.

"Oh, I haven't had time to powder my nose," she would say, scrabbling through her handbag, which she kept on a shelf beneath the bar.

"I suppose you've been off on one of your errands of mercy," said Mr. Willis.

"Don't be silly. I've had a very nice tea party with my old lady in the almshouse. What errand of mercy is there about that? Oh, you really shouldn't. What a gorgeous colour!"

Every evening now, he brought her a rose. When he had left the bar to go back to his lodgings for supper, the other customers teased her. "Your boy friend stayed late tonight," Eric would say.

"He's sweet," she protested. "No truly. Such lovely old-world manners, and he's so genuine."

The evening before her birthday, he came in as usual, admired her new blouse, and gave her a yellow rosebud. "And that may be the last," he said. "Oh, you aren't going away!" she exclaimed, looking so disconcerted that he smiled with pleasure.

"No, but the roses have already gone. Unless we have another crop later on."

"What a relief. You really frightened me. I can do without the roses at a pinch, but we couldn't do without you."

"You're always kind. I enjoy our chats. I couldn't do without them, either."

She turned her head away, as if she dared not meet his eyes.

"How's your old lady?" he asked. In the silence that had fallen he was conscious of his heart beating. It was a loud and hollow sound, like an old grandfather clock, and he spoke quickly lest she, too, should hear it. They were alone in the bar, as they so often were for the first quarter of an hour after opening time.

"My old lady?" she repeated, and seemed to be dragging her thoughts back from a long way away. Then she smiled at him. "Oh, she's very well."

"Have you seen her lately?"

"Well, not many days go by when I don't pop in."

But she had not popped in for a long time. There had been other things to occupy her mind, and shopping had become a pleasure again.

"You must be sure to come in tomorrow and have a drink with me," she said. "It's my birthday."

Instead of pinning the rosebud to her blouse, she put it in a glass of water. "I'll keep it for tomorrow night," she said.

He leant across the bar and took the rose from the glass and wiped it carefully on his handkerchief. Then, hoping he would not blush, he tucked it into her blouse.

The next morning, two dozen shop roses arrived by messenger.

When the bus turned round at the church and set off on its journey back to the town, Evie always felt marooned. Until it returned, in two hours' time, there was no escape.

It was three o'clock on a late autumn afternoon—soft, misty weather. In the churchyard, graves were lost under the fallen leaves. There were pockets of web on the brambles and unseen strands of it in the air. From the bus-stop, Evie could see her great-aunt at work in the churchyard, raking leaves off the grave. She was wearing a forage cap of emerald-green wool that she had knitted herself, and she had tied a pinafore over her winter coat.

"Well, girl," she said, when Evie joined her. "I wasn't expecting you."

"Mother thought the news ought to come from me," Evie said. She sat down on a slab of polished granite and gazed at her aunt's astonishing hat. "I'm getting engaged on Sunday," she said. "Norman's bringing his mother and father to tea, and giving me the ring then. It's a diamond with two amethysts."

"And when's the wedding?"

Evie looked vague. "Oh, I don't know about that. Both Norman and I favour long engagements." She stood up quickly, hearing footsteps and not wanting to be seen sitting on a grave.

Phyllis Butcher was taking a short cut through the churchyard on her way from the post office. She nodded as she passed them, hurrying towards the lych-gate.

"*She's* offhand," Evie said. "There were two women talking about her on the bus. She was in the telephone box outside the post office as we went by. They were saying that she goes down there nearly every afternoon to ring someone up, although they've got the phone at the pub. I must say she looks the type. Does she still keep pestering you?"

"She hasn't been in since the summer. Fill that vase from the tap over there, will you?"

Evie took the stone urn, which was inscribed "In Loving Memory," and made her way between graves to the water tap by the church wall. When she came back, the grave was raked free of leaves and Mrs. Swan was untying the string round a bunch of bronze chrysanthemums.

"I imagine her one of those people—gushing one moment and cutting you dead the next," Evie said, her thoughts still on Phyllis Butcher. "Every time I came last summer, she was stuck there in the kitchen. And putting you under an obligation with all those presents."

"I didn't see any obligation in it."

"I told Mother about her, and she was quite annoyed. It wasn't her place to carry on like that."

"I was sorry for her," Mrs. Swan replied. "She did me no harm." She knelt down to arrange the flowers in the urn. "There, that looks nice, I think. I'm always pleased when the chrysanthemums come. Charlie was so fond of them."

She straightened her back and pushed stray ends of hair under her cap. "If you bring the rake, I'll take the basket. We'll make a cup of tea, and you can tell me about your plans."

They walked slowly to the lych-gate. The last of the yellow leaves were drifting down. On some graves, the chestnut fans lay flat, like outspread hands.

IN THE SUN

"OH, HEAVENS!" said Deirdre Wallace, stepping out of the car with some of her Moroccan trophies—a water-carrier's hat from Marrakesh hanging on a string from her wrist, a native basket, and an ugly, stamped-leather bag.

Her husband, Bunny, snatched at a crumpled chiffon scarf as it loosened from her shoulders in the wind from the sea. He was a soldierly-looking little man, with receding hair; had gone bald very early; was now in his fifties. *So English*, the other visitors at the hotel would be bound to say—not only because of his clothes, but on account of every stalwart movement he made.

Deirdre, before stepping into the coolness of the hotel, looked about her in dismay. She preferred something more Arab—an old Sultan's palace, for instance; or some ancient house inside a medina, with broken mosaics, and wrought-iron lanterns casting fancy patterns on the walls. So far, she had had an instinct for finding such places. This hotel looked like being their first mistake.

Beyond a bougainvillaea-hedge, people were actually playing tennis in this broiling sun. Scarlet Thames-valley geraniums bordered the drive—though more brilliant than any in England, and exuberantly climbing the trunks of trees.

Driving through the town, Deirdre had remarked how very much it was in the style of the departed French, with its *boulevards*, *ronds-points*, shuttered villas named Les Mimosas, Les Rosiers, La Terrasse. There were more bicycles than in Oxford, where the Wallaces lived.

Arab women in *djellabahs* and *yashmaks* looked absurd riding them, Deirdre thought.

Despite the *palmeraie* near which it was built, the new white hotel looked very European. "It might be anywhere in the world," Deirdre complained, "from Nice to the Bahamas—or Torquay."

Beside a peacock-blue swimming-pool, sunbathers were spread out like starfish on brightly cushioned furniture. Limbs stirred occasionally, but hardly a word was spoken. One lone swimmer stood as if bemused on the diving-board, then suddenly flung himself with a deep, crashing sound into the water. The shock of this interruption subsided into peaceful blowing noises, gentle splashes, as the swimmer surfaced, shook the bright water from his face and then, as if once more bemused, began to swim slowly, aimlessly about the pool. No one opened an eye to look at him.

A porter, wearing a somewhat fancy-dress version of Moorish costume, took their suitcases to the lift. A man and woman, in beach clothes, carrying sunbathing paraphernalia stepped out of it. "English," Deirdre murmured to Bunny, as they stood side by side in the lift, ascending.

Bunny was secretly, guiltily, a little glad to see someone from his own country. His French was not as good as Deirdre's, and he spoke it and listened to it under a sense of strain. It would be a relief to chat in his own language—in the bar before dinner, perhaps.

"Very luxe," Deirdre said, but not in a tone of satisfaction, as she glanced about the large, cool bedroom. Bunny wound up the shutters and stepped on to the balcony. The pool, with its coloured umbrellas, was below him. No one was swimming now, but wet footprints round the edges were drying quickly. They vanished one after the other on the hot concrete.

The English couple were arranging themselves ready for their afternoon's sunbathing. They removed their wraps and lay back in their deckchairs—a stout pair, already well on with their tanning. The sun beat down. Arabs, at this time of the day, were squatting in the shade, or safely indoors.

While she was waiting for Bunny to change into his swimming-trunks, Deirdre wandered out into the stone-paved corridor, moving slowly along from window to window, looking at the distant hills, the pink and paprika landscape. The heat seemed to move, to rise and fall, making the dusty air whirl giddily.

A commotion beneath one of the windows made her lean out. A smell of rotting fruit rose from below. This was the back of the hotel and a rough road ran close to it, leading to the cemetery. As she leant out of the window, Deirdre could see beneath her a swarm of children picking over a cart of refuse, disturbing the flies. The sight of this sickened her. "Oh, it is quite upsetting," she told herself. Especially was she moved by one little girl standing apart from the others, tearing pieces off a crust of bread. She was barefooted as they all were, but wore a crumpled party dress of violet-coloured velvet. This, too, had probably come off a rubbish cart, Deirdre thought. It was threadbare, like some old banner hanging in a chapel.

"It was so upsetting," she told Bunny as they went down in the lift. "The back of the hotel might be in a different sphere from the front."

The company about the swimming-pool was still somnolent. The large couple they had seen in the lift had been joined now by two other people—a man and a woman—and a lazy conversation had begun.

Deirdre took Bunny's wrap and went to sit in the shade under a blue umbrella. Very smartly, Bunny stepped on to the diving-board, sprang outwards and did a belly-flop into the still water. The French visitors cried out with good-natured shouts of anguish. Most of the English pretended that nothing had happened. Bunny came up through the water with a crimson chest. Deirdre blushed.

The Troughtons and the Crouches had struck up a desultory holiday friendship. They chatted when they met about the hotel, and joined one another for drinks before dinner, but did not yet go on expeditions together. The Troughtons, for that matter, very rarely went on expeditions. They had come here to get a tan, and seriously developed it from breakfast until the moment when the sun suddenly dropped out of the sky at six o'clock.

"Yes, they were getting into the lift as we got out," Mrs. Troughton told Mrs. Crouch, who had turned her attention to the newcomers on the other side of the pool. "So English," she murmured. "Simply couldn't be anything else."

Bunny flailed about in the water—a splashy, disorganised crawl—and Deirdre sat under the umbrella in her white blouse, her flowered dirndl skirt, a book in her hands, which she read with so little attention that she had not turned a page. Her fond, dreamy gaze was more often upon Bunny. Admiringly, she watched him quietly floating on his back, the little hairy patch on his chest exposed to the sun, his eyes closed.

When at last he came out of the water, Deirdre handed him his robe. Something about her devoted attitude irritated Mrs. Crouch. She doubted if they were married to one another, she said; but Mrs. Troughton could not think why else they would be on holiday together.

Other people greatly engaged Mrs. Crouch, and her husband shared her interest—a rather unmannish trait, Mrs. Troughton thought. Her own husband was not, on holiday, interested in anything. Separated from the Stock Market, his mind became a vacuum. A paperbacked thriller was part of his sunbathing equipment, but he had not so far opened it. His hands were always covered with sun-tan oil, and for much of the time he dozed.

"Doesn't she remind you of Miss Simpson, Daddy?" Mrs. Crouch suggested to her husband, gazing across the pool at Deirdre Wallace.

"*He* reminds me of someone," Mrs. Troughton said, thinking what awful company one sometimes fell in with on holiday—and often, through proximity and one's tolerant holiday spirit, became quite absorbed in their lives. "Someone I've seen somewhere or seen a photograph of," she added.

"Miss Simpson was Janice's music mistress," Mrs. Crouch explained. No need to explain who Janice was. The Troughtons knew all about Janice, who was training to be a nurse. They knew about the hospital, too—the matron, sisters, patients. Mrs. Troughton thought she could find her way blindfold about it...poor staff nurse found crying in the sluice; old Mr. Norwich's registrar kicking up a rumpus in Casualty. She would also be quite at home in the other Crouch girl's, Carol's, office, and in their house (or home—as Mrs. Crouch always called it) in Guildford, with its frilled nylon curtains at seven-and-elevenpence a yard; its sun-lounge and bar—quilted plastic décor done by Mr. Crouch...*Leslie*...*Daddy*...himself.

Well, they were a nice homeloving pair, Mrs. Troughton thought, though this *Daddy* business grated rather. The world would be better with more such peaceable, easily pleased creatures in it.

"Don't you think so, *Daddy*? The image of Miss Simpson."

He looked at Deirdre over the top of his spectacles and agreed. Part of Brenda's unflagging interest in other people was to be constantly finding likenesses between them. She had at the very beginning—last Saturday—decided that Ralph Troughton was a younger, shorter General de Gaulle, and that his Peggy might have been an identical twin to their doctor's wife back home.

That was how Mrs. Crouch had introduced herself to them, sitting at the bar before dinner. "Oh, you must think me terribly rude," she said. "I just found myself staring at you. It quite took my breath away when you walked in. You're so like our doctor's wife back home—we live in Guildford—I thought for a moment..."

Mrs. Troughton was easy, benign, friendly. She smiled. "Here we go," she thought. It will be like those Tillotsons in Majorca and the funny couple in Corfu. She was quite prepared to be genial for a fortnight. Her placid disposition was never disturbed by other people. At home, in London, she protected Ralph from such intrusions; on holiday it was unnecessary, he was not really there.

Mr. Troughton now stirred himself, slapped a fly away from his ankle, got stiffly up and stretched. "Time for a drink," he said. "Last dip," he added. He had few words to spare.

He dived in expertly from the side of the pool, swam powerfully across it, and hauled himself out. The others, feeling rather dazed and enervated by the sun, began to collect their belongings.

After dinner, the Wallaces drank coffee in the hotel courtyard. Light fell from wrought-iron lanterns and printed scrolled shadows on the white walls around them, together with the shadows of giant leaves. A fountain dribbled water back into a pool. An orange dropped from a tree.

Next to them at dinner sat a young American and his Moroccan wife—perhaps on their honeymoon, it was thought. His wife dealt deftly with every situation, speaking in Arabic, French or Spanish. She was as curt with waiters as Deirdre had earlier watched her being with rug-sellers and beggars who hung about the entrance to the hotel. Her shift was of a pale lime-green silk and clung to her, showing her beautiful, wide-apart breasts.

Now she and her husband were sitting across the courtyard, under a climbing-rose tree. She was feeding a thin grey cat with popcorn. Deirdre, who loved cats, had tried to make this one come to her, but it had edged away at her touch. The popcorn made it thirsty, and it kept pattering off to the fountain pool in the middle of the courtyard to have a drink. A boy had hosed the paving-stones. Although they had dried at once, there was still the delicious smell of wet stone.

Deirdre refilled Bunny's coffee-cup and then sat back. He was glancing too often at the young Moroccan woman, almost staring at her at the moment, and to underline his inattention, Deirdre twisted her fingers in her lap and looked fixedly down at them. The message was received. With a little start of confusion, Bunny said, "I was just remembering when you had a dress that colour."

"What colour?" asked Deirdre, glancing round the courtyard.

"That yellowish green."

"When?"

"Oh, I can't remember. Probably years ago."

"Not that colour, I'm quite sure. It wouldn't suit me in the least."

"Oh well…" he said vaguely, taking up his coffee-cup, his eyes anywhere but on that lime-green dress under the roses.

"But," she persisted, "what on earth was it like?"

He regretted mentioning it. He had made a mistake, and she was beginning to think it was some other woman's dress he had remembered. It had been a difficult evening.

In the bar before dinner, she had looked huffily at the other visitors as if cross with them for being English; then had turned away to chat in French with the Arab barman. "Until we came here, we hadn't seen a single English person since we left Ouezzane."

When they reached home after their holidays, she liked to tell people that hardly a word of English had offended their ears from start to finish. Now she would not be able to—for she would not exaggerate, or tell a lie.

Bunny had smiled and said good-evening when Ralph Troughton had come into the bar, and Ralph had nodded back quite genially, settling himself on a high stool and helping himself to olives. It was soon plain, however, that Deirdre was annoying him, monopolising the attentions of the barman as she was, asking him what was the Arabic for peanuts, for cherries, for everything she could see around her.

"Large Scotch," said Ralph Troughton, when he could get a word in.

Deirdre turned her eyes to him and then away.

It was always the same, Bunny thought wistfully, and without bitterness. She drove people from him, shooed them off, as if he were private ground. Sometimes he longed to have a conversation with someone else, another man—this one drinking whisky, for instance.

At dinner, they had found themselves sitting next to the Crouches. The Troughtons, earlier established in the hotel, had a table by the veranda overlooking the swimming-pool and beyond that the dark seashore.

Deirdre recognised Mrs. Crouch as the one who had stared so much at them that afternoon, had been talking about them, had murmured to her companions, Deirdre thought, when poor Bunny had done his belly-flop. To punish her, when she was overheard remarking to her husband how strange it seemed that the scarecrows in the fields should be dressed as Arabs, Deirdre put her tongue in her cheek and smiled, giving a glance under her lids at Bunny.

The food was extremely boring, but Mrs. Crouch was either hungry or easily pleased. That her chop should be tender was enough for her, and several times she told her husband how tender it was.

"Do you remember the *tajine de poulet aux amandes* in Fes?" Deirdre asked Bunny, leaving most of her own chop, putting her knife and fork together. He could see that she had taken a great dislike to Mrs. Crouch.

Now, sitting in the courtyard, listening to nightingales, looking through leaves at the stars—for safety—they both felt tired; tired by one another. Deirdre was exhausted by trying to interest him and keep him happy, trying, in fact, to make up for all the rest of the world; to be a world in herself.

"Shall we hire a *calèche* and drive round for a bit?" Bunny suggested. The Crouches and Troughtons had come out into the courtyard and were settling down at a nearby table. He had written them off. They were not for him.

"Oh, I should love to," said Deirdre. She seemed in ecstasies at the idea and hurried upstairs to select one of her many stoles.

The air was beautifully soft and smelt of orange blossom, as they drove in the *calèche* down the *boulevard*, across the *rond-point* and into the old part of the town. Under the walls, by one of the gates into the medina, a circle of men were sitting on the ground, wrapped round in their *djellabahs*, listening to an old man who was reading to them from a large book. Light from a paraffin flare waved over the pages, over their intent faces. They were absorbed, like children, and did not lift their eyes to Deirdre and Bunny jolting by in their *calèche*.

"It is so beautiful," whispered Deirdre, taking Bunny's hand.

They drove round the walls, and when they came back past the gateway, the circle of Arabs had broken up; the men were dispersing in silence, going their own ways thoughtfully, through the quiet streets, still under the spell of what they had heard.

"It is what we came to see," Deirdre said, with a sweep of her hand at the white walls, beyond them the tower of a mosque topped with a stork's nest. "Not that boring new hotel, not all those tiresome English people. We can have plenty of them at home."

Yet don't, thought Bunny sadly...

It was becoming colder and the fronds of the trees in the palmeraie clashed softly together. Moonlight was enough to read by. It blanched Deirdre's face as she lifted it to look at the stars, it glinted on some metal threads woven into her stole.

The streets were quiet. The only sound was of the horse's hoofs on the road, the creaking of the *calèche*, and then, as they drew near, dance music coming from the hotel.

The Troughtons and the Crouches were just setting out for a stroll before bed. They felt drowsy from the day's sun and non-exertion.

As they went down the steps of the hotel, they saw Bunny helping Deirdre from the *calèche*...her radiant smile as she took his hand.

"*Of course* they aren't married," Mrs. Crouch murmured as she and Mrs. Troughton fell into step together.

"I'd like to go in one of those, Ralph," Mrs. Troughton said, over her shoulder. But she didn't suppose they'd ever bother...

Peggy Troughton sat up in bed and drank her coffee; croissant crumbs scattered on her sunburned chest.

"And his name is Bunny. Isn't that wonderful?" she asked her husband, who was pottering about, getting into his swimming-trunks and sandals, ready for the day's lying-out in the sun. He was rather irritable in the mornings when he was on holiday, having slept most of the day and, so, badly at night.

"What do you think he does?" Peggy Troughton went on.

"Does? What do you mean *does*?"

"I think he travels in lingerie. Or he might own a launderette. It's obvious that *she* has the money, don't you think?"

"What money?"

"Well, for this sort of holiday, for instance, and all those moonstones and seed pearls and garnets that she wears in the evening."

"Poor sod, whatever he does," Ralph said. He found Deirdre's airs and graces intolerable. Her pale-blue eyes, baby hair, and crushed scarves irritated him. Not that she ever talked to him, but she talked *at* him.

"Very henpecked," Peggy agreed. "His accent isn't quite right. A bit too much of a good thing."

She put her breakfast-tray aside and got heavily out of bed. When she had pulled off her nightgown she stood in front of the long mirror, turned round slowly, trying to look over her fat shoulders at her sunburned back. Between the top of her thighs and the lower part of her breasts her flesh was as white as lard.

"Ralph, I'm not peeling, am I? Don't tell me I'm peeling. I am itching all down my spine."

He came across the room and peered at her, as if he were making up his mind about a joint of meat, not looking at a woman, his wife. The red skin across her shoulders was puckered and creased from the crushed-up night-gown.

"Looks a bit angry," he said. "I should give your back a rest today."

But she could not bear to waste a whole day—and what else was there to do?

Going into the bathroom, she said, "And the way she drags him off to those mosques. And all that shopping, and going into those smelly *souks*."

It was another world that these Europeans briefly made—nothing to do with the country they were in, and little to do with the one from which they had come. Everything was centred on the sun cult and its rituals—the oiling, the turning, the rules for exposure and non-exposure, the setbacks—particularly blisters—the whole absorbing process.

They were mostly middle-aged married people who lolled about the swimming-pool all day. The young French girls—the bikini brigade, as Leslie Crouch called them—went to the shore and lay on the sands where a group of straw umbrellas was planted above tide level.

Deirdre was rather relieved when Bunny decided to swim in the sea for a change. There he would have to wade out and she would be spared the anxiety of the dive in.

She went with him, taking her book. She would not bathe herself. The last time she had put on a swimsuit, she had felt absurd, too thin—not the kind of thinness of the young bikini girls, but a wide flatness which looked ridiculous or pathetic; her skin, which never tanned, looked almost mauve. She suffered, deprived of her floating stoles, her floppy hats.

On their way, they passed Mr. and Mrs. Troughton. She was oiling his back, finishing with an affectionate little pat. Then, sternly turbaned and wearing her sunglasses, she opened a book and began to read to him. She had pulled down the straps of her sunsuit and all that showed of her large bosom was reddish brown. The morning air smelt heavily of sun-tan oil.

"A very large lobster," Deirdre whispered to Bunny when they had passed by. "She only needs a dollop of mayonnaise."

They made their way through some dusty oleanders, across the shore road and on to the beach. When they had taken off their sandals, their feet sank deeply into the sharp, hot sand. They plodded slowly through it down towards the water's edge.

Bunny's forehead was peeling, so he wore a little white jockey cap with a long peak. As he strutted, very upright, arms swinging, on the hard ribbed sand they had come to, he resembled some kind of bird. Deirdre thought Mrs. Troughton had looked amused as they passed by, but it was difficult to be sure. Sunglasses take so much expression from the face.

"People come out here," said Deirdre, glaring at the bodies about her, "and bake themselves all day, only glad if they can go back home the colour that they punish other people for being."

"So true," said Bunny.

Without discussing where they should sit, they moved apart from the others and spread towels out on the sand. Bunny removed his hat and shirt, and went trotting down to the sea, his crooked arms jerking back and forth like a long-distance runner's.

Languid, shallow waves came in, gathering little crests of foam, spilling over and fanning out on the sands. After quite a long time, Deirdre could still see Bunny wading out, not even knee-deep in the water.

Quite close to where Deirdre sat guarding his towel and shirt, two young girls came and flopped down on the sand. They were smoothly brown, slimwaisted. One had a pale appendectomy scar showing above the little triangle of bikini. She rolled her almost bare, oiled body over to switch on her transistor-set and a French song blared out.

Not entirely because of this, Deirdre gathered up her things and moved away into the shade beneath an umbrella. She sat there primly, reading; sometimes glancing at the sea, her shiny, white legs tucked under her flowered skirt. When she saw Bunny coming out of the water, she stood up and waved to him. He altered his course and came towards the umbrella.

"Some shade," she explained, handing him his towel. "And that awful transistor-set. They oughtn't to be allowed."

He patted his wet, sunburned face with the towel, glanced towards the two girls, and then quickly back at Deirdre. "You look very pretty sitting under this umbrella," he said. "I wish I had brought the camera."

On Friday it was their last evening. The Crouches and the Troughtons were leaving too, and seemed to be in an especially festive mood. Trying to make less of their jollity, Deirdre worked hard at her now. She was animated, smiling at Bunny and raising her wine-glass to her lips, as if at some deep and secret understanding between them. She gave her dazzled attention to every word he said—as if his fascination for her was endless.

"What can she see in him?" Mrs. Crouch asked her husband, exasperated by curiosity.

"Or *he* in *her*?"

"No, but I mean, to keep it up like this? She must be very new to the game. Don't tell me any woman can find her husband as enthralling as that all the time. Or any man his wife, for that matter. Well, the novelty has to wear off."

"I can't see why she has to try so hard. Don't look now. She just tapped him on the hand as if he'd said something *risqué*. Naughty, naughty."

"Perhaps she has to try so hard because they're not married. She may be in a very insecure position. He may have a real wife somewhere."

"We shall never know."

"Well, they've kept themselves to themselves so much," Mrs. Crouch complained, taking her husband's arm.

"*She's* kept *him* to *herself*."

When they had had coffee in the courtyard, Deirdre went upstairs to tidy her hair. The hotel lounge was being arranged for dancing, the chairs pushed back and the rugs rolled up.

She did her hair, put on an extra necklace, then went out on to the balcony, feeling suddenly limp, headachy. The dance band had begun to play. From below, she could hear the rhythmic beat which depressed her and made her feel nervy.

She wished that the evening was over, or that they might go away from the hotel on another drive in a *calèche*—just quiet—and she and Bunny on their own; but she had not liked to suggest it.

At last, she went downstairs, and rather self-consciously made her way to the lounge. Bunny was dancing with the American's Moroccan bride, who was again wearing the lime-green shift. He looked miserable and embarrassed when he saw Deirdre hesitating by the door, seemed to be trying to send a message to her, as if to say, with his anxious expression, "Wait, I shall come to you as soon as ever I can."

But she did not wait. She turned and went out into the deserted court-yard and sat down, shivering beside the fountain. Bunny found her there, nursing the little grey cat, for warmth, and consolation.

"Did you *see* her face?" Mrs. Crouch asked her husband, as they reversed nattily out of the way of the large bulldozing Troughtons. "He's obviously not allowed to dance with other women."

"Certainly not with the second most beautiful woman in the room," said Mr. Crouch, gazing down at Brenda's faded hair...

"I couldn't avoid it," said Bunny.

"Avoid what?" asked Deirdre faintly.

"He came up to me in the bar and insisted on buying me a drink. She was with him. We stood chatting. They are on their honeymoon. Then the band struck up. He said he didn't dance."

The fountain dribbled. A nightingale was singing. She lifted the cat and kissed its fur.

"It was the least I could do," he went on. He could not say how grateful he had been for someone else to have spoken to him at last.

"Will you come and dance with me?" he asked.

"I'd rather not."

"To please me," he implored.

Carefully she put the cat down, brushed her lap and went before him to the lounge.

Bunny was quite deft at all the old-fashioned dances. Deirdre was taken into his arms as if into a stranger's embrace. She had no sense of rhythm. Stiffly she shuffled, stumbled, blushed. He smiled gallantly and held her tighter, guiding her as adroitly as he could.

To make up for everything, she smiled. She smiled until her cheeks ached. Then she whispered, "After this, can we go for a walk?"

On the next day, on Saturday, the new, pale intake from the north began to arrive. The porter kept bringing down luggage for departing guests and piling it up in the hall—suitcases, and other loot such as camel saddles, rolled-up rugs and brass trays.

The Crouches and Troughtons came in from their last sunbathe, and there were the Wallaces in the hall, ready to depart. At this moment, the American came leaping up the steps with an armful of lilies, and just as Deirdre was going through the hall door he put them into her arms and said, with the most beautiful smile, "In homage!"

Mrs. Troughton took off her sunglasses and stared at him.

He had gone down the steps and opened the car door for her, and Bunny wrote something on a piece of paper and handed it through the window.

"In *homage*!" Mrs. Crouch repeated unbelievingly.

None of them had talked to the American before. His honeymoon state seemed to have insulated him; but when he came back into the hotel, Mrs. Crouch could not contain herself. "Everyone departing," she said dramatically, throwing wide her arms. "After lunch, we're off ourselves."

"I hope you have a good trip," he said politely. He was still holding the piece of paper in his hand.

"Kind regards, Gerald Wallace, Morocco '64," Mrs. Troughton, a little behind him, read.

"For my young brother," he said, waving the paper. "Sure he'll be thrilled. I nerved myself last night and introduced myself. Maybe he gets tired of that, but he was pleasant all right, very pleasant."

"Gerald Wallace," Mrs. Crouch said faintly. "But how did you know?"

"Well, there's the face in the photographs, and the name."

"*Gerald Wallace?*" Mrs. Troughton said, when the American had left them. "Well, really! That Bunny business put us off the scent. To think that Ralph's been reading his book all the holiday—carrying it around, anyway! Where is it, my love?" She took the paperback and looked at the photograph on the cover.

"That must have been taken at least fifteen years ago. All that hair! Well, who would have thought it. How can that man have recognised him?"

"Well, he did," said Mrs. Crouch rather snappily. This was the nearest she had ever been to a celebrity, and she had let him slip through her fingers . . .

At lunch—since it could not now create a precedent—the Crouches were invited to join the Troughtons at their table.

They could talk of nothing else. "I wish I'd asked for his autograph," said Mrs. Crouch, the most incredulous of them all. "Oh, the girls would have been fascinated, intrigued. Of course, Janice has got Sir Malcolm Sargent, you know. I could kick myself."

"It's awfully odd, really," said Mrs. Troughton. "Such a mild, henpecked little man, writing all those exotic stories."

"How does he get off the chain to find out about the underworld—all that violence?" asked Ralph Troughton.

"To think it's the last meal," said his wife, gazing out of the window at the familiar scene, so soon to be a thing of the past.

"All those spies and loose women, Buenos Aires and those sorts of places. Casablanca, Monte Carlo."

"We didn't get to Casablanca after all, Ralph," said Mrs. Troughton.

"International harlots," said Mrs. Crouch, flushing with excitement.

"The last dates," said her husband, taking a few.

"Well, we have tripped up," his wife said, in a more resigned voice. Then, as if suddenly she couldn't get home fast enough, she put down her napkin and asked, "Have we time for coffee?"

She was back in Guildford in her mind, all the tiresome travelling suddenly over, and she was saying to the girls, and her daily help, and her friends at the bridge club, "Now you'll never guess who we met on holiday. Staying in the hotel." They would never guess, and when they were told, they would crowd in with questions that she would be able to answer.

"Now you've got our address," she said to the Troughtons. "And we shall never forgive you if you don't drop in any time you're in Guildford."

Mrs. Troughton let it go. Dreamily, she peeled an orange—knew that she was unlikely to be in Guildford, whereas everybody was in London at some time or another—especially in the part in which she and Ralph had their flat.

The Crouches went upstairs to finish packing, and Mrs. Troughton smiled at her husband as if to say, "What odd people! But it's over now." They would certainly go out to see them off in the car, before they got ready to leave themselves; but really the Crouches had already changed into shades—like the Tillotsons in Majorca and those people whose name they had forgotten in Corfu.

Guildford was gloomy, an anticlimax. The sun-lounge was dark and the large windows streaming with rain. The girls were glad to see their parents, and they listened dutifully—even appreciatively—to the holiday stories. A most united family.

The very next morning, after their homecoming, Mrs. Crouch went out to the public library to look up Gerald Wallace in *Who's Who*: WALLACE, Gerald, *author*; *b.* 3 *July* 1912. Looked older, thought Mrs. Crouch. What a long list of books! European War—despatches three times. Who would have thought it? We were as wrong as could be, Mrs. Crouch decided, peering at the rather small print, her finger underlining it. So very wrong. It was twenty-seven years ago that he had married Deirdre Imogen Burnett—his one and only wife.

Mrs. Crouch left the library, put up her umbrella and picked her way through the streets to the coffee-shop.

"Goodness, how brown you are!" her friends said enviously, who were waiting for her among the horse-brasses and copper warming-pans.

"Did you have a marvellous time?" they asked.

She sat down and drew off her gloves, smiling as if to herself; then she raised her head and looked round the table at her friends' pale faces and, "Guess," she began, "guess who..."

VRON AND WILLIE

HERE WAS London—Willie, Vron and Aunt in the station hotel restaurant. Aunt had brought them from the country, to settle them in their new homes; but before taking them—Vron to the hostel, Willie to lodgings—she had stopped at one or two discreet-looking bars and, finally, at a shabby corner public house—discretion, by then, having ceased to count for anything.

Vron and Willie loved her in a vague way, rather as they had after a fashion still loved their animal pets when the novelty of them had worn off: but it was from a sense of responsibility that they had come back to the station with her, to see her safely on to the train. It was, after all, because of them that she had taken to drink, although they had always suspected that she must in the first place have been a little that way inclined.

It was early evening and the restaurant, luckily, was almost empty. A pale light fell on the white table-cloth and the silvery dish-covers the waitress lifted off their in-between-meals food—poached eggs on toast, with baked beans under the eggs for Willie and sardines (the waitress had looked aghast) for Vron.

They watched Aunt put her knife uncertainly into her egg; and, as the yolk ran out, she seemed to recoil. Nevertheless, they intended her to eat something. Having stowed her in the train, with food in her, they could feel at peace, and forget her. At the other end, the village taxi-driver would meet her, and he knew her habits. They might call at the Bell on their way home. Safely there—the Bell *or* home—she was in her own country. There were people to lift a finger.

"But will you ever find your way back?" she now asked *them*, and for the fifth or sixth time. "Keep seeing one another to and fro could go on all night."

"I *dote* on sardines," said Vron. "I feel I could never have enough of them. Even when they make me sick, the minute after, I'm ready for them again. What could *you* never have enough of, Willie? Aunt?"

Well, the latter of course she knew, and Willie never answered such questions, which seemed to him like talking for the sake of talking.

"I do hope you'll both be all right," Aunt said. She carefully lifted her fork to her mouth, and runny yolk dropped through the prongs on to her blouse. Vron inexpertly dabbed at her.

"I shall miss them," Aunt thought. (In fits and starts, but such very terrible fits and starts.) The angelic siblings, who had never quarrelled, whose rare gravity, even, was amiable. They had the charmed relationship she and their mother had had until the hour of her death. That was a grief, a lack, which did not come and go in fits and starts; but remained, like a long, tired yawn, in the depth of her heart.

She glanced mistily at the two—Vron and Willie—the fluorescent light falling on their silky, beige hair, their pale, composed faces. Vron ate her disgusting mixture with style—as she did everything—appreciatively, but without absorption. Then Aunt put her knife and fork together, defeated. She longed to be home. She sat quite still, with bent head, attempting to assemble facts; but it was like trying to catch goldfish with her hand—the facts slithered from her grasp. She was at the end of her tether, not daring to ask questions, lest she had asked them before, and before that, and had perhaps all day done nothing else but ask. However, no clue from her muddled mind coming to aid her, she said suddenly, in an off-hand voice, barely saying it, looking at the same time into her handbag, "Let me see, I *did* give you your money, didn't I? You're all *right*?"

"Yes, Aunt," they said, not glancing at one another—their manners towards her too good for that.

Willie paid the waitress, and Vron put Aunt's arms back into her coatsleeves; then, one on each side of her, they made their way to the platform. The train was in, and they found an empty, first-class compartment.

"Don't wait, darlings," she said, leaning out of the window. They looked so pale and slight, standing there together, looking up at her. Could she be doing the right thing, she wondered; leaving them in London, so young, only just left school? Today, London had seemed like a jungle to her, with noisy, discordant public houses, terrifying traffic, jostling throngs. Other hazards of London, not being in her experience, she did not envisage for them.

But of course her decision was right, she told herself firmly. To go to London had been just what she and her sister had so badly wanted to do—and had not been allowed.

She closed her eyes for a moment, feeling exhausted. She had done her best. She had brought them up, almost from babyhood, the poor little orphans; and *she* had done so, who was quite out of her depth in such a situation, with such responsibilities. Now she could be proud of them—of their goodness and charm.

But there was one more thing to be settled—surely? At the back of her mind, a certain question shifted about. Matters were getting worse; now that she could not even remember what the question was. She leant forward out of the window.

"Darlings, I forget ... did I ... ?"

"Yes, Aunt, you did," they said together.

"Darling Aunt,

The hostel was so frightful, that I have moved to a room at Miss Bassage's, next to Willie's. I know that you will think this the best thing to do; for you could not have borne it yourself where I was. I was so home-sick; it was a thousand times worse than school. Those awful girls drink hot chocolate all the time, and I got spots on my face, trying to join in. They wash one another's hair, and talk about sex until I was sick at heart."

"That's good," Willie said, interrupting Vron's reading of the letter. "We know our aunt."

She had never married; but she rather resented sex than feared it. It was what had stolen her sister from her.

"Very good about the chocolate, too," Willie added. Neither he nor Vron had ever had spots. For their transparent and unblemished skin, they were, Aunt said, indebted to their mother. Their father, it seemed, had been rubicund.

"It was true, all that," Vron said rapidly, then read on. "'Simply, it wasn't what I have been brought up to. Don't for a moment blame yourself, Aunt dear. No one could have guessed, unless there, what went on behind the façade.' I shall leave about leaving the other place until next week," she said, looking across at Willie.

The other place was the secretarial school where—so soon, Aunt would learn—the girls did not only *talk* about sex.

"Give it a fair chance," Willie said slyly, agreeing.

None of their schools had been good enough for these angels, as Aunt had so very often said, when trouble after trouble had mounted up. *She* knew what they were like, and who could know better? She was misunderstood herself. They formed a little misunderstood family, and had been almost entirely happy.

Willie, applauding his sister's way of cutting loose from her tedious commitments, could find, for the present, no way of severing himself from his own. Daily—almost daily—he went on the Underground to work in a land agent's office in Knightsbridge. One of the partners of the firm was related to Aunt. Willie was vague as to the exact relationship; had not listened when it was explained to him. He hoped it was not too close as to cause unpleasantness when at last, as he must, he found he could bear no more.

"He's like an old bull," he told Vron. "His face the colour of this." They were drinking *cappuccinos* in a coffee-bar, and he stared into his cup with disgust, as if at Mr. Waterhouse's creased old face. "Straggly moustache; hunched-up shoulders," he went on.

Luckily, Mr. Waterhouse did not come often to the office. It was the only thing in his favour.

On the day of this conversation, Willie had been so tempted by the prospect of the sort of day Vron was going to have—doing hardly anything, that is, and nothing she did not want to do—that he could not bring himself to set out for the office. He felt snuffles coming in his head. It was not that he ever found it necessary to lie to himself; but he had been interested to discover that, by a steady concentration, almost self-hypnotism, he could produce symptoms, could make himself sneeze, even raise his temperature, certainly increase his pulse.

Miss Bassage—to whom he first rehearsed—had said it would be folly to go out at all on such a drizzly morning; but at twelve o'clock he and Vron set forth.

London enchanted them—even on such a dreary day as this, with the windows of the Scherzo coffee-bar steamed over, and umbrellas going by in the street. They sat at a corner table, backed by a blown-up print of the Grand Canal at Venice. The ceiling was hung with strings of onions, Chianti bottles, and bunches of plastic grapes. Every now and then, the coffee-machine gave out a dreadful gasp, like a giant's death-rattle.

Although rather impeded by financial worries, Vron and Willie were very happy this noon-day. Aunt's money was harder to come by at their new distance from it. No letters from them to her had yet been answered. Their allowances arrived—the sum judged suitable by Aunt's old solicitor—but the past, of having what they wanted, had not fitted them for cheese-paring, or putting sums aside. In London, surrounded by so many new needs that they had hardly before pictured (such as coffee-bars, cinemas, record-shops), their condition could have been vexatious but for their sunny dispositions.

"This is the life," said Willie, and put his lips to the creamy froth of his coffee.

Beautiful, glossy Danish buns were put on the next table, and he turned his head away quickly from the sight. He could too well imagine biting into the flaky, soft texture of them, tasting the thin sugary icing, smelling the spice. His imagination was like some extra, unfair pain he had to bear—one of the few things that separated him from Vron, who seemed free of it. "Very nice," she had said, as they had stood looking into a shop window earlier that morning. When she turned away, he had turned away, too; but reluctantly, and with pictures still in his head—they would remain—of what he would look like in the striped *matelot's* sweater—bands of dark blue and white—cut high and straight across at the neck. It would make a different person of him for two pounds ten.

Used only to school tuck-shops and the village post office, London was too much for them. Some sort of saliva of the spirit flowed continually, excruciatingly. At every turn was something saying mutely, Behold! There were beckoning fingers, luring suggestions, and no Aunt, any longer, to provide.

Vron, more philosophical, less sensitive, was able to watch—though with detestation—the woman at the next table helping herself to another bun, biting daintily at it, dabbing her lips with her paper napkin, into which she then screwed her sticky fingers.

"I might go and work there," Vron said presently. While Willie's eyes had been fixed on the *matelot* sweater, hers had strayed to the notice in the corner of the window, advertising for what was termed a "saleslady."

There was something from her childhood which gave glamour to the idea of serving in a shop. She remembered the satisfaction of turning a garden seat into a counter and standing behind it to count acorns and put them in a paper bag, to hand them across the seat to Willie, taking leaves from him, and giving back smaller ones for change. The shopkeeper had a more positive role than the customer. To work in a big store must be the game on an exotic scale.

Willie had not noticed the advertisement and, as soon as she told him, his heart eased. Pounds, several pounds, perhaps many pounds (he really had no idea), would be added to their pittance.

"Let's go straight away," he said. He pushed aside his empty cup, edged round the table and went to the cash desk. Vron tilted her head back, sucking the last of the froth from her cup, and wiping her hand across her mouth, followed him out into the street.

"I simply took it. It was perfectly easy," said Vron. "It was there. *You* wanted it. I took it." Impatience, posing as patience, gave precision to her words.

"But it was hanging up in the window."

"It was *displayed* in the window," she corrected him. "Not this one, though. Inside there were dozens. Different colours, too. But I thought you would prefer the blue."

"Oh, yes," he said quickly, blinking his eyes at the thought of anything but this colour. "I only like the blue." Having said this, he had accepted the situation, accepted the sweater. He began to tear off his shirt excitedly.

They were in his room, where the gas-ring was, and Vron emptied a tin of baked beans into a saucepan and began to heat them.

The two rooms they had on the second floor were at the end of a dark passage. (Also use of bathroom, one flight down; and, by special arrangement, kitchen on ground floor.) They had never made any especial arrangements, preferring to keep out of Miss Bassage's way. ("Pack," they had nicknamed her, between themselves.) They saw her only by chance, as they went through the hall, on their way in or out. They kept their own rooms tidy—or otherwise, according to their whim—and ate in hamburger bars, or else, as on this evening, opened a tin of something at home.

Once upon a time they had been more ambitious about food, and Miss Bassage, meeting them as they came home from the market— Vron with an armful of leeks to make soup—had cried out in horror, "*Do* my eyes deceive me? You surely aren't going to *cook* those? You'll smell the whole house out."

They had watched with fascination the bead of mucus wavering on the end of her nose, trembling more and more, as her indignation rose.

"Isn't she scrawny?" Willie said, as they reached their own

landing. He had to hold his stomach for a while, so pained was he by kept-back laughter.

It was true that they had certainly stunk the house out with the leeks, which boiled and boiled in the only saucepan, but never turned themselves into soup.

Thinking of this failure, Vron stirred the safe and easy beans, her smooth hair hanging down round her pale face. She yawned, as she crouched there by the gas-ring, so tired, most awfully tired. All day long, she was at everybody's beck and call, running errands, taking messages. Not once had she been allowed to sell anything and, as soon as one o'clock on Saturday came, she was going to take her wages, and a pair of doe-skin gloves she had her eye on for a present to Aunt, and then Price & Trounsell would never see her again.

"It's so quiet," Willie complained, pacing about the room as she heated the beans. It was indeed quiet in this faded cul-de-sac, much quieter than the country. There were no animal noises, for a start. This was a respectable district. Aunt's solicitor's friend's nephew had once lodged here as a student of something or other, and Miss Bassage had been like a guardian angel to him, had even taken him to the Chapel social, and to an amateur performance of *The Pirates of Penzance*.

Willie looked out of the window at all the railings and steps, the high, narrow houses, some with old, dusty ivy on the walls, and all of yellowish-grey bricks. It was not the kind of London in whose glittering swirl they were elsewhere caught up.

"We ought to have one of those little transistor-sets," he said, turning to Vron. She looked up from the saucepan, shaking her hair away from her face. Their eyes rested on one another's for a moment; but not a word was said.

Aunt was delighted with the doe-skin gloves—in fact, so gladdened that she wept. Although they were several sizes too small, she carried them to the pub and showed them to people; and continued to, one evening after another, always forgetting she had done so before. She passed them round to be admired. Sometimes, she left them behind, and had them back next day. Although winks were exchanged, her gloves were treated with reverence, with murmurs tinged with simulated envy. And they grew soiled from constant handling.

"Such an unerring instinct," Aunt would say. "That comes from *our* side. We have always had this feeling for quality. Their mother was just like the Princess with a pea in her bed."

Her cronies had never known her to be coarse before, and they always waited for this pronouncement with an especial, wicked glee.

Aunt's life was now a contented one. She believed that she had faced her duties fairly and squarely, and at last was justly freed from them. She had reared her sister's paragons, and brought them to perfection. She took credit for their grace, their good manners, their clear complexions. (Hadn't there been something quite lately about Vron drinking hot chocolate—so ruinous to the skin? But she, her aunt, had very properly put a stop to it.)

Puzzling letters had recently come about Vron, from the hostel and the secretarial school, written on a note of uncalled-for tartness, and almost as if in reply to letters from herself to them.

But the catspaw they occasioned soon was smoothed. The young ones' footwork had been put in. That remedy they had made habitual Aunt turned to as a matter of course. She had thrown the letters on the fire and made for the sideboard. Standing there, she poured out brandy into a large glass and drank quickly, her hand still on the uncorked bottle, and very soon it seemed that the letters were a long-ago matter, which she had dealt with and settled satisfactorily.

It was like an illumination to Vron—the idea that having left Price & Trounsell's did not cut her off entirely from the pleasures of shoplifting. Obviously, there were other shops. She realised that all of London lay at hand, glittering with treasures. Her grace and deftness, her small alert body, her way of weaving herself unerringly through a crowd, made the pursuit seem almost pre-ordained. She had a vocation for it, she felt; and it was not long before Willie heard his own call.

At first, they took only what seemed to them necessities—a tin of baked beans from the back of the display, because they were hungry; or the little transistor-set (under the folded raincoat on Willie's arm), because number seven Enniskillen Grove was too quiet for their liking. But soon, these children of the Princess who had the pea under the mattresses developed an exquisite taste in shop-lifting. They chose the softest cashmere sweaters in beautiful shades of slate blue and apricot; silk shirts; little pots of Beluga caviare. They had not eaten caviare before, but a nice instinct led Vron's hand to the Beluga. "It opens up a new kingdom," said Willie, spooning it from the jar.

"Shall we try *pâté de foie gras* tomorrow?" Vron suggested.

"No, it's frightfully cruel," he said, looking shocked.

They sampled a very small bottle of cherry brandy, taking it from a table-spoon like medicine; pulling faces. They were rather prim and disapproving where alcohol was concerned. It seemed to them that it was the clever ones who did not drink, and it was quite clear to them that those who did so were exploited. In the old days, they had only to pour more and more brandy into Aunt's glass, topping it up constantly, to get practically anything they wanted. She usually gave in. If she did not, they pretended that she had, and she would easily be convinced. "But, Aunt, don't you remember promising last night?" In shame, she would quickly agree that it had been so; had for a moment slipped her memory.

Muzzy, and just where they wanted her, she deteriorated. They flourished. And the lessons they most needed and respected were those they had taught themselves.

"I shall speak to Charlie Garter," Miss Bassage said, in her angry, wobbly voice, standing with her fists on her hips, blocking their way to the stairs.

"Who he?" asked Willie insolently, bending to tie his shoe-lace just to his liking, as if the last thing in the world he wanted to do was to go upstairs.

"Police Constable Garter to you," Miss Bassage said.

Vron noted tears of anger in her eyes. Of *anger*! she thought. Such an unusual manifestation. *She* knew who P.C. Garter was. She took more interest in people than did Willie. She had seen the constable going up Enniskillen Grove, padding along with his slow pace. She had recognised him at once when she met him coming out of Miss Bassage's kitchen to the hall where she, Vron, stood with a little tray of *petits fours* she had just pinched scattered on the floor.

"Allow me," said P.C. Garter stopping. He looked quite different, she thought, holding his helmet in one hand, snatching up thieved *petits fours* with the other; really looked so unfamiliar, bare-headed. She felt quite shy of him in this informal situation, as if she had caught him off his guard.

He had just been having a cup of tea with Miss Bassage, she guessed. They went to the same Wesleyan Chapel. Miss Bassage had stood watching him, with the look which should be accompanied by purring.

She was not purring now.

"I shall write to your aunt," she went on.

Willie was still arranging his shoe-laces. ("Oh, they *rile* me," she would tell P.C. Garter later on. "They just *rile* me.")

"Do my ears deceive me?" Vron asked, unwinding a marabou stole from her neck. "Oh, dear! That dewdrop!" she thought.

"A little common consideration. You're not the only people in the world, nor in this house, either."

Someone in a room below had complained of the noise; for Vron and Willie would come back from their forays in the early evening, dump the loot, turn up the wireless very loud, and dance. They danced non-stop, as gay as birds in April.

Really, Vron thought, her feet were itching already, while she stood there whirling the marabou stole in circles.

"Or *go—you—will*," Miss Bassage ended, stepping across the hall at last, slamming the kitchen door. She had threatened P.C. Garter, their aunt, and expulsion. She could think of nothing else, and what she *had* thought of would surely be enough.

With hands over their mouths, Vron and Willie bolted upstairs, flung themselves into the room, laughing convulsively.

"It's 'akimbo,' isn't it, like this?" Willie asked, imitating Miss Bassage.

They collapsed into chairs, writhing with laughter, and Vron stuffed her stole into her mouth, then wiped her eyes with it.

But they were too hungry to go on laughing for long. Vron fetched the bread-knife, and cut a couple of lobsters in half. While they ate them, they felt at peace; they enjoyed the contentment of those who have discovered their real way of life; the deepest satisfaction.

"What *else* do we want?" Vron asked, looking round the crowded room.

"Those portable record-players are rather neat," said Willie, putting a lobster claw on the floor, and stamping on it. "Not too big, either."

"And to think of all the records we could get," said Vron. "And dead easy, too."

After supper, they switched on the transistor-set and danced, obliged to make up a kind of very slow twist to the last movement of Brahms' Symphony Number One.

"You see what I mean about the record-player?" said Vron. "This is hopeless."

They danced on, however, and with vigour, not hearing someone banging furiously on the ceiling below.

"So light, you could eat it with your teeth out," said P.C. Garter, praising Miss Bassage's Victoria sponge.

"Oh, I fancied it wasn't quite up to the usual," she said, flushing with pleasure.

At this moment, Vron and Willie were going upstairs, with the record-player in a large rush basket, hidden under packets of popcorn. Soon all hell was let loose. The tenant in the room below banged at his ceiling until he was breathless with exertion and anger. Then he descended the stairs and knocked on Miss Bassage's kitchen door.

"Well, *this* is final," she said grimly. "This has done it. They'll have to go. I wrote to their aunt, but not a word from her. I've *warned* them enough."

Her eyes strayed to P.C. Garter, sitting there so happily, drinking tea, his helmet on the horsehair sofa behind him. She hesitated. "A word from you," she suggested. "With the authority of the law behind it." For, indeed, how *could* she turn them out into the street, at their age, having had Willie, at least, practically put into her care?

"Quite unofficial, of course," she added.

P.C. Garter rose and took up his helmet. As he and Miss Bassage climbed the two flights of stairs, the clamour from above grew louder, beat down on them. Miss Bassage put her hands over her ears.

The dancing stopped as he flung open the door. Vron and Willie froze like statues. Their faces were pink, making their green eyes look greener; their hair was tangled.

The record came to an end; and in the sudden silence, P.C. Garter said, "*Well*, now," and took a slow stride or two forward, crunching on popcorn which was scattered over the floor. Neither Vron nor Willie moved. Miss Bassage's eyes, astonished, flew about the room. P.C. Garter's, more calculating and interested, travelled slowly, at loot piled on loot; chairs, bed, cupboard and chest tops heaped with plunder.

"Well, well, *well*," he said, taking a turn about the room, picking up a large pot of caviare and reading the label aloud. "Well, well, well," he said again. All the time, he was watched by the statues, followed by the thoughtful-looking bright green eyes, in the now pale faces.

When Aunt was asked questions about the children—often by malicious, winking people who already knew the answer—she would think for a little, trying to gather what was left of her ravelled wits, and say at last, "They are continuing their education." And this was true.

THE VOICES

WHEN THE voices began again, Laura decided that she had let things go too far to demonstrate the thinness of the walls by coughing. To have to speak in whispers from then on might spoil their holiday, and would take something from her own. As they talked, she could hear movements about the room, the rattling of coat-hangers in the wardrobe. The conversation was discursive, languid, and there were long, tired silences.

She had never seen them, had never come across them in the passage or waiting for the lift, and was amused to know so much about two women she had never met. For instance, she knew that Edith's little trouble had cleared up at last, and she was glad about that. It had seemed a pity to waste two days of a holiday, from fear of leaving the hotel. Amy had seemed to be kindness itself, hardly venturing out except on little errands, and having trays of plain food sent up for her friend. "It's the oil, all that oil," Laura often heard.

She spent the hot part of the day in her bedroom, writing letters or lying on the bed, listening, keeping quiet. When she opened the shuttered windows, the noise of Athens roared in—traffic, pneumatic drills, the chipping of steel on masonry, bells tolling—and in flowed, too, the steady heat, the glare from the sky, and greasy smells from the kitchen below. When she had failed to find any fresh air, Laura closed the windows and flopped back on the bed to listen.

"It was just a sort of mince with a batter," Amy said.

"Really more of a custard," said Edith.

"'Mousaká,' they called it."

"Mousaká," Edith said. She was the less gentle one. She liked to know more, and dominated. Taller, Laura thought. She imagined Amy rather plump and soft. Her voice was high and floating, very sweet. Edith's was abrupt and deeper. It was Amy who had been so affected by the stairs when the lift was out of order. She had puffed and blown for a long time after they reached their room. It was the morning that they visited the Acropolis (a view of which Laura could have by leaning right out over the courtyard and craning her neck upwards), and both were worn-out, but exalted. To think they had really seen it, after all these years, they said over and over again.

To Laura, at first, they had sounded like school-mistresses; but the summer term could not be ended yet. They might have retired; yet she pictured them leading some kind of busy life together—"my colleague," they might say in introductions to other people—"a colleague of mine." It was clear that their holiday had been planned for a long time and Laura was glad that, apart from Edith's little trouble at the beginning, it was being a success. They went off to Delphi, having what they called "mugged it up" first, and Laura wondered anxiously if Delphi would come up to expectations. It had, and more. Sounion, in spite of a thunderstorm (perhaps because of it, Amy suggested), had greatly impressed, and even the food was what everyone—and especially a certain Colonel Benson—had warned them that it would be.

From Myconos ("just a little bit touristy") they had apparently brought back a quantity of peasant art—the prices of it were much compared and discussed—and Laura could imagine them making their excursions draped in crudely striped stoles, their hair covered with bright scarves, guide-books and sun-tan oil in fringed and tasselled shoulder-bags.

On the other side of the wall, they often mildly argued. "We paid no credence to Colonel Benson about drinking the water," Amy had said, when Edith had her bout of diarrhoea.

"I paid no credence then. I pay no credence now," said Edith sharply. "It is a long time since the Colonel was in Athens. It was the oil—'This oil's *off*,'" I remember saying to you the first evening we were here. In that place with the wine vats. It was rancid."

Amy had murmured something in reply, but for once Laura could not hear.

Sometimes, when Laura awoke in the morning, the voices were going on as if they had not stopped all night; other days, there was silence, broken by Alexis bringing their breakfast.

"Good-morning, good-morning, ladies," he would call out in a warning, lilting voice, and Laura imagined the scramble for bed-wraps, the sheets drawn up to their chins as they gravely replied in the other language: "*Kali méra*, Alexis." When he had gone, Laura would hear long yawns, the sounds of breakfast beginning, and the start of the day's conversation.

"How kind Madame Petropoulos was," said Amy. "I made a note of the restaurant she recommended. *Where* did she say to get the rose-petal jam from?"

Edith had made a note of that somewhere. They had acquired a habit of writing everything down, for there was a great deal they were in danger of forgetting. They had brought a letter of introduction to Madame Petropoulos and had been greatly excited about their visit to her. Amy had even been tempted to wear the stole she had bought as a present for her niece.

Madame Petropoulos had a flat high up in a building at the foot of Mount Lycabettos (such a pull up from the hotel; they had arrived quite winded and then had to climb the flights of marble stairs), and they had sat out on a balcony and looked at the view—the Acropolis golden in the evening light, the mountains violet and Salamis darkening in the glittering sea. They had described it over and over to one another as they went to bed the previous night, rather over-excited, like children. It had been a high spot of their holiday. This morning, they began to marvel at it again. "We must remember to send her a Christmas card," Amy said. "Although I don't think they make as much of it as we do."

"Don't *speak* of Christmas," Edith begged her, with the English dread of it in her voice.

"We needn't have worried about the language. I must confess I was quite nervous at bringing out my few sentences."

She had been rehearsing these—compiled from the phrase book—for days beforehand; but Edith, whom Laura suspected of fearing to make a fool of herself, would not try. "We know that Madame Petropoulos can speak English. Colonel Benson told us so," she had reminded Amy, interrupting her rehearsal of "Athens pleases us very much. We go to Delphi." (Everything in the phrase book was in the present tense, but she hoped to be understood.) "Delphi pleases us very much. Myconos pleases us very much. And Sounion."

To her girlish wonder and—it appeared to Laura—Edith's annoyance, the phrases had seemed to be understood and had gone down well. Madame Petropoulos had responded with warm surprise, had said, in fact: "Now I do not know whether to speak to you in English or Greek."

"Such a lot of gold teeth when she laughed," Amy said afterwards, repeating what she had said. "And clasping her hands and shaking them over her head like that reminded me of those boxers we saw on the television."

"*You* saw," Edith said.

"But the *view*—the colours changing all the time and then suddenly the lights going on out at sea."

"I think we stayed too long. I kept trying to catch your eye."

"I simply forgot time existed."

Laura could hear breakfast-trays being put aside, and then creakings and rustlings about the room, water running. She lay very still in bed, her arms laced under her head, and wondered what to do with her day. She also had letters of introduction and invitations, but she had done nothing about them. The habit of inertia is a hard one to shake off, the accidie of mind and body torments as it takes hold. After a long illness, her parents had persuaded her to go away—perhaps as a holiday for themselves as well. For her, it was too soon; travel had not broken into her apathy; flying in, she had gazed down at the islands with indifference, though their tawny beauty would at one time have moved her to tears. Since then, she had wasted the holiday, mooning about in the morning sunshine, lunching at the same place every day, resting in the afternoon. It was a much more real holiday—this one she enjoyed vicariously through the bedroom wall.

When Amy and Edith had gone out, she telephoned for her own breakfast and ate it sitting up in the hard bed—spreading the pieces of dry bread with melting butter, drinking coffee from a large, thick cup.

It was such a silence, now that the next room was empty. They had gone down to the travel agency in the Square to arrange a trip to Mycenae. *I* ought to do that, Laura thought. As things were turning out, she would have nothing to say for herself when she returned home. "Did you go there? Did you see such and such?" And to those questions, she would say, "No, no, no," her voice rising irritably. "I just stayed in my room and listened to two old ladies chattering."

She dressed and went out and wandered about the busy streets. The day was well on for other people. After a time, she found herself in a cool flower market with watered pavings. She walked all round it, breathing the scented air, made her way out of it by a different narrow street, and soon was lost. Some buildings looked familiar from other similarly aimless wanderings, but she could form no pattern from them. She could not even read the letters of the street names, or those above the shops. The feeling of isolation was the worst she had suffered since her illness, and she was ready to sit down on some church steps she had arrived at and weep until someone rescued her. She was too much of a burden to be managed by herself alone.

In the end, she found a taxi and was driven back to the hotel. When she reached her room, she was a little comforted to find that Edith and Amy had also returned, were busily counting coins as they did after all their expeditions. When they had settled everything fairly down to the last drachma, they began to sort out the picture-postcards they had bought.

"There is quite an art in timing them," Edith said in a humorous voice. "If you send them off too soon, one's friends are apt to think one is at a loss to know how to pass the time, that there is nothing better to do, that one can only think of people back home, and are perhaps homesick. Then, too late seems like a last-minute thought and a dreadful risk that they may arrive after one arrives oneself."

"I think *now* is just about right," Amy said.

"And another thing is that they must all be posted together. I haven't forgotten that rumpus when we went to Rimini and some people in the village got them early and others thought they had been forgotten."

"Don't you think we might send Colonel Benson's off a little earlier than the rest? After all, he's been so kind. It would be a small mark of appreciation."

"Perhaps a couple of days," Edith conceded. "I thought this one of the Evzones for him—it was about the nearest I could find to anything of a military nature."

"And this Archaic statue for Mrs. Campion, don't you think? It is *so* like her daughter-in-law."

"Funny that that smile looks so beautiful on a statue, and is simply infuriating on a real person."

Laura, lying on her bed, nodded to herself and smiled a different smile.

"We will go after tea and get the stamps," said Amy, making it sound quite an expedition.

So somewhere, Laura thought, they had organised tea-time, as they had organised everything else. She felt ashamed of herself, not able to imagine *them* wanting to sit down on the steps of a church and weep.

There were some silences in the next room while—Laura supposed—they wrote their postcards. She hoped all those people in whatever village it was would value the trouble that had been taken.

"The temple of Poseidon *is* later than the Parthenon, isn't it?" asked Edith.

"I am almost sure; but you could look it up. Who is that for?"

"The Vicar."

"I am just putting personal things. 'Sitting here in the sun, drinking *retzina*.'"

Laura turned her face to the pillow, laughing silently.

"But you aren't," said Edith. "Oh, there is so little space on a post-card, and so much to say."

When they had gone out to tea, Laura had a shower and went for a walk in the Royal Gardens. Dusky, dappled light was shed through leaves and petals, and peacocks stepped fastidiously over fallen, rotting oranges under the trees. She sat on a seat and watched the passers-by—beautifully dressed babies in perambulators pushed by English-looking nannies in uniform, young couples hand in hand, older men wearing sunglasses, swinging keyrings, treading ponderously. One of them passed several times, staring at her with curiosity, but her indifferent English air puzzled and at last defeated him.

The sun went down quickly, and when she got up at last and came out of the Gardens the temples on the Acropolis had turned from golden to a shadowy brown.

The next morning, after Alexis's high-spirited "Good-morning, ladies," Laura heard Edith and Amy mugging up Mycenae from the guide-book. They were to set out the next day, early in the morning, and Laura decided that she, too, must go somewhere. She felt like knocking on the wall to ask them where. Delphi, she knew, they had especially enjoyed. It had been described as picturesque.

"We now enter a circular chamber shaped like a beehive," Edith read from the guide-book in a voice unlike the one she used in conversation.

"I can't take in so much beforehand," Amy complained. "I like to read about it *after* I've been there."

"And *I* don't like going round a site with a book in my hands," said Edith. She then must have dropped the guide-book on the floor, because Amy exclaimed about the pressed flowers that had fallen out.

"And I get the royal family so muddled up," she said, panting a little, perhaps on her knees, gathering up wafery, dry wild flowers. "Agamemnon and so forth."

"Perfectly straightforward," Edith replied. "Agamemnon returns from the war, Aegysthus and Clytemnestra murder *him*; Orestes murders Clytemnestra; Electra—"

"Your *hands*!" interrupted Amy. "Just look at your hands. All the time you were saying that, they weren't still for a moment. You laugh at *me*; but, goodness, you are even worse."

"I don't do it in the street," said Edith coldly.

It was then that Laura, diverted and off-guard, suddenly sneezed. Reaching for a handkerchief to stifle it, she was too late, and knocked over a glass of water.

There was a deep, long silence in the next room. She imagined them staring at one another, hardly daring to stir. It was some time before they began to whisper and move stealthily about the room.

Sitting in the bus, on her way back from Delphi, Laura wondered how Edith and Amy had enjoyed Mycenae. Enjoy it she knew they would; their enthusiasm would reduce the ancient horrors, dispassionately they would relate old histories as if describing house parties at Balmoral.

Laura felt put to shame by their toughness. At Delphi, brooded over by towering crags, diminished, overawed, she had tried to put herself in their state of mind in the same place—happily darting from one wild flower to another, describing—as they had—the scenery as picturesquely mountainous. They had even had someone sick on the bus, as Laura had, but were led by this simply to talk of national characteristics. Greeks had poor stomachs; they had known this beforehand; hadn't Colonel Benson himself said so?

When she reached the hotel, Laura found flowers in her room and an invitation to a party. She wondered if she might not accept it after all. The journey to Delphi, however shattering, had been a beginning. It might now be pleasant to talk again to someone in her own language. Yet she had not been so very lonely. Edith and Amy had been just the undemanding company she would have wished for, and she hoped that they were not still talking in whispers on her account.

She awoke early the next morning, and there was silence in the next room. She lay and waited for the coming of breakfast and the beginnings of conversation. "Perhaps they have finished talking about Mycenae by now, and I shall never find out about it," she thought.

When Alexis came along the passage and opened the door of the next room, his voice was less warning than usual, Laura thought, and less genial. "Good-morning, good-morning," he called, falsely bright.

Someone groaned and yawned. "Good-morning to you," a man's voice replied—an American voice.

Laura was quite shocked. As soon as Alexis had gone away down the passage, she began to cough sharply. She telephoned for her breakfast, making as much noise about it as she could when it arrived.

So they have gone, she thought. They have followed their post-cards back home, and Colonel Benson will hear about Mycenae and the rest, not I.

THE DEVASTATING BOYS

LAURA was always too early; and this was as bad as being late, her husband, who was always late himself, told her. She sat in her car in the empty rail-way station approach, feeling very sick, from dread.

It was half-past eleven on a summer morning. The country station was almost spellbound in silence, and there was, to Laura, a dreadful sense of self-absorption—in herself—in the stillness of the only porter standing on the platform, staring down the line: even—perhaps especially—in inanimate things; all were menacingly intent on being themselves, and separately themselves—the slanting shadow of railings across the platform, the glossiness of leaves, and the closed door of the office looking more closed, she thought, than any door she had ever seen.

She got out of the car and went into the station walking up and down the platform in a panic. It was a beautiful morning. If only the children weren't coming then she could have enjoyed it.

The children were coming from London. It was Harold's idea to have them, some time back, in March, when he read of a scheme to give London children a summer holiday in the country. This he might have read without interest, but the words "Some of the children will be coloured" caught his eye. He seemed to find a slight tinge of warning in the phrase; the more he thought it over, the more he was convinced. He had made a long speech to Laura about children being the great equalisers, and that we should learn from them, that to insinuate the stale prejudices of their elders into their fresh, fair minds was such a sin that he could not think of a worse one.

He knew very little about children. His students had passed beyond the blessed age, and shades of the prison-house had closed about them. His own children were even older, grown-up and gone away; but, while they were young, they had done nothing to destroy his faith in them, or blur the idea of them he had in his mind, and his feeling of humility in their presence. They had been good children carefully dealt with and easy to handle. There had scarcely been a cloud over their growing-up. Any little bothers Laura had hidden from him.

In March, the end of July was a long way away. Laura, who was lonely in middle-age, seemed to herself to be frittering away her days, just waiting for her grandchildren to be born: she had agreed with Harold's suggestion. She would have agreed anyway, whatever it was, as it was her nature—and his—for her to do so. It would be rather exciting to have two children to stay—to have the beds in Imogen's and Lalage's room slept in again. "We could have two boys, or two girls," Harold said. "No stipulation, but that they must be coloured."

Now *he* was making differences, but Laura did not remark upon it. All she said was, "What will they do all the time?"

"What our own children used to do—play in the garden, go for picnics..."

"On wet days?"

"Dress up," he said at once.

She remembered Imogen and Lalage in her old hats and dresses, slopping about in her big shoes, see-sawing on high heels, and she had to turn her head away, and there were tears in her eyes.

Her children had been her life, and her grandchildren one day would be; but here was an empty space. Life had fallen away from her. She had never been clever like the other professors' wives, or managed to have what they called "outside interests." Committees frightened her, and good works made her feel embarrassed and clumsy.

She *was* a clumsy person—gentle, but clumsy. Pacing up and down the platform, she had an ungainly walk—legs stiffly apart, head a little poked forward because she had poor sight. She was short and squarely-built and her clothes were never right; often she looked dishevelled, sometimes even battered.

This morning, she wore a label pinned to her breast, so that the children's escort would recognise her when the train drew in; but she felt self-conscious about it and covered it with her hand, though there was no one but the porter to see.

The signal dropped, as if a guillotine had come crashing down, and her heart seemed to crash down with it. "Two boys!" she thought. Somehow, she had imagined girls. She was used to girls, and shy of boys.

The printed form had come a day or two ago and had increased the panic which had gradually been gathering. Six-year-old boys, and she had pictured perhaps eight-or ten-year-old girls, whom she could teach to sew and make cakes for tea, and press wild flowers as she had taught Imogen and Lalage to do.

Flurried and anxious entertaining at home; interviewing head-mistresses; once—shied away from failure—opening a sale-of-work in the village—these agonies to her diffident nature seemed nothing to the nervousness she felt now, as the train appeared round the bend. She simply wasn't good with children—only with her own. *Their* friends had frightened her, had been mouse-quiet and glum, or had got out of hand, and she herself had been too shy either to in-trude or clamp down. When she met children—perhaps the small grandchildren of her acquaintances, she would only smile, perhaps awkwardly touch a cheek with her finger. If she were asked to hold a baby, she was fearful lest it should cry, and often it would, sensing lack of assurance in her clasp.

The train came in and slowed up. "Suppose that I can't find them," she thought, and she went anxiously from window to win-dow, her label uncovered now. "And suppose they cry for their moth-ers and want to go home."

A tall, authoritative woman, also wearing a label, leant out of a window, saw her and signalled curtly. She had a compartment full of little children in her charge to be delivered about Oxfordshire. Only two got out on to this platform, Laura's two, Septimus Smith and Benny Reece. They wore tickets, too, with their names printed on them.

Benny was much lighter in complexion than Septimus. He was obviously a half-caste and Laura hoped that this would count in Harold's eyes. It might even be one point up. They stood on the platform, looking about them, holding their little cardboard cases.

"My name is Laura," she said. She stooped and clasped them to her in terror, and kissed their cheeks. Sep's in particular was extraordinarily soft, like the petal of a poppy. His big eyes stared up at her, without expression. He wore a dark, long-trousered suit, so that he was all over sombre and unchildlike. Benny had a mock-suède coat with a nylon-fur collar and a trilby hat with a feather. They did not speak. Not only was she, Laura, strange to them, but they were strange to one another. There had only been a short train-journey in which to sum up their chances of becoming friends.

She put them both into the back of the car, so that there should be no favouritism, and drove off, pointing out—to utter silence—places on the way. "That's a café where we'll go for tea one day." The silence was dreadful. "A caff," she amended. "And there's the little cinema. Not very grand, I'm afraid. Not like London ones."

They did not even glance about them.

"Are you going to be good friends to one another?" she asked.

After a pause, Sep said in a slow grave voice, "Yeah, I'm going to be a good friend."

"Is this the country?" Benny asked. He had a chirpy, perky Cockney voice and accent.

"Yeah, this is the countryside," said Sep, in his rolling drawl, glancing indifferently at some trees.

Then he began to talk. It was in an aggrieved sing-song. "I don't go on that train no more. I don't like that train, and I don't go on that again over my dead body. Some boy he say to me, 'You don't sit in that corner seat. I sit there.' I say, 'You don't sit here. I sit here.' 'Yeah,' I say, 'you don't own this train, so I don't budge from here.' Then he dash my comic down and tore it."

"Yep, he tore his comic," Benny said.

"'You tear my comic, you buy me another comic,' I said. 'Or else. Or *else*,' I said." He suddenly broke off and looked at a wood they were passing. "I don't go near those tall bushes. They full of snakes what sting you."

"No, they ain't," said Benny.

"My mam said so. I don't go."

"There aren't any snakes," said Laura, in a light voice. She, too, had a terror of them, and was afraid to walk through bracken. "Or only little harmless ones," she added.

"I don't go," Sep murmured to himself. Then, in a louder voice, he went on. "He said, 'I don't buy no comic for you, you nigger,' he said."

"He never said that," Benny protested.

"Yes, 'You dirty nigger,' he said."

"He never."

There was something so puzzled in Benny's voice that Laura immediately believed him. The expression on his little monkey-face was open and impartial.

"I don't go on that train no more."

"You've got to. When you go home," Benny said.

"Maybe I don't go home."

"We'll think about that later. You've only just arrived," said Laura, smiling.

"No, I think about that right now."

Along the narrow lane to the house, they were held up by the cows from the farm. A boy drove them along, whacking their messed rumps with a stick. Cow-pats plopped on to the road and steamed there, zizzing with flies. Benny held his nose and Sep, glancing at him, at once did the same. "I don't care for this smell of the country-side," he complained in a pinched tone.

"No, the countryside stinks," said Benny.

"Cows frighten me."

"They don't frighten me."

Sep cringed against the back of the seat, whimpering; but Benny wound his window right down, put his head a little out of it, and shouted, "Get on, you dirty old sods, or else I'll show you."

"Hush," said Laura gently.

"He swore," Sep pointed out.

They turned into Laura's gateway, up the short drive. In front of the house was a lawn and a cedar tree. From one of its lower branches hung the old swing, on chains, waiting for Laura's grandchildren.

The boys clambered out of the car and followed her into the hall, where they stood looking about them critically; then Benny dropped his case and shot like an arrow towards Harold's golf-bag and pulled out a club. His face was suddenly bright with excitement and Laura, darting forward to him, felt a stab of misery at having to begin the "No"s so soon. "I'm afraid Harold wouldn't like you to touch them," she said. Benny stared her out, but after a moment or two gave up the club with all the unwillingness in the world. Meanwhile, Sep had taken an antique coaching-horn and was blowing a bubbly, uneven blast on it, his eyes stretched wide and his cheeks blown out. "Nor that," said Laura faintly, taking it away. "Let's go upstairs and un-pack."

They appeared not at all overawed by the size of this fairly large house; in fact, rather unimpressed by it.

In the room where once, as little girls, Imogen and Lalage had slept together, they opened their cases. Sep put his clothes neatly and carefully into his drawer; and Benny tipped the case into his—comics, clothes and shoes, and a scattering of peanuts. "I'll tidy it later," Laura thought.

"Shall we toss up for who sleeps by the window?" she suggested.

"I don't sleep by no window," said Sep. "I sleep in *this* bed; with *him*."

"I want to sleep by myself," said Benny.

Sep began a babyish whimpering, which increased into an an-guished keening. "I don't like to sleep in the bed by myself. I'm scared to. I'm real scared to. I'm scared."

This was entirely theatrical, Laura decided, and Benny seemed to think so, too; for he took no notice.

"A fortnight!" Laura thought. This day alone stretched endlessly before her, and she dared not think of any following ones. Already she felt ineffectual and had an inkling that they were going to despise her. And her brightness was false and not infectious. She longed for Harold to come home, as she had never longed before.

"I reckon I go and clean my teeth," said Sep, who had broken off his dirge.

"Lunch is ready. Afterwards would be more sensible, surely?" Laura suggested.

But they paid no heed to her. Both took their toothbrushes, their new tubes of paste, and rushed to find the bathroom. "I'm going to bathe myself," said Sep. "I'm going to bathe all my skin, and wash my head."

"Not *before* lunch," Laura called out, hastening after them; but they did not hear her. Taps were running and steam clouding the window, and Sep was tearing off his clothes.

"He's bathed three times already," Laura told Harold.

She had just come downstairs, and had done so as soon as she heard him slamming the front door.

Upstairs, Sep was sitting in the bath. She had made him a lacy vest of soap-froth, as once she had made them for Imogen and Lalage. It showed up much better on his grape-dark skin. He sat there, like a tribal warrior done up in war-paint.

Benny would not go near the bath. He washed at the basin, his sleeves rolled up: and he turned the cake of soap over and over uncertainly in his hands.

"It's probably a novelty," Harold said, referring to Sep's bathing. "Would you like a drink?"

"Later perhaps. I daren't sit down, for I'd never get up again."

"I'll finish them off. I'll go and see to them. You just sit there and drink this."

"Oh, Harold, how wonderfully good of you."

She sank down on the arm of a chair, and sipped her drink, feeling stunned. From the echoing bathroom came shouts of laughter, and it was very good to hear them, especially from a distance. Harold was being a great success, and relief and gratitude filled her.

After a little rest, she got up and went weakly about the room, putting things back in their places. When this was done, the room still looked wrong. An unfamiliar dust seemed to have settled all over it, yet, running a finger over the piano, she found none. All the same, it was not the usual scene she set for Harold's home-coming in the evenings. It had taken a shaking-up.

Scampering footsteps now thundered along the landing. She waited a moment or two, then went upstairs. They were in bed, in separate beds; Benny by the window. Harold was pacing about the room, telling them a story: his hands flapped like huge ears at either side of his face; then he made an elephant's trunk with his arm. From the beds, the children's eyes stared unblinkingly at him. As Laura came into the room, only Benny's flickered in her direction, then back at once to the magic of Harold's performance. She blew a vague, unheeded kiss, and crept away.

"It's like seeing snow begin to fall," Harold said at dinner. "You know it's going to be a damned nuisance, but it makes a change."

He sounded exhilarated; clashed the knife against the steel with vigour, and started to carve. He kept popping little titbits into his mouth. Carver's perks, he called them.

"Not much for me," Laura said.

"What did they have for lunch?"

"Fish-cakes."

"Enjoy them?"

"Sep said, 'I don't like that.' He's very suspicious, and that makes Benny all the braver. Then he eats too much, showing off."

"They'll settle down," Harold said, settling down himself to his dinner. After a while, he said, "The little Cockney one asked me just now if this were a private house. When I said 'Yes,' he said, 'I thought it was, because you've got the sleeping upstairs and the talking downstairs.' Didn't quite get the drift."

"Pathetic," Laura murmured.

"I suppose where they come from, it's all done in the same room."

"Yes, it is."

"Pathetic," Harold said in his turn.

"It makes me feel ashamed."

"Oh, come now."

"And wonder if we're doing the right thing—perhaps unsettling them for what they have to go back to."

"My dear girl," he said. "Damn it, those people who organise these things know what they're doing."

"I suppose so."

"They've been doing it for years."

"Yes, I know."

"Well, then . . ."

Suddenly she put down her knife and fork and rested her forehead in her hands.

"What's up, old thing?" Harold asked, with his mouth full.

"Only tired."

"Well, they've dropped off all right. You can have a quiet evening."

"I'm too tired to sit up straight any longer." After a silence, lifting her face from her hands, she said, "Thirteen more days! What shall I do with them all that time?"

"Take them for scrambles in the woods," he began, sure that he had endless ideas.

"I tried. They won't walk a step. They both groaned and moaned so much that we turned back."

"Well, they can play on the swing."

"For how long, how *long*? They soon got tired of that. Anyhow, they quarrel about one having a longer turn than the other. In the end, I gave them the egg-timer."

"That was a good idea."

"They broke it."

"Oh."

"Please God, don't let it rain," she said earnestly, staring out of the window. "Not for the next fortnight, anyway."

The next day, it rained from early morning. After breakfast, when Harold had gone off, Laura settled the boys at the dining-room table with a snakes-and-ladders board. As they had never played it, she had to draw up a chair herself, and join in. By some freakish chance, Benny threw one six after another, would, it seemed, never stop; and Sep's frustration and fury rose. He kept snatching the dice-cup away from Benny, peering into it, convinced of trickery. The game went badly for him and Laura, counting rapidly ahead, saw that he was due for the longest snake of all. His face was agonised, his dark hand, with its pale scars and scratches, hovered above the board; but he could not bring himself to draw the counter down the snake's horrid speckled length.

"I'll do it for you," Laura said. He shuddered, and turned aside. Then he pushed his chair back from the table and lay, face-down on the floor, silent with grief.

"And it's not yet ten o'clock," thought Laura, and was relieved to see Mrs. Milner, the help, coming up the path under her umbrella. It was a mercy that it was her morning.

She finished off the game with Benny, and he won; but the true glory of victory had been taken from him by the vanquished, lying still and wounded on the hearth-rug. Laura was bright and cheerful about being beaten, trying to set an example; but she made no impression.

Presently, in exasperation, she asked, "Don't you play games at school?"

There was no answer for a time, then Benny, knowing the question wasn't addressed to him, said, "Yep, sometimes."

"And what do you do if you lose?" Laura asked, glancing down at the hearth-rug. "You can't win all the time."

In a muffled voice, Sep at last said, "I don't win any time. They won't let me win any time."

"It's only luck."

"No, they don't *let* me win. I just go and lie down and shut my eyes."

"And are these our young visitors?" asked Mrs. Milner, coming in with the vacuum-cleaner. Benny stared at her; Sep lifted his head from his sleeve for a brief look, and then returned to his sulking.

"What a nasty morning I've brought with me," Mrs. Milner said, after Laura had introduced them.

"You brought a nasty old morning all right," Sep agreed, mumbling into his jersey.

"But," she went on brightly, putting her hands into her overall pockets, "I've also brought some lollies."

Benny straightened his back in anticipation. Sep, peeping with one eye, stretched out an arm.

"That's if Madam says you may."

"They call me 'Laura.'" It had been Harold's idea and Laura had foreseen this very difficulty.

Mrs. Milner could not bring herself to say the name and she, too, could foresee awkwardnesses.

"No, Sep," said Laura firmly. "Either you get up properly and take it politely, or you go without."

She wished that Benny hadn't at once scrambled to his feet and stood there at attention. Sep buried his head again and moaned. All the sufferings of his race were upon him at this moment.

Benny took his sweet and made a great appreciative fuss about it.

All the china had gone up a shelf or two, out of reach, Mrs. Milner noted. It was like the old days, when Imogen's and Lalage's friends had come to tea.

"Now, there's a good lad," she said, stepping over Sep, and plugging in the vacuum-cleaner.

"Is that your sister?" Benny asked Laura, when Mrs. Milner had brought in the pudding, gone out again, and closed the door.

"No, Mrs. Milner comes to help me with the housework—every Tuesday and Friday."

"She must be a very kind old lady," Benny said.

"Do you like that?" Laura asked Sep, who was pushing jelly into his spoon with his fingers.

"Yeah, I like this fine."

He had suddenly cheered up. He did not mention the lolly, which Mrs. Milner had put back in her pocket. All the rest of the morning, they had played excitedly with the telephone—one upstairs, in Laura's bedroom; the other downstairs, in the hall—chattering and shouting to one another, and running to Laura to come to listen.

That evening, Harold was home earlier than usual and could not wait to complain that he had tried all day to telephone.

"I know, dear," Laura said. "I should have stopped them, but it gave me a rest."

"You'll be making a rod for everybody's back, if you let them do just what they like all the time."

"It's for such a short while—well, relatively speaking—and they haven't got telephones at home, so the question doesn't arise."

"But other people might want to ring you up."

"So few ever do, it's not worth considering."

"Well, someone did today. Helena Western."

"What on earth for?"

"There's no need to look frightened. She wants you to take the boys to tea." Saying this, his voice was full of satisfaction, for he admired Helena's husband. Helena herself wrote what he referred to as "clever-clever little novels." He went on sarcastically, "She saw you with them from the top of a bus, and asked me when I met her later in Blackwell's. She says she has absolutely *no* feelings about coloured people, as some of her friends apparently have." He was speaking in Helena's way of stresses and breathings. "In fact," he ended, "she rather goes out of her way to be extra pleasant to them."

"So she does have feelings," Laura said.

She was terrified at the idea of taking the children to tea with Helena. She always felt dull and overawed in her company, and was afraid that the boys would misbehave and get out of her control, and then Helena would put it all into a novel. Already she had put Harold in one; but, luckily, he had not recognised his own transformation from professor of archaeology to barrister. Her simple trick worked, as far as he was concerned. To Harold, that character, with his vaguely left-wing opinions and opinionated turns of phrase, his quelling manner to his wife, his very appearance, could have nothing to do with him, since he had never taken silk. Everyone else had recognised and known, and Laura, among them, knew they had.

"I'll ring her up," she said; but she didn't stir from her chair, sat staring wearily in front of her, her hands on her knees—a very resigned old woman's attitude; Whistler's mother. "I'm *too* old," she thought. "I'd be too old for my own grandchildren." But she had never imagined *them* like the ones upstairs in bed. She had pictured biddable little children, like Lalage and Imogen.

"They're good at *night*," she said to Harold, continuing her thoughts aloud. "They lie there and talk quietly, once they're in bed. I wonder what they talk about. Us, perhaps." It was an alarming idea.

In the night she woke and remembered that she had not telephoned Helena. "I'll do it after breakfast," she thought.

But she was still making toast when the telephone rang, and the boys left the table and raced to the hall ahead of her. Benny was first and, as he grabbed the receiver, Sep stood close by him, ready to shout some messages into the magical instrument. Laura hovered anxiously by, but Benny warned her off with staring eyes. "Be polite," she whispered imploringly.

"Yep, my name's Benny," he was saying.

Then he listened, with a look of rapture. It was his first real telephone conversation, and Sep was standing by, shivering with impatience and envy.

"Yep, that'll be OK," said Benny, grinning. "What day?"

Laura put out her hand, but he shrank back, clutching the receiver. "I got the message," he hissed at her. "Yep, he's here," he said, into the telephone. Sep smiled self-consciously and drew himself up as he took the receiver. "Yeah, I am Septimus Alexander Smith." He gave his high, bubbly chuckle. "Sure I'll come there." To prolong the conversation, he went on, "Can my friend Benny Reece come, too? Can Laura come?" Then he frowned, looking up at the ceiling, as if for inspiration. "Can my father Alexander Leroy Smith come?"

Laura made another darting movement.

"Well, no, he can't then," Sep said, "because he's dead."

This doubled him up with mirth, and it was a long time before he could bring himself to say good-bye. When he had done so, he quickly put the receiver down.

"Someone asked me to tea," he told Laura. "I said, 'Yeah, sure I come.'"

"And me," said Benny.

"Who was it?" Laura asked, although she knew.

"I don't know," said Sep. "I don't know *who* that was."

When later and secretly, Laura telephoned Helena, Helena said, "Aren't they simply *devastating* boys?"

"How did the tea party go?" Harold asked.

They had all arrived back home together—he, from a meeting; Laura and the boys from Helena's.

"They were good," Laura said, which was all that mattered. She drew them to her, one on either side. It was her movement of gratitude towards them. They had not let her down. They had played quietly at a fishing game with real water and magnetised tin fish, had eaten unfamiliar things, such as anchovy toast and brandy-snaps, without any expression of alarm or revulsion: they had helped carry the tea-things indoors from the lawn. Helena had been surprisingly clever with them. She made them laugh, as seldom Laura could. She struck the right note from the beginning. When Benny picked up sixpence from the gravelled path, she thanked him casually and put it in her pocket. Laura was grateful to her for that and proud that Benny ran away at once so unconcernedly. When Helena had praised them for their good behaviour, Laura had blushed with pleasure, just as if they were her own children.

"She is really very nice," Laura said later, thinking still of her successful afternoon with Helena.

"Yes, she talks too much, that's all."

Harold was pleased with Laura for having got on well with his colleague's wife. It was so long since he had tried to urge Laura into academic circles, and for years he had given up trying. Now, sensing his pleasure, her own was enhanced.

"When we were coming away," Laura said, "Helena whispered to me, 'Aren't they simply *dev*astating?'"

"You've exactly caught her tone."

At that moment, they heard from the garden, Benny also exactly catching her tone.

"Let's have the bat, there's a little pet," he mimicked, trying to snatch the old tennis-racquet from Sep.

"You sod off," drawled Sep.

"Oh, my dear, you shake me rigid."

Sep began his doubling-up-with-laughter routine; first, in silence, bowed over, lifting one leg then another up to his chest, stamping the ground. It was like the start of a tribal dance, Laura thought, watching him from the window; then the pace quickened, he skipped about, and laughed, with his head thrown back, and tears rolled down his face. Benny looked on, smirking a little, obviously proud that his wit should have had such an effect. Round and round went Sep, his loose limbs moving like pistons. "Yeah, you shake me rigid," he shouted. "You shake me entirely rigid." Benny, after hesitating, joined in. They circled the lawn, and disappeared into the shrubbery.

"She *did* say that. Helena," Laura said, turning to Harold. "When Benny was going on about something he'd done she said, 'My dear, you shake me entirely rigid.'" Then Laura added thoughtfully, "I wonder if they are as good at imitating *us*, when they're lying up there in bed, talking."

"A sobering thought," said Harold, who could not believe he had any particular idiosyncrasies to be copied. "Oh, God, someone's broken one of my sherds," he suddenly cried, stooping to pick up two pieces of pottery from the floor. His agonised shout brought Sep to the French windows, and he stood there, bewildered.

As the pottery had been broken before, he hadn't bothered to pick it up, or confess. The day before, he had broken a whole cup and nothing had happened. Now this grown man was bowed over as if in pain, staring at the fragments in his hand. Sep crept back into the shrubbery.

The fortnight, miraculously, was passing. Laura could now say, "This time next week." She would do gardening, get her hair done, clean all the paint. Often, she wondered about the kind of homes the other children had gone to—those children she had glimpsed on the train; and she imagined them staying on farms, helping with the animals, looked after by buxom farmers' wives—pale London children, growing gratifyingly brown, filling out, going home at last with roses in their cheeks. She could see no difference in Sep and Benny.

What they had really got from the holiday was one another. It touched her to see them going off into the shrubbery with arms about one another's shoulders, and to listen to their peaceful murmuring as they lay in bed, to hear their shared jokes. They quarrelled a great deal, over the tennis-racquet or Harold's old cricket-bat, and Sep was constantly casting himself down on the grass and weeping, if he were out at cricket, or could not get Benny out.

It was he who would sit for hours with his eyes fixed on Laura's face while she read to him. Benny would wander restlessly about, waiting for the story to be finished. If he interrupted, Sep would put his hand imploringly on Laura's arm, silently willing her to continue.

Benny liked her to play the piano. It was the only time she was admired. They would dance gravely about the room, with their bottles of Coca-Cola, sucking through straws, choking, heads bobbing up and down. Once, at the end of a concert of nursery-rhymes, Laura played "God Save the Queen," and Sep rushed at her, trying to shut the lid down on her hands. "I don't like that," he keened. "My mam don't like 'God Save the Queen' neither. She say 'God save *me*.'"

"Get out," said Benny, kicking him on the shin. "You're shaking me entirely rigid."

On the second Sunday, they decided that they must go to church. They had a sudden curiosity about it, and a yearning to sing hymns.

"Well, take them," said liberal-minded and agnostic Harold to Laura.

But it was almost time to put the sirloin into the oven. "We did sign that form," she said in a low voice. "To say we'd take them if they wanted to go."

"Do you *really* want to go?" Harold asked, turning to the boys, who were wanting to go more and more as the discussion went on. "Oh, God!" he groaned—inappropriately, Laura thought.

"What religion are you, anyway?" he asked them.

"I am a Christian," Sep said with great dignity.

"Me, too," said Benny.

"What time does it begin?" Harold asked, turning back to Laura.

"At eleven o'clock."

"Isn't there some kids' service they can go to on their own?"

"Not in August, I'm afraid."

"Oh, God!" he said again.

Laura watched them setting out; rather overawed, the two boys; it was the first time they had been out alone with him.

She had a quiet morning in the kitchen. Not long after twelve o'clock they returned. The boys at once raced for the cricket-bat, and fought over it, while Harold poured himself out a glass of beer.

"How did it go?" asked Laura.

"Awful! Lord, I felt such a fool."

"Did they misbehave, then?"

"Oh, no, they were perfectly good—except that for some reason Benny kept holding his nose. But I knew so many people there. And the Vicar shook hands with me afterwards and said, 'We are especially glad to see *you*.' The embarrassment!"

"It must have shaken you entirely rigid," Laura said, smiling as she basted the beef. Harold looked at her as if for the first time in years. She so seldom tried to be amusing.

At lunch, she asked the boys if they had enjoyed their morning.

"Church smelt nasty," Benny said, making a face.

"Yeah," agreed Sep. "I prefer my own country. I prefer Christians."

"Me, too," Benny said. "Give me Christians any day."

"Has it been a success?" Laura asked Harold. "For them, I mean."

It was their last night—Sep's and Benny's—and she wondered if her feeling of being on the verge of tears was entirely from tiredness. For the past fortnight, she had reeled into bed, and slept without moving.

A success for *them*? She could not be quite sure; but it had been a success for her, and for Harold. In the evenings, they had so much to talk about, and Harold, basking in his popularity, had been genial and considerate.

Laura, the boys had treated as a piece of furniture, or a slave, and humbly she accepted her place in their minds. She was a woman who had never had any high opinions of herself.

"No more cricket," she said. She had been made to play for hours—always wicket-keeper, running into the shrubs for lost balls while Sep and Benny rested full-length on the grass.

"He has a lovely action," she had said to Harold one evening, watching Sep taking his long run up to bowl. "He might be a great athlete one day."

"It couldn't happen," Harold said. "Don't you see, he has rickets?"

One of her children with rickets, she had thought, stricken.

Now, on this last evening, the children were in bed. She and Harold were sitting by the drawing-room window, talking about them. There was a sudden scampering along the landing and Laura said, "It's only one of them going to the toilet."

"The *what*?"

"They ticked me off for saying 'lavatory,'" she said placidly. "Benny said it was a bad word."

She loved to make Harold laugh, and several times lately she had managed to amuse him, with stories she had to recount.

"I shan't like saying good-bye," she said awkwardly.

"No," said Harold. He got up and walked about the room, examined his shelves of pottery fragments. "It's been a lot of work for you, Laura."

She looked away shyly. There had been almost a note of praise in his voice. "Tomorrow," she thought. "I hope I don't cry."

At the station, it was Benny who cried. All the morning he had talked about his mother, how she would be waiting for him at Paddington station. Laura kept their thoughts fixed on the near future.

Now they sat on a bench on the sunny platform, wearing their name-labels, holding bunches of wilting flowers, and Laura looked at her watch and wished the minutes away. As usual, she was too early. Then she saw Benny shut his eyes quickly, but not in time to stop two tears falling. She was surprised and dismayed. She began to talk brightly, but neither replied. Benny kept his head down, and Sep stared ahead. At last, to her relief, the signal fell, and soon the train came in. She handed them over to the escort, and they sat down in the compartment without a word. Benny gazed out of the further window, away from her, rebukingly; and Sep's face was expressionless.

As the train began to pull out, she stood waving and smiling; but they would not glance in her direction, though the escort was urging them to do so, and setting an example. When at last Laura moved away, her head and throat were aching, and she had such a sense of failure and fatigue that she hardly knew how to walk back to the car.

It was not Mrs. Milner's morning, and the house was deadly quiet. Life, noise, laughter, bitter quarrelling had gone out of it. She picked up the cricket-bat from the lawn and went inside. She walked about, listlessly tidying things, putting them back in their places.

Then fetched a damp cloth and sat down at the piano and wiped the sticky, dirty keys.

She was sitting there, staring in front of her, clasping the cloth in her lap, when Harold came in.

"I'm taking the afternoon off," he said. "Let's drive out to Minster Lovell for lunch."

She looked at him in astonishment. On his way across the room to fetch his tobacco pouch, he let his hand rest on her shoulder for a moment.

"Don't fret," he said. "I think we've got them for life now."

"Benny cried."

"Extraordinary thing. Shall we make tracks?"

She stood up and closed the lid of the keyboard. "It was awfully nice of you to come back, Harold." She paused, thinking she might say more; but he was puffing away, lighting his pipe with a great fuss, as if he were not listening. "Well, I'll go and get ready," she said.

elderly helpless—there was never an empty corner or time of real silence.

White people and coloured people now walked in twos and threes along St. Luke's Road to the church on the corner. The peal of bells jangled together, faltered, then faded. Church-goers stepped up their pace. The one slow bell began and, when that stopped, the road was almost empty. For a time, there were only the children below playing some hopping game up and down the steps.

It was a very wide road. Fifty years ago, all those four-storeyed houses had been lived in by single families—with perhaps a little servant girl sleeping in an attic—in a room on the same floor as Jasper's. The flights of broken front steps led up to the porches with scabby pillars and—always—groups of dirty milk bottles. The sky was no-colour above the slate roofs and chimney-pots and television aerials, and the street looked no-colour, too—the no-colour of most of Jasper's Sunday mornings in London. Either the sky pressed down on him, laden with smog or rain or dark, lumbering clouds, or it vanished, it simply wasn't there, was washed away by rain, or driven somewhere else by the wind.

He was bored with the street, and began to get dressed. He went down several times to the lavatory on the half-landing, but each time the door was bolted. He set about shaving—trimming his moustache neatly in a straight line well above his full, up-tilted lip. He washed a pair of socks and some handkerchiefs. When he had dusted the window, he spread the wet handkerchiefs, stretched and smoothed, against the pane to dry, having no iron. Then—in between times he was trying the lavatory door without luck—he fried a slice of bread in a little black pan over the gas-ring and, when it was done, walked about the room eating it, sometimes rubbing the tips of his greasy fingers in his frizzy hair, which was as harsh as steel wool.

He was a tall, slender young man, and his eyes had always looked mournful, even when he was happier, though hungry, at home in his own country. Tomorrow, he would be twenty-six. He remained, so far, solitary, worked hard, and grieved hard over his mistakes. He

TALL BOY

THIS SUNDAY had begun well, by not having begun too early. Jasper Jones overslept—or, rather, slept later than usual, for there was nothing to get up for—and so had got for himself an hour's remission from the Sunday sentence. It was after half-past ten and he had escaped, for one thing, the clatter of the milk-van, a noise which for some reason depressed him. But church bells now began to toll—to him an even more dispiriting sound, though much worse in the evening.

The curtains drawn across the window did not meet. At night, they let a steamy chink of light out on to the darkness, and this morning let a grey strip of daylight in.

Jasper got out of bed and went to this window. It was high up the house, and a good way down below, in the street, he could see some children playing on the crumbling front steps, and two women wearing pale, tinselly saris and dark overcoats, hurrying along the other side of the road.

In this part of London, nationalities clung together—Poles one street, African negroes in the next. This road—St. Luke's—mostly Pakistani. Jasper thought he was the only West Indian way along it. *His* people were quite distant—in the streets near railway-bridge, where the markets were, where he had been to find a room.

This bed-sitter was his world. There was distinction in having it all to himself. In such a neighbourhood, few did. He had never in his life known such isolation. Back in his own country, his home bulged with people—breadwinners or unemployed, children saved, and sent money back home to Mam. Poverty from the earliest days—which makes some spry and crafty—had left him diffident and child-like.

At last—having found the lavatory door open—he set out for his usual Sunday morning walk. People were coming out of St. Luke's, standing in knots by the porch, taking it in turns to shake hands with the Vicar. Their clothes—especially the women's—were dauntingly respectable. One Sunday, Jasper had rather fearfully gone to the service, but the smell of damp stone, the mumbled, hurried prayers, the unrhythmical rush and gabble of psalms dismayed him. He had decided that this sense of alienation was one he could avoid.

Pubs had just opened, and he went into one—the Victoria and Albert—and ordered a glass of beer. This he did for passing time and not for enjoyment. Sweet, thick drinks were too expensive, and this warmish, wry-tasting one, for which he tried to acquire a liking, was all he could afford. It made him wonder about Londoners, though, as that church service had. There seemed to be inherent in them a wish for self-punishment he could not understand—a greyness of soul and taste, to match the climate. Perhaps in total depression there was safety. His own depression—of fits and starts—held danger in it, he guessed.

The barman went round the tables collecting glasses, carrying away five in each hand, fingers hooked into them. The pub was filling up. As soon as the door swung to, it was pushed open again. After a time, people coming in had rain on their shoulders, and wiped it from their faces. The sight of this was a small calamity to Jasper, who had planned to spend at least half an hour queasily sipping his beer. Now he would have to drain his glass quickly and go, because of his shoes and the need to have them dry for the morning—and his suit.

The rain brushed the streets, swept along by the wind. He changed into a run, shoulders high and his head held back to stop the rain running down his spine, so that it spurted instead from his eyelids and his moustache. His arms going like pistons, his knees lifted high, he loped slowly, easily. In one way, he loved and welcomed the rain, for giving him the chance to run. He always wanted to run, but people stared when he did so, unless he were running for a bus. Running for running's sake was an oddity. He was worried only about his suit and shoes, and the shoes were already soaked, and there was a soapy squelch in his socks.

He reached home, panting and elated, and sprang lightly up the three flights of stairs. When he had hung up his damp suit and put on his working overalls, stuffed his wet shoes with newspaper and set them to dry, soles facing the gas-ring, steaming faintly, he began to mix up his dinner. Two rashers of bacon went into the frying-pan, then he took a handful or two of flour and rubbed in some dripping. He shaped the dough carefully into balls with his long, pale-palmed hands, and put them into the bacon fat. They were as near as he could get to his mother's fried dumplings. Perhaps, just at this moment, she would be making them at home, dumplings and sweet potato pudding. He imagined home having the same time as England. He would have felt quite lost to his loved ones if, when he woke in the night, he could not be sure that they were lying in darkness, too; and, when his own London morning came, theirs also came, the sun streamed through the cracks of their hut in shanty-town, and the little girls began to chirp and skip about. He could see them clearly now, as he knelt by the gas-ring—their large, rolling eyes, their close-cropped, frizzy hair. Most of the time, they had bare patches on their scalps from sores they would not leave alone, those busy fingers scratching, slapped down by Mam. They all had names of jewels, or semi-precious stones—Opal, Crystal and Sapphyra, his little sisters. He smiled, and gently shook his head, as he turned the dumplings with a fork.

All the afternoon, the rain flew in gusts against the window. If he could not go out and walk about the streets, there was nothing to do. He took the chair to the window, and looked through the blurred pane at the street below; but there was no life down there—only an occasional umbrella bobbing along, or a car swishing by slowly, throwing up puddle-water with a melancholy sound.

The launderette round the corner was open on Sunday afternoons and evenings, and sometimes he took his dirty shirts and overalls and sat there before the washing-machine, waiting, his hands hanging loose between his knees, and the greenish, fluorescent light raining down on him. He might make a dash towards it, if the rain eased up a little. His heart began to ache for the bright launderette, as if for a dear dream.

Half-way through the afternoon, he quite suddenly experienced utter desolation. He knew the signs of it coming, and he closed his eyes and sat warily still, feeling silence freezing in his ear-drums. Then he got up quietly and began to pad up and down the room; stopping at the far wall from the window, he leant against the wall and rhythmically banged his forehead against it, his eyes shut tight again, his lips parted. Very soon, a sharp rapping came back from the other side—his only human recognition of the day. He reeled away from the wall, and sat on the edge of the bed, sighing dramatically, for something to do.

What light there had been during the day seemed to be diminishing. Time was going. Sunday was going. He lay on his back on the bed, while the room darkened, and he counted his blessings—all off by heart, he knew them well. There was nothing wrong. He was employed. He had a room, and a good suit, and his shoes would soon be dry. There was money going back home to Mam. No one here, in England, called him "Nigger," or put up their fists to him. That morning, he had sat there in the pub without trouble. There *was* no trouble. Once, at work, they had all laughed at him when he was singing "I'm Dreaming of a White Christmas" as he loaded a van; but it was good-humoured laughter. *Tall Boy* they called him; but they had nick-names for some of the others, too—Dusty and Tiny and Buster.

Jasper thought about each of them in turn, trying to picture their Sundays from Monday morning chat that he always listened to carefully. The single ones tinkered with their motor-bikes, then went out on them, dressed in black mock leather, with a white-helmeted girl on the pillion. The married ones mended things, and put up shelves, they "went over to Mother's to tea," and looked at the telly as soon as the religious programmes were over. Dusty had even built a greenhouse in his back garden, and grew chrysanthemums. But, whatever they did, all were sorry when Monday morning came. They had not longed for it since Friday night, as Jasper had.

The rain fell into the dark street. Whether it eased up or not, he had to catch the last post. He fetched pen and ink and the birthdaycard for himself that he had chosen with great care, gravely conscious of the rightness of receiving one. He dipped the pen in the ink, then sat back, wondering what to write. He would have liked to sign it "From a well-wisher," as if it were to come out of the blue; but this seemed insincere, and he prized sincerity. After a while, he simply wrote, "With greetings from Mr. Jasper Jones," stamped the envelope, and went again to the window to look at his Sunday enemy, the rain.

In the end, he had to make a dash for it, splashing up rain from the wet pavements as he ran with long, loose strides through the almost deserted streets.

He thought Monday morning tea-break talk the best of the week. He could not sincerely grouse with the others about beginning work again, so he listened happily to all they had to say. This had a comforting familiarity, like his dreams of home—the game of darts, the fish-and-chips, Saturday night at White City, and *Sunday Night at the Palladium* on telly while the children slap-dashed through the last of their homework; beef was roasted, a kitchen chair repainted and a fuse mended, mother-in-law was visited; someone had touched a hundred on the motorway, and was ticked off by his elders and betters; there had been a punch-up outside the Odeon, but few sexual escapades this week—as far as the young ones were concerned—because of the weather.

"What about you, Tall Boy?" Buster asked.

Jasper smiled and shrugged. "Well, I just had a quiet time," he said.

The birthday-card had not arrived that morning. At first, he had been disappointed, for the lack of it made his birthday seem not to have happened, but now he had begun to look forward to finding it there when he got home from work. He kept fingering the knot of his tie, and opening the collar of his overalls more.

"Hey, Tall Boy, what the devil you got there?" Dusty came over, stared at Jasper's tie, then appeared to be blinded by it, reeling away theatrically, saying "Strewth!," his hands over his eyes.

Some of the others joined in in a wonderful, warm sort of abuse— just how they talked to one another, and which made Jasper so happy, grinning, putting up his fists at them, dancing up and down on his toes like a boxer.

"No, come off it, mate," Dusty said, recovering a little. "You can't wear that."

"It's hand-painted," said Jasper. "I got it for my birthday."

"So it's his birthday," Dusty said, turning to the others. He advanced slowly, menacingly towards Jasper, stuck out his finger and prodded his tie. "You know what that means, don't you?"

To prolong the delight of being in the middle of it all, Jasper pretended that he did not.

"It means," said Dusty slowly, knocking his fist against Jasper's chest. "It means, Tall Boy, you got to buy the cakes for tea."

"Yeah, that's right," said Buster. "You buy the cakes."

"I know, I know," said Jasper in his sing-song voice. He threw back his head and gave his high bubbling laugh, and jingled coins in both his pockets.

The weather had brightened and, as Jasper walked home from work, groups of women were sitting out on the steps of houses, waiting for their husbands to come home, shouting warnings to their children playing on the pavements.

Traffic at this hour was heavy and the streets were crowded, as London was emptying out its workers—thousands of arteries drawing them away, farther and farther from the heart of the city, out to the edges of the countryside.

At home, his birthday-card was waiting for him, and there was a miracle there, too; something he hardly dared to pick up—one of the rare letters from home, come on the right day. He sat down on the edge of the bed and opened it. Mam could never write much. It was a great labour and impatience to her to put pen to paper, and here was only a line or two to say the money had arrived safely and all were well. She did not mention his birthday. When she was writing, it must have been far ahead, and out of mind.

The letter was folded round a photograph. Who had taken it, he could not imagine; but there were the three little girls, his sisters, sitting on the steps of the wooden house—Opal, Crystal and Sapphyra. They were grinning straight at him, and Sapphyra's middle top teeth were missing. She looked quite different, he thought for a moment; then decided no, she was the same—the lovely same. He stared at the photograph for a long time, then got up with a jerk, and put it on the shelf by his bed, propped against the alarm clock, and his birthday-card beside it.

He went to the window and pushed down the sash and leant out, his elbows resting on the frame. The noise of children playing came up. He had a peaceful feeling, listening to the street sounds, looking at a golden, dying light on the rooftops across the road.

He stayed there until the gold went out of the light, and he felt suddenly hungry. Then he shut the window, unhooked the frying-pan and took an opener to a tin of beans. He smiled as he edged the opener round the rim. "They liked the cakes," he kept on thinking. The cakes he'd bought for tea.

He squatted by the gas-ring, turning the beans about in the pan, humming to himself. He was glad he'd bought the tie—otherwise they'd never have known, and he could never have treated them. The tie had been a good idea. He might give it another airing, this nice, dry evening—stroll among the crowds outside the Odeon and the bowling alley.

He ate the beans out of the pan, spooning them up contentedly as he sat on the bed, staring at Opal and Crystal and Sapphyra, who grinned cheekily back at him, sitting in a neat row, their bare feet stuck out in front of them, out of focus, and sharp black shadows falling on their white dresses.

IN AND OUT THE HOUSES

KITTY Miller, wearing a new red hair-ribbon, bounced along the vicarage drive, skipping across ruts and jumping over puddles.

Visiting took up all of her mornings in the school holidays. From kitchen to kitchen, round the village, she made her progress, and, this morning, felt drawn towards the vicarage. Quite sure of her welcome, she tapped on the back door.

"Why, Kitty Miller!" said the Vicar, opening it. He looked quite different from in church, Kitty thought. He was wearing an open-necked shirt and an old, darned cardigan. He held a tea-towel to the door-handle, because his fingers were sticky. He and his wife were cutting up Seville oranges for marmalade and there was a delicious, tangy smell about the kitchen.

Kitty took off her coat, and hung it on the usual peg, and fetched a knife from the dresser drawer.

"You are on your rounds again," Mr. Edwards said. "Spreading light and succour about the parish."

Kitty glanced at him rather warily. She preferred him not to be there, disliking men about her kitchens. She reached for an orange, and watching Mrs. Edwards for a moment out of the corners of her eyes, began to slice it up.

"What's new?" asked the Vicar.

"Mrs. Saddler's bad," she said accusingly. He should be at that bedside, she meant to imply, instead of making marmalade. "They were saying at the Horse and Groom that she won't last the day."

"So we are not your first call of the morning?"

She had, on her way here, slipped round the back of the pub and into the still-room, where Miss Betty Benford, eight months pregnant, was washing the floor, puffing and blowing as she splashed grey soapy water over the flags with a gritty rag. When this job was done—to Miss Betty's mind, not Kitty's—they drank a cup of tea together and chatted about the baby, woman to woman. The village was short of babies, and Kitty visualised pushing this one out in its pram, taking it round with her on her visits.

In his office, the landlord had been typing the luncheon menus. The keys went down heavily, his finger hovered, and stabbed. He often made mistakes, and this morning had typed "Jam Fart and Custard." Kitty considered—and then decided against—telling the Vicar this.

"They have steak-and-kidney pie on the set menu today," she said instead.

"My favourite!" groaned the Vicar. "I *never* get it."

"You had it less than a fortnight ago," his wife reminded him.

"And what pudding? If it's treacle tart I shall cry bitterly."

"Jam tart," Kitty said gravely. "And custard."

"I quite like custard, too," he said simply.

"Or choice of cheese and biscuits."

"I should have cheese and biscuits," Mrs. Edwards said.

It was just the kind of conversation Kitty loved.

"Eight-and-sixpence," she said. "Coffee extra."

"To be rich! To be rich!" the Vicar said. "And what are *we* having, my dear? Kitty has caused the juices to run."

"Cold, of course, as it's Monday."

He shuddered theatrically, and picked up another orange. "My day off, too!"

Kitty pressed her lips together primly, thinking it wrong for clergymen to have days off, especially with Mrs. Saddler lying there, dying.

The three of them kept glancing at one another's work as they cut the oranges. Who was doing it finely enough? Only Mrs. Edwards, they all knew.

"I like it fairly chunky," the Vicar said.

When it was all done, Kitty rinsed her hands at the sink, and then put on her coat. She had given the vicarage what time she could spare, and the morning was getting on, and all the rest of the village waiting. She was very orderly in her habits and never visited in the afternoons, for then she had her novel to write. The novel was known about in the village, and some people felt concerned, wondering if she might be another little Daisy Ashford.

With the Vicar's phrases of gratitude giving her momentum, Kitty tacked down the drive between the shabby laurels, and out into the lane.

"The Vicar's having cold," she told Mrs. De Vries, who was preparing a *tajine* of chicken in a curious earthenware pot she had brought back from Morocco.

"Poor old Vicar," Mrs. De Vries said absent-mindedly, as she cut almonds into slivers. She had a glass of something on the draining-board and often took a sip from it. "Do run and find a drink for yourself, dear child," she said. She was one of the people who wondered about Daisy Ashford.

"I'll have a bitter lemon, if I may," Kitty said.

"Well, do, my dear. You know where to find it."

As Kitty knew everything about nearly every house in the village, she did not reply; but went with assurance to the bar in the hall. She stuck a plastic straw in her drink, and returned to the kitchen sucking peacefully.

"Is there anything I can do?" she enquired.

"No, just tell me the news. What's going on?"

"Mr. Mumford typed 'Jam Fart and Custard' on the menu card."

"Oh, he didn't! You've made me do the nose-trick with my gin. The *pain* of it!" Mrs. De Vries snatched a handkerchief from her apron pocket and held it to her face. When she had recovered, she said, "I simply can't wait for Tom to come home, to tell him that."

Kitty looked modestly gratified. "I called at the vicarage, too, on my way."

"And what were *they* up to?"

"They are up to making marmalade."

"Poor darlings! They *do* have to scrimp and scratch. Church mice, indeed!"

"But isn't home-made marmalade nicer than shop?"

"Not all *that* much."

After a pause, Kitty said, "Mrs. Saddler's on her way out."

"Who the hell's Mrs. Saddler?"

"At the almshouse. She's dying."

"Poor old thing."

Kitty sat down on a stool and swung her fat legs.

"Betty Benford is eight months gone," she said, shrugging her shoulders.

"I wish you'd tell me something about people I *know*," Mrs. De Vries complained, taking another sip of gin.

"Her mother plans to look after the baby while Betty goes on going out to work. Mrs. Benford, you know."

"Not next door's daily?"

"She won't be after this month."

"Does Mrs. Glazier know?" Mrs. De Vries asked, inclining her head towards next door.

"Not yet," Kitty said, glancing at the clock.

"My God, she'll go up the wall," Mrs. De Vries said with relish. "She's had that old Benford for years and years."

"What do you call that you're cooking?"

"It's a *tajine* of chicken."

"Mrs. De Vries is having *tajine* of chicken," Kitty said next door five minutes later.

"And what might that be when it's at home?"

Kitty described it as best she could, and Mrs. Glazier looked huffy. "Derek wouldn't touch it," she said. "He likes good, plain, English food, and no messing about."

She was rolling out pastry for that evening's steak-and-kidney pie.

"They're having that at the Horse and Groom," Kitty said.

"*And* we'll have sprouts. *And* braised celery," Mrs. Glazier added, not letting Mrs. De Vries get away with her airs and graces.

"Shall I make a pastry rose to go on the top of the pie?" Kitty offered. "Mrs. Prout showed me how to."

"No, I think we'll leave well alone."

"Do you like cooking?" Kitty asked in a conversational tone.

"I don't mind it. Why?"

"I was only thinking that then it wouldn't be so hard on you when Mrs. Benford leaves."

Mrs. Benford was upstairs. There was a bumping, droning noise of a vacuum-cleaner above, in what Kitty knew to be Mrs. Glazier's bedroom.

Mrs. Glazier, with an awful fear in her heart, stared, frowning, at Kitty, who went on, "I was just telling Mrs. De Vries that after Mrs. Benford's grandchild's born she's going to stay at home to mind it."

The fact that next door had heard this stunning news first made the blow worse, and Mrs. Glazier put a flour-covered hand to her forehead. She closed her eyes for a moment. "But why can't the girl look after the little—baby herself?"

Kitty took the lid off a jar marked "Cloves" and looked inside, sniffing. "Her daughter earns more money at the Horse and Groom than her mother earns here," she explained.

"I suppose you told Mrs. De Vries that too."

Kitty went to the door with dignity. "Oh, no! I never talk from house to house. My mother says I'll have to stop my visiting, if I do. Oh, by the way," she called back, "you'd better keep your dog in. The De Vrieses' bitch is on heat."

She went home and sat down to lamb and bubble-and-squeak.

"The Vicar's having cold, too," she said.

"And that's *his* business," her mother said warningly.

A few days later, Kitty called on Mrs. Prout.

Mrs. Prout's cottage was one of Kitty's favourite visits. Many years ago, before she was married, Mrs. Prout had been a school-teacher, and she enjoyed using her old skills to deal with Kitty. Keeping her patience pliant, she taught her visitor new card games (and they were all educational), and got her on to collecting and pressing wild flowers. She would give her pastry-trimmings to cut into shapes, and showed her how to pop corn and make fudge. She was extremely kind, though firm, and Kitty respected the rules—about taking off her Wellingtons and washing her hands and never calling on Mondays or Thursdays, because these were turning-out days when Mrs. Prout was far too busy to have company.

They were very serious together. Mrs. Prout enjoyed being authoritative to a child again, and Kitty had a sense of orderliness which obliged her to comply.

"They sent this from the vicarage," she said, coming into the kitchen with a small pot of marmalade.

"How jolly nice!" Mrs. Prout said. She took the marmalade, and tilted it slightly, and it moved. Rather sloppy. But she thought no worse of the Vicar's wife for that. "That's really *jolly* nice of them," she said, going into the larder. "And they shall have some of my apple jelly, in fair return. *Quid pro quo*, eh? And one good turn deserves another."

She came out of the larder with a different little pot and held it to the light; but the clear and golden content did not move when she tipped it sideways.

"What's the news?" she asked.

"Mrs. Saddler still lingers on," Kitty said. She had called at the almshouse to enquire, but the district nurse had told her to run off and mind her own business. "I looked in at the Wilsons' on my way here. Mrs. Wilson was making a cheese-and-onion pie. Of course, they're vegetarians; but I have known him to sneak a little chicken into his mouth. I was helping to hand round at the De Vrieses' cocktail party, and he put out his hand towards a patty. 'It's chicken,' I said to him in a low voice. 'Nary a word,' he said, and he winked at me and ate it."

"And now you *have* said a word," Mrs. Prout said briskly.

"Why, so I have," Kitty agreed, looking astonished.

Mrs. Prout cleared the kitchen table in the same brisk way, and said, "If you like, now, I'll show you how to make ravioli. We shall have it for our television supper."

"Make ravioli," cried Kitty. "You can't *make* ravioli. Mrs. Glazier buys it in a tin."

"So Mrs. Glazier may. But I find time to make my own."

"I shall be fascinated," Kitty said, taking off her coat.

"Then wash your hands, and don't forget to dry them properly. Isn't it about time you cut your nails?" Mrs. Prout asked, in her schoolmistressy voice, and Kitty, who would take anything from her, agreed. ("We all know Mrs. Prout is God," her mother sometimes said resentfully.)

"Roll up those sleeves, now. And we'll go through your tables while we work."

Mrs. Prout set out the flour-bin and a dredger and a pastry-cutter and the mincer. Going back and forth to the cupboard, she thought how petty she was to be pleased at knowing that by this time tomorrow, most of the village would be aware that she made her own ravioli. But perhaps it was only human, she decided.

"Now this is what chefs call the *mise en place*," she explained to Kitty, when she had finished arranging the table. "Can you remember that? *Mise en place*."

"*Mise en place*," Kitty repeated obediently.

"Shall I help you prepare the *mise en place*?" Kitty enquired of Mrs. Glazier.

"Mr. Glazier wouldn't touch it. I've told you he will only eat English food."

"But you have ravioli. That's Italian."

"I just keep it as a stand-by," Mrs. Glazier said scornfully. She was very huffy and put out these days, especially with Mrs. De Vries next door and her getting the better of her every time. Annette De Vries was French, and didn't they all know it. Mrs. Glazier, as a result, had become violently insular.

"I can make ravioli," Kitty said, letting the *mise en place* go, for she was not absolutely certain about it. "Mrs. Prout has just been teaching me. She and Mr. Prout have television trays by the fire, and then they sit and crack walnuts and play cards, and then they have hot milk and whisky and go to bed. I think it is very nice and cosy, don't you?"

"Mr. Glazier likes a proper sit-down meal when *he* gets back. Did you happen to see Tiger anywhere down the lane?"

"No, but I expect he's next door. I told you their bitch is on heat. You ought to shut him up."

"It's their affair to shut *theirs* up."

"Well, I'm just calling there, so I'll shoo him off."

She had decided to cut short this visit. Mrs. Glazier was so bad-tempered these days, and hardly put herself out at all to give a welcome, and every interesting thing Kitty told her served merely to annoy.

"And I must get on with my jugged hare," Mrs. Glazier said, making no attempt to delay the departure. "It should be marinating in the port wine by now," she added grandly. "And I must make the soup and the croutons."

"Well, then, I'll be going," Kitty said, edging towards the door.

"And apricot mousse," Mrs. Glazier called out after her, as if she were in a frenzy.

"Shall I prepare your *mise en place*?" Kitty enquired of Mrs. De Vries, trying her luck again.

"My! We *are* getting professional," said Mrs. De Vries, but her mind was really on what Kitty had just been telling her. "Soup and jugged hare!" she was thinking. "What a dreadful meal!"

She was glazing a terrine of chicken livers and wished that all the village might see her work of art, but having Kitty there was the next best thing.

"What's that?" she asked, as Kitty put the jar of apple jelly on the table.

"I have to take it to the vicarage on my way home. It's some of Mrs. Prout's apple jelly."

Mrs. De Vries gave it a keen look, and notched up one point to Mrs. Prout. She notched up another when she heard about the ravioli, and wondered if she had underestimated the woman.

"I shooed that Tiger away," Kitty said.

"The wretched cur. He is driving Topaze insane."

Kitty mooched round the kitchen, peeking and prying. Mrs. De Vries was the only one in the village to possess a *mandoline* for cutting vegetables. There was a giant pestle and mortar, a wicker breadbasket, ropes of Spanish onions, and a marble cheese-tray.

"You can pound the fish for me, if you have the energy," said Mrs. De Vries.

As this was not a house where she was made to wash her hands first, Kitty immediately set to work.

"I was just going to have pears," Mrs. De Vries said, in a half-humorous voice. "But if the Glaziers are going in for apricot mousse I had better pull my socks up. That remark, of course, is strictly *entre nous.*"

"Then Mrs. De Vries pulled her socks up, and made a big apple tart," Kitty told her mother.

"I have warned you before, Kitty. What you see going on in people's houses, you keep to yourself. Or you stay out of them. Is that finally and completely understood?"

"Yes, Mother," Kitty said meekly.

"My dear girl, I couldn't eat it. I couldn't eat another thing," said Mr. Glazier, confronted by the apricot mousse. "A three-course meal. Why, I shouldn't sleep all night if I had any more. The hare alone was ample."

"I think Mr. De Vries would do better justice to his dinner," said Mrs. Glazier bitterly. She had spent all day cooking and was exhausted. "It's not much fun slaving away and not being appreciated. And what on earth can I do with all the left-overs?"

"Finish them up tomorrow and save yourself a lot of trouble."

Glumly, Mrs. Glazier washed the dishes, and suddenly thought of the Prouts sitting peacefully beside their fire, cracking walnuts, playing cards. She felt ill-done-by, as she stacked the remains of dinner in the fridge, but was perfectly certain that lie as she might have to to Kitty in the morning, the whole village should not know that for the second day running the Glaziers were having soup, and jugged hare, and apricot mousse.

Next day, eating a slice of apple tart, Kitty saw Mrs. De Vries test the soup and then put the ladle back into the saucepan. "What the eye doesn't see, the heart cannot grieve over," Mrs. De Vries said cheerfully. She added salt, and a turn or two of pepper. Then she took more than a sip from the glass on the draining-board, seeming to find it more to her liking than the soup.

"The vicarage can't afford drinks," Kitty said.

"They *do* confide in you."

"I said to the Vicar, 'Mrs. De Vries drinks gin while she is cooking,' and he said, 'Lucky old her.'"

"There will be a lot of red faces about this village if you go on like this," said Mrs. De Vries, making her part of the prophecy come true at once. Kitty looked at her in surprise. Then she said—Mrs. De Vries's flushed face reminding her—"I think next door must be having the change of life. She is awfully grumpy these days. Nothing pleases her."

"You are too knowing for your years," Mrs. De Vries said, and she suddenly wished she had not been so unhygienic about the soup. Too late now. "How is your novel coming along?" she enquired.

"Oh, very nicely, thank you. I expect I shall finish it before I go back to school, and then it can be published for Christmas."

"We shall all look forward to that," said Mrs. De Vries, in what Kitty considered an unusual tone of voice.

"Mrs. De Vries cuts up her vegetables with a *mandoline*," Kitty told Mrs. Glazier some days later.

"I always knew she must be nuts," said Mrs. Glazier, thinking of the musical instrument.

Seeing Kitty dancing up the drive, she had quickly hidden the remains of a shepherd's pie at the back of a cupboard. She was more than ever ruffled this morning, because Mrs. Benford had not arrived or sent a message. She had also been getting into a frenzy with her ravioli and, in the end, had thrown the whole lot into the dustbin. She hated waste, especially now that her house-keeping allowance always seemed to have disappeared by Wednesday, and her husband was, in his dyspeptic way, continually accusing her of extravagance.

Kitty had been hanging about outside the almshouses for a great part of the morning, and had watched Mrs. Saddler's coffin being carried across the road to the church.

"Only one wreath and two relations," she now told Mrs. Glazier. "That's what comes of being poor. What are you having for dinner tonight? I could give you a hand."

"Mr. Glazier will probably be taking me to the Horse and Groom for a change," Mrs. Glazier lied.

"They are all at sixes and sevens there. Betty Benford started her pains in the night. A fortnight early. Though Mr. Mumford thinks she may have made a mistake with her dates."

Then Mrs. Benford would never come again, Mrs. Glazier thought despondently. She had given a month's notice the week before, and Mrs. Glazier had received it coldly, saying, "I think I should have been informed of this before it became common gossip in the village." Mrs. Benford had seemed quite taken aback at that.

"Well, I mustn't hang around talking," Mrs. Glazier told Kitty. "There's a lot to do this morning, and will be from now on. When do you go back to school?"

"On Thursday."

Mrs. Glazier nodded, and Kitty felt herself dismissed. She sometimes wondered why she bothered to pay this call, when everyone else made her so welcome; but coming away from the funeral she had seen Mrs. De Vries driving into town, and it was one of Mrs. Prout's turning-out days. She had hardly liked to call at the vicarage under the circumstances of the funeral, and the Horse and Groom being at sixes and sevens had made everyone there very boring and busy.

"I hope you will enjoy your dinner," she said politely to Mrs. Glazier. "They have roast Surrey fowl and all the trimmings."

When she had gone, Mrs. Glazier took the shepherd's pie from its hiding place, and began to scrape some shabby old carrots.

"Kitty, will you stop chattering and get on with your pudding," her mother said in an exasperated voice.

Kitty had been describing how skilfully the undertaker's men had lowered Mrs. Saddler's coffin into the grave, Kitty herself peering from behind the tombstone of Maria Britannia Marlowe—her favourite dead person on account of her name.

It was painful to stop talking. A pain came in her chest, severe enough to slow her breathing, and gobbling the rice pudding made it worse. As soon as her plate was cleared she began again. "Mrs. Glazier has the change of life," she said.

"How on earth do you know about such things?" her mother asked on a faint note.

"As *you* didn't tell me, I had to find out the hard way," Kitty said sternly.

Her mother pursed her lips together to stop laughing, and began to stack up the dishes.

"How Mrs. De Vries will miss me!" Kitty said dreamily, rising to help her mother. "I shall be stuck there at school doing boring things, and she'll be having a nice time drinking gin."

"Now *that* is enough. You are to go to your room immediately," her mother said sharply, and Kitty looked at her red face reflectively, comparing it with Mrs. Glazier's. "You will have to find some friends of your own age. You are becoming a little menace to everyone with your visiting, and we have got to live in this village. Now upstairs you go, and think over what I have said."

"Very well, Mother," Kitty said meekly. If she did not have to help Mother with the washing-up, she could get on with her novel all the sooner.

She went upstairs to her bedroom and spread her writing things out on the table and soon, having at once forgotten her mother's words, was lost in the joy of authorship.

Her book was all about little furry animals, and their small adventures, and there was not a human being in it, except the girl, Katherine, who befriended them all.

She managed a few more visits that holiday; but on Thursday she went back to school again, and then no one in the village knew what was happening any more.

FLESH

PHYL WAS always one of the first to come into the hotel bar in the evenings, for what she called her *aperitif,* and which, in reality, amounted to two hours' steady drinking. After that, she had little appetite for dinner, a meal to which she was not used.

On this evening, she had put on one of her beaded tops, of the kind she wore behind the bar on Saturday evenings in London, and patted back her tortoiseshell hair. She was massive and glittering and sunburned—a wonderful sight, Stanley Archard thought, as she came across the bar towards him.

He had been sitting waiting for her. They had found their own level in one another on about the third day of the holiday. Both being heavy drinkers drew them together. Before that had happened, they had looked one another over warily as, in fact, they had all their fellow-guests.

Travelling on their own, speculating, both had watched and wondered. Even at the airport, she had stood out from the others, he remembered, as she had paced up and down in her emerald-green coat. Then their flight number had been called, and they had gathered with others at the same channel, with the same pink labels tied to their hand luggage, all going to the same place; a polite, but distant little band of people, no one knowing with whom friendships were to be made—as like would no doubt drift to like. In the days that followed, Stanley had wished he had taken more notice of Phyl from the beginning, so that at the end of the holiday he would have that much more to remember. Only the emerald-green coat had stayed in his mind. She had not worn it since—it was too warm—

and he dreaded the day when she would put it on again to make the return journey.

Arriving in the bar this evening, she hoisted herself up on a stool beside him. "Well, here we are," she said, glowing, taking one peanut; adding, as she nibbled, "Evening, George," to the barman. "How's tricks?"

"My God, you've caught it today," Stanley said, and he put his hands up near her plump red shoulders as if to warm them at a fire. "Don't overdo it," he warned her.

"Oh, I never peel," she said airily.

He always put in a word against the sunbathing when he could. It separated them. She stayed all day by the hotel swimming-pool, basting herself with oil. He, bored with basking—which made him feel dizzy—had hired a car and spent his time driving about the island, and was full of alienating information about the locality, which the other guests—resenting the hired car, too—did their best to avoid. Only Phyl did not mind listening to him. For nearly every evening of her married life she had stood behind the bar and listened to other people's boring chat: she had a technique for dealing with it and a fund of vague phrases. "Go on!" she said now, listening—hardly listening—to Stanley, and taking another nut. He had gone off by himself and found a place for lunch: *hors d'œuvre*, nice-sized slice of veal, two veg, *crème caramel*, half bottle of rosé, coffee—twenty-two shillings the lot. "Well, I'm blowed," said Phyl, and she took a pound note from her handbag and waved it at the barman. When she snapped up the clasp of the bag it had a heavy, expensive sound.

One or two other guests came in and sat at the bar. At this stage of the holiday they were forming into little groups, and this was the jokey set who had come first after Stanley and Phyl. According to them all sorts of funny things had happened during the day, and little screams of laughter ran round the bar.

"Shows how wrong you can be," Phyl said in a low voice. "I thought they were ever so starchy on the plane. I was wrong about you, too. At the start, I thought you were...you know...one of *those*. Going about with that young boy all the time."

Stanley patted her knee. "On the contrary," he said, with a meaning glance at her. "No, I was just at a bit of a loose end, and he seemed to cotton-on. Never been abroad before, he hadn't, and didn't know the routine. I liked it for the first day or two. It was like taking a nice kiddie out on a treat. Then it seemed to me he was sponging. I'm not mean, I don't think; but I don't like that—sponging. It was quite a relief when he suddenly took up with the Lisper."

By now, he and Phyl had nicknames for most of the other people in the hotel. They did not know that the same applied to them, and that to the jokey set he was known as Paws and she as the Shape. It would have put them out and perhaps ruined their holiday if they had known. He thought his little knee-pattings were of the utmost discretion, and she felt confidence from knowing her figure was expensively controlled under her beaded dresses when she became herself again in the evenings. During the day, while sun-bathing, she considered that anything went—that, as her mind was a blank, her body became one also.

The funny man of the party—the awaited climax—came into the bar, crabwise, face covered slyly with his hand, as if ashamed of some earlier misdemeanour. "Oh, my God, don't look round. Here comes trouble!" someone said loudly, and George was called for from all sides. "What's the poison, Harry? No, my shout, old boy. George, if you *please*."

Phyl smiled indulgently. It was just like Saturday night with the regulars at home. She watched George with a professional eye, and nodded approvingly. He was good. They could have used him at the Nelson. A good quick boy.

"Heard from your old man?" Stanley asked her.

She cast him a tragic, calculating look. "You must be joking. He can't *write*. No, honest, I've never had a letter from him in the whole of my life. Well, we always saw each other every day until I had my hysterectomy."

Until now, in conversations with Stanley, she had always referred to "a little operation." But he had guessed what it was—well, it always was, wasn't it?—and knew that it was the reason for her being on holiday. Charlie, her husband, had sent her off to recuperate. She had sworn there was no need, that she had never felt so well in her life—was only a bit weepy sometimes late on a Saturday night. "I'm not really the crying sort," she had explained to Stanley. "So he got worried, and sent me packing."

"You clear off to the sun," he had said, "and see what that will do."

What the sun had done for her was to burn her brick-red, and offer her this nice holiday friend. Stanley Archard, retired widower from Hove.

She enjoyed herself, as she usually did. The sun shone every day, and the drinks were so reasonable—they had many a long discussion about that. They also talked about his little flat in Hove; his strolls along the front; his few cronies at the Club; his sad, orderly and lonely life.

This evening, he wished he had not brought up the subject of Charlie's writing to her, for it seemed to have fixed her thoughts on him and, as she went chatting on about him, Stanley felt an indefinable distaste, an aloofness.

She brought out from her note-case a much-creased cutting from the *Morning Advertiser*. "Phyl and Charlie Parsons welcome old friends and new at the Nelson, Southwood. In licensed hours only!" "That was when we changed Houses," she explained. There was a photograph of them both standing behind the bar. He was wearing a dark blazer with a large badge on the pocket. Sequins gave off a smudged sparkle from her breast, her hair was newly, elaborately done, and her large, ringed hand rested on an ornamental beer-handle. Charlie had his hands in the blazer pockets, as if he were there to do the welcoming, and his wife to do the work: and this, in fact, was how things were. Stanley guessed it, and felt a twist of annoyance in his chest. He did not like the look of Charlie, or anything he had heard about him—how, for instance, he had seemed like a fish out of water visiting his wife in hospital. "He used to sit on the edge of the chair and stare at the clock, like a boy in school," Phyl had said, laughing. Stanley could not bring himself to laugh, too. He had leant forward and taken her knee in his hand and wobbled it sympathetically to and fro.

No, she wasn't the crying sort, he agreed. She had a wonderful buoyancy and gallantry, and she seemed to knock years off his age by just *being* with him, talking to him.

In spite of their growing friendship, they kept to their original, separate tables in the hotel restaurant. It seemed too suddenly decisive and public a move for him to join her now, and he was too shy to carry it off at this stage of the holiday, before such an alarming audience. But after dinner, they would go for a walk along the sea-front, or out in the car for a drink at another hotel.

Always, for the first minute or two in a bar, he seemed to lose her. As if she had forgotten him, she would look about her critically, judging the set-up, sternly drawing attention to a sticky ring on the counter where she wanted to rest her elbow, keeping a professional eye on the prices.

When they were what she called "nicely grinned-up," they liked to drive out to a small headland and park the car, watching the swinging beam from a lighthouse. Then, after the usual knee-pattings and neck-strokings, they would heave and flop about in the confines of the Triumph Herald, trying to make love. Warmed by their drinks, and the still evening and the romantic sound of the sea idly turning over down below them, they became frustrated, both large, solid people, she much corseted and, anyhow, beginning to be painfully sunburned across the shoulders, he with the confounded steering-wheel to contend with.

He would grumble about the car and suggest getting out on to a patch of dry barley grass; but she imagined it full of insects; the chirping of the cicadas was almost deafening.

She also had a few scruples about Charlie, but they were not so insistent as the cicadas. After all, she thought, she had never had a holiday-romance—not even a honeymoon with Charlie—and she felt that life owed her just one.

After a time, during the day, her sunburn forced her into the shade, or out in the car with Stanley. Across her shoulders she began to peel, and could not bear—though desiring his caress—him to touch her. Rather glumly, he waited for her flesh to heal, told her "I told you so"; after all, they had not for ever on this island, had started their second, their last week already.

"I'd like to have a look at the other island," she said, watching the ferry leaving, as they sat drinking nearby.

"It's not worth just going there for the inside of a day," he said meaningfully, although it was only a short distance.

Wasn't this, both suddenly wondered, the answer to the too-small car, and the watchful eyes back at the hotel. She had refused to allow him into her room there. "If anyone saw you going in or out? Why, they know where I live. What's to stop one of them coming into the Nelson any time, and chatting Charlie up?"

"Would you?" he now asked, watching the ferry starting off across the water. He hardly dared to hear her answer.

After a pause, she laughed. "Why not?" she said, and took his hand. "We wouldn't really be doing any harm to anyone." (Meaning Charlie.) "Because no one could find out, could they?"

"Not over there," he said, nodding towards the island. "We can start fresh over there. Different people."

"They'll notice we're both not at dinner at the hotel."

"That doesn't prove anything."

She imagined the unknown island, the warm and starlit night and, somewhere, under some roof or other, a large bed in which they could pursue their daring, more than middle-aged adventure, unconfined in every way.

"As soon as my sunburn's better," she promised. "We've got five more days yet, and I'll keep in the shade till then."

A chambermaid advised yoghourt, and she spread it over her back and shoulders as best she could, and felt its coolness absorbing the heat from her skin.

Damp and cheesy-smelling in the hot night, she lay awake, cross with herself. For the sake of a tan, she was wasting her holiday—just to be a five minutes' wonder in the bar on her return, the deepest brown any of them had had that year. The darker she was, the more *abroad* she would seem to have been, the more prestige she could command. All summer, pallid herself, she had had to admire others.

Childish, really, she decided, lying rigid under the sheet, afraid to move, burning and throbbing. The skin was taut behind her knees, so that she could not stretch her legs; her flesh was on fire.

Five more days, she kept thinking. Meanwhile, even this sheet upon her was unendurable.

On the next evening, to establish the fact that they would not always be in to dinner at the hotel, they complained in the bar about the dullness of the menu, and went elsewhere.

It was a drab little restaurant, but they scarcely noticed their surroundings. They sat opposite one another at a corner table and ate shell-fish briskly, busily—he, from his enjoyment of the food; she, with a wish to be rid of it. They rinsed their fingers, quickly dried them and leant forward and twined them together—their large placid hands, with heavy rings, clasped on the table-cloth. Phyl, glancing aside for a moment, saw a young girl, at the next table with a boy, draw in her cheekbones to suppress laughter then, failing, turn her head to hide it.

"At *our* age," Phyl said gently, drawing away her hands from his. "In public, too."

She could not be defiant; but Stanley said jauntily, "I'm damned if I care."

At that moment, their chicken was placed before them, and he sat back, looking at it, waiting for vegetables.

As well as the sunburn, the heat seemed to have affected Phyl's stomach. She felt queasy and nervy. It was now their last day but one before they went over to the other island. The yoghourt—or time—had taken the pain from her back and shoulders, though leaving her with a dappled, flaky look, which would hardly bring forth cries of admiration or advance her prestige in the bar when she returned. But, no doubt, she thought, by then England would be too cold for her to go sleeveless. Perhaps the trees would have changed colour. She imagined—already—dark Sunday afternoons, their three o'clock lunch done with, and she and Charlie sitting by the electric log fire in a lovely hot room smelling of oranges and the so-called hearth littered with peel. Charlie—bless him—always dropped off among a confusion of newspapers, worn out with banter and light ale, switched off, too, as he always was with her, knowing that he could relax—be nothing, rather—until seven o'clock, because it was Sunday. Again, for Phyl, imagining home, a little pang, soon swept aside or, rather, swept aside *from*.

She was in a way relieved that they would have only one night on the little island. That would make it seem more like a chance escapade than an affair, something less serious and deliberate in her mind. Thinking about it during the day-time, she even felt a little apprehensive; but told herself sensibly that there was really nothing to worry about: knowing herself well, she could remind herself that an evening's drinking would blur all the nervous edges.

"I can't get over that less than a fortnight ago I never knew you existed," she said, as they drove to the afternoon ferry. "And after this week," she added, "I don't suppose I'll ever see you again."

"I wish you wouldn't talk like that—spoiling things," he said heavily, and he tried not to think of Hove, and the winter walks along the promenade, and going back to the flat, boiling himself a couple of eggs, perhaps; so desperately lost without Ethel.

He had told Phyl about his wife and their quiet happiness together for many years, and then her long, long illness, during which she seemed to be going away from him gradually; but it was dreadful all the same when she finally did.

"We could meet in London on your day off," he suggested.

"Well, maybe." She patted his hand, leaving that disappointment aside for him.

There were only a few people on the ferry. It was the end of summer, and the tourists were dwindling, as the English community was reassembling, after trips "back home."

The sea was intensely blue all the way across to the island. They stood by the rail looking down at it, marvelling, and feeling like two people in a film. They thought they saw a dolphin, which added to their delight.

"Ethel and I went to Jersey for our honeymoon," Stanley said. "It poured with rain nearly all the time, and Ethel had one of her migraines."

"I never had a honeymoon," Phyl said. "Just the one night at the Regent Palace. In our business, you can't both go away together. This is the first time I've ever been abroad."

"The places I could take you to," he said.

They drove the car off the ferry and began to cross the island. It was hot and dusty, hillsides terraced and tilled; green lemons hung on the trees.

"I wouldn't half like to actually *pick* a lemon," she said.

"You shall," he said, "somehow or other."

"And take it home with me," she added. She would save it for a while, showing people, then cut it up for gin and tonic in the bar one evening, saying casually, "I picked this lemon with my own fair hands."

Stanley had booked their hotel from a restaurant, on the recommendation of a barman. When they found it, he was openly disappointed; but she managed to be gallant and optimistic. It was not by the sea, with a balcony where they might look out at the moonlit waters or rediscover brightness in the morning; but down a dull side street, and opposite a garage.

"We don't *have* to," Stanley said doubtfully.

"Oh, come on! We might not get in anywhere else. It's only for sleeping in," she said.

"It *isn't* only for sleeping in," he reminded her.

An enormous man in white shirt and shorts came out to greet them. "My name is Radam. Welcome," he said, with confidence. "I have a lovely room for you, Mr. and Mrs. Archard. You will be happy here, I can assure you. My wife will carry up your cases. Do not protest, Mr. Archard. She is quite able to. Our staff has slackened off at the end of the season, and I have some trouble with the old ticker, as you say in England. I know England well. I am a Bachelor of Science of England University. Once had digs in Swindon."

A pregnant woman shot out of the hotel porch and seized their suitcases, and there was a tussle as Stanley wrenched them from her hands. Still serenely boasting, Mr. Radam led them upstairs, all of them panting but himself.

The bedroom was large and dusty and overlooked a garage.

"Oh, God, I'm sorry," Stanley said, when they were left alone. "It's still not too late, if you could stand a row."

"No. I think it's rather sweet," Phyl said, looking round the room. "And, after all, don't blame yourself. You couldn't know any more than me."

The furniture was extraordinarily fret-worked, as if to make more crevices for the dust to settle in; the bedside-lamp base was an old gin bottle filled with gravel to weight it down, and when Phyl pulled off the bed cover to feel the bed she collapsed with laughter, for the pillow-cases were embroidered "Hers" and "Hers."

Her laughter eased him, as it always did. For a moment, he thought disloyally of the dead—of how Ethel would have started to be depressed by it all, and he would have hard work jollying her out of her dark mood. At the same time, Phyl was wryly imagining

Charlie's wrath, how he would have carried on—for only the best was good enough for him, as he never tired of saying.

"He's quite right—that awful fat man," she said gaily. "We shall be very happy here. I dread to think who he keeps 'His' and 'His' for, don't you?"

"I don't suppose the maid understands English," he said, but warming only slightly. "You don't expect to have to read off pillowcases."

"I'm sure there *isn't* a maid."

"The bed is very small," he said.

"It'll be better than the car."

He thought, "She is such a woman as I have never met. She's like a marvellous Tommy in the trenches—keeping everyone's pecker up." He hated Charlie for his luck.

"I shan't ever be able to tell anybody about 'Hers' and 'Hers,'" Phyl thought regretfully—for she dearly loved to amuse their regulars back home. Given other circumstances, she might have worked up quite a story about it.

A tap on the door, and in came Mr. Radam with two cups of tea on a tray. "I know you English," he said, rolling his eyes roguishly. "You can't be happy without your tea."

As neither of them ever drank it, they emptied the cups down the hand basin when he had gone.

Phyl opened the window and the sour, damp smell of new cement came up to her. All round about, building was going on; there was also the whine of a saw-mill, and a lot of clanking from the garage opposite. She leant farther out, and then came back smiling into the room, and shut the window on the dust and noise. "He was quite right—that barman. You can see the sea from here. It's down the bottom of the street. Let's go and have a look as soon as we've unpacked."

On their way out of the hotel, they came upon Mr. Radam, who was sitting in a broken old wicker chair, fanning himself with a folded newspaper.

"I shall prepare your dinner myself," he called after them. "And shall go now to make soup. I am a specialist of soup."

They strolled in the last of the sun by the glittering sea, looked at the painted boats, watched a man beating an octopus on a rock. Stanley bought her some lace-edged handkerchiefs, and even gave the lace-maker an extra five shillings, so that Phyl could pick a lemon off one of the trees in her garden. Each bought for the other a picture-postcard of the place, to keep.

"Well, it's been just about the best holiday I ever had," he said. "And there I was in half a mind not to come at all." He had for many years dreaded the holiday season, and only went away because every-one he knew did so.

"I just can't remember when I last had one," she said. There was not—never would be, he knew—the sound of self-pity in her voice.

This was only a small fishing-village; but on one of the headlands enclosing it and the harbour was a big new hotel, with balconies overlooking the sea, Phyl noted. They picked their way across a rub-bly car-park and went in. Here, too, was the damp smell of cement; but there was a brightly lighted empty bar with a small dance floor, and music playing.

"We could easily have got in here," Stanley said. "I'd like to wring that bloody barman's neck."

"He's probably some relation, trying to do his best."

"I'll best him."

They seemed to have spent a great deal of their time together hoisting themselves up on bar stools.

"Make them nice ones," Stanley added, ordering their drinks. "Perhaps he feels a bit shy and awkward, too," Phyl thought.

"Not very busy," he remarked to the barman.

"In one week we close."

"Looks as if you've hardly opened," Stanley said, glancing round.

"It's not *his* business to get huffy," Phyl thought indignantly, when the young man, not replying, shrugged and turned aside to polish some glasses. "Customer's always right. He should know that. Politics, religion, colour-bar—however they argue together, they're all of them always right, and if you know your job you can joke them out of it and on to something safer." The times she had done that, making a fool of herself, no doubt, anything for peace and quiet. By the time the elections were over, she was usually worn out.

Stanley had hated her buying him a drink back in the hotel; but she had insisted. "What all that crowd would think of me!" she had said; but here, although it went much against her nature, she put aside her principles, and let him pay; let him set the pace, too. They became elated, and she was sure it would be all right—even having to go back to the soup-specialist's dinner. They might have avoided that; but too late now.

The barman, perhaps with a contemptuous underlining of their age, shuffled through some records and now put on "Night and Day." For them both, it filled the bar with nostalgia.

"Come *on*!" said Stanley. "I've never danced with you. This always makes me feel . . . I don't know."

"Oh, I'm a terrible dancer," she protested. The Licensed Victuallers' Association annual dance was the only one she ever went to, and even there stayed in the bar most of the time. Laughing, however, she let herself be helped down off her stool.

He had once fancied himself a good dancer; but, in later years, got no practice, with Ethel being ill, and then dead. Phyl was surprised how light he was on his feet; he bounced her round, holding her firmly against his stomach, his hand pressed to her back, but gently, because of the sunburn. He had perfect rhythm and expertise, side-stepping, reversing, taking masterly control of her.

"Well, I never!" she cried. "You're making me quite breathless."

He rested his cheek against her hair, and closed his eyes, in the old, old way, and seemed to waft her away into a different dimension. It was then that he felt the first twinge, in his left toe. It was doom to him. He kept up the pace, but fell silent. When the record ended, he hoped that she would not want to stay on longer. To return to the hotel and take his gout pills was all he could think about. Some intuition made her refuse another drink. "We've got to go back to the soup-specialist some time," she said. "He might even be a good cook."

"Surprise, surprise!" Stanley managed to say, walking with pain towards the door.

Mr. Radam was the most abominable cook. They had—in a large cold room with many tables—thin greasy chicken soup, and after that the chicken that had gone through the soup. Then peaches; he brought the tin and opened it before them, as if it were a precious wine, and no hanky-panky going on. He then stood over them, because he had much to say. "I was offered a post in Basingstoke. Two thousand pounds a year, and a car and a house thrown in. But what use is that to a man like me? Besides, Basingstoke has a most detestable climate."

Stanley sat, tight-lipped, trying not to lose his temper; but this man, and the pain, were driving him mad. He did not—dared not—drink any of the wine he had ordered.

"Yes, the Basingstoke employment I regarded as not *on*," Mr. Radam said slangily.

Phyl secretly put out a foot and touched one of Stan's—the wrong one—and then thought he was about to have a heart attack. He screwed up his eyes and tried to breathe steadily, a slice of peach slithering about in his spoon. It was then she realised what was wrong with him.

"Oh, sod the peaches," she said cheerfully, when Mr. Radam had gone off to make coffee, which would be the best they had ever tasted, he had promised. Phyl knew they would not complain about the horrible coffee that was coming. The more monstrous the egoist, she had observed from long practice, the more normal people hope to uphold the fabrication—either for ease, or from a terror of any kind of collapse. She did not know. She was sure, though, as she praised the stringy chicken, hoisting the unlovable man's self-infatuation a notch higher, that she did so because she feared him falling to pieces.

Perhaps it was only fair, she decided, that weakness should get preferential treatment. Whether it would continue to do so, with Stanley's present change of mood, she was uncertain.

She tried to explain her thoughts to him when, he leaving his coffee, she having gulped hers down, they went to their bedroom. He nodded. He sat on the side of the bed, and put his face into his hands.

"Don't let's go out again," she said. "We can have a drink in here. I love a bedroom gin, and I brought a bottle in my case." She went busily to the wash-basin, and held up a dusty tooth-glass to the light.

"You have one," he said.

He was determined to keep unruffled, but every step she took across the uneven floorboards broke momentarily the steady pain into burning splinters.

"I've got gout," he said sullenly. "Bloody hell, I've got my gout."

"I thought so," she said. She put down the glass very quietly and came to him. "Where?"

He pointed down.

"Can you manage to get into bed by yourself?"

He nodded.

"Well, then!" She smiled. "Once you're in, I know what to do."

He looked up apprehensively, but she went almost on tiptoe out of the door and closed it softly.

He undressed, put on his pyjamas, and hauled himself on to the bed. When she came back, she was carrying two pillows. "Don't laugh, but they're 'His' and 'His,'" she said. "Now, this is what I do for Charlie. I make a little pillow house for his foot, and it keeps the bedclothes off. Don't worry, I won't touch."

"On this one night," he said.

"You want to drink a lot of water." She put a glass beside him. "'My husband's got a touch of gout,' I told them down there. And I really felt quite married to you when I said it."

She turned her back to him as she undressed. Her body, set free at last, was creased with red marks, and across her shoulders the bright new skin from peeling had ragged, dirty edges of the old. She stretched her spine, put on a transparent nightgown and began to scratch her arms.

"Come here," he said, unmoving. "I'll do that."

So gently she pulled back the sheet and lay down beside him that he felt they had been happily married for years. The pang was that this was their only married night and his foot burned so that he thought that it would burst. "And it will be a damn sight worse in the morning," he thought, knowing the pattern of his affliction. He began with one hand to stroke her itching arm.

Almost as soon as she had put the light off, an ominous sound zigzagged about the room. Switching on again, she said, "I'll get that devil, if it's the last thing I do. You lie still."

She got out of bed again and ran round the room, slapping at the walls with her *Reader's Digest*, until at last she caught the mosquito, and Stanley's (as was apparent in the morning) blood squirted out.

After that, once more in the dark, they lay quietly. He endured his pain, and she without disturbing him rubbed her flaking skin.

"So this is our wicked adventure," he said bitterly to the moonlit ceiling.

"Would you rather be on your own?"

"No, no!" He groped with his hand towards her.

"Well, then . . ."

"How can you forgive me?"

"Let's worry about you, eh? Not me. That sort of thing doesn't matter much to me nowadays. I only really do it to be matey. I don't know . . . by the time Charlie and I have locked up, washed up, done the till, had a bit of something to eat . . ."

Once, she had been as insatiable as a flame. She lay and remembered the days of her youth; but with interest, not wistfully.

Only once did she wake. It was the best night's sleep she'd had for a week. Moonlight now fell over the bed, and on one chalky white-washed wall. The sheet draped over them rose in a peak above his feet, so that he looked like a figure on a tomb. "If Charlie could see me now," she suddenly thought. She tried not to have a fit of giggles for fear of shaking the bed. Stanley shifted, groaned in his sleep, then went on snoring, just as Charlie did.

He woke often during that night. The sheets were as abrasive as sand-paper. "I knew this damn bed was too small," he thought. He shifted warily on to his side to look at Phyl who, in her sleep, made funny little whimpering sounds like a puppy. One arm flung above her head looked, in the moonlight, quite black against the pillow. Like going to bed with a coloured woman, he thought. He dutifully took a sip or two of water and then settled back again to endure his wakefulness.

"Well, *I* was happy," she said, wearing her emerald-green coat again, sitting next to him in the plane, fastening her safety-belt.

His face looked worn and grey.

"Don't mind me asking," she went on, "but did he charge for that tea we didn't order?"

"Five shillings."

"I *knew* it. I wish you'd let me pay my share of everything. After all, it was me as well wanted to go."

He shook his head, smiling at her. In spite of his prediction, he felt better this departure afternoon, though tired and wary about himself.

"If only we were taking off on holiday now," he said, "not coming back. Why can't we meet up in Torquay or somewhere? Something for me to look forward to," he begged her, dabbing his mosquito-bitten forehead with his handkerchief.

"It was only my hysterectomy got me away this time," she said.

They ate, they drank, they held hands under a newspaper, and presently crossed the twilit coast of England, where farther along grey Hove was waiting for him. The trees had not changed colour much and only some—she noticed, as she looked down on them, coming in to land—were yellower.

She knew that it was worse for him. He had to return to his empty flat; she, to a full bar, and on a Saturday, too. She wished there was something she could do to send him off cheerful.

"To me," she said, having refastened her safety-belt, taking his hand again. "To me, it was lovely. To me it was just as good as if we had."

SISTERS

ON A THURSDAY morning, soon after Mrs. Mason returned from shopping—in fact she had not yet taken off her hat—a neat young man wearing a dark suit and spectacles, half-gold, half-mock tortoiseshell, and carrying a rolled umbrella, called at the house, and brought her to the edge of ruin. He gave a name, which meant nothing to her, and she invited him in, thinking he was about insurance, or someone from her solicitor. He stood in the sitting-room, looking keenly about him, until she asked him to sit down and tell her his business.

"Your sister," he began. "Your sister Marion," and Mrs. Mason's hand flew up to her cheek. She gazed at him in alarmed astonishment, then closed her eyes.

In this town, where she had lived all her married life, Mrs. Mason was respected, even mildly loved. No one had a word to say against her, so it followed there were no strong feelings either way. She seemed to have been made for widowhood, and had her own little set, for bridge and coffee mornings, and her committee-meetings for the better known charities—such as the National Society for the Prevention of Cruelty to Children, and the Royal Society for the Prevention of Cruelty to Animals.

Her husband had been a successful dentist, and when he died she moved from the house where he had had his practice, into a smaller one in a quiet road nearby. She had no money worries, no worries of any kind. Childless and serene, she lived from day to day. They were almost able to set their clocks by her, her neighbours said, seeing her leaving the house in the mornings, for shopping and coffee at the

Oak Beams Tea Room, pushing a basket on wheels, stalking rather on high-heeled shoes, blue-rinsed, rouged. Her front went down in a straight line from her heavy bust, giving her a stately look, the weight throwing her back a little. She took all of life at the same pace—a sign of ageing. She had settled to it a long time ago, and all of her years seemed the same now, although days had slightly varying patterns. Hers was mostly a day-time life, for it was chiefly a woman's world she had her place in. After tea, her friends' husbands came home, and then Mrs. Mason pottered in her garden, played patience in the winter, or read historical romances from the library. "Something light," she would tell the assistant, as if seeking suggestions from a waiter. She could never remember the names of authors or their works, and it was quite a little disappointment when she discovered that she had read a novel before. She had few other disappointments—nothing much more than an unexpected shower of rain, or a tough cutlet, or the girl at the hairdresser's getting her rinse wrong.

Mrs. Mason had always done, and still did, everything expected of women in her position—which was a phrase she often used. She baked beautiful Victoria sponges for bring-and-buy sales, arranged flowers, made *gros-point* covers for her chairs, gave tea parties, even sometimes, daringly, sherry parties with one or two husbands there, much against their will—but this was kept from her. She was occasionally included in other women's evening gatherings for she made no difference when there was a crowd, and it was an easy kindness. She mingled, and chatted about other people's holidays and families and jobs. She never drank more than two glasses of sherry, and was a good guest, always exclaiming appreciatively at the sight of canapés, "My goodness, *someone's* been busy!"

Easefully the time had gone by.

This Thursday morning, the young man, having mentioned her sister, and seen her distress, glanced at one of the needlework cushions, and rose for a moment to examine it. Having ascertained that it was her work (a brief, distracted nod), he praised it, and sat down again.

Then, thinking the pause long enough, he said, "I am writing a book about your sister, and I did so hope for some help from you."

"How did you know?" she managed to ask with her numbed lips. "That she was, I mean."

He smiled modestly. "It was a matter of literary detection—my great hobby. My life's work, I might say."

He had small, even teeth, she noticed, glancing at him quickly. They glinted, like his spectacles, the buttons on his jacket and the signet ring on his hand. He was a hideously glinty young man, she decided, looking away again.

"I have nothing to say of any interest."

"But anything you say will interest us."

"Us?"

"Her admirers. The reading public. Well, the world at large." He shrugged.

"The world at large" was menacing, for it included this town where Mrs. Mason lived. It included the Oak Beams Tea Room, and the Societies of Prevention.

"I have nothing to say." She moved, as if she would rise.

"Come! You had your childhoods together. We know about those only from the stories. The beautiful stories. That wonderful house by the sea."

He looked at a few shelves of books beside him, and seemed disappointed. They were her late husband's books about military history.

"It wasn't so wonderful," she said, for she disliked all exaggeration. "It was a quite ordinary, shabby house."

"Yes?" he said softly, settling back in his chair and clasping his ladylike hands.

The shabby, ordinary house—the rectory—had a path between cornfields to the sea. On either side of it now were caravan sites. Her husband, Gerald, had taken her back there once when they were on holiday in Cornwall. He, of course, had been in the know. She had been upset about the caravans, and he had comforted her. She wished that he were here this morning to deal with this terrifying young man.

Of her childhood, she remembered—as one does—mostly the still hot afternoons, the cornflowers and thistles and scarlet pimpernels, the scratchy grass against her bare legs as they went down to the beach. Less clearly, she recalled evenings with shadows growing longer, and far-off sounding voices calling across the garden. She could see the picture of the house with windows open, and towels and bathing-costumes drying on upstairs sills and canvas shoes, newly whitened, drying too, in readiness for the next day's tennis. It had all been so familiar and comforting; but her sister, Marion, had complained of dullness, had ungratefully chafed and rowed and rebelled—although using it all (twisting it) in later years to make a name for herself. It had never, never been as she had written of it. And she, Mrs. Mason, the little Cassie of those books, had never been at all that kind of child. These more than forty years after, she still shied away from that description of her squatting and peeing into a rock-pool, in front of some little boys Marion had made up. "Cassie! Cassie!" her sisters had cried, apparently, in consternation. But it was Marion herself who had done that, more like. There were a few stories she could have told about Marion, if she had been the one to expose them all to shame, she thought grimly. The rock-pool episode was nothing, really, compared with some of the other inventions—"experiments with sex," as reviewers had described them at the time. It was as if her sister had been compelled to set her sick fancies against a background that she knew.

Watching Mrs. Mason's face slowly flushing all over to blend with her rouged cheekbones, the young man, leaning back easily, felt he had bided his time long enough. Something was obviously being stirred up. He said gently—so that his words seemed to come to her like her own thoughts—"A few stories now, please. Was it a happy childhood?"

"Yes. No. It was just an ordinary childhood."

"With such a genius among you? How *awfully* interesting!"

"She was no different from any of the rest of us." But she *had* been, and so unpleasantly, as it turned out.

"Really *extraordinarily* interesting." He allowed himself to lean forward a little, then, wondering if the slightest show of eagerness might silence her, he glanced about the room again. There were only two photographs—one of a long-ago bride and bridegroom, the other of a pompous-looking man with some sort of chain of office hanging on his breast.

It was proving very hard-going, this visit; but all the more of a challenge for that.

Mrs. Mason, in her silvery-grey wool dress, suddenly seemed to him to resemble an enormous salmon. She even had a salmon shape—thick from the shoulders down and tapering away to surprisingly tiny, out-turned feet. He imagined trying to land her. She was demanding all the skill and tenacity he had. This was very pleasurable. Having let him in, and sat down, her good manners could find no way of getting rid of him. He was sure of that. Her good manners were the only encouraging thing, so far.

"You know, you are really not at all what I expected," he said boldly, admiringly. "Not in the very least like your sister, are you?"

What he had expected was an older version of the famous photograph in the Collected Edition—that waif-like creature with the fly-away fringe and great dark eyes.

Mrs. Mason now carefully lifted off her hat, as if it were a coronet. Then she touched her hair, pushing it up a little. "I was the pretty one," she did not say; but, feeling some explanation was asked for, told him what all the world knew. "My sister had poor health," she said. "Asthma and migraines, and so on. Lots of what we now call allergies. I never had more than a couple of days' illness in my life." She remembered Marion always being fussed over—wheezing and puking and whining, or stamping her feet up and down in temper and frustration, causing scenes, a general rumpus at any given moment.

He longed to get inside her mind; for interesting things were going on there he guessed. Patience, he thought, regarding her. She was wearing opaque grey stockings; to hide varicose veins, he thought. He knew everything about women, and mentally unclothed her. In a leisurely fashion—since he would not hurry anything—he stripped off her peach-coloured slip and matching knickers, tugged her out of her sturdy corselette, whose straps had bitten deep into her plump shoulders, leaving a permanent indentation. He did not even jib at the massive, mottled flesh beneath, creased, as it must be, from its rigid confinement, or the suspender imprints at the top of her tapering legs. Her navel would be full of talcum powder.

"It was all so long ago. I don't want to be reminded," she said simply.

"Have you any photographs—holiday snapshots, for instance? I adore looking at old photographs."

There was a boxful upstairs, faded sepia scenes of them all paddling—dresses tucked into bloomers—or picnicking, with sandwiches in hand, and feet out of focus. Her father, the Rector, had developed and printed the photographs himself, and they had not lasted well. "I don't care to live in the past," was all she said in reply.

"Were you and Marion close to one another?"

"We were sisters," she said primly.

"And you kept in touch? I should think that you enjoyed basking in the reflected glory." He knew that she had not kept in touch, and was sure by now that she had done no basking.

"She went to live in Paris, as no doubt you know."

Thank heavens, Mrs. Mason had always thought, that she *had* gone to live in Paris, and that she herself had married and been able to change her name. Still quite young, and before the war, Marion had died. It was during Mr. Mason's year as Mayor. They had told no one.

"Did you ever meet Godwin? Or any of that set?"

"Of course not. My husband wouldn't have had them in the house."

The young man nodded.

Oh, that dreadful clique. She was ashamed to have it mentioned to her by someone of the opposite sex, a complete stranger. She had been embarrassed to speak of it to her own husband, who had been so extraordinarily kind and forgiving about everything connected with Marion. But that raffish life in Paris in the thirties! Her sister living with the man Godwin, or turn and turn about with others of her set. They all had switched from one partner to the other; some-times—she clasped her hands together so tightly that her rings hurt her fingers—to others of the same sex. She knew about it; the world knew; no doubt her friends knew, although it was not the sort of thing they would have discussed. Books had been written about that Paris lot, as Mrs. Mason thought of them, and their correspondence published. Godwin, and Miranda Braun, the painter, and Grant Opie, the American, who wrote obscene books; and many of the others. They were all notorious: that was Mrs. Mason's word for them.

"I think she killed my father," she said in a low voice, almost as if she were talking to herself. "He fell ill, and did not seem to want to go on living. He would never have her name mentioned, or any of her books in the house. She sent him a copy of the first one—she had left home by then, and was living in London. He read some of it, then took it out to the incinerator in the garden and burned it. I re-member it now, his face was as white as a sheet."

"But *you* have read the books surely?" he asked, playing her in gently.

She nodded, looking ashamed. "Yes, later, I did." A terrified curi-osity had proved too strong to resist. And, reading, she had discov-ered a childhood she could hardly recognise, although it was all there: all the pieces were there, but shifted round as in a kaleido-scope. Worse came after the first book, the stories of their girlhood and growing up and falling in love. She, the Cassie of the books, had become a well-known character, with all her secrets laid bare; though they were really the secrets of Marion herself and not those of the youngest sister. The candour had caused a stir in those far-off days. During all the years of public interest, Mrs. Mason had kept her silence, and lately had been able to bask indeed—in the neglect which had fallen upon her sister, as it falls upon most great writers at some period after their death. It was done with and laid to rest, she had thought—until this morning.

"And you didn't think much of them, I infer," the young man said.

She started, and looked confused. "Of what?" she asked, drawing back, tightening his line.

"Your sister's stories."

"They weren't true. We were well-brought-up girls."

"Your other sister died, too."

He *had* been rooting about, she thought in dismay. "She died before all the scandal," Mrs. Mason said grimly. "She was spared."

The telephone rang in the hall, and she murmured politely and got up. He heard her, in a different, chatty voice, making arrangements and kind enquiries, actually laughing. She rang off presently, and then stood for a moment steadying herself. She peered into a glass and touched her hair again. Full of strength and resolution, she went back to the sitting-room and just caught him clipping a pen back into the inside of his jacket.

"I'm afraid I shall have to get on with some jobs now," she said clearly, and remained standing.

He rose—had to—cursing the telephone for ringing, just when he was bringing her in so beautifully. "And you are sure you haven't even one little photograph to lend me," he asked. "I would take enormous care of it."

"Yes, I am quite sure." She was like another woman now. She had been in touch with her own world, and had gained strength from it.

"Then may I come to see you again when you are not so busy?"

"Oh, no, I don't think so." She put out an arm and held the door-handle. "I really don't think there would be any point."

He really felt himself that there would not be. Still looking greedily about him, he went into the hall towards the front door. He had the idea of leaving his umbrella behind, so that he would have to return for it; but she firmly handed it to him. Even going down the path to the gate, he seemed to be glancing from side to side, as if memorising the names of flowers.

"I said nothing, I said nothing," Mrs. Mason kept telling herself, on her way that afternoon to play bridge. "I merely conveyed my disapproval." But she had a flustered feeling that her husband would not have agreed that she had done only that. And she guessed that the young man would easily make something of nothing. "She killed my father." She had said that. It would be in print, with her name attached to it. He had been clever to ferret her out, the menacing young man and now he had something new to offer to the world—herself. What else had she said, for heaven's sake? She was walking uphill, and panted a little. She could not for the life of her remember if she had said any more. But, ah yes! How her father had put that book into the incinerator. Just like Hitler, some people would think. And her name and Marion's would be linked together. Ex-Mayoress, and that rackety and lustful set. Some of her friends would be openly cool, others too kind, all of them shocked. They would discuss the matter behind her back. There were even those who would say they were "intrigued" and ask questions.

Mrs. Oldfellow, Mrs. Fitch and Miss Christy all thought she played badly that afternoon, especially Mrs. Oldfellow who was her partner. She did not stay for sherry when the bridge was over but excused herself, saying that she felt a cold coming on. Mrs. Fitch's offer to run her back in the car she refused, hoping that the fresh air might clear her head.

She walked home in her usual sedate way; but she could not rid herself of the horrible idea they were talking about her already.

HÔTEL DU COMMERCE

THE HALLWAY, with its reception desk and hat-stand, was gloomy. Madame Bertail reached up to the board where the keys hung, took the one for room eight, and led the way upstairs. Her daughter picked up the heavier suitcase, and began to lurch lopsidedly across the hall with it until Leonard, blushing as he always (and understandably) did when he was obliged to speak French, insisted on taking it from her.

Looking offended, she grabbed instead Melanie's spanking-new wedding present suitcase, and followed them grimly, as *they* followed Madame Bertail's stiffly corseted back. Level with her shoulder-blades, the corsets stopped and the massive flesh moved gently with each step she took, as if it had a life of its own.

In Room Eight was a small double bed and wallpaper with a paisley pattern, on which what looked like curled-up blood-red embryos were repeated every two inches upon a sage-green background. There were other patterns for curtains and chair covers and the thin eiderdown. It was a depressing room, and a smell of some previous occupier's Ambre Solaire still hung about it.

"I'm so sorry, darling," Leonard apologised, as soon as they were alone.

Melanie smiled. For a time, they managed to keep up their spirits. "I'm so tired, I'll sleep anywhere," she said, not knowing about the mosquito hidden in the curtains, or the lumpiness of the bed, and other horrors to follow.

They were both tired. A day of driving in an open car had made them feel, now they had stopped, quite dull and drowsy. Conversation was an effort.

Melanie opened her case. There was still confetti about. A crescent-shaped white piece fluttered on to the carpet, and she bent quickly and picked it up. So much about honeymoons was absurd—even little reminders like this one. And there had been awkwardnesses they could never have foreseen—especially that of having to make their way in a foreign language. (*Lune de miel* seemed utterly improbable to her.) She did not know how to ask a maid to wash a blouse, although she had pages of irregular verbs somewhere in her head, and odd words, from lists she had learnt as a child—the Parts of the Body, the Trees of the Forest, the Days of the Week—would often spring gratifyingly to her rescue.

When she had unpacked, she went to the window and leant out, over a narrow street with lumpy cobbles all ready for an early-morning din of rattling carts and slipping hooves.

Leonard kept glancing nervously at her as he unpacked. He did everything methodically, and at one slow pace. She was quick and untidy, and spent much time hanging about waiting for him, growing depressed, then exasperated, leaning out of windows, as now, strolling impatiently in gardens.

He smoked in the bedroom: she did not, and often thought it would have been better the other way about, so that she could have had something to do while she waited.

He hung up his dressing-gown, paused, then trod heavily across to his suitcase and took out washing things, which he arranged neatly on a shelf. He looked at her again. Seen from the back, hunched over the window-sill, she seemed to be visibly drooping, diminishing, like melting wax; and he knew that her mood was because of him. But a lifetime's habit—more than that, something inborn—made him feel helpless. He also had a moment of irritation himself, seeing her slippers thrown anyhow under a chair.

"Ready, then," he said, in a tone of anticipation and decision.

She turned eagerly from the window, and saw him take up his

comb. He stood before the glass, combing, combing his thin hair, lapsing once more into dreaminess, intent on what he was doing. She sighed quietly and turned back to look out of the window.

"I can see a spire of the Cathedral," she said presently; but her head was so far out of the window—and a lorry was going by—that he did not hear her.

"Well, we've *had* the Cathedral," she thought crossly. It was too late for the stained glass. She would never be able to make him see that every minute counted, or that there should not be some preordained method but, instead, a shifting order of priorities. Unpacking can wait; but the light will not.

By the time they got out for their walk, and saw the Cathedral, it was floodlit, bone-white against the dark sky, bleached, flat, stagey, though beautiful in this unintended and rather unsuitable way. Walking in the twisting streets, Leonard and Melanie had glimpsed the one tall spire above roof-tops, then lost it. Arm in arm, they had stopped to look in shop windows, at glazed pigs' trotters, tarts full of neatly arranged strawberries, sugared almonds on stems, in bunches, tied with ribbons. Leonard lingered, comparing prices of watches and cameras with those at home in England; Melanie, feeling chilly, tried gently to draw him on. At last, without warning, they came to the square where the Cathedral stood, and here there were more shops, all full of little plaster statues and rosaries, and antiques for the tourists.

"Exorbitant," Leonard kept saying. "My God, how they're out to fleece you!"

Melanie stood staring up at the Cathedral until her neck ached. The great rose window was dark, the light glaring on the stone façade too static. The first sense of amazement and wonder faded. It was part of her impatient nature to care most for first impressions. On their way south, the sudden, and far-away sight of Chartres Cathedral across the plain, crouched on the horizon, with its lop-sided spires, like a giant hare, had meant much more to her than the close-up details of it. Again, for *that*, they had been too late. Before they reached the town, storm-clouds had gathered. It might as well have been dusk inside the Cathedral. She, for her part, would not have stopped to fill up with petrol on the road. She would have risked it, parked the car anywhere, and run.

Staring up at *this* Cathedral, she felt dizzy from leaning backwards, and swayed suddenly, and laughed. He caught her close to him and so, walking rather unevenly, with arms about the other's waist, moved on, out of the square, and back to the hotel.

Such moments, of more-than-usual love, gave them both great confidence. This time, their mood of elation lasted much longer than a moment.

Although the hotel dining-room was dark, and they were quite alone in it, speaking in subdued voices, their humour held; and held, as they took their key from impassive Madame Bertail, who still sat at the desk, doing her accounts; it even held as they undressed in their depressing room, and had no need to hold longer than that. Once in bed, they had always been safe.

"Don't tell me! Don't tell me!"

They woke at the same instant and stared at the darkness, shocked, wondering where they were.

"Don't tell me! I'll spend my money how I bloody well please."

The man's voice, high and hysterical, came through the wall, just behind their heads.

A woman was heard laughing softly, with obviously affected amusement.

Something was thrown, and broke.

"I've had enough of your nagging."

"I've had enough of *you*," the woman answered coolly.

Melanie buried her head against Leonard's shoulder and he put an arm round her.

"I had enough of *you*, a very long time ago," the woman's voice went on. "I can't honestly remember a time when I *hadn't* had enough of you."

"What I've gone through!"

"What *you've* gone through?"

"Yes, that's what I said. What *I've* gone through."

"Don't shout. It's so common." She had consciously lowered her own voice, then said, forgetting, in almost a shout, "It's a pity for both our sakes, you were so greedy. For Daddy's money, I mean. That's all you ever cared about—my father's money."

"All *you* cared about was getting into bed with me."

"You great braggart. I've always loathed going to bed with you. Who wouldn't?"

Leonard heaved himself up in bed, and knocked on the damp wallpaper.

"I always felt sick," the woman's voice went on, taking no notice. She was as strident now as the man; had begun to lose her grip on the situation, as he had done. "And God knows," she said, "how many other women you've made feel sick."

Leonard knocked louder, with his fist this time. The wall seemed as soft as if it were made from cardboard.

"I'm scared," said Melanie. She sat up and switched on the light. "Surely he'll kill her, if she goes on like that."

"You little strumpet!" The man slurred this word, tried to repeat it and dried up, helplessly, goaded into incoherence.

"Be careful! Just be careful!" A dangerous, deliberate voice hers was now.

"Archie Durrant? Do you think I didn't know about Archie Durrant? Don't take me for a fool."

"I'll warn you; don't put ideas into my head, my precious husband. At least Archie Durrant wouldn't bring me to a lousy place like this."

She then began to cry. They reversed their rôles and he in his turn became the cool one.

"He won't take you anywhere, my pet. Like me, he's had enough. *Un*like me, *he* can skedaddle."

"Why doesn't someone *do* something!" asked Melanie, meaning, of course, that Leonard should. "Everyone must be able to hear. And they're English, too. It's so shaming, and horrible."

"Go on, then, skedaddle, skedaddle!" The absurd word went on and on, blurred, broken by sobs. Something more was thrown—something with a sharp, hard sound; perhaps a shoe or book.

Leonard sprang out of bed and put on his dressing-gown and slippers.

"Slippers!" thought Melanie, sitting up in bed, shivering.

As Leonard stepped out into the passage, he saw Madame Bertail coming along it, from the other direction. She, too, wore a dressing-gown, corded round her stout stomach: her grey hair was thinly braided. She looked steadily at Leonard, as if dismissing him, classing him with his loose compatriots, then knocked quickly on the door and at once tried the door-handle. The key had been turned in the lock. She knocked again, and there was silence inside the room. She knocked once more, very loudly, as if to make sure of this silence, and then, without a word to Leonard, seeming to feel satisfied that she had dealt successfully with the situation, she went off down the corridor.

Leonard went back to the bedroom and slowly took off his dressing-gown and slippers.

"I think that will be that," he said, and got back into bed and tried to warm poor Melanie.

"You talk about your father's money," the man's voice went on, almost at once. "But I wouldn't want any truck with that kind of money."

"You just want it."

Their tone was more controlled, as if they were temporarily calmed. However, although the wind had dropped they still quietly angled for it, keeping things going for the time being.

"I'll never forget the first time I realised how you got on my nerves," he said, in the equable voice of an old friend reminiscing about happier days. "That way you walk upstairs with your bottom waggling from side to side. My God, I've got to walk upstairs and downstairs behind that bottom for the rest of my life, I used to think."

"Such triviality!" Melanie thought fearfully, pressing her hands against her face. To begin with such a thing—for the hate to grow from it—not nearly as bad as being slow and keeping people waiting.

"I wasn't seriously loathing you then," the man said in a conversational tone. "Even after that fuss about Archie Durrant. I didn't seriously *hate* you."

"Thank you very much, you ... cuckold."

If Leonard did not snore at that moment, he certainly breathed sonorously.

During that comparative lull in the next room, he had dropped off to sleep, leaving Melanie wakeful and afraid.

"She called him a cuckold," she hissed into Leonard's ear.

"No, the time, I think," said the man behind the wall, in the same deadly flat voice, "the time I first really hated you, was when you threw the potatoes at me."

"Oh, yes, that was a *great* evening," she said, in tones chiming with affected pleasure.

"In front of my own mother."

"She seemed to enjoy it as much as I did. Probably longed for years to do it herself."

"That was when I first realised."

"Why did you stay?" There was silence. Then, "Why stay now? Go on! Go now! I'll help you to pack. There's your bloody hairbrush for a start. My God, you look ridiculous when you duck down like that. You sickening little coward."

"I'll kill you."

"Oh God, he'll kill her," said Melanie, shaking Leonard roughly.

"You won't, you know," shouted the other woman.

The telephone rang in the next room.

"Hello?" The man's voice was cautious, ruffled. The receiver was quietly replaced. "You see what you've done?" he said. "Someone ringing up to complain about the noise you're making."

"You don't think I give a damn for anyone in a crumby little hotel like this, do you?"

"Oh, my nerves, my nerves, my nerves," the man suddenly

groaned. Bed-springs creaked, and Melanie imagined him sinking down on the edge of the bed, his face buried in his hands.

Silence lasted only a minute or two. Leonard was fast asleep now. Melanie lay very still, listening to a mosquito coming and going above her head.

Then the crying began, at first a little sniffing, then a quiet sobbing.

"Leonard, you must wake up. I can't lie here alone listening to it. Or *do* something, for heaven's sake."

He put out a hand, as if to stave her off, or calm her, without really disturbing his sleep, and this gesture infuriated her. She slapped his hand away roughly.

"There's nothing I can do," he said, still clinging to the idea of sleep; then, as she flounced over in the bed, turning her back to him, he resignedly sat up and turned on the light. Blinking and tousled, he stared before him, and then leaned over and knocked on the wall once more.

"*That* won't do any good," said Melanie.

"Well, their door's locked, so what else can I do?"

"Ring up the police."

"I can't do that. Anyhow, I don't know how to in French."

"Well, try. If the hotel was on fire, you'd do something, wouldn't you?"

Her sharp tone was new to him, and alarming.

"It's not really our business."

"If he kills her? While you were asleep, she called him a cuckold. I thought he was going to kill her then. And even if he doesn't, we can't hope to get any sleep. It's perfectly horrible. It sounds like a child crying."

"Yes, with temper. Your feet are frozen."

"Of course, they're frozen." Her voice blamed him for this.

"My dear, don't let *us* quarrel."

"I'm so tired. Oh, that—damned mosquito." She sat up, and tried to smack it against the wall, but it had gone. "It's been such an awful day."

"I thought it was a perfectly beautiful day."

She pressed her lips together and closed her eyes, drawing herself away from him, as if determined now, somehow or other, to go to sleep.

"Didn't you like your day?" he asked.

"Well, you must have known I was disappointed about the Cathedral. Getting there when it was too dark."

"I didn't know. You didn't give me an inkling. We can go first thing in the morning."

"It wouldn't be the same. Oh, you're so hopeless. You hang about, and hang about, and drive me mad with impatience."

She lay on her side, well away from him on the very edge of the bed, facing the horribly patterned curtains, her mouth so stiff, her eyes full of tears. He made an attempt to draw her close, but she became rigid, her limbs were iron.

"You see, she's quietening down," he said. The weeping had gone through every stage—from piteous sobbing, gasping, angry moans, to—now—a lulled whimpering, dying off, hardly heard. And the man was silent. Had he dropped senseless across the bed, Melanie wondered, or was he still sitting there, staring at the picture of his own despair.

"I'm so sorry about the Cathedral. I had no idea..." said Leonard, switching off the light, and sliding down in bed. Melanie kept her cold feet to herself.

"We'll say no more about it," she said, in a grim little voice.

They slept late. When he awoke, Leonard saw that Melanie was almost falling out of bed in her attempt to keep away from him. Disquieting memories made him frown. He tried to lay his thoughts out in order. The voices in the next room, the nightmare of weeping and abuse; but worse, Melanie's cold voice, her revelation of that harboured disappointment; then, worse again, even worse, her impatience with him. He drove her nearly mad, she had said. Always? Since they were married? When?

At last Melanie awoke, and seemed uncertain of how to behave. Unable to make up her mind, she assumed a sort of non-behaviour to be going on with, which he found most mystifying.

"Shall we go to the Cathedral?" he asked.

"Oh, I don't think so," she said carelessly. She even turned her back to him while she dressed.

There was silence from the next room, but neither of them referred to it. It was as if some shame of their own were shut up in there. The rest of the hotel was full of noises—kitchen clatterings and sharp voices. A vacuum-cleaner bumped and whined along the passage outside, and countrified traffic went by in the cobbled street.

Melanie's cheeks and forehead were swollen with mosquito bites, which gave her an angry look. She scratched one on her wrist and made it water. They seemed the stigmata of her irritation.

They packed their cases.

"Ready?" he asked.

"When you are," she said sullenly.

"Might as well hit the trail as soon as we've had breakfast," he said, trying to sound optimistic, as if nothing were wrong. He had no idea of how they would get through the day. They had no plans, and she seemed disinclined to discuss any.

They breakfasted in silence in the empty dining-room. Some of the tables had chairs stacked on them.

"You've no idea where you want to go, then?" he asked.

She was spreading apricot jam on a piece of bread and he leant over and gently touched her hand. She laid down the knife, and put her hand in her lap. Then picked up the bread with her left hand and began to eat.

They went upstairs, to fetch their cases and, going along the passage, could see that the door of the room next to theirs now stood wide open. Before they reached it, a woman came out and hesitated in the doorway, looking back into the room. There was an appearance of brightness about her—her glowing face, shining hair, starched dress. Full of gay anticipation as it was, her voice, as she called back into the room, was familiar to Melanie and Leonard.

"Ready, darling?"

The other familiar voice replied. The man came to the doorway, carrying the case. He put his arm round the woman's waist and they went off down the passage. Such a well turned-out couple, Melanie thought, staring after them, as she paused at her own doorway, scratching her mosquito bites.

"Let's go to that marvellous place for lunch," she heard the man suggesting. They turned a corner to the landing, but as they went on downstairs, their laughter floated up after them.

MISS A. AND MISS M.

A NEW MOTORWAY had made a different landscape of that part of England I loved as a child, cutting through meadows, spanning valleys, shaving off old gardens and leaving houses perched on islands of confusion. Nothing is recognisable now: the guest-house has gone, with its croquet-lawn; the cherry orchard; and Miss Alliot's and Miss Martin's week-end cottage. I should think that little is left anywhere, except in *my* mind.

I was a town child, and the holidays in the country had a sharp delight which made the waiting time of school term, of traffic, of leaflessness, the unreal part of my life. At Easter, and for weeks in the summer, sometimes even for a few snatched days in winter, we drove out there to stay—it wasn't far—for my mother loved the country, too, and in that place we had put down roots.

St. Margaret's was the name of the guest-house, which was run by two elderly ladies who had come down in the world, bringing with them quantities of heavily riveted Crown Derby, and silver plate. Miss Louie and Miss Beatrice.

My mother and I shared a bedroom with a sloping floor and threadbare carpet. The wallpaper had faint roses, and a powdery look from damp. Oil-lamps or candles lit the rooms, and, even now, the smell of paraffin brings it back, that time of my life. We were in the nineteen twenties.

Miss Beatrice, with the help of a maid called Mabel, cooked deliciously. Beautiful creamy porridge, I remember, and summer puddings, suckling pigs and maids-of-honour and marrow jam. The guests sat at one long table with Miss Louie one end and Miss Beatrice the other, and Mabel scuttling in and out with silver domed dishes. There was no wine. No one drank anything alcoholic, that I remember. Sherry was kept for trifle, and that was it, and the new world of cocktail parties was elsewhere.

The guests were for the most part mild, bookish people who liked a cheap and quiet holiday—schoolmasters, elderly spinsters, sometimes people to do with broadcasting who, in those days, were held in awe. The guests returned, so that we had constant friends among them, and looked forward to our reunions. Sometimes there were other children. If there were not, I did not care. I had Miss Alliot and Miss Martin.

These two were always spoken of in that order, and not because it was easier to say like that, or more euphonious. They appeared at luncheon and supper, but were not guests. At the far end of the orchard they had a cottage for week-ends and holidays. They were schoolmistresses in London.

"Cottage" is not quite the word for what was little more than a wooden shack with two rooms and a veranda. It was called Breezy Lodge, and draughts did blow between its ramshackle clap-boarding.

Inside, it was gay, for Miss Alliot was much inclined to orange and yellow and grass-green, and the cane chairs had cushions patterned with nasturtiums and marigolds and ferns. The curtains and her clothes reflected the same taste.

Miss Martin liked misty blues and greys, though it barely mattered that she did. She had a small smudged-looking face with untidy eyebrows, a gentle, even submerged nature. She was a great—but quiet—reader and never seemed to wish to talk of what she had read. Miss Alliot, on the other hand, would occasionally skim through a book and find enough in it for long discourses and an endless supply of allusions. She wrung the most out of everything she did or saw and was a great talker.

That was a time when one fell in love with who ever was *there*. In my adolescence the only males available to me for adoration were such as Shelley or Rupert Brooke or Owen Nares. A rather more real passion could be lavished on prefects at school or the younger mistresses.

Miss Alliot was heaven-sent, it seemed to me. She was a holiday goddess. Miss Martin was just a friend. She tried to guide my reading, as an elder sister might. This was a new relationship to me. I had no elder sister, and I had sometimes thought that to have had one would have altered my life entirely, and whether for better or worse I had never been able to decide.

How I stood with Miss Alliot was a reason for more pondering. Why did she take trouble over me, as she did? I considered myself sharp for my age: now I see that I was sharp only for the age I *lived* in. Miss Alliot cultivated me to punish Miss Martin—as if she needed another weapon. I condoned the punishing. I basked in the doing of it. I turned my own eyes from the troubled ones under the fuzzy brows, and I pretended not to know precisely what was being done. Flattery nudged me on. Not physically fondled, I was fondled all the same.

In those days before—more than forty years before—the motorway, that piece of countryside was beautiful, and the word "countryside" still means there to me. The Chiltern Hills. Down one of those slopes below St. Margaret's streamed the Cherry Orchard, a vast delight in summer of marjoram and thyme. An unfrequented footpath led through it, and every step was aromatic. We called this walk the Echo Walk—down through the trees and up from the valley on its other side to larch woods.

Perched on a stile at the edge of the wood, one called out messages to be rung back across the flinty valley. Once, alone, I called out, "I love you," loud and strong, and "I love you" came back faint, and mocking. "Miss Alliot," I added. But that response was blurred. Perhaps I feared to shout too loudly, or it was not a good echo name. I tried no others.

On Sunday mornings I walked across the fields to church with Miss Martin. Miss Alliot would not join us. It was scarcely an intellectual feast, she said, or spiritually uplifting, with the poor old Vicar mumbling on and the organ asthmatic. In London, she attended St. Ethelburga's in the Strand, and spoke a great deal of a Doctor Cobb. But, still more, she spoke of the Townsends.

For she punished Miss Martin with the Townsends too.

The Townsends lived in Northumberland. Their country house was grand, as was to be seen in photographs. Miss Alliot appeared in some of these shading her eyes as she lay back in a deck chair in a sepia world or—with Suzanne Lenglen bandeau and accordion-pleated dress—simply standing, to be photographed. By whom? I wondered. Miss Martin wondered, too, I thought.

Once a year, towards the end of the summer holiday (mine: theirs) Miss Alliot was invited to take the train north. We knew that she would have taken that train at an hour's notice, and, if necessary, have dropped everything for the Townsends.

What they consisted of—the Townsends—I was never really sure. It was a group name, both in my mind and in our conversations. "Do the Townsends play croquet?" I enquired, or "Do the Townsends change for dinner?" I was avid for information. It was readily given.

"I know what the Townsends would think of *her*," Miss Alliot said, of the only common woman, as she put it, who had ever stayed at St. Margaret's. Mrs. Price came with her daughter, Muriel, who was seven years old and had long, burnished plaits, which she would toss—one, then the other—over her shoulders. Under Miss Alliot's guidance, I scorned both Mrs. Price and child, and many a laugh we had in Breezy Lodge at their expense. Scarcely able to speak for laughter, Miss Alliot would recount her "gems," as she called them. "Oh, she *said* . . . one can't believe it, little Muriel . . . Mrs. Price *insists* on it . . . changes her socks and knickers twice a day. She likes her to be nice and fresh. And . . ." Miss Alliot was a good mimic, "'she always takes an apple for recess.' What in God's name is recess?"

This was rather strong language for those days, and I admired it.

"It's 'break' or…" Miss Martin began reasonably. This was her mistake. She slowed things up with her reasonableness, when what Miss Alliot wanted, and I wanted, was a flight of fancy.

I tried, when those two were not there, to gather foolish or despicable phrases from Mrs. Price, but I did not get far. (I suspect now Miss Alliot's inventive mind at work—rehearsing for the Townsends.)

All these years later, I have attempted, while writing this, to be fair to Mrs. Price, almost forgotten for forty years; but even without Miss Alliot's direction I think I should have found her tiresome. She boasted to my mother (and no adult was safe from my eavesdropping) about her hysterectomy, and the gynaecologist who doted on her. "I always have my operations at the Harbeck Clinic." I was praised for that titbit, and could not run fast enough to Breezy Lodge with it.

I knew what the medical words meant, for I had begun to learn Greek at school—Ladies' Greek, as Elizabeth Barrett Browning called it, "without any accents." My growing knowledge served me well with regard to words spoken in lowered tones. "My operations! How Ralph Townsend will adore that one!" Miss Alliot said.

A Townsend now stepped forward from the general family group. Miss Martin stopped laughing. I was so sharp for my years that I thought she gave herself away by doing so, that she should have let her laughter die away gradually. In that slice of a moment she had made clear her sudden worry about Ralph Townsend. Knowing as I did then so much about human beings, I was sure she had been meant to.

Poor Miss Martin, my friend, mentor, church-going companion, mild, kind and sincere—I simply used her as a stepping-stone to Miss Alliot.

I never called them by their first names, and have had to pause a little to remember them. Dorothea Alliot and Edith Martin. "Dorothea" had a fine ring of authority about it. Of course, I had the Greek meaning of that, too, but I knew that Miss Alliot was the giver her-self—of the presents and the punishments.

My mother liked playing croquet and cards, and did both a great deal at St. Margaret's. I liked going across the orchard to Breezy Lodge. There, both cards and croquet were despised. We sat on the veranda (or, in winter, round an oil-stove which threw up petal patterns on the ceiling) and we talked—a game particularly suited to three people. Miss Alliot always won.

Where to find such drowsy peace in England now is hard to discover. Summer after summer through my early teens, the sun shone, bringing up the smell of thyme and marjoram from the earth—the melting tar along the lane and, later, of rotting apples. The croquet balls clicked against one another on the lawn, and voices sounded lazy and far-away. There were droughts, when we were on our honour to be careful with the water. No water was laid on at Breezy Lodge, and it had to be carried from the house. I took this duty from Miss Martin, and several times a day stumbled through the long grass and buttercups, the water swinging in a pail, or slopping out of a jug. As I went, I disturbed clouds of tiny blue butterflies, once a grass snake.

Any excuse to get to Breezy Lodge. My mother told me not to intrude, and I was offended by the word. She was even a little frosty about my two friends. If for some reason they were not there when we ourselves arrived on holiday I was in despair, and she knew it and lost patience.

In the school term I wrote to them and Miss Martin was the one who replied. They shared a flat in London, and a visit to it was spoken of, but did not come about. I used my imagination instead, building it up from little scraps as a bird builds a nest. I was able to furnish it in unstained oak and hand-woven rugs and curtains. All about would be jars of the beech-leaves and grasses and berries they took back with them from the country. From their windows could be seen, through the branches of a monkey-puzzle tree, the roofs of the school—Queen's—from which they returned each evening.

That was their life on their own where I could not intrude, as my mother would have put it. They had another life of their own in which I felt aggrieved at not participating: but I was not invited to. After supper at St. Margaret's, they returned to Breezy Lodge, and did not ask me to go with them. Games of solo whist were begun in the drawing-room, and I sat and read listlessly, hearing the clock tick and the maddening mystifying card-words—"*Misère*" "Abundance"—or "going a bundle," "prop and cop," and "*Misère Ouverte*" (which seemed to cause a little stir). I pitied them and their boring games, and I pitied myself and my boring book—imposed holiday reading, usually Sir Walter Scott, whom I loathed. I pecked at it dispiritedly and looked about the room for distraction.

Miss Louie and Miss Beatrice enjoyed their whist, as they enjoyed their croquet. They really were hostesses. We paid a little—astonishingly little—but it did not alter the fact that we were truly guests, and they entertained us believing so.

"Ho...ho...hum...hum," murmured a voice, fanning out a newly-dealt hand, someone playing for time. "H'm, h'm, now let me see." There were relaxed intervals when cards were being shuffled and cut, and the players leant back and had a little desultory conversation, though nothing amounting to much. On warm nights, as it grew later, through the open windows moths came to plunge and lurch about the lamps.

Becoming more and more restless, I might go out and wander about the garden, looking for glow-worms and glancing at the light from Breezy Lodge shining through the orchard boughs.

On other evenings, after Miss Beatrice had lit the lamps, Mrs. Mayes, one of the regular guests, might give a Shakespeare recital. She had once had some connection with the stage and had known Sir Henry Ainley. She had often heard his words for him, she told us, and perhaps, in consequence of that, had whole scenes by heart. She was ageing wonderfully—that is, hardly at all. Some of the blonde was fading from her silvery-blonde hair, but her skin was still wild-rose, and her voice held its great range. But most of all, we marvelled at how she remembered her lines. I recall most vividly the Balcony

Scene from *Romeo and Juliet*. Mrs. Mayes sat at one end of a velvet-covered *chaise-longue*. When she looped her pearls over her fingers, then clasped them to her bosom, she was Juliet, and Romeo when she held out her arms, imploringly (the rope of pearls swinging free). Always she changed into what, in some circles, was then called semi-evening dress, and rather old-fashioned dresses they were, with bead embroidery and loose panels hanging from the waist. Once, I imagined, she would have worn such dresses *before* tea, and have changed again later into something even more splendid. She had lived through grander days: now, was serenely widowed.

Only Mrs. Price did not marvel at her. I overheard her say to my mother, "She must be forever in the limelight, and I for one am sick and tired, *sick* and *tired*, of Henry Ainley. I'm afraid I don't call actors 'sir.' I'm like that." And my mother blushed, but said nothing.

Miss Alliot and Miss Martin were often invited to stay for these recitals; but Miss Alliot always declined.

"One is embarrassed, being recited *at*," she explained to me. "One doesn't know where to look."

I always looked at Mrs. Mayes and admired the way she did her hair, and wondered if the pearls were real. There may have been a little animosity between the two women. I remember Mrs. Mayes joining in praise of Miss Alliot one day, saying, "Yes, she is like a well-bred race-horse," and I felt that she said this only because she could not say that she was like a horse.

Mrs. Price, rather out of it after supper, because of Mrs. Mayes, and not being able to get the hang of solo whist, would sulkily turn the pages of the *Illustrated London News*, and try to start conversations between scenes or games.

"*Do* look at *this*." She would pass round her magazine, pointing out something or other. Or she would tiptoe upstairs to see if Muriel slept, and come back to report. Once she said, *à propos* nothing, as cards were being re-dealt, "Now who can clasp their ankles with their fingers? Like *that*—with no gaps." Some of the ladies dutifully tried, but only Mrs. Price could do it. She shrugged and laughed. "Only a bit of fun," she said, "but they do say that's the right proportion. Wrists, too, that's easier, though." But they were all at cards again.

One morning, we were sitting on the lawn and my mother was stringing redcurrants through the tines of a silver fork into a pudding-basin. Guests often helped in these ways. Mrs. Price came out from the house carrying a framed photograph of a bride and bridegroom—her son, Derek, and daughter-in-law, Gloria. We had heard of them.

"You don't look old enough," my mother said, "to have a son that age." She had said it before. She always liked to make people happy. Mrs. Price kept hold of the photograph, because of my mother's stained fingers, and she pointed out details such as Gloria's veil and Derek's smile and the tuberoses in the bouquet. "Derek gave her a gold locket, but it hasn't come out very clearly. Old enough! You are trying to flatter me. Why my husband and I had our silver wedding last October. Muriel was our little after-thought."

I popped a string of currants into my mouth and sauntered off. As soon as I was out of sight, I sped. All across the orchard, I murmured the words with smiling lips.

The door of Breezy Lodge stood open to the veranda. I called through it, "Muriel was their little after-thought."

Miss Martin was crying. From the bedroom came a muffled sobbing. At once, I knew that it was she, never could be Miss Alliot. Miss Alliot, in fact, walked out of the bedroom and shut the door.

"What is wrong?" I asked stupidly.

Miss Alliot gave a vexed shake of her head and took her walking-stick from its corner. She was wearing a dress with a pattern of large poppies, and cut-out poppies from the same material were appliquéd to her straw hat. She was going for a walk, and I went with her, and she told me that Miss Martin had fits of nervous hysteria. For no reason. The only thing to be done about them was to leave her alone until she recovered.

We went down through the Cherry Orchard and the scents and the butterflies were part of an enchanted world. I thought that I was completely happy. I so rarely had Miss Alliot's undivided attention.

She talked of the Townsends, and I listened as if to the holy intimations of a saint.

"I thought you were lost," my mother said when I returned.

Miss Alliot always wore a hat at luncheon (that annoyed Mrs. Price). She sat opposite me and seemed in a very good humour, taking trouble to amuse us all, but with an occasional allusion and smile for me alone. "Miss Martin has one of her headaches," she explained. By this time I was sure that this was true.

The holidays were going by, and I had got nowhere with *Quentin Durward*. Miss Martin recovered from her nervous hysteria, but was subdued.

Miss Alliot departed for Northumberland, wearing autumn tweeds. Miss Martin stayed on alone at Breezy Lodge, and distempered the walls primrose, and I helped her. Mrs. Price and Muriel left at last, and a German governess with her two little London pupils arrived for a breath of fresh air. My mother and Mrs. Mayes strolled about the garden. Together they did the flowers, to help Miss Louie, or sat together in the sunshine with their *petit point*.

Miss Martin and I painted away, and we talked of Miss Alliot and how wonderful she was. It was like a little separate holiday for me, a rest. I did not try to adjust myself to Miss Martin, or strive, or rehearse. In a way, I think she was having a well-earned rest herself; but then I believed that she was jealous of Northumberland and would have liked some Townsends of her own to retaliate with. Now I know she only wanted Miss Alliot.

Miss Martin was conscientious; she even tried to take me through *Quentin Durward*.

She seemed to be concerned about my butterfly mind, its skimming over things, not stopping to understand. I felt that knowing things ought to "come" to me, and if it did not, it was too bad. I believed in instinct and intuition and inspiration—all labour-saving things.

Miss Martin, who taught English (my subject, I felt), approached the matter coldly. She tried to teach me the logic of it—grammar. But I thought "ear" would somehow teach me that. Painless learning I wanted, or none at all. She would not give up. She was the one who was fond of me.

We returned from our holiday, and I went back to school. I was moved up—by the skin of my teeth, I am sure—to a higher form. I remained with my friends. Some of those had been abroad for the holidays, but I did not envy them.

Miss Martin wrote to enquire how I had got on in the *Quentin Durward* test, and I replied that as I could not answer one question, I had written a general description of Scottish scenery. She said that it would avail me nothing, and it did not. I had never been to Scotland, anyway. Of Miss Alliot I only heard. She was busy producing the school play—*A Tale of Two Cities*. Someone called Rosella Byng-Williams was very good as Sidney Carton, and I took against her at once. "I think Dorothea has made quite a discovery," Miss Martin wrote—but I fancied that her pen was pushed along with difficulty, and that she was due for one of her headaches.

Those three "i's"—instinct, intuition, inspiration—in which I pinned my faith were more useful in learning about people than logic could be. Capricious approach to capricious subject.

Looking back, I see that my mother was far more attractive, lovable, than any of the ladies I describe; but there it was—she was my mother.

Towards the end of that term, I learnt of a new thing, that Miss Alliot was to spend Christmas with the Townsends. This had never been done before: there had been simply the early autumn visit—it seemed that it had been for the sake of an old family friendship, a one-sided one, I sharply guessed. Now, what had seemed to be a yearly courtesy became something rather more for conjecture.

Miss Martin wrote that she would go to Breezy Lodge alone, and pretend that Christmas wasn't happening—as lonely people strive to. I imagined her carrying pails of cold water through the wet, long grasses of the orchard, rubbing her chilblains before the oil-stove. I began to love her as if she were a child.

My mother was a little flustered by my idea of having Miss Martin to stay with us for Christmas. I desired it intensely, having reached a point where the two of us, my mother and I alone, a Christmas done just for me, was agonising. What my mother thought of Miss Martin I shall never know now, but I have a feeling that schoolmistresses rather put her off. She expected them all to be what many of them in those days were—opinionated, narrow-minded, set in their ways. She had never tried to get to know Miss Martin. No one ever did.

She came. At the last moment before her arrival I panicked. It was not Miss Alliot coming, but Miss Alliot would hear all about the visit. Our house was in a terrace (crumbling). There was nothing, I now saw, to commend it to Miss Martin except, perhaps, water from the main and a coal fire.

After the first nervousness, though, we had a cosy time. We sat round the fire and ate Chinese figs and sipped ginger wine and played paper games which Miss Martin could not manage to lose. We sometimes wondered about the Townsends and I imagined a sort of Royal-Family-at-Sandringham Christmas with a giant tree and a servants' ball, and Miss Alliot taking the floor in the arms of Ralph Townsend—but then my imagination failed, the picture faded: I could not imagine Miss Alliot in the arms of any man.

After Christmas, Miss Martin left and then I went back to school. I was too single-minded in my devotion to Miss Alliot to do much work there, or bother about anybody else. My infatuation was fed by her absence, and everything beautiful was wasted if it was not seen in her company.

The Christmas invitation bore glorious fruit. As a return, Miss Martin wrote to ask me to stay at Breezy Lodge for my half-term holiday. Perfect happiness invaded me, remembered clearly to this day. Then, after a while of walking on air, the bliss dissolved. Nothing in the invitation, I now realised, had been said of Miss Alliot.

Perhaps she was off to Northumberland again, and I was to keep Miss Martin company in her stead. I tried to reason with myself that even that would be better than nothing, but I stayed sick with apprehension.

At the end of the bus-ride there on a Saturday morning, I was almost too afraid to cross the orchard. I feared my own disappointment as if it were something I must protect myself—and incidentally Miss Martin—from. I seemed to become two people—the one who tapped jauntily on the door, and the other who stood ready to ward off the worst. Which did not happen. Miss Alliot herself opened the door.

She was wearing one of her bandeaux and several ropes of beads and had a rather gypsy air about her. "The child has arrived," she called back into the room. Miss Martin sat by the stove mending stockings—an occupation of those days. They were Miss Alliot's stockings—rather thick and biscuit-coloured.

We went over to St. Margaret's for lunch and walked to the Echo afterwards, returning with branches of catkins and budding twigs. Miss Alliot had a long, loping stride. She hit about at nettles with her stick, the fringed tongues of her brogues flapped—she had long, narrow feet, and trouble with high insteps, she complained. The bandeau was replaced by a stitched felt hat in which was stuck the eye-part of a peacock's feather. Bad luck, said Miss M. Bosh, said Miss A.

We had supper at Breezy Lodge, for Miss Alliot's latest craze was for making goulash, and a great pot of it was to be consumed during the week-end. Afterwards, Miss Martin knitted—a jersey of complicated Fair Isle pattern for Miss Alliot. She sat in a little perplexed world of her own, entangled by coloured wools, her head bent over the instructions.

Miss Alliot turned her attention to me. What was my favourite line of poetry, what would I do if I were suddenly given a thousand pounds, would I rather visit Rome or Athens or New York, which should I hate most—being deaf or blind; hanged or drowned; are cats not better than dogs, and wild flowers more beautiful than garden ones, and Emily Brontë streets ahead of Charlotte? And so on. It was heady stuff to me. No one before had been interested in my opinions. Miss Martin knitted on. Occasionally, she was included in the questions, and always appeared to give the wrong answer.

I slept in their bedroom, on a camp-bed borrowed from St. Margaret's. (And how was I ever going to be satisfied with staying *there* again? I wondered.)

Miss Alliot bagged (as she put it) the bathroom first, and was already in bed by the time I returned from what was really only a ewer of water and an Elsan. She was wearing black silk pyjamas with DDA embroidered on a pocket. I bitterly regretted my pink nightgown, of which I had until then been proud. I had hastily brushed my teeth and passed a wet flannel over my face in eagerness to get back to her company and, I hoped, carry on with the entrancing subject of my likes and dislikes.

I began to undress. "People are kind to the blind, and impatient with the deaf," I began, as if there had been no break in the conversation. "You are so right," Miss Alliot said. "And people matter most."

"But if you couldn't see ... well, this orchard in spring," Miss Martin put in. It was foolish of her to do so. "You've already seen it," Miss Alliot pointed out. "Why this desire to go on repeating your experiences?"

Miss Martin threw in the Parthenon, which she had *not* seen, and hoped to.

"Still people matter most," Miss Alliot insisted. "To be cut off from them is worse than to be cut off from the Acropolis."

She propped herself up in bed and with open curiosity watched me undress. For the first time in my life I realised what dreadful things I wore beneath my dress—lock-knit petticoat, baggy school bloomers, vest with Cash's name tape, garters of stringy elastic tied in knots, not sewn. My mother had been right ... I should have sewn them. Then, for some reason, I turned my back to Miss Alliot and put on my nightgown. I need not have bothered, for Miss Martin was there between us in a flash, standing before Miss Alliot with Ovaltine.

On the next day—Sunday—I renounced my religion. My doubts made it impossible for me to go to church, so Miss Martin went alone. She went rather miserably, I was forced to notice. I can scarcely believe that any deity could have been interested in my lack of devotion, but it was as if, somewhere, there was one who was. Freak weather had set in and, although spring had not yet begun, the sun was so warm that Miss Alliot took a deck chair and a blanket and sat on the veranda and went fast asleep until long after Miss Martin had returned. (She *needed* a great deal of sleep, she always said.) I pottered about and fretted at this waste of time. I almost desired my faith again. I waited for Miss Martin to come back, and, seeing her, ran out and held a finger to my lips, as if Miss Alliot were royalty, or a baby. Miss Martin nodded and came on stealthily.

It was before the end of the summer term that I had the dreadful letter from Miss Martin. Miss Alliot—hadn't we both feared it?— was engaged to be married to Ralph Townsend. Of course, that put paid to my examinations. In the event of more serious matters, I scrawled off anything that came into my head. As for questions, I wanted to answer them only if they were asked by Miss Alliot, and they must be personal, not factual. As usual, if I didn't know what I was asked in the examination paper, I did a piece about something else. I imagined some *rapport* being made, and that was what I wanted from life.

Miss Martin's letter was taut and unrevealing. She stated the facts—the date, the place. An early autumn wedding it was to be, in Northumberland, as Miss Alliot had now no family of her own. I had never supposed that she had. At the beginning of a voyage, a liner needs some small tugs to help it on its way, but they are soon dispensed with.

Before the wedding, there were the summer holidays, and the removal of their things from Breezy Lodge, for Miss Martin had no heart, she said, to keep it on alone.

During that last holiday, Miss Martin's face was terrible. It seemed to be fading, like an old, old photograph. Miss Alliot, who was not inclined to jewellery ("Would you prefer diamonds to Rembrandts?" she had once asked me), had taken off her father's signet ring and put in its place a half hoop of diamonds. Quite incongruous, I thought.

I was weeks older. Time was racing ahead for me. A boy called Jamie was staying at St. Margaret's with his parents. After supper, while Mrs. Mayes's recitals were going on, or the solo whist, he and I sat outside the drawing-room on the stairs, and he told me blood-chilling stories, which I have since read in Edgar Allan Poe.

Whenever Jamie saw Miss Alliot, he began to hum a song of those days—"Horsy, keep your tail up." My mother thought he was a bad influence, and so another frost set in.

Sometimes—not often, though—I went to Breezy Lodge. The Fair Isle sweater was put aside. Miss Martin's having diminished, diminished everything, including Miss Alliot. Nothing was going on there, no goulash, no darning, no gathering of branches.

"Yes, she's got a face like a horse," Jamie said again and again.

And I said nothing.

"But he's *old*." Miss Martin moved her hands about in her lap, regretted her words, fell silent.

"Old? How old?" I asked.

"He's seventy."

I had known that Miss Alliot was doing something dreadfully, dangerously wrong. She could not be in love with Ralph Townsend; but with the Townsends entire.

On the day they left, I went to Breezy Lodge to say good-bye. It looked squalid, with the packing done—something horribly shabby, ramshackle about it.

Later, I went with Jamie to the Echo and we shouted one another's names across the valley. His name came back very clearly. When we returned, Miss Alliot and Miss Martin had gone for ever.

Miss Alliot was married in September. Miss Martin tried sharing her London flat with someone else, another schoolmistress. I wrote to her once, and she replied.

Towards Christmas my mother had a letter from Miss Louie to say that she had heard Miss Martin was dead—"by her own hand," she wrote, in her shaky handwriting.

"I am HORRIFIED," I informed my diary that night—the five-year diary that was full of old sayings of Miss Alliot, and descriptions of her clothes.

I have quite forgotten what Jamie looked like—but I can still see Miss Alliot clearly, her head back, looking down her nose, her mouth contemptuous, and poor Miss Martin's sad, scribbly face.

THE FLY-PAPER

ON WEDNESDAYS, after school, Sylvia took the bus to the out-skirts of the nearest town for her music lesson. Because of her docile manner, she did not complain of the misery she suffered in Miss Harrison's darkened parlour, sitting at the old-fashioned upright piano with its brass candlesticks and loose, yellowed keys. In the highest register there was not the faintest tinkle of a note, only the hollow sound of the key being banged down. Although that distant octave was out of her range, Sylvia sometimes pressed down one of its notes, listening mutely to Miss Harrison's exasperated railings about her—Sylvia's—lack of aptitude, or even concentration. The room was darkened in winter by a large fir tree pressing against—in windy weather tapping against—the window, and in summer even more so by holland blinds, half-drawn to preserve the threadbare carpet. To add to all the other miseries, Sylvia had to peer short-sightedly at the music-book, her glance going up and down between it and the keyboard, losing her place, looking hunted, her lips pursed.

It was now the season of the drawn blinds, and she waited in the lane at the bus-stop, feeling hot in her winter coat, which her grand-mother insisted on her wearing, just as she insisted on the music les-sons. The lane buzzed in the heat of the late afternoon—with bees in the clover, and flies going crazy over some cow-pats on the road.

Since her mother's death, Sylvia had grown glum and sullen. She was a plain child, plump, mature for her eleven years. Her greasy hair was fastened back by a pink plastic slide; her tweed coat, of which, last winter, she had been rather proud, had cuffs and collar of mock ocelot. She carried, beside her music case, a shabby handbag, once her mother's.

The bus seemed to tremble and jingle as it came slowly down the road. She climbed on, and sat down on the long seat inside the door, where a little air might reach her.

On the other long seat opposite her, was a very tall man; quite old, she supposed, for his hair was carefully arranged over his bald skull. He stared at her. She puffed with the heat and then, to avoid his glance, she slewed round a little to look over her shoulder at the dusty hedges—the leaves all in late summer darkness. She was sure that he was wondering why she wore a winter's coat on such a day, and she unbuttoned it and flapped it a little to air her armpits. The weather had a threat of change in it, her grandmother had said, and her cotton dress was too short. It had already been let down and had a false hem, which she now tried to draw down over her thighs.

"Yes, it is very warm," the man opposite her suddenly said, as if agreeing with someone else's remark.

She turned in surprise, and her face reddened, but she said nothing.

After a while, she began to wonder if it would be worth getting off at the fare-stage before the end of her journey and walk the rest of the way. Then she could spend the money on a lolly. She had to waste half-an-hour before her lesson, and must wander about somewhere to pass the time. It would be better to be wandering about with a lolly to suck. Her grandmother did not allow her to eat sweets—bathing the teeth in acid, she said it was.

"I believe I have seen you before," the man opposite said. "Either wending your way to or from a music lesson, I imagine." He looked knowingly at her music case.

"To," she said sullenly.

"A budding Myra Hess," he went on. "I take it that you play the piano, as you seem to have no instrument secreted about your person."

She did not know what he meant, and stared out of the window, frowning, feeling so hot and anguished.

"And what is your name?" he asked. "We shall have to keep it in mind for the future when you are famous."

"Sylvia Wilkinson," she said under her breath.

"Not bad. Not bad, Sylvia. No doubt one day I shall boast that I met the great Sylvia Wilkinson on a bus one summer's afternoon. Name-dropping, you know. A harmless foible of the humble."

He was very neat and natty, but his reedy voice had a nervous tremor. All this time, he had held an unlighted cigarette in his hand, and gestured with it, but made no attempt to find matches.

"I expect at school you sing the beautiful song, 'Who is Sylvia?' Do you?"

She shook her head without looking at him and, to her horror, he began to sing, quaveringly, "Who is Sylvia? What is she-he?"

A woman sitting a little farther down the bus turned and looked at him sharply.

He's mad, Sylvia decided. She was embarrassed, but not nervous, not nervous at all, here in the bus with other people, in spite of all her grandmother had said about not getting into conversations with strangers.

He went on singing, wagging his cigarette in time.

The woman turned again and gave him a longer stare. She was homely-looking, Sylvia decided—in spite of fair hair going very dark at the roots. She had a comfortable, protective manner, as if she were keeping an eye on the situation for Sylvia's sake.

Suddenly, he broke off his singing and returned her stare. "I take it, madam," he said, "that you do not appreciate my singing."

"I should think it's hardly the place," she said shortly. "That's all," and turned her head away.

"Hardly the place!" he said, in a low voice, as if to himself, and with feigned amazement. "On a fair summer's afternoon, while we bowl merrily along the lanes. Hardly the place—to express one's joy of living! I am sorry," he said to Sylvia, in a louder voice. "I had not realised we were going to a funeral."

Thankfully, she saw that they were coming nearer to the outskirts of the town. It was not a large town, and its outskirts were quiet.

"I hope you don't mind me chatting to you," the man said to Sylvia. "I am fond of children. I am known as being *good* with them. Well known for that. I treat them on my own level, as one should."

Sylvia stared—almost glared—out of the window, twisted round in her seat, her head aching with the stillness of her eyes.

It was flat country, intersected by canals. On the skyline were the clustered chimneys of a brick-works. The only movement out there was the faintest shimmering of heat.

She was filled by misery; for there seemed nothing in her life now but acquiescence to hated things, and her grandmother's old ways setting her apart from other children. Nothing she did was what she wanted to do—school-going, church-going, now this terrible music lesson ahead of her. Since her mother's death, her life had taken a sharp turn for the worse, and she could not see how it would ever be any better. She had no faith in freeing herself from it, even when she was grown-up.

A wasp zigzagged across her and settled on the front of her coat. She was obliged to turn. She sat rigid, her head held back, her chin tucked in, afraid to make a movement.

"Allow me!" The awful man opposite had reached across the bus, and flapped a crumpled handkerchief at her. The wasp began to fuss furiously, darting about her face.

"We'll soon settle you, you little pest," the man said, making matters worse.

The bus-conductor came between them. He stood carefully still for a moment, and then decisively clapped his hands together, and the wasp fell dead to the ground.

"Thank you," Sylvia said to him, but not to the other.

They were passing bungalows now, newly built, and with unmade gardens. Looking directly ahead of her, Sylvia got up, and went to the platform of the bus, standing there in a slight breeze, ready for the stopping-place.

Beyond the bus-shelter, she knew that there was a little general shop. She would comfort herself with a bright red lolly on a stick. She crossed the road and stood looking in the window, at jars of boiled sweets, and packets of detergents and breakfast cereals. There was a notice about ice-creams, but she had not enough money.

She turned to go into the empty, silent shop when the now familiar and dreaded voice came from beside her. "Would you care to partake of an ice, this hot afternoon?"

He stood between her and the shop, and the embarrassment she had suffered on the bus gave way to terror.

"An ice?" he repeated, holding his head on one side, looking at her imploringly.

She thought that if she said "yes," she could at least get inside the shop. Someone must be there to serve, someone whose protection she might depend upon. Those words of warning from her grandmother came into her head, cautionary tales, dark with unpleasant hints.

Before she could move, or reply, she felt a hand lightly but firmly touch her shoulder. It was the glaring woman from the bus, she was relieved to see.

"Haven't you ever been told not to talk to strangers?" she asked Sylvia, quite sharply, but with calm common sense in her brusqueness. "*You'd* better be careful," she said to the man menacingly. "Now come along, child, and let this be a lesson to you. Which way were you going?"

Sylvia nodded ahead.

"Well, best foot forward, and keep going. And *you*, my man, can kindly step in a different direction, or I'll find a policeman."

At this last word, Sylvia turned to go, feeling flustered, but important.

"You should *never*," the woman began, going along beside her. "There's some funny people about these days. Doesn't your mother warn you?"

"She's dead."

"Oh, well, I'm sorry about that. My God, it's warm." She pulled her dress away from her bosom, fanning it. She had a shopping-basket full of comforting, homely groceries, and Sylvia looked into it, as she walked beside her.

"Wednesday's always my day," the woman said. "Early closing here, so I take the bus up to Horseley. I have a relative who has the little general store there. It makes a change, but not in this heat."

She rambled on about her uninteresting affairs. Once, Sylvia glanced back, and could see the man still standing there, gazing after them.

"I shouldn't turn round," the woman said. "Which road did you say?"

Sylvia hadn't, but now did so.

"Well, you can come my way. That would be better, and there's nothing much in it. Along by the gravel-pits. I'll have a quick look round before we turn the corner."

When she did so, she said that she thought they were being followed, at a distance. "Oh, it's disgraceful," she said. "And with all the things you read in the papers. You can't be too careful, and you'll have to remember that in the future. I'm not sure I ought not to inform the police."

Along this road, there were disused gravel-pits, and chicory and convolvulus. Rusty sorrel and rustier tin-cans gave the place a derelict air. On the other side, there were allotments, and ramshackle tool-sheds among dark nettles.

"It runs into Hamilton Road," the woman explained.

"But I don't have to be there for another half-hour," Sylvia said nervously. She could imagine Miss Harrison's face if she turned up on the doorstep all that much too soon, in the middle of a lesson with the bright-looking girl she had often met leaving.

"I'm going to give you a nice cup of tea, and make sure you're all right. Don't you worry."

Thankfully, she turned in at the gate of a little red-brick house at the edge of the waste land. It was ugly, but very neat, and surrounded by holly-hocks. The beautifully shining windows were draped with frilly, looped-up curtains, with plastic flowers arranged between them.

Sylvia followed the woman down a side path to the back door, trying to push her worries from her mind. She was all right this time, but what of all the future Wednesdays, she wondered—with their perilous journeys to be made alone.

She stood in the kitchen and looked about her. It was clean and cool there. A budgerigar hopped in a cage. Rather listlessly, but not knowing what else to do, she went to it and ran her finger-nail along the wires.

"There's my baby boy, my little Joey," the woman said in a sing-song, automatic way, as she held the kettle under the tap. "You'll feel better when you've had a cup of tea," she added, now supposedly addressing Sylvia.

"It's very kind of you."

"Any woman would do the same. There's a packet of Oval Marie in my basket, if you'd like to open it and put them on this plate."

Sylvia was glad to do something. She arranged the biscuits carefully on the rose-patterned plate. "It's very nice here," she said. Her grandmother's house was so dark and cluttered; Miss Harrison's even more so. Both smelt stuffy, of thick curtains and old furniture. She did not go into many houses, for she was so seldom invited anywhere. She was a dull girl, whom nobody liked very much, and she knew it.

"I must have everything sweet and fresh," the woman said complacently.

The kettle began to sing.

"I've still got to get home," Sylvia thought in a panic. She stared up at a fly-paper hanging in the window—the only disconcerting thing in the room. Some of the flies were still half alive, and striving hopelessly to free themselves. But they were caught for ever.

She heard footsteps on the path, and listened in surprise; but the woman did not seem to hear, or lift her head. She was spooning tea from the caddy into the tea-pot.

"Just in time, Herbert," she called out.

Sylvia turned round as the door opened. With astonished horror, she saw the man from the bus step confidently into the kitchen.

"Well done, Mabel!" he said, closing the door behind him. "Don't forget one for the pot." He smiled, smoothing his hands together, surveying the room.

Sylvia spun round questioningly to the woman, who was now bringing the tea-pot to the table, and she noticed for the first time that there were three cups and saucers laid there.

"Well, sit down, do," the woman said, a little impatiently. "It's all ready."

VIOLET HOUR AT THE FLEECE

THEY WERE the first in. The landlord followed them into the little side bar with two pints of stout-and-mild on a tin tray, then rattled with a poker at the fire which had been quenched with a welter of coal. It was an empty gesture, a mere pass made in the direction of hospitality. When he had gone: "Well!" she said, turning from a picture of Lord Kitchener, tears in her eyes.

"You haven't been in here since I went," he said.

"How did you know?"

"Because you walked up to that picture as if you were saying: 'Ah, Lord Kitchener, my old friend!' If you were here every night you wouldn't have done that." He handed her a glass of beer and went to the window. The cobbles outside, between pub and church, were full of shadows, the sun struck only the gilt weathervane on the steeple. Now the quarter was marked with rounded leaden notes. Thrushes sang from gravestones and umbrella trees.

"The violet hour. Who said that? Sappho?"

"Sappho. I like the sound of Sappho. The last time I was in here ..."

"The day before war. A Saturday. They were all here—the man in the bowler hat and his wife ..."

"The one in the corner with the paste sandwiches, reading ..."

"One moment!" She flicked her fingers. "*Extinct Civilisations*! That was it. Over there," she pointed, "two girls drinking. *Good* girls! There hadn't started to be tarts about then. Not here, I mean."

"Are there now?"

She laughed. "And *you* said: 'We'll always remember this because it is a Date. It is something children will have to learn for history.'"

"Poor little sods."

"'When I am eighty,'" you said, 'I shall tell people I remember that day. I sat drinking at the Fleece with Sarah Fletcher...'"

"So I shall tell my children that."

"And they will be madly bored, and you will say, 'That stout old woman who lives now, I believe, at Tunbridge Wells.'"

"No. I shall say, 'I was drinking with Sarah Fletcher, a beautiful lady and my very dear friend.'"

"No one has talked like that to me for four years."

She sat down at the table and he came and sat down beside her. They slipped into the old habit of drinking together, elbow against elbow, their beer going down level as it used.

"How've you been for... ?" he tapped the glass.

"I haven't much..."

"Nor me. How does it go down?"

"It seems no different, though I suppose it is."

"How is your son?" he asked politely.

"His milk teeth are coming out. Funny and touching when he grins. I love it in him. Not in other children, though."

"And your daughter?"

"You speak very stiffly." She laughed.

"Say 'silly sod' as you used."

"No. I've stopped saying that."

As he tapped the table with a half-crown, he was thinking how grimy his hand looked, and curled the nails into his palm, against the coin.

"I hated all the maleness, chaps undressing together, being hearty," he said suddenly. "I always felt thin and blue. Good luck!" He lifted his filled glass. "But the worst thing was Christmas dinners. All sitting there being pleased and cheery with our nice dinners and the officers being decent, but each one of us his own private self. 'Poor men and soldiers unable to rejoice.' Perhaps not, though. Perhaps all enjoying themselves like hell. God, this is boring. Before I came tonight, I thought I wouldn't tell any soldier stories. You see, you don't like me to talk like it."

She wiped a little moustache of froth from her mouth. "I want you to tell me some time, but it separates me from you, and just now it is hard enough to get back again."

"I thought we were doing fine."

"I thought so too."

"And then there always *were* things to separate us. Your posh friends and your political notions. These endureth for ever, but being a soldier soon stops."

"I can think of the fighting and your being hungry and the hospital all right, but I can't hear about the Christmas dinner. I can't think about that."

"I enjoyed it like mad really. Look, now the fire's going to burn for us."

The coals shuddered and collapsed and a few flames, pale like irises, grew up between them.

"Do you still cry as much as you used?"

"No." At once, the tears rushed up into her eyes.

The landlord came in now, and placed a log on top of the flames, which wavered and sank down. It was a damp green log, with ivy still clinging to its bark.

"Tell me more, then, about being a soldier."

"No, it's just madly boring and stupid, living miles below the subsistence level, and the chaps being so coarse, much worse even than the way posh girls like you are coarse. And when they're not being coarse, they're bloody touching and have S.W.A.K. on the backs of their letters and make you feel ashamed. It's only all being together. Then office jobs—copy lists of numbers on to ration cards, so boring you make mistakes . . . do a pile and then say, 'Oh, God! October has only thirty days,' correct them all, smudges and blots and then, 'Oh damn! It's November has thirty.' And being in a sort of dirty post-office place, dust, broken nibs, ink bottles empty, falling over and full of fluff. And stuffy. You're not listening. Let's have some more beer. Darling, what are you looking at?"

"I was watching the ivy on that log turning bronze."

"I hate ivy. Christ! The trouble is, I've no more money."

She felt in her coat pockets. It was a thick white coat with a fine bloom of dirt upon it.

"Angel! I do like taking money from a nice girl."

"Ivy. My mother's favourite. She used to like to spend two or three hours fixing it all up in a jar against a white wall."

"Your mother did do the hell of a lot of high-class things, but don't go on about *her*. You'll only cry."

"I remember her doing that, in a long dress and *she* was crying because her mother and father had gone away for ever. I saw the back of her. I was eight. Her hair was shiny black and soft and done up like a Japanese woman's. It would be a good thing to paint. How tired I am of the fronts of people! Particularly bosoms. The back could be most expressive. You could tell by the arms and the listless way of holding the ivy that she was weeping because her father had left her in an ugly house with a nasty husband. The Victorians would have gone round to the other side and left an opened letter lying on the table and written 'Parting' on the frame—or 'Solitude.' But Toulouse-Lautrec and I like it best the other way round . . . and *you* don't like it at all. You've had your bellyful of it, in fact."

"No, but I'm always afraid of you crying when you speak about your mother, and when you begin to harp on bosoms and your inferiority. It worries me when you cry. It must be a thing you do a lot in your family. It's all right now while you're young and beautiful, but very uncomfortable for everyone once you're past forty."

A woman came in and drew red serge curtains and switched on the light. It rained cruelly down on them. He curled his fingers out of sight again.

"Mike!" he suddenly cried with false *bonhomie*.

She put up her cheek for her husband to kiss, which he would not do in a pub.

"How are you, old man?"

"Fine. Fine, thanks."

"Quite fit again?"

"Rather! You?"

"Pretty good."

"What to drink?"

"No. Can't stop. Coming, Sarah?"

"One for the road?"

"No, nor the ditch. Many thanks, all the same. OK, Sarah?"

She looked at them both with a feeling of contempt. Men together. Or, perhaps, just men before a woman. "They speak symbols," she thought. "It isn't a language at all. They make strange, half-savage noises at one another."

She said good-bye and the two of them went out into the last few moments of the violet hour. Her husband held open the car door. She sank back into the seat, watching sullenly the road before her, regretting the bright pub.

"OK?" He fidgeted at the dashboard and they were away. The buildings made strange shapes against the darkening sky.

"Oh, crying!" he protested. "Oh, stop for God's sake. Oh, Christ!"

OTHER NEW YORK REVIEW CLASSICS

For a complete list of titles, visit www.nyrb.com or write to:
Catalog Requests, NYRB, 435 Hudson Street, New York, NY 10014

* *Also available as an electronic book.*